# V

*Based on the epic television drama that enthralled 80 million viewers . . .*

". . . some telling comments about life on earth. There is valid social commentary on our misuse of water, our dependence on mass communications, our commercialization of daily life."
—*The Christian Science Monitor*

". . . thrilling, thought-provoking and paced like a motor race. What separates *V* . . . is that it is more than an eye-popping adventure. It is an allegory about fascist takeover . . . a mesmerizing nightmare."
—*The Washington Post*

". . . an enormously engrossing experience."
—*Los Angeles Herald Examiner*

". . . intelligent, imaginative, engrossing."
—*New York Daily News*

". . . interesting, suspenseful."
—*Los Angeles Times*

"V"

A KENNETH JOHNSON PRODUCTION
IN ASSOCIATION WITH WARNER BROS. TELEVISION
A WARNER COMMUNICATIONS COMPANY

Based on a Movie-For-Television
Parts 1 & 2:

Written by Kenneth Johnson

"V"

A BLATT/SINGER PRODUCTION
IN ASSOCIATION WITH WARNER BROS. TELEVISION
A WARNER COMMUNICATIONS COMPANY

Based on a Movie-For-Television

Part 3:

Teleplay by Brian Taggert and Peggy Goldman
Story by Lillian Weezer & Peggy Goldman &
Faustus Buck & Diane Frolov and Harry &
Renee Longstreet
Based on characters by Kenneth Johnson

Part 4:

Teleplay by Brian Taggert and Diane Frolov
Story by Lillian Weezer & Diane Frolov &
Peggy Goldman & Faustus Buck
Based on characters by Kenneth Johnson

Part 5:

Teleplay by Brian Taggert and Faustus Buck
Story by Lillian Weezer & Faustus Buck &
Diane Frolov & Peggy Goldman
Based on characters by Kenneth Johnson

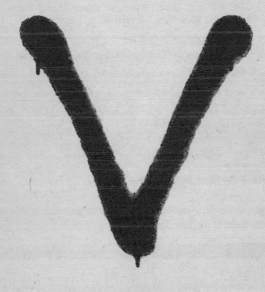

# A.C. CRISPIN

**PINNACLE BOOKS**  **NEW YORK**

V

*Copyright © 1984 by Warner Bros. Inc.*

An original Pinnacle Books edition, published for the first time anywhere.

First printing/May 1984

ISBN: 0-523-42237-7

Can. ISBN: 0-523-43231-3

*Printed in the United States of America*

PINNACLE BOOKS, INC.
1430 Broadway
New York, New York 10018

9    8    7    6    5    4    3    2    1

This book is dedicated to the Whileaway Writers
Co-op, that irrepressible, egalitarian Gang of Six
I'm fortunate enough to have as friends—movers,
shakers, and artists all.

Anne
Debby
O'Malley
Shana
Teresa

I'd like to extend a special acknowledgment to my editor, Harriet P. McDougal, Vice-President of TOR Books, for her encouragement, advice, and paw-holding during the writing of this book.

Warmest thanks are also due Pixie Lamppu, who really *cared*, and helped whenever possible.

# Book One

---

# TOMORROW

# Chapter 1

The guerilla encampment was set up in the remains of an old village. The mud and cinderblock huts, the remains of a bombed-out church—even a pottery shop, wares still baking in the summer heat—all seemed to huddle, forlorn, a dying, bullet-torn thing.

Tony Wah Chong Leonetti wiped at the sweat on his forehead as he parked the ancient jeep beneath a sagging thatched overhang. "Looks the same . . . Why do they always look the same?" he mumbled.

"Why do what always look the same?" Mike Donovan shifted his camera to his shoulder and panned it quickly around the camp, his alert green eyes searching for the best angles, the most telling shots.

"Guerilla hideouts. No matter what country—Laos, Cambodia, Vietnam—they all manage to look the same. Guess people on the run are basically alike, never mind their nationality." He rummaged in the back seat, dragged out a bag containing his sound equipment. Mumbling softly to himself, he tested the mike, listened to the playback in his earphones, finally nodding in satisfaction. Donovan, meanwhile, had climbed out of the jeep to meet a dark-haired woman who was approaching, her AK-47 not quite pointing at them.

Her voice was hard, her eyes reddened with dust and exhaustion. "You are Donovan?" she asked in broken English. "Juan told us you would be coming."

3

Donovan nodded.

"Carlos is not here right now. You must wait."

Donovan looked doubtfully at the dusty camp. "How long?"

"I do not know. Wait." Purposefully she turned on her heel and left.

Donovan looked back at Tony. "Hope he's on his way. I'm starved, and the prospects for chow don't look very promising, do they?"

Tony sighed. "I suppose we could always grab one of those chickens over there."

Donovan grinned, looking suddenly much younger. "Wouldn't be the first time, would it?"

"No—" Leonetti turned. "Did I hear an engine?"

"You sure did." Donovan began checking the settings on his camera.

A truck, heavily laden with armed guerillas, trundled bumpily into camp. Groans from the wounded mixed with shouts of greeting broke the hot silence as other fighters emerged from the broken buildings and ran toward the vehicle. Donovan and Leonetti followed, stepping aside as men and women carrying stretchers passed them.

"Looks like they weren't so lucky, wherever they've been," Tony observed, listening to the babble of rapid Spanish and the moans of the injured. Some of the forms handed down from the truck didn't stir.

Donovan trained his camera on a bloody face, feeling, not for the first time, like a ghoul—living off the suffering and death of others—then thought, as he always did, that suffering and death served no useful purpose at all if nobody knew of them. His job was to see that people knew what was happening.

One man was shouting orders above the din. Tony glanced over. "Carlos?"

Mike Donovan nodded. "Must be." Raising his voice, he called, "Excuse me, are you Carlos? Juan said you would talk to us about the attack last night. How bad was it? How about your losses?"

The man swung down from the truck. He looked to be in his mid-thirties, and he might have been handsome if not for the sweat and blood streaking his face. He brushed irritably at a

wound by his left eye, causing fresh red to well and drip. At
Donovan's hail, he turned, glared at them. "Of *course* we
suffered losses, man. You don't go up against a force like theirs
without expecting losses!" Angrily he turned, striding past the
truck. The sleepy camp was now a welter of activity, as men
and women struggled to load gear into trucks and jeeps.

Leonetti moved his microphone in a circle, picking up the
sounds of the camp—the running feet, the squawk of frightened chickens, the heavy thumps as the fighters loaded the
trucks. He glanced over at Donovan. "Looks like they're
moving out, Mike. Think we should take the hint?"

Donovan, intent on a shot, nodded abstractedly, then
focused on the leader. He was shouting:

*"Saquen primero los camiones de municiones!"*

Tony shook his head. "What'd he say?"

Donovan started after Carlos. "'Get the ammunition trucks
out first.'"

"Oh, shit," Tony mumbled. "They must be expecting
trouble."

Donovan was already out of earshot. Catching up to the
guerilla commander, he shouted, "How many losses?"

The man's mouth twisted into an ugly line. "Seven men and
women killed. A dozen wounded." Looking back at his
fighters, he shouted, "Jesus—*muebe el jeep! Lo esta tapando
todo!*"

Donovan looked over at the offending vehicle to make sure
Carlos wasn't referring to the old wreck he and Tony had
finagled, was reassured that it was another. He took a close shot
of the man's face as he directed the evacuation. "You're
wounded too."

As if realizing for the first time that he was on camera, that
what he said would be relayed to millions of television
viewers, Carlos looked directly into the lens, his words biting.
"These wounds are *nothing* compared to the wounds they've
inflicted on my country." One of the medics approached, tried
to dab at his eye, but Carlos brushed him aside to continue.
"But we're gonna fight them. Till we win, man. You got that?
Fight till El Salvador is *free*! Nothin's going to stop us! *You got
that?*"

"Yeah," Donovan said, "I got that."

A sudden shriek tore the air behind them. Donovan and the

guerilla leader whirled to see an army helicopter roaring toward them, nearly skimming the tops of the trees surrounding the camp. Machine guns spattered bullets like deadly raindrops as the gunship began a strafing run straight down the dusty middle of the camp. Several people went down with the first blasts, and their screams battled the thunderous roar of the chopper, the staccato bursts of the guns.

Without realizing how he'd gotten there, Donovan found himself belly-down behind a broken wall, camera still perched on his shoulder. He began following the path of the attack chopper, panning the camera carefully as the helicopter turned and came back for another run. He was dimly aware of a blur beside him—a blur that resolved itself into Tony, sweating and covered with dust, but still gamely clutching his sound gear.

He could barely hear his partner's voice over the chaos. "This don't look so good, Mike."

Donovan couldn't believe the shot he was getting of the gunship, guns blazing, as it roared back through the village. His voice grated from the dust he'd swallowed, but his tone was jubilant. "You kidding, man? It's great!"

Across the camp a truck exploded as the gas tank was hit— and at almost the same moment the woman who had first spoken to them doubled up with a shriek. Several people ran to help her; others began firing back at the enemy. Bullets kicked up dirt only feet away, and Tony Leonetti grabbed Donovan's arm. "Come on—the hell with the great shots!"

They ran, weaving and dodging, hampered by their gear. Yet it was so much a part of them that neither newsman thought of abandoning the equipment. They dodged behind another wall, closer to a building, huddled against a new assault from the chopper.

Tony flinched as a bullet whanged past him. "Donovan— you're gonna get me killed this time, I swear to God!"

Donovan turned and grinned, his teeth flashing in his dirty face. "Hell, Tony, you're going to get another Emmy!"

"I'm gonna get a bullet in my earphone!" Leonetti shouted back, grimly keeping his sound equipment operating. "Tell my wife my last thoughts were of—"

"Look!" Donovan's shout cut through Tony's words. "Look at him!"

Carlos had run to a downed comrade just as the helicopter

turned, bearing down on him. Bullets began peppering the ground before them. The guerilla leader stood, his .45 automatic pistol in both hands, coolly sighting along the barrel at the approaching chopper. As it came within range, swooping even lower for the kill, he squeezed off several rounds, aiming for the pilot, clearly visible behind the glass bubble of the cockpit.

Just as it seemed that the next burst of machine-gun fire would destroy the leader, the gunship pilot sagged limply in his seat. The helicopter wavered, dipped, then slipped over the treetops, losing altitude with every second. The ground shook with the force of the explosion, and Donovan could feel a puff of warm air against his face, even at this distance. "Unbelievable! I don't believe it! Did you see that?"

Tony nodded vigorously, grabbing his arm. "What's *really* unbelievable is that we're still alive, chum! Come *on!*"

Donovan was still shooting as his companion dragged him into their beat-up vehicle, which was still, amazingly, intact. Leonetti gunned the motor, hearing the beating thunder of another helicopter closing on the camp, now blazing with gunfire and flames from exploded vehicles. Letting out the clutch with a jerk, he sent the jeep fishtailing through the camp, heading back toward the road they'd traveled earlier that morning. He glanced over at the cameraman, then grinned half in admiration, half in exasperation. Donovan was training his camera back the way they'd come, leaning backwards to catch a shot of the helicopter as it followed them.

"I wish we had a Tyler mount!" he shouted as the camera bounced on his shoulder.

Tony Leonetti sighed. "I wish we had a tank." But Donovan, still shooting, didn't hear him. The jeep careened along the road, crossed a creek, raising a spray of water Suddenly the vehicle lurched sickeningly as a rocket exploded near them, sluicing water over the jeep and its occupants.

Donovan's voice reached Tony dimly, though the soundman knew his friend must be shouting at the top of his lungs. "Hang in there, Tony! This isn't any worse than Cambodia!"

The Asian laughed, shaking his head. "At least if you bought it there, I could'a passed for one of them! Where the hell did that chopper go?"

The question was answered as they topped a small rise in the road. The chopper was hanging a few feet above the ground, waiting for them.

Tony turned the wheel quickly, but not before the copter fired a burst. The jeep swerved again as Leonetti gasped, grabbing at his arm. Donovan quickly reached for the wheel, steadying the careening vehicle as the chopper lifted off overhead. Glancing quickly at his partner's arm, the cameraman saw a new blotch of scarlet staining Tony's hibiscus-flowered shirt. "You okay?" he shouted, as his partner took over the driving again.

"You kidding?" The wind whipped Tony's black hair back from his sweatband. "I'm loving every minute of this!"

Suddenly another rocket went off directly in their path. The jeep, already overbalanced, slipped sideways, overturning in the ditch beside the road. Overhead they could hear the thunder of the chopper as it homed in on them.

Donovan was thrown atop his partner, out of the overturned jeep, but the soft dirt of the roadside kept them from being more than shaken up. All of the cameraman's instincts reacted to the beat-beat of the helicopter blades. They had to reach the shelter of the trees!

Donovan scrambled up, camera still clutched firmly. Turning, he pulled the soundman to his feet, noting with part of his mind that the gas line had ruptured and that flames were licking along the splattered fuel.

He was alarmed by Tony's pallor beneath his tan. "Can you run?"

Tony turned to see the fire. "I have a choice?"

"I'm going to draw their fire. You haul ass over to those trees. They'll give you a little protection." He cast a quick glance upward at the helicopter, which had turned and was heading back for them. He threw himself forward. "Go, Tony!"

"No, Mike! We go together—"

Donovan was already running. "Get your can in gear! Go!" Behind him he could hear Tony heading for the trees.

Donovan zigged across the mud flat, hearing the bullets beginning to spang almost on his heels. Even as he increased his speed, he realized that there was nothing ahead of him except another bend of the creek—broad, shallow, but nearly impossible to run in. Rusting in the middle of it was the hulk of a once-orange pickup, Swiss-cheesed with hundreds of bullet holes.

*Hide in the shelter of that?* he wondered, thinking that the truck would provide little cover from the bullets. But there was no place else to run.

He turned, cradling the camera, only to see the chopper settle down to within a few feet of the water as delicately as a broody hen arranging herself on her nest. *Shit,* he thought, *this is it.* In sheer defiance—with a wild thought that perhaps the chopper didn't realize he was a newsman—Donovan raised the camera and began shooting directly at the faces of the two men in the helicopter. His eye narrowed on the viewfinder of the camera as the chopper moved even closer and Donovan peered sharply at the man sitting next to the pilot.

*It can't be! Ham Tyler—what the hell is he doing here?* The former CIA agent was now part of a highly secret branch of covert U.S. security operations. He had dogged Donovan's heels before—in Laos. Donovan had heard rumors that the right-wing "patriot" (*his* term, not Donovan's) was responsible for some of the more notorious mop-ups of guerilla forces here in El Salvador, but hadn't been able to verify them.

But even as Mike Donovan recognized the man in the co-pilot's seat, the helicopter abruptly lifted, turned, and went zipping away. *Huh? Now why the hell—*

Donovan turned to see if by some miracle a tank had rolled up behind him (*in total silence?! Don't be foolish, Mike . . .*) and nearly dropped his precious camera. Even as he heard the low, pulsing hum, his startled eyes took in the huge shape drifting toward him over the distant mountains, dwarfing even their vastness.

Donovan felt his jaw sag; his mind screamed that he must've bought it—he couldn't still be *alive* and seeing this. Automatically his finger tightened on the shooting button, and he heard the camera record the incredible vision.

An oblate spheroid, just as he'd heard it described in those UFO stories, but it was so *big!* His fuddled mind tried to absorb the enormity of the ship, but as it loomed closer and closer, his sense of proportion simply gave out. A mile in diameter? More. Two miles? More— *Big—*

Finally it stopped, hanging in mid-air like an impossible dream. Donovan heard Tony shouting behind him, and turned to wave reassuringly at the soundman. As he slogged through the water toward his friend, one thought ran through Donovan's head like a broken record: *How many people in history have been saved from having their asses shot off by a flying saucer?*

The white mouse sat up on his hind legs, whiskers twitching, as he heard the cage door rattle. Food time? But his stomach told him no, it was not food time. Instead he felt a hand grasp him gently, lift him carefully, then turn him over. He recognized the scent, the voice that spoke, and did not struggle.

"Come on, Algernon. Show Doctor Metz your tummy."

"Remarkable!" Doctor Rudolph Metz leaned over to scrutinize the mouse's furry belly, then picked up a magnifying glass to inspect it more closely. "The lesion's nearly healed!"

The blonde young woman in the lab coat smiled, pleased by Metz's reaction. "Yes. In a few more days it should be completely normal." She stroked the mouse's head with one finger, then gently put him back in the cage.

Doctor Metz raised bushy salt-and-pepper brows, regarding her as intently as he had the mouse. "You know how long my research staff has been searching for that formula, Juliet?"

Juliet Parrish smiled, but shook her head. "It wasn't all my doing. Ruth helped a lot."

Ruth Barnes looked up from a microscope across the lab. "I heard that, and don't you believe it, Rudolph. She did it all."

"Well, I was very lucky." The fourth-year medical student carefully examined the latch on the mouse cage, not meeting the older man's eyes.

Metz nodded. "Luck happens in science, but usually only when accompanied by hard work and inspiration. The truth here, Juliet, is that you are very, very gifted. Research comes naturally to you."

Coming from Doctor Metz, this was an extraordinary compliment, and Juliet couldn't stop the flush of pleasure that warmed her face. Glancing over at Ruth, she saw the older woman give her a "thumbs up" sign of approval.

Metz watched the mouse as he frisked around his cage. "And furthermore, I warn you that Ruth and I are going to try and steal you from the med school. If you could devote your full time to biochemistry, you might—"

The laboratory door slammed back against the wall with a bang, making them all jump. Silhouetted in the doorway was a breathless young black man. "Have you heard about them?"

"Heard about what, Ben?" Doctor Metz was puzzled.

Doctor Benjamin Taylor flipped on the television set that sat high on a shelf in the lab. The small portable's face filled with Dan Rather's well-known countenance—at this moment, a very grave countenance:

". . . but wherever the reports have come from—Paris, Rome, Geneva, Buenos Aires, Tokyo—descriptions of the craft have all been identical. And  " he broke off, plainly listening to a voice in his earphone, "I'm told that our affiliate station KXT in San Francisco now has this visual."

The screen filled with the image of a huge vessel looming in across San Francisco harbor, filling the screen, so vast that the Golden Gate Bridge below it looked like a Tinker Toy. The three in the laboratory could hear the awe in Rather's voice-over:

"Yes, there it is—Good Lord, the size of it! Ladies and gentlemen, this picture is coming to you *live* from San Francisco."

Almost at the same moment, the three scientists heard a low, pulsing hum, barely within the range of human ears. The mice, however, shrilled and began to race frantically around their cages.

Juliet glanced over at Ben. "Do you think—"

As if in answer to her question, Dan Rather spoke from the television screen: "I'm also getting confirmation that *another* of the giant ships is moving in over Los Angeles!"

"Oh, God," Ruth said. The three scientists stared at each other.

Anthropologist Robert Maxwell leaned closer to his prize, brushing carefully at a vacant eye socket with far greater gentleness than he used when bathing his three-year-old daughter. Even so, Arch Quinton put up a cautioning hand. "Gently, gently, Robert. She's a verra' special lady . . ." His Scots' burr was most pronounced when he was excited, and Maxwell grinned to himself, thinking that he'd never seen the older man more ecstatic over a discovery—though Quinton would die rather than break out of that "dour Scot" cover he affected.

"So your examination of the hip socket verified that she was female?" he asked. At Quinton's nod, he continued, dabbing carefully at the blackened, jagged teeth, "Upper Pleistocene, for sure, Arch. Much older than any we've uncovered at this site, wouldn't you agree?"

Quinton nodded. "The artifacts seem t' bear you out, lad. Also, look at her forehead, here—" His hand, which had been raised to brush gently at the wispy fragments of hair, paused, then turned into a point. "Robert, look at that!"

Even before Robert Maxwell could turn, he heard the sound— a vibrating pulse throbbing in his body as well as his ears. He turned to see a giant craft, silver-blue, sliding toward them as smoothly as if it ran on an invisible track. His hand tightened convulsively on the brush, and he pressed his body closer to the cliff, as though he would interpose himself between his find and the spaceship.

Elias Taylor squatted on the fire escape, glancing quickly around to make sure he was unobserved. Not much chance that anyone would be home, since it was the middle of the day, but Elias had never been caught yet, and didn't intend to break his record. Satisfied, he quickly taped the small pane over, his movements neat and economical. Then, a quick tap with a rock and—presto! The young man's teeth looked doubly white against his dark countenance as he grinned. Easy. Elias liked jobs that were easy.

Once inside the apartment, he trotted through the tiny rooms, looking for items that would be easy to carry, simple to fence. A Walkman caught his eye, and he flipped it on, listening intently to make sure that the tone was good.

A sock stuffed under the mattress of an unmade bed yielded nearly a hundred in cash. Elias grinned again as he counted it, shaking his head. *They always hide the bread in the same places. Most folks have no imagination . . .*

The only other thing that interested Taylor was a portable television. He turned it on, grimacing as he saw it was only black-and-white. *Cheap suckers, I swear,* he thought, ready to turn it off and make his exit. Black-and-whites were so cheap that it wasn't worth his energy to steal them anymore. His fingers hovered over the "off" switch, arrested by the image on the screen, what looked like (but couldn't be!) a *live* shot of a big UFO! Hastily he turned the sound up.

". . . along the Champs Elysees. We repeat, this picture is coming live from Paris, where yet another giant UFO is moving overhead."

Elias sat, eyes widening, as the picture changed to a squadron of jet fighters scrambling into the air. The voice continued:

"The Pentagon reports that fighters from the Tactical Air Command bases around the United States have approached these monstrous UFO's, but all jets reported interference with their onboard guidance and electrical systems, forcing them to break off their attempts."

The scene shifted to a mob rushing madly along a street, cars jammed in the middle, honking insanely—complete and utter chaos. Even the cops looked spaced-out, and no wonder, thought Elias, seeing another of the giant ships hanging (how the hell did they *do* that trick?) overhead. The scene reminded him tantalizingly of another, something he'd seen in the past, in a movie. As the camera panned to reveal the Washington Monument, Elias whistled softly to himself. "Shit," he mumbled, "it's old Klaatu and Gort come to Earth for real this time!"

The announcer was still talking: ". . . making it impossible to get within a mile of the craft. Missiles fired at the ships simply go astray, then detonate harmlessly well out of range. Police and troops are trying to maintain an orderly evacuation of the nation's capital . . ."

"Hell, too," mumbled Elias. "That sure don't look orderly to me!" He fingered the Walkman, wondering how this new development would affect the prices Reggie would give him on this stuff . . .

". . . and all the other cities that are threatened by this unprecedented happening, but roads and highways everywhere are jammed with traffic. Accidents have paralyzed all or most of the major arteries. Other craft are known to be approaching or hovering over at least seven other major U.S. cities— Houston, New York, San Francisco, New Orleans—yes, and this is now confirmed, Los Angeles . . ."

*"L.A.?!"* Elias nearly dropped the Walkman, rousing to realize that he was in a stranger's living room, and that the rightful owner might reappear any moment. Hastily he slid one leg over the windowsill, afraid to look up.

He heard it before he saw it. Clutching the Walkman, Elias decided to take the rest of the day off.

Mike Donovan pulled a blanket over Tony's gently snoring form, and moved forward to the Learjet's cockpit. Dropping into the co-pilot's seat, he glanced at the instruments. "Ahead of schedule," he commented.

Joe Harnell, the pilot, nodded. "How's your friend?"

"He's fine. The Scotch and codeine put him out. I can take her for a while, if you want to stretch your legs."

"Ever flown one before?" The pilot glanced quickly at Donovan.

"I've piloted almost everything except the shuttle, one time or another. Used to fly recon in the Nam. Did you find out where we can set down?"

The pilot stood up, watching as Donovan took over the controls, then nodded approvingly, before answering the newsman's question. "Yeah. So far Dulles is still open. We'd better take it. They're shutting down all over."

Donovan considered. "No, I got a hunch that New York is going to be the place to be as far as news goes. How about JFK?"

"Closed."

Donovan shrugged, grinning. "Let's open it. They can't roll up the runways, can they?"

"Hell, too. The FAA would have our—"

Donovan snapped his fingers. "No, I've got a better idea! La Guardia's much better!"

Harnell stared at him. "You nuts? That'd mean flying this sucker right *under* the goddamn thing!"

"Yeah! Think of the shots I could get!"

"No way, Mike."

Donovan grinned at him. "Come on, think of the bucks the film will be worth! I'll share the credit with you . . ."

Harnell stared at him in disbelief. Donovan gave him a wink and went to get his camera.

* * *

The next morning the Bernstein family, Stanley, Lynn, their son Daniel, and Stanley's father, Abraham, watched in amazement as Mike Donovan's film showed the view of the underside of the great craft that hung over New York City. Like the one in Los Angeles, where the Bernsteins lived, it had remained stationary and silent throughout the long (and at least for Lynn Bernstein) sleepless night.

Daniel, who was eighteen, was fascinated by the spacecraft. All his life he'd been waiting for something exciting to happen to him, and here it finally had. Never mind that it had happened to the rest of the world too—something told him that this was what he'd been waiting for. He turned excitedly to his father, a thin-haired, sad-eyed man with a permanent stoop and the beginnings of a potbelly.

"They say it's a good five miles in diameter, Dad!"

His mother, Lynn, a nervous woman who might have been attractive if not for the deep lines between her eyes and her permanently thinned lips, wrung her hands in her lap, saying for the hundredth time to nobody in particular, "We ought to leave the city, don't you think?"

Stanley Bernstein glared at his son. "I told you before, Lynn, where would we go? The roads are jammed, they say. Besides, as the President pointed out, we ought to avoid panic. They haven't done anything to indicate they're hostile."

Old Abraham shifted uneasily on the couch. "I wonder if there is any place *left* to hide. Even the Germans during the war had no ships like these."

"Father," Stanley said reprovingly, "that doesn't help—"

Their attention shifted abruptly back to the television screen. A somewhat hoarse but still professional Dan Rather was saying: ". . . They have reported the same occurrence now in Rome . . . and Rio de Janeiro . . . Moscow . . . Yes, the reports are flooding in—that same tone is being repeated all over the world from the spacecraft hanging over our cities—"

The Bernsteins heard the pulsing signal simultaneously from the television pickup and also from outside their suburban Los Angeles home. A tone, swiftly echoing, then changing to a voice!

"Twenty-one . . . twenty . . . nineteen . . . eighteen . . ." The strangely resonant voice continued the countdown while the news commentator explained that all over the world people were hearing the same thing—each in the appropriate local tongue.

". . . five . . . four . . . three . . . two . . . one." After a second's pause, the voice continued, "Citizens of the planet Earth . . . we bring you greetings. We come in peace. May we respectfully request the Secretary General of your United Nations please come to the top of the United Nations Building in New York at 0100 Greenwich Mean Time this evening. Thank you."

Stanley blinked. "What time is that?"

Dan Rather answered, obligingly, from the television. "The voice we have just heard requested the presence of the Secretary General at the top of the United Nations Building in New York City at eight o'clock this evening."

Lynn clutched frantically at her husband's hand. "What will this mean, Stanley?"

Daniel turned to grin at her, ecstatic. "It means something is gonna happen, Mom . . . finally! Isn't it *great*?"

# Chapter 2

Sunset was a dim red memory on the New York western sky as Mike Donovan panned his camera across the lights of Manhattan. Late summer wind whipped his already-rumpled hair—the breeze was stiff this high up. The top of the United Nations Building. Donovan checked his watch again. Seven-fifty and forty-five seconds. Not quite ten minutes to go.

The roof door slammed, admitting yet another crowd of journalists and technicians. Mike spotted a familiar black head and hurried over to greet Tony Leonetti, helping his friend carry his equipment over to the roped-off line. Donovan noted Leonetti's grimace as he moved his shoulder.

"You sure you're gonna make it, Tony?"

Tony grinned. "The news event of the *century*? Man, I ain't about to miss it!"

"Mike?" Both men turned as a woman's voice reached them.

Donovan's eyes held hers as she walked toward them, a tall, very well-groomed woman in her early thirties. Everything about her, from her expertly applied makeup and hairstyle to her level, measuring gaze, proclaimed her as one of the most prominent television reporters in the business. "Uh, hello, Kristine."

"Hello, Mike. Hi, Tony." She nodded pleasantly to Tony, who returned her greeting. "I heard you drew the TV pool. Me too."

Donovan smiled knowingly. "I thought I recognized your card in the pile downstairs. Figured you wouldn't miss this one."

She returned his smile a little sheepishly. "So where are we setting up?"

He pointed to the roped-off line beyond which stood a contingent of UN military police. With a nod, Tony excused himself to set up his equipment. Donovan hesitated, looking over at the bustle of camera crews, their faces ranging from strained worry to hectic gaiety. From far below he could hear the ever-present wail of sirens.

Kristine took his arm. "Mike? Let's get set up."

He started, "Yeah. I was just . . . thinking."

Her glance was knowing. "So was I. You could've at least said good-bye before you left that morning."

"I did. You were on the phone, hustling somebody for an assignment, and didn't hear me."

She paused, turned to him, her green eyes eloquent. "I'm sorry."

Donovan smiled, a little tensely. "So was I."

Their eyes held for several seconds, then she looked away. "What time is it?"

Donovan checked his watch. "Seven fifty-six."

Kristine hurried away to check her last-minute preparations. Donovan busied himself with his camera settings. The minutes crawled by.

At seven fifty-nine, a distinguished white-haired man emerged, flanked by armed escorts. Donovan recognized him as the Secretary General and watched as he waved to the roof-top troops to lower their weapons. Donovan trained his camera on the gigantic floodlit shape of the alien craft hovering far above them, so enormous it dwarfed the tallest of the sky-scrapers. He could hear someone counting down under his breath.

One of the newsmen was speaking into a mike: ". . . and a hush has fallen . . . not just here, I am sure, but around the world . . ."

"Nine . . . eight . . . seven . . . six . . ."

*Five*, thought Donovan, *four, three, two, one—*

". . . as eight o'clock strikes . . . 0100 Greenwich Mean time."

Donovan stared upward, the viewfinder of his camera pressed against his eye. His eye watered as he tried not to blink.

There! Something—hard to make out in that silver-blue vastness—a tiny dark opening! Donovan allowed himself that blink, then squinted back at the ship.

He zoomed in, centering directly on the opening, watched it fill with something—something that resolved into a streamlined shape that detached swooping down toward them. Donovan could hear Kristine's cool, professional tones, and with one part of his mind admired her control—he knew she was as nervous as any of them, but her poise argued that she did this every day. "The smaller craft is moving at an angle downward, now across Third Avenue and Thirty-Ninth—coming directly toward the UN Building."

Donovan pivoted to follow the craft as it slowed prior to landing. It gleamed white, with small dark triangles that could have been opaqued windows at regular intervals. On what looked to be its nose was a red symbol of some kind, a combination of dots and lines, like nothing the cameraman had ever seen before, but holding a haunting familiarity nevertheless. The craft descended with barely a whoosh of displaced air to mark its passage.

Kristine continued her commentary: "Now the craft is drifting to a stop some ten feet in the air above our heads . . . Now it's landing . . . The air itself feels strange . . . vibrating slightly . . ."

A panel opened at the bottom side of the craft, just as the assembled crowd heard a voice—a strangely resonant, slightly echoing voice: "Herr General Sekreterare . . ." Donovan shifted the camera to pick up the Secretary General as the man stepped to the front of the crowd, his face set in lines of calm determination, his back very straight.

The voice continued: "*Var intre radd kom upp for trappan.*" At the same moment a short ramp extruded onto the rooftop, resting there securely.

Kristine's voice reached Donovan, still poised, calm, but with a new tightness. "I think the voice spoke Swedish—that's the Secretary General's native language . . ." She listened intently to a button in her ear. "Yes, I have the translation now . . . 'Mr. Secretary General . . . do not be afraid . . . Please climb the ramp.'"

Beneath his shock of white hair, the elderly man's face was set, his strides coming with a steady precision. He reached the ramp and began climbing, step by step, until he reached the top and disappeared. The armed guards raised their weapons. Donovan realized he'd been holding his breath only when his vision began to blur. He let it out slowly, his eye riveted to the camera's viewfinder, and waited.

There was a stirring at the top of the stairs, shadows moving within darkness. Then—a face! The Secretary General emerged, moving with a quick vigor that was in huge contrast to the rigid strides he had taken to reach the craft.

Murmurs filled the rooftop, but Kristine's authoritative tones cut through them: "There he is! The Secretary General is reappearing! He is apparently unharmed, waving cheerfully to the onlookers here on the roof of the UN Building . . . Just a minute. It looks as though he's going to address the crowd . . ."

The older man's educated, slightly-accented tones reached Donovan clearly as he focused on the speaker's face. "My fellow citizens of Earth . . . these Visitors assure me that they come in peace and that they wish to honor all the covenants of our United Nations Charter. As you'll see, they are much like us . . . although their voices *are* unusual. They first asked me to speak on their behalf, but I felt everyone would be more comfortable if their Supreme Commander, who is aboard this vessel, spoke directly to you all. His voice will be heard around the world, in every language necessary."

The Secretary General turned back to look up the stairs. Donovan focused past him on the dark opening in the belly of the shuttle. Movement—then he was seeing booted feet in the viewfinder, legs, a normal-seeming trunk, two arms, a head—

Donovan gasped, his fingers tightening on the camera. He'd expected differences, and there were none! At first glance, the alien appeared to be a normal human male of middle years, with thick gray hair and keen blue eyes. He was wearing high black boots, looking for all the world like ordinary English riding boots, and a reddish-colored coverall that was cut much the same as a pilot's flight suit. It had five diagonal black stripes across the breast.

Kristine's commentary was analytical and precise: "Roughly six feet tall . . . I'd estimate one hundred sixty pounds

. . . He seems to have some difficulty seeing in the glare of the floodlights here . . . He's stopping now, halfway down the ramp . . . I think he's about to speak . . ."

The man's voice reached them clearly, but its unusual timbre—sort of a vibrating resonance—was even more apparent live, like this, than it had been over the airwaves.

"I trust you will forgive me . . . but our eyes are unaccustomed to this sort of brightness . . ." Reaching into a pocket of the coverall, he took out a pair of surprisingly normal-looking dark glasses and put them on.

"As the Secretary General has told you, we have come in peace to all mankind on Earth . . . Our planet is the fourth in distance from the star which you call Sirius. It is some 8.7 light-years from your Earth. This is the first time we have journeyed from our system, and you are the first intelligent life form we've encountered." He paused, then a very warm smile brightened his features. "We are very pleased to meet you!"

Donovan could hear the murmur of relief and welcome rising audibly from the assembled journalists and dignitaries. He continued shooting, zooming in for a closeup as the man took a few strides toward him before resuming: "Our names would sound peculiar to you, so we—my fellow Visitors and I—have chosen simple names from Earth. My name is John."

The Visitor smiled again. "The Secretary General referred to me as a 'Supreme Commander.' Actually, I'm just sort of an admiral. I'm responsible for this small fleet around your planet . . ."

*Small fleet?* Donovan tightened his fingers on the camera, suddenly conscious that his hands were sweating.

"We've sent other unmanned craft before us, some of which have monitored the Earth for quite a while, so we could learn your languages—but some of us are not as skilled as others, so we hope you will be patient with us. We have come here on behalf of Our Great Leader . . . who governs our united planet with benevolence and wisdom . . . We have come because we need your help."

*Benevolence and wisdom,* thought Donovan cynically. *Sounds like a real party hack. They ought to do just fine down here. John may end up our next President . . .*

"Our planet is in serious environmental difficulty. Far, far worse than yours. It's reached a stage where we will be unable to survive without immediate assistance. There are certain chemicals and compounds which we need to manufacture—which alone can save our struggling civilization. You can help us manufacture these. And in return, we'll gladly share with you the fruits of all our knowledge."

*The fruits of all our knowledge . . . Who the hell have they got for a speechwriter?*

"Now that contact is established, we would like to meet with individual governments so that we may present requests for certain operating plants around the world to be retooled for manufacture of the compound we need . . ."

Donovan thought fleetingly of his stepfather's plant, could visualize his mother, Eleanor, goading that poor SOB Arthur to try and land a Visitor contract. *Wonder what kind of compound they're talking about?*

"And we'll reward your generosity, as I have said, by educating your industrial and scientific complex to the limits of our knowledge—helping solve your environmental, agricultural, and health dilemmas—then we'll leave you, as we came, in peace."

*Talk about offering us heaven on a silver platter—what would they do if we told them to stick it in their non-pointed ears?*

"I know that if circumstances were reversed, and you had come to visit us, I'd feel a burning curiosity to see the inside of your spacecraft right away. With that in mind, we'd like to have the Secretary General and five of your journalists accompany us back aboard our Mother Ship, for what will be the first of many opportunities to get to know us better."

Donovan felt a tap on his shoulder, and looked up from his camera's viewfinder to see one of the Secretary General's aides at his side. "Your card came up, Mr. Donovan," the man said in accented English.

"Hot damn!" Hastily Donovan checked his equipment, then ducked under the rope at the man's signal. As he began walking toward the ship, Kristine and Tony fell in beside him.

"What'd he mean, my card came up?" Donovan asked them in a low voice as they crossed the rooftop.

"They chose the journalists by lot," Kristine explained. "Sam Egan and Jeri Taylor got it too."

"We really got the luck!"

"Yeah," Tony agreed dryly. Donovan turned to ask him what he meant, but Leonetti was already mounting the ramp. Donovan hastened after him.

The Visitor leader, "John," was waiting for them at the top of the ramp. Donovan was the last to climb it as he hung back to get a good shot of the other journalists meeting and shaking hands with the alien. Then he sprinted up the ramp for his own turn, hastily resting his camera on his left shoulder so he could free his right hand. *God,* he thought, impressed in spite of himself, *I'm getting to shake the hand of someone born under a different sun . . . even though he looks human, he's not . . .*

John's hand was markedly cool, the skin firm and smooth. He nodded pleasantly. "Mr. Donovan. I saw your films of the underside of our Mother Ship. Most impressive . . . and quite daring."

Donovan felt like a kid receiving a chuckle and a pat on the shoulder from an adult. "That's right, you said you monitored our television. How long have you been doing that?"

Behind the Visitor's dark glasses Donovan could see the man's blue eyes appraise him coolly. John smiled. "For several of your solar years, now. I promise you we'll satisfy your curiosity, Mike. We'll have lots of time to communicate during our visit here."

"I'm glad to hear it." Donovan moved along. He stepped into the shuttle, grabbing a closeup of John's face as he smiled graciously at Kristine, before sitting down beside the news-woman.

*The guy wears authority like a shroud,* Donovan thought, wrenching his eyes away from the leader with an almost physical effort.

The interior of the craft was disappointing. It looked like a cross between the Learjet and one of those shuttle vehicles that transport passengers to planes. Seats lined the walls, cushioned seats covered in what appeared to be (and probably was) very ordinary dark brown fabric—*a good color choice,* Donovan thought, remembering his own carpet shopping when he'd set up his apartment last year after the divorce—*doesn't show dirt.*

Thinking of his divorce made Donovan recall—with a guilty start—that he hadn't called Sean in almost three days. *Since before this thing started. The event of the century, and you haven't phoned to see how your only child is reacting.* He made a swift mental promise to call first thing tomorrow morning, and to visit over the weekend. He wondered if Sean had seen him walk up those stairs and enter the alien shuttle—then smiled. He knew he had. Sean was his Dad's biggest cheering section. *Even Marjorie's bitterness can't change that.*

Kristine Walsh was sitting across the cabin from him, still deep in conversation with John. Donovan wondered what they were talking about—she was smiling that wide, candid grin that Mike knew she reserved for people she really liked. He felt an irrational stab of jealousy. *Cut it out, idiot. You're here for a story, not a romantic interlude.*

Quickly he panned the camera around the inside, wishing he had more light. The Visitors evidently kept their illumination levels at what most humans would think of as "late-night television" dimness. Donovan could see clearly enough, but reading would have been uncomfortable after more than a few minutes.

*But I thought Sirius was a really bright star . . . Have to check it out with the observatory when I get back . . . I suppose their planet could have a heavy cloud cover or something . . .*

Two other Visitors, young men about Donovan's age, stuck their heads into the main cabin, and John nodded. Moments later, Donovan felt a slight movement as the craft evidently took off. He wished the windows weren't darkened—what a shot it would make to catch the UN Building rooftop receding, and that giant saucer drawing closer!

The alien craft was silent and seemed nearly motionless. Donovan wondered how the Visitors powered their ships. Jargon from "Cosmos" episodes and science fiction stories zipped through his mind—*matter/antimatter, ion drives, tesseracts, space warps*—

Tony turned to him. "Scared, Mike?"

"Are you?"

"Yeah, a little maybe. This is a big day for the whole planet."

"It's funny how you start thinking of this place as a planet—only one of God knows how many—since they came along."

"I've noticed that. What you'd call a cosmic consciousness-raiser, I guess."

"Yeah. But to answer your question—yeah, I'm a little scared too."

There was an almost imperceptible bump, then the craft stopped. Donovan gathered up his camera, setting it to compensate as much as possible for the anticipated lack of lighting. "Here we go."

They stepped out into a large, open area. Rows of shuttles like the one they'd arrived in were lined up on either side. The large docking bay looked very similar to those Donovan had seen aboard the biggest of the Navy's aircraft carriers. The white craft gleamed faintly, reflecting a dim blue from the overall lighting and the painted floor. John explained that each docking bay held about three dozen shuttles, and that there were two hundred or more of them scattered through the great Mother Ships that made up the fleet. Donovan heard Kristine relaying this information in her voice-over recording as he wheeled slowly, panning his camera.

The Visitor leader touched Kristine's arm. "This way. I'll take you to see the Main Control Room."

Donovan trailed behind them so he could shoot the overhead catwalk with the journalists climbing up to it. Then he hurried to catch up.

As they moved above the docking bay, a dark-haired, extremely attractive woman entered from a side door and stood waiting for them. Donovan zoomed in on her. Even with the low lighting level it was impossible to mistake the authority in her dark eyes, an authority which seemed as much a part of her as her sculpted cheekbones and generous mouth. Kristine's voice reached Donovan as they walked toward the Visitor woman.

"You have both males and females in your crew?"

John sounded faintly surprised. "Well, yes, of course. This is Diana . . . she is second in command."

The brunette nodded pleasantly at them. Donovan gave her another closeup. She turned to accompany them on the tour.

The control room looked faintly like the conning tower of a nuclear submarine, but larger, with perhaps a dozen men and women busily working at large multi-lighted consoles before viewscreens. A few showed glimpses of Manhattan below, but most were filled with instrument graphs and readouts. All the crewmembers were dressed in the reddish coveralls, with slight variations in the breast designs that apparently designated rank and station. Mike panned the camera quickly, for the Supreme Commander did not pause, but kept moving.

"Next we'll see what you'd call our engine room."

"Does that screen over there keep you in touch with the other ships in your 'small fleet'?" John turned to see which readout Kristine was pointing to.

"Yes, Kristine." Diana's voice, barring the alien reverberation, was a husky contralto. "Most of the others monitor and activate the functions of the ship. It's quite routine and unspectacular, really."

*Sure,* thought Donovan, zooming in for a shot of the two women. *If you happen to be from another star . . .*

They moved along the catwalk until it led into a tunnel. The dark walkway extended for nearly forty paces—Donovan counted them. He realized, with a prickle touching the short hairs at the nape of his neck, that he was behaving as if he were scouting enemy territory. *Don't be paranoid, Mike. They've come in peace, remember?*

The only features worth noting in the tunnel were several doors painted a brilliant, chromatic yellow. Donovan examined them through the viewfinder, but saw nothing beyond their color to indicate that they were special.

"And those doors we just passed?" Kristine was asking Diana.

"Restricted areas—a lot of radioactivity. Our gravity drive, as you've seen, is quite effective, but it takes up nearly half the ship."

"How fast can this baby go?" Donovan asked. It was the first time he'd spoken, and Diana looked over at him.

"We can travel at speeds close to that of light itself."

Donovan thought of asking if they'd proved or disproved Einstein's theory, but stopped when he realized they might well not know who Einstein was.

They emerged onto a catwalk high above a considerable number of gleaming, golden-hued cylinders. The place looked vaguely like a refinery, with tracings of pipework running everywhere. A few technicians moved among the giant cylinders, examining and recording information from readouts and dials.

Diana was continuing, "The other half of the ship contains

the living quarters for the crew, as well as storage areas to hold
the chemicals we'll be manufacturing here on Earth. They'll be
contained within enormous cryogenic tanks to keep them—"

"Cryogenic?" Kristine paused in her voice-over.

"Super-cooled. For maximum efficiency in storage."

John chuckled. "You'll have to forgive Diana, Kristine.
Like all scientists, she tends to forget at times that not all of us
are as well-versed in technical language as she is."

"Now, you also mentioned living quarters for the crew,"
Kristine continued her voice-over. "How many of your people
are on this ship?"

Diana hesitated for barely a second, but Donovan didn't
miss her quick, sideways glance at her commander. "It
. . . varies . . . Several thousand."

*On this ship alone? How many does that make on all fifty or
so ships?* Donovan bit his lip, glancing over at Kristine, but
she was intent on her next question.

"Can we talk to some of them?"

John smiled. "You can. You'll have a lot of opportunity for
that."

The tour ended a few minutes later back in the docking bay.
Diana, not John, accompanied the journalists and the Secretary
General back down to the UN Building.

Sitting aboard the Visitor shuttle (as far as Donovan could
tell, it was the same one they'd come up in—but it was
impossible to be sure), Donovan stretched, rubbing the
muscles at the back of his neck.

"What time is it?" he asked Tony, seeing his friend check
his watch.

The soundman grinned. "About nine-thirty. The night is still
embryonic, Mike old buddy."

Donovan fought back a yawn. "'Zat *all*? Christ, why am I
so tired? I feel like I've been awake for *days*."

"You have been. Unless you sacked out on the plane back
from El Salvador."

"Nope. I was too busy playing nursemaid to you."

"Bull. I saw those closeups of the Mother Ship. You were
playing daredevil pilot and hotshot cameraman again."

"That's me," Donovan acknowledged the ribbing with a
grin. He patted the camera. "I can hardly wait to get this on the
air."

"What do you think it'll be worth?" Tony, the practical one in the partnership, wanted to know.

"Just about anything we want to ask for it, old friend. I'll leave the extent of our greed up to you, as the business manager."

Tony nodded thoughtfully, then, taking out a pocket calculator, busied himself with the pleasant task of figuring out the profit margin this venture would net them.

The five journalists and the Secretary General were relatively sheltered from the press until they'd turned their tapes and films over to the networks. Donovan, Tony, and Kristine watched their story air in a "Special Bulletin" broadcast by satellite.

"Do you think we'll place first in the Nielsens?" Tony studied Donovan's films of the docking bay with a wide grin.

"Maybe . . ." Kristine grinned back. "What about it, Mike? Do you think we managed to beat out 'Dallas'?"

"I dunno," Donovan took a slightly tipsy swig from his third can of Coors. "You're talking about tough competition, lady. I mean, this is *only* the news event of the *century*."

As soon as the broadcast was finished, somebody brought out bottles of champagne. The corks popped with almost the same frequency as the machine-gun bullets had just—yesterday? The day before? Time seemed to Donovan to have swerved, looped, gone sidereal.

He thought about traveling at the speed of light—what that might be like. What would it be like to pilot one of those big Mother Ships? Probably it would be such a group effort that you wouldn't get the thrill of handling the ship yourself.

"Mike?" He looked up a little blearily to see Kristine standing in front of him, realized he'd nearly dozed off.

"What time is it?" He looked around. The party was in full swing.

"Almost midnight. Want to come over to my place for a nightcap?"

He almost said no, that he'd better go find a hotel, that he was tired, but found himself agreeing. "Sure. You got a VCR?"

"Of course. You bringing the tape?"

"Of course!"

It had been several months since he'd been up to Kristine's

apartment. The view was breathtaking here on the upper East Side. He looked out at the glimmer of the water, watching the play of headlights far below. And above, of course, there was the floodlit enormity of the Visitor ship. Donovan stood looking at it, hardly able to believe he'd actually been up there, just a few hours ago.

Kristine emerged from the kitchen with several green bottles, and two delicately stemmed glasses. Donovan grinned. "*More* champagne?" The cork went off with a pop, and wine foamed out. He hurried to get his glass under the bottle as they sat down together in her luxurious velour conversation pit.

Kristine laughed. "Sure! How often do we get to celebrate our coverage of the event of the century?"

"Yeah." Donovan shook his head, then sipped carefully at the champagne. "I can't believe how the three of us just lucked into it!"

Kristine giggled. Mike had never seen her before when she'd had this much to drink. "Luck had nothing to do with it. I stacked the deck they drew from, so we'd get the pool!"

"Oh, come on!" He didn't know whether to believe her or not—or whether to hug her or give her a lecture. Stacked the deck?

"Yeah, I really did." She laughed, kicking off her shoes. She'd shed her businesslike tan blazer, and the white blouse she wore looked soft, feminine. He noticed that she'd unbuttoned it at the throat.

Donovan turned away from her, sipping his champagne. She edged back into the pit beside him, picking up the remote-control device for the television set. "Did you put the tape in, Mike?"

"But you saw it on the network . . ."

"Yeah, wasn't it terrific! Play it again, Sam. One more time!"

She turned on the unit, reaching for the bottle at the same time. Donovan felt something cold splash on his leg, and yelped. "Kris! Try to get it into the glass, for Chrissake!"

She made a face at the newsman on the screen. "We don't want to listen to *you*. Fast forward!" The television screen blurred and rippled.

Donovan laughed. "Your *life* is on fast forward, honey."

They watched their tour of the Mother Ship, as captured by

Donovan's camera. Kristine turned a mock-accusing face on Mike as Diana appeared on the screen. "There she is. Your girlfriend. You gave her more closeups than me!"

Donovan grinned at her, making no attempt to deny it. "She's got everything . . . brains . . . looks . . ."

"And a figure that doesn't quit," Kristine laughed, watching Diana in profile. "But would you want your sister to marry a Sirian?"

She punched the "fast forward" button again, then when the screen resolved, Diana was looking straight at them, at close range. "See!" Kristine turned to Donovan, her glass held threateningly aloft. "*Another* closeup!"

Donovan, laughing, tried to fend her off, but she was too quick for him, splashing a cold spatter of wine down the back of his neck. He made a grab for her, trying not to spill his own wine, finally managing to snag one of her wrists. Her empty glass dropped, falling onto the thickly sculpted carpet.

Both of them were laughing as they struggled for the remaining champagne glass. Somehow Mike found himself sprawled on the couch, with Kristine pulled down on top of him—and the champagne still in his possession. The glass was still—miraculously—full, but Donovan had lost interest in drinking any more of it. He was too conscious of Kristine's gaze. Their eyes were only inches away.

Her voice was husky. "Mike . . . why didn't it work for us before?"

He shook his head, shrugging wordlessly, realizing that if he didn't intend to spend the night here, he ought to call a halt to this right now. It wasn't fair to Kris otherwise. But somehow, he couldn't summon the words.

"I'd like to try again, Mike." She leaned toward him. Her mouth tasted sweet from the wine.

Donovan kissed her back, closing his eyes. Her body was alive and warm against his as he pulled her down beside him. One hand caught in the soft tumble of her hair as he drew her even closer. His other hand searched for the end table. He managed to set the glass down without spilling it.

# Chapter 3

Robert Maxwell frowned at his wife, Kathleen. "I thought Robin had to be there by now!"

Kathleen was clearly rattled, but made an effort to project her usual calm confidence. "Take it easy, honey. She'll be ready in just a moment. Did you back the car out?"

"Yes!" Maxwell knew he was being bearish, but couldn't help it. His first chance to get a close look at the Visitors, and his daughter was holding him up. Teenagers! "What's the delay, Kathy?"

"She found a spot on her band uniform, and she's trying to get it out. Calm down, honey."

Their twelve-year-old, Polly, came down the stairs carrying her three-year-old sister, Katie. Maxwell gathered up his youngest, giving her an affectionate kiss, enjoying her soap-and-water cleanliness. "Mmmm, you look pretty, sweetheart. Thanks for getting her ready, Polly."

"That's okay, Dad. She sure didn't want to wear that pink dress and those ruffled panties, though." Polly grinned at Katie, who shared her older sister's rough-and-tough ideas of apparel.

Kathleen shook her head at Maxwell as he stooped to put his little girl down. "Don't. Just keep hold of her. If you put her down she'll be filthy inside of thirty seconds."

Maxwell straightened, Katie giggling in his arms. "Your mommy's pretty smart, isn't she, Punkin? You, the World's

31

Champion Dirt Magnet? Huh?'' Katie grinned unabashedly at her father and planted a moist kiss squarely on his upper lip.

"Mother, where's my hat?" Seventeen-year-old Robin erupted down the stairs in a flash of white and maroon, trimmed liberally with black braid. Polly picked up her sister's flute case and handed it to her.

"Here it is, dear." Kathleen picked up the furry scarlet hat.

"Let's *go*, gang! We were supposed to be there five minutes ago!"

Maxwell drove the station wagon quickly, surely, toward the plant managed by their neighbor, Arthur Dupres. In the three weeks since the Visitors had arrived, they'd selected a number of plants to be retooled for the production of their urgently needed chemical compound. The Richland Chemical Corporation owned the first such plant to be declared operational by the Visitor Scientific Commander, Diana. Consequently, the place was thronged with news media and crowds awaiting the landing of the Visitor shuttle. Luckily Maxwell was able to park the station wagon near the school buses transporting the band equipment.

Hurriedly he handed Robin her flute case, as Kathleen adjusted the furry uniform hat on her daughter's dark head. "Do I look all right?" Robin squinted at the station wagon's outside mirror.

"You're gorgeous, kid," her father said, thinking that his habitual answer was becoming more truthful every day. With her blue-green eyes, fluffy dark hair and pretty features, his daughter had most of the boys in her class at Rosemont High School vying for her attention. Unfortunately, Robin was only too aware of this—a fact Maxwell found disturbing.

Watching her race over to where the band was forming up its lines, he sighed. *There's still a child in there*, he thought, *but not for long*.

Carrying Katie on his shoulder, Maxwell, his wife, and Polly headed for the reviewing stand. Late as they were for band formation, they were still earlier than the majority of the crowd, so were able to get good seats. Maxwell unslung his binocular case and took out his glasses.

"Bob!" Kathleen frowned, pushing her dark blonde hair off her forehead. "You're not going to use those things, are you?"

Maxwell focused the glasses, squinting, so he'd get the best view of the raised platform that had been set up for the opening ceremonies. "I sure am," he said.

"Doesn't that strike you as rather rude?"

"Nobody will even notice me. And we're sitting too far away from the platform for anyone to look up here."

Kathleen looked troubled. "Well, I still think—"

Maxwell put the glasses back in their case. "Honey, nobody's going to be looking at me! Everyone's going to be craning their necks for a glimpse of the Visitors! Arch Quinton told me last week that the telephoto shots of some of the Visitors showed some 'interesting anomalies,' as he put it. I want to see if I can spot what he was talking about."

"Why didn't you ask him?"

"You know Arch when he's got something on his mind. He was about as informative as the Stone of Scone."

"Maxwell!"

Both Maxwells turned at the hail, to see a balding man dressed in an expensive suit waving to them from the other side of the viewing stand. As they watched, a woman dressed in a quietly elegant hat and suit joined him.

With Polly and Katie in tow, Robert and Kathleen picked their way down the bleachers. At the bottom Maxwell held out his hand, "Hello, Arthur. Congratulations on the big day. The eyes of the world are on Richland today, eh?"

"They certainly are." Eleanor Dupres took her husband's arm proudly. "*I* was the one who suggested it. The very first night, when John first mentioned they needed chemicals, I said to Arthur that he ought to call up Richland and volunteer his plant for Visitor use. I pointed out that it was his civic duty, in a way. So he did, and now all this is happening . . . I think it's wonderful!"

"It certainly is," Kathleen said hastily, deliberately brushing Robert's arm with hers as she reached out to clasp Eleanor's hand warmly. Maxwell took a deep breath and manfully managed to smother the broad grin that Eleanor's speeches invariably invoked in him.

"Oh, and by the way, Robert and Kathleen," Eleanor said, oblivious to the Maxwells' byplay, "I'm giving a little party tonight to honor the Visitors. Several of them have consented to join us, and I wonder if you could come too."

Maxwell tried not to let his excitement show. "We'd love to, Eleanor. What time?"

"About eight. Nothing too formal . . . just evening wear required. See you then."

Eleanor and Arthur departed in the direction of the reviewing stand. Maxwell waited until they were out of earshot, then let out a whoop. "All *right!* I'll get to meet them close up!"

Kathleen gave him a mock glare. "You and your big mouth, Bob." Her light tones dropped into a deadly imitation of Eleanor's effusive ones. " 'Just evening wear required.' What the hell am I going to dig up to wear on six hours' notice?"

"You'll look gorgeous, honey, you always do," Maxwell said automatically, his mind already filling with visions of conversations with the Visitors about their evolutionary origins. So far, no scientific observers had been invited aboard the Visitor ships—just journalists and politicians. What a chance for him!

"And even if I *do* manage to scrape something up for myself, I can't figure what *you're* going to wear."

"What about that new sports jacket we got this past spring?"

Kathleen snorted rudely. "Did you even *notice* what you did to the cuffs that day you and Arch stopped off to visit the dig for 'just a few minutes'—when the few minutes turned into *three hours*? Talk about the original absentminded professors!"

"Oh, yeah." Maxwell looked chagrined. "Maybe I should go out and pick up a new one this afternoon, after the opening ceremonies."

Kathleen shook her head. "Sorry, hon. We can't afford it. But don't worry. I think the old Navy one is clean, and it will do."

Maxwell dropped an impulsive kiss onto her forehead. "Thank you, honey. I don't deserve you, you know that?"

Her clear green eyes softened a bit. "Sure you do. I love you, Bob."

"And I love you." They exchanged a fond look—a look which was interrupted by Polly's shout.

"Mom! Can Katie have a soda?"

"Later, Polly." They turned to climb the bleachers again.

"But *Mommy*, I'm *thirsty!*"

Kathleen sighed. "I said later, Katie. You can have some of those grapes Mommy brought."

The band began tuning up, and the bleachers filled rapidly. Maxwell saw a white van pull up, and several technicians began setting up gear. Several people got out of the van, and Maxwell, who was using his binoculars again, recognized two of them immediately.

"Look, honey, it's Michael Donovan and Kristine Walsh!"

"Let me see!" Kathleen took the binoculars eagerly. "Hmmm . . . Somehow they look shorter than when you see them on television."

"She's an attractive woman," Maxwell said, squinting at the journalist.

Kathleen gave him an amused look. "Who would you rather meet? Ms. Walsh, or Diana?"

"Diana," Maxwell grinned. "Preferably with a specimen glass behind my back."

She laughed. "The anthropologist to the end. Are you trying to tell me you haven't noticed how gorgeous she is?"

Maxwell chuckled. "I didn't say *that*."

The band struck up a wavering but recognizable rendition of the "Star Wars" theme. Someone in the bleachers shouted, "There it is!"

Maxwell looked up to see one of the Visitor shuttlecraft approaching from the giant ship that hovered over Los Angeles. The Mother Ship was such a normal sight by now that the L.A. skyline would have looked odd without it.

"What are they using to provide the raw materials for their chemical, do you know?" the man sitting next to Maxwell asked.

"I understand that they're using garbage and other wastes," Maxwell answered. "But I've never heard much of an explanation of what the chemical *is*, or what they're going to use it for."

The man, a heavyset black man in his late fifties, grunted. "That reminds me of a really bad joke I heard. 'Bout aliens that eat garbage and piss gasoline. Do you ever—I dunno—worry 'bout all this?"

Maxwell frowned through the binoculars as the shuttlecraft door opened and the Visitor technicians began filing through and assembling in ranks. Each carried a large, cumbersome-looking container of some kind. His mind distracted by his attempts to study their features under the caps and dark glasses, he almost forgot the man's question until Kathleen nudged him. "Worry? About what? They've shown their peaceful intentions."

The black man rubbed thoughtfully at his salt-and-pepper moustache. "I dunno. What *have* they really shown us? Where's all this scientific jazz they're supposed to be showing us? They've been here three weeks now, and we barely know any more about them than the first day they talked to us."

Maxwell squinted, recognizing Diana in the crowd. The Visitor technicians continued to file from the craft. Now a second shuttlecraft settled down and began disgorging red-garbed Visitors. Polly nudged him. "Hey, Dad, I just heard a joke."

"Ummmm?" Maxwell tried to focus the binoculars on the troops of Visitors. How many were out there now? The band continued to labor through "Star Wars"—Maxwell winced as he heard a flutist hit a sour note and hoped fervently it wasn't Robin.

"How many Visitors does it take to change a lightbulb?"

Maxwell craned his neck. "I don't know. How many?"

Polly laughed with all of a twelve-year-old's enthusiasm. "None! They *like* the dark!"

Maxwell laughed politely, heard the black man chuckling at his side. Visitors continued to file out of the craft, the band continued to play.

"How many of them *are* there, Robert?" Kathleen asked.

The black man turned to her. "I been wonderin' that myself. How many you counted?"

Maxwell stared at the growing sea of red coveralls, frowning. "I don't know. A lot."

"Yeah," said the black man. "A helluva lot."

Robin Maxwell was doing her best to keep playing in time with the band while her head turned to watch the Visitors file past her. She wasn't going to miss the chance to see them this close! She hit a sour note and winced—hoping the rest of the band had covered up her mistake. Still, she couldn't look away from the Visitor technicians walking past her.

There were a lot of them—Robin wondered what the various black stripes and insignia on their uniforms meant. What had

Daniel Bernstein said? Something about the markings denoting rank and type of work.

She wrinkled her attractive nose, thinking of Daniel. He'd been acting so *dumb* since the Visitors had come. They were all he could talk about. Used to be that all he'd wanted to talk about was whether or not she'd go out with him . . . not that Robin had any intention of *that*. Daniel was a nice kid, good-looking too, but that's all he was—a kid. True, he was almost nineteen, nearly eighteen months older than Robin herself, but he acted like a kid.

In the six months since Daddy had allowed her to go out on real car dates with boys, she'd already decided she wasn't going to waste her time going out with kids. Why, the last time she'd driven over to the University library with Daddy, two really cute freshmen had tried to pick her up as she walked across the quadrangle.

Robin smiled around the mouthpiece of her flute, remembering. "Star Wars" continued around her. Mr. Elderbaum, the bandleader, didn't look particularly pleased by the performance. But heck, they'd had less than a week to rehearse!

For sure, there were a lot of Visitors going by her, Robin thought. She wondered vaguely how many, then she hit a flat note without even noticing, and a second later she lowered the flute and simply stood there, staring.

He was the most gorgeous boy she'd ever seen—hair the color of bronze, and eyes—it was hard to make out behind the dark glasses, but Robin squinted until she was sure. Blue. A beautiful sky blue. He was standing beside the shuttlecraft hatch, evidently directing some of the Visitor technicians as they formed their ranks.

For long moments Robin stared, unaware that she was smiling. Just before he turned to move on, the Visitor's eyes met hers for a second. Robin felt the quick flush in her cheeks as his gaze touched hers.

Then he was gone, and she was alone once more with the band, and the seemingly never-ending "Star Wars." Robin put the flute back to her lips, picking up her place, but her playing was completely automatic.

*What a* fox *he was,* she thought. *A bitchin'* fox. She hoped that somehow, someday, she'd see him again . . .

\* \* \*

On the catwalk overhead, two men wearing hardhats stood, watching the red-coveralled forms file by. One, a heavy-shouldered black man, shook his head, "Damn!"

His companion, a wispy-haired white whose stomach proclaimed his fondness for beer and armchair football, turned to him. "What's the matter, Caleb?"

"What's the *matter*?" Caleb Taylor pointed indignantly. "Look at them, man! There's so many of those suckers they can hardly fit onto the parking lot! First we got to fight you honkies for jobs, then the Mexicans—and now these creeps have come to work with us, and they ain't even *from* this planet!"

Bill Graham laughed. "Don't be so paranoid, Caleb!"

After a second Taylor chuckled wryly. "If you'd had to worry 'bout layoffs as many times as I have, Bill, you'd be paranoid too. You know blacks are most often the first to go, don't try and tell me any different. In the days when I had a wife and two kids to feed, I used to sweat every time things got a little slow here at Richland."

"Well, it's sure different for you now," Bill pointed out. "Ben's doing so well at the hospital that you won't have to touch your pension from this place if you don't want to."

"I don't know 'bout that," Caleb said thoughtfully. "I've never lived off another person, and I'm not about to start. Even if Ben *is* a doctor. Shit, he could get married and move to Boston or something, and what would Elias and I do then?"

"Is Ben finally getting serious about someone?"

Caleb Taylor snorted. "You kidding? He's so wrapped up in medicine that the only time he ever *looks* at a woman is when she's stripped an' lying on an examining table!"

Graham made a juicy noise with his lips. "Hey, for all I know, that's as good a way as any to get some—"

"Shit, don't you ever suggest that to Ben! He's so dedicated to that Hippocratic oath of his that he wouldn't even know you were jokin'. He'd probably nail you one before you could explain it to him!"

Both men laughed. "Speaking of Elias, how's he doing?" Graham asked.

Caleb Taylor turned back to stare morosely down at the Visitor ranks. "Hell, Bill, I don't know. He barely even sleeps at home anymore. He ain't worked in months, yet the other day

I asked him if he could pay the paperboy, and he whipped a roll
out of his pants you could choke an alligator with!"

"Uh oh."

"That's what I said, believe me, man. I don't know where he
goes durin' the day, what he does—and I'm scared to ask for
fear he'll tell me, and then what would I do?"

"I'm sorry, Caleb. Funny about those two boys—Ben's such
a success, and Elias—"

"Yeah. Don't I know it."

They watched the presentation ceremony for several minutes
in silence. Graham changed the subject. "Did you hear that
about half of the plants they've arranged for will be used to
desalinate the sea water, not to produce the chemical?"

"Yeah? Which will they be doin' here at Richland?"

"Both."

"How many plants they going to be using?"

"I don't know. They're still negotiating. A lot of them.
Almost every seacoast plant in the world was contacted, I
understand. How many of them they'll pick is anyone's
guess."

Caleb frowned, staring intently down at the Visitor ranks,
his lips moving soundlessly. "What're you doing, Caleb?"
Graham asked, trying to follow his friend's gaze.

"Countin' those suckers. *Damn*, there are a lot of 'em!"

Juliet Parrish looked over Dennis Lowell's tanned, muscular
shoulder at the television screen, which showed one of the
Visitor leaders, "Steven," talking to the well-known television
reporter, Kristine Walsh. He was explaining that most of the
Visitor plants chosen would be located on the Earth's coast-
lines.

As Juliet watched, her fingers continued their rhythmic
knead and pull at Lowell's back. "Look at that mob, Denny.
I'm glad we decided to stay here and watch this on the set. We
wouldn't be able to see a thing if we'd driven over there."

Denny, absorbed in the *Wall Street Journal*, merely grunted
assent. Juliet smiled down at his dark head, continuing her
massage. Her fingers moved downward and together, rubbing
in short, circular motions over the *vertebrae lumbaris* area.
She had a sudden, insistent urge to kiss the back of his neck,
but resisted. Denny didn't like being interrupted while he was

studying the market—and although stocks and bonds frankly bored Parrish, she went out of her way not to let him know it.

"Mmmmm—that's good," mumbled Denny.

Juliet smiled again. "Well, after five years of anatomy, it *should* be."

"No—I meant the market. It's really surging up. The Visitors have been good for the economy. I think we've got some good times ahead."

Juliet sighed, smiling ruefully. Denny loved his work as a stockbroker as much as she loved medicine. Someday, no doubt, he'd be very, very rich, he was so good at what he did. If they married—*if*—she'd share that with him. Though she'd never given a damn about money. If it hadn't been for that scholarship she'd gotten, she'd be in debt far worse than she was . . .

If she had her choice she'd join Vista or the Peace Corps—or maybe WHO—after her internship was complete. Or go back to China, where she'd studied on an exchange program for six months. But if she did, she'd lose Denny. She knew it, even though she'd never brought up the subject. Denny wasn't the kind to wait two or three years. She grimaced. Few men were, these days. Most guys she'd ever been attracted to had faded into the woodwork after learning she was a med student, at the top of her class. Her biochemistry research with Doctor Metz had only worsened matters. Then she'd met Denny . . .

He was one of the few men she'd met who enjoyed being with a woman who he acknowledged was probably smarter than he was. And Juliet, after the months and years of dedicated study, had found herself liking the changes he introduced in her life. Quiet homemade meals and intimate restaurants, instead of TV dinners and textbooks. Parties with a few congenial friends. Backpacking and camping when she had a free weekend. Old Bogart and Gable movies on his VCR.

She studied the face of the Visitor on the television screen through slightly narrowed eyes, wishing she could meet one of them, talk him or her into donating some blood samples. What did their DNA look like? Assuming they *had* DNA . . .

They probably did. After all, they looked so *much* like us. Except for their voices, you could put one in a business suit and drop him or her on Wall Street and nobody would bat an eye.

*In a way,* Juliet Parrish thought, *I'd have liked it better if they had purple tentacles or something.* She noticed a black face among the hordes of Visitors ranked beside the shuttle, and frowned. *Weird. They even have the same racial differences. Wonder if Ben Taylor's watching?*

Her eyes roamed the rows and rows of red coveralls, searching for any anomalies, noting the lack of visible facial scars or blemishes. *There are so many of them, and each one is perfect.* She didn't realize that her fingers had tightened on Dennis Lowell's back until he gasped and jumped. "Hey, watch it, honey! That's too hard!"

She kissed the back of his neck, feeling with relief the solidity and warmth of his flesh. "Sorry, Den. Let's turn off the television, okay?"

"Why? This is an historical occasion."

She reached for the remote control, clicked it off, her hands then sliding around his body very slowly. " 'Cause I've got something better than making mere history in mind."

" 'Zat so?"

Neither of them noticed they were crumpling the *Wall Street Journal.*

The night air was brisk and delicious, just cool enough to make Robert Maxwell forget his usual distaste for a coat and tie. He held Kathleen's arm as the two of them walked up the street and through the gate to the Dupres house. The house itself was mostly dark; laughter and conversation were emanating from the garden out back. They took the flagstoned path around the side of the house.

The garden was festooned with outdoor lamps, mosquitoes, and people. Maxwell sniffed appreciatively at the good smells—he'd gotten home from the ceremonies too late to eat.

He scooped a couple of glasses of wine off a tray as the waiter passed him, handing one to Kathleen. "Thanks," she whispered, her green eyes traveling around the guests, evaluating the women's clothes. "Do I look all right?"

"Gorgeous. That dress really suits you, honey." It did, too. Red was one of Kathy's best colors—and that shimmering shawl he'd brought home from Pakistan set it off perfectly.

A chiffon wave of blue that turned out to be Eleanor with both arms spread wide engulfed them, seemingly from out of nowhere. "Robert, Kathleen! *So* glad you could make it! Do come meet our guests of honor!"

"Nice party, Eleanor," Maxwell said, brushing unobtrusively at a mosquito.

"Delightful," murmured Kathleen.

"Didn't the ceremonies go off *splendidly*? Steven was saying to me a few minutes ago that the ceremonies and the party have been among the nicest they've encountered. I told Arthur we must do this again."

"Mother," said a male voice almost in Maxwell's ear.

He turned, as did Eleanor and Kathleen, to find himself facing the journalists he'd seen that afternoon—Mike Donovan, Kristine Walsh, and an Asian man. At the latter's side stood a slender, brown-haired woman.

"I beg your pardon?" began Maxwell, but Eleanor, with a moue of annoyance, cut him off.

"What is it, Michael?"

"Kris and Tony and I have a special interview with Diana to tape, so we'll have to be going."

"Oh. I'd hoped to be able to introduce you around, Michael." Eleanor was obviously displeased. Just as obviously, Donovan was unaffected by her pique.

"Sorry. The shuttle is supposed to pick us up at nine, over at the plant parking lot." For the first time the newsman seemed to notice the Maxwells standing awkwardly before him, and extended his hand. "My name's Mike Donovan. Kristine Walsh, Tony and Fran Leonetti. Nice to meet you."

Maxwell shook hands, nodding. "Robert Maxwell. My wife, Kathleen. Our pleasure."

Murmured greetings filled the air, until they were replaced almost without pause by murmured farewells. Maxwell watched as the three journalists left the party, stopping briefly to speak with Arthur Dupres. Robert turned back to his hostess.

"Eleanor, I had no idea that Michael Donovan the newsman is your son. Why, he's one of the most well-known cameramen in the country!"

Eleanor sniffed. "You'd think he could have stayed long enough to meet the rest of my guests."

"Uh, yeah." Maxwell, discomfited, looked sidelong at Kathleen, who gallantly rose to the occasion.

"Speaking of guests, Eleanor, isn't that one of your guests of honor over there? Robert and I would *love* to meet him!"

Eleanor brightened. "Yes, that's Steven. He brought a young woman with him—quite an attractive girl. I'll introduce you."

They threaded through the crowd in their hostess' blue wake until they reached the dark-haired, slenderly built man in the red coveralls. In the gentle illumination of the patio torches, he'd removed his dark glasses. He was nodding and smiling as Arthur introduced him to guests.

Eleanor took the Visitor's arm. "Steven dear, here are two people you simply *must* meet. Robert Maxwell and his wife, Kathleen Maxwell. Robert is quite a prominent anthropologist."

Maxwell extended his hand, felt his fingers gripped firmly by cool, resilient flesh. *Markedly cool*, Maxwell thought, shaking hands. *Body temperature about 85° or so.*

Kathleen, smiling warmly, also shook hands. Steven smiled, then spoke in that resonating near-echo voice that sounded so strange coming from such human lips. "An-thro-polo-gist? What kind of work do you do, Mr. Maxwell?"

"Robert," Maxwell said. "Please call me Robert, Steven. An anthropologist is a scientist who studies the development of man from his earliest hominid ancestors to our current version of *homo sapiens.*"

As Maxwell spoke, Steven stiffened perceptibly, his smile fading. *Now what the hell did I say wrong?* Robert wondered. He cast a sidelong look at Kathleen, only to realize from her anxious expression that she, too, had noticed the Visitor's reaction.

A moment only, then the alien was smiling graciously again. "You must forgive us—we have studied your language very closely, but inevitably there are words we do not know."

"No problem," Maxwell said, brushing at a ubiquitous buzzing near his ear. "Damn mosquitoes . . ."

Eleanor, who had vanished a few seconds earlier, suddenly reappeared, brandishing a tray of hors d'oeuvres. Maxwell thanked her, trying not to seem too greedy as he helped himself to several. As he chewed on a water chestnut, bacon, and chicken liver concoction, Steven, with a polite smile, carefully selected a carrot stick and munched cautiously on it. He shook his head graciously as Eleanor proffered meatballs, chicken wings teriyaki, and sausage—each time her offers were met by Steven's headshake and polite smile.

*Totally avoids cooked foods and meats*, thought Maxwell, slapping unobtrusively at another buzz. *And we're being eaten by mosquitoes—but he's not . . .*

Edging back through the crowd until he was again beside the Visitor, Maxwell cleared his throat. "Are there many scientists aboard your ships?"

Steven nodded. "Yes. What you would call engineers of all sorts—chemical, cryogenic, structural—plus many other specialties."

"Do you have any scientists that would be the equivalent of anthropologists?"

"Yes, of course. But they were not needed for this mission, which required technical skills."

"Well, do you mind if I ask you a few questions about your culture?"

Steven smiled. "Not at all."

"What is your planet like?"

"Much like yours. It is somewhat larger, as our star is larger. It is made up of many of the same kinds of minerals."

"And your evolution? Did your people evolve from a common ancestor with other anthropoids? You know—manlike apes and monkeys?"

"Oh, I see. Well, I am no anthropologist, you understand, but I think our anthropologists have concluded that our evolution was quite similar to yours."

"Great!" Maxwell nodded eagerly. "What kind of government do you have?"

"We have no nations, as you have. Just all the peoples of our world, united under the leadership of our Great Leader."

"How does he govern?"

"By divining the will of the people, and using it to lead us effectively."

"I see. What kind of social unit, then?"

"Social unit?" Steven cocked his head questioningly.

"Well, our basic social unit is the family. A male and female, pledged to live and work together for their mutual benefit, plus any resulting offspring."

"Matings with outsiders are considered undesirable?"

"That's right. Monogamy."

The Visitor nodded. "Monogamy is also our way. One male, one female, children, living together."

"I really appreciate getting a chance to talk to you, Steven."

The Visitor's eyes moved past Maxwell to fix on a table in the middle of the patio near the pool. Kathleen sat at the table, smiling at a young woman with long, fair hair in a red coverall.

"Your wife?" asked Robert, thinking how attractive the Visitor woman was.

"No." Steven smiled. "Barbara is a sub-leader in the unit I command. She was assigned to assist me. We work together."

"I see," said Maxwell. He was trying to sort through the questions jumbling through his mind. "What sort of—"

"Hello, Robert!" Arthur Dupres boomed, shaking hands fervently. "I see you've met Steven. Do you mind if I steal him from you?" He winked broadly at the Visitor. "Got some folks from Richland who just arrived, and they're dying to meet you. And if I know old Bob here, he was plying you with questions on your social structure and habits, eh?"

Maxwell forced a grin. "Can't blame me for being curious, Arthur. First time I ever met a gentleman who also happened to be an extraterrestrial!"

Taking Steven's arm, Arthur led him over to a group of men and women standing near the entrance to the garden. As they walked by the cage containing Eleanor's prize lovebirds, the creatures fluttered desperately, dashing themselves against the wire bars.

*Now* that's *weird*, the anthropologist thought, watching the birds' agitation subside. *What caused* that? Frowning, he walked over to study the birds, wondering if there were a cat skulking in the bushes. But the bushes at the corner of the garden were empty of anything except fallen blossoms and cigarette butts.

Arthur was coming back his way, and Maxwell quickly stepped aside as his host, Steven firmly ensconced at his side, passed him.

This time Robert Maxwell kept his eyes on the lovebirds the entire time, and there was no doubt what was causing their panic. No doubt at all.

It was Steven, the Visitor.

# Chapter 4

Arch Quinton frowned down at the folder on his battered old desk in the University Anthropology Department, then picked up the phone. Punching buttons with quick, nervous fingers, he waited impatiently as the connection was made. A ring! He gave a quick grimace of relief—the line had been busy for nearly an hour. *Probably Robin. Teenagers,* thought Quinton sourly.

After four rings, he heard a surprised voice. "Hello?"

"Robin, this is Doctor Quinton. I apologize for calling so late. Is Robert in bed?"

"No, I'm sorry, Doctor Quinton, he and my mom are out for the evening. They went to a party over at the Dupreses'. You want him to call you when he gets home?"

"No, that's all right, lass. I'll be headin' out now, since it's—" He checked his watch. Good Lord, it was after midnight! "It's late," he said. "I'll call him tomorrow, if he's not reached me first."

"Yes, sir," said Robin. "I'm leaving a note you called. Is it important?"

"Sort of," said Quinton, not wishing to alarm her, "but nothing that can't wait for tomorrow. I've something in my current files he'll find interesting. Good night, lass."

"Night, Dr. Quinton."

With a sigh Quinton cradled the instrument, then turned back to the folder labeled, simply, "John."

47

He turned over the large, blown-up glossies of the Visitor leader, some of them marked with a numbered grid, to the infrared shots at the back of the folder. These were his prizes. A photography major on the University paper had taken and developed them using special equipment and a telephoto lens during one of the Visitor leader's many press conferences.

Quinton shook his head slowly, thoughtfully, as he studied the heat patterns the infrared photos revealed. *They're* not right, he thought. *Something about the skull . . . misshapen . . . bone too thick . . . especially at the top of the head- . . . Wish they were clearer, then I'd really have something . . . Maxwell may say I'm crazy.* He frowned, taking out a magnifying glass and examining the grid-patterned shot with painstaking attention.

*Even in this shot, the shadows indicate anomalies in the bone . . . I've got t' have an X-ray. Then there'd be no doubt . . .*

Picking up his ancient pipe, he tamped and lit it, staring thoughtfully at the folder. Then he pushed the photos back into it and shut it, dropping it into his "current" box with the happy face and the slogan his godchild, Polly, had presented him with: "Archeology: can you dig it?"

As he sat there, he felt weariness settle over him like a muffling blanket. Best to go home, get a good night's rest, think about it tomorrow, he decided. Knocking his pipe out in the ashtray, he stood up, feeling the hours of intensive study in the cramped muscles of his neck and back. His stomach rumbled, reminding him that the cheeseburger his grad assistant had brought him for lunch was now almost twelve hours in the past.

Wondering if he was too tired to stop for something to eat, he slung his coat across his shoulders and left, carefully locking the office door, then the back gate. The parking lot was silent and deserted. Quinton stopped for a moment by the back gate, looking up at the stars. It was a clear night for Los Angeles—they were very distinct. He could even make out the densest part of the Milky Way stretching overhead. His eyes shifted to the eastern part of the sky, but Canis Major wouldn't be visible for a month yet, at least. The Great Dog, containing the brightest star in the heavens, Sirius, with a magnitude of

− 1.58. A white scorching star, some 8.7 light-years away, a back-fence neighbor, as galactic distances go.

Arch Quinton's eyes began to blur, and he rubbed them wearily. Sirius. Just a local star a month ago. Now . . . what?

His hands were cold in the night wind as he fumbled with the keys to his Granada. Opening the door, he swung in, started the engine, then turned to back the car out of its space.

Sitting in the back seat was a man wearing a red coverall. The dash lights reflected an eerie green from his dark glasses. Quinton opened his mouth to scream . . .

# Chapter 5

The Visitor was not having a good day. This morning he'd awakened to find that his original assignment of a chemical plant near Saudi Arabia had been changed: he was now assigned to the Richland plant in a place called Los Angeles. Even his name, Ahmed, had been changed—he was now William."

Now, the bulky cryo storage unit held before him like a heavy shield, he clutched his orders in his fingertips and staggered, blinking, from the shuttle.

The lights were so *bright*! He'd been warned, but with everything else that had happened, he'd forgotten. This was his first time down on the surface of this new world. Blinking, he stumbled forward until he could set the gray unit on the pavement and find his dark glasses.

Thanks be to the Leader, he had them. Blinking, William slipped them on. The glare became manageable. His back muscles complaining, William picked up the c-unit again, starting off in search of his assigned area, mentally struggling to remember the snippets of English he'd picked up from hearing the officers talk among themselves. John had given the order that crewmembers must practice their assigned Earth languages at all times in order to gain proficiency as quickly as possible. Ahmed—no, *William*, he must remember *William*—had learned to think in Arabic.

And now this! William found a flight of metal stairs in front of him and began cautiously to climb them. The gravity of Earth was slightly lower than that of his native planet—one hardly felt it on a straightaway, but the difference could cause stumbles on an incline.

He peered again at the assigned station on the card inscribed with his technician's data and personal background. The plant seemed a warren of steel-gray and orange piping and hurrying people. He realized he'd have to ask directions—

An impact jarred him backward. "Hey! Watch out where the hell you're going!"

William almost slipped on the foot-polished treads of the stair, but managed to keep his balance. Looking up, he saw a dark-skinned man (the humans called that shade of skin "black," though to William it looked like a warm brown) wearing a yellow hardhat with "Taylor" stenciled across it. The Visitor struggled for words. "Uh . . . Oh, excuse, please. Uh . . . help, please."

William wasn't very familiar with human expressions, but he thought he remembered this one. It was termed a "frown," and if the Visitor wasn't mistaken, it was a way of displaying displeasure. "Help what?" the human growled.

"Please," said William, thinking furiously and finally hitting on the right word—he hoped. "I am just."

"Just what?" asked the man, still frowning.

"Yes," nodded William emphatically. "Just."

The man growled again. "Aw, get out of my way!" He pushed William roughly aside. "Damn stupid alien!"

The Visitor watched him leave, trying to translate the man's words. Directions to the Cryogenics Transfer Unit? Somehow William was pretty sure not. He even suspected that Taylor's words constituted an insult of some kind.

Sighing, William looked around, hoping from this elevation to spot some sign of his destination.

Nothing. Another whistle blew from a nearby speaker, making him jump. He "heard" the raucous blast throughout his body, and it "felt" even more unpleasant than it sounded.

He abandoned the stairs and wandered forlornly across the cement, looking over at the shuttles for some sign of someone he could talk to. He was even beginning to consider disobeying orders and asking directions in his native language (though that would definitely be a last-resort tactic), if he could find another of his people. He rounded a series of cylindrical containers that appeared to be used as repositories for waste (a notion which puzzled him—why simply store waste? It was a valuable energy source).

Ahead of him he saw several larger transports parked, and made his way toward them. His back ached, and, to his distress, he realized he was beginning to feel hungry. He would not be able to eat until after his shift, back in his quarters. Those were the rules.

He trudged around to the nose of one of the transports, peering at the vehicle. Nobody inside. He turned, growing ever more frustrated, conscious now that he was *very* late for his work shift. Everyone said that Steven, who was in charge of operations here, was someone to avoid angering. What was he going to do?

Hesitantly he rapped on the black opaqueness of the viewscreen, hoping that someone might be in the back of the shuttle.

A voice spoke from behind him. "Hi there. Are you okay?"

Turning, he saw a human standing behind him. The blue dress and the rounded protuberances beneath the front of it told him this one was female. Her hair was dark gold and blew around her head in fluffy profusion. Her eyes were almost exactly the same color as her planet's lower atmospheric regions in favorable weather conditions. She smiled—William was quite sure that was what she was doing, and was also sure, although why he couldn't say, that he vastly preferred this expression to the one Taylor had treated him to.

"I am just," he told her simply.

"Yeah?" She cocked her head inquiringly. "What?"

"Just," William repeated as clearly and meaningfully as he could.

Her smile faded slightly. "Just . . . just?"

William had the distinct impression he wasn't communicating properly. "Yes. *Just.*"

She frowned—though not in the same way Taylor had. "Just what?"

William had been hoping so strongly that she'd understand that he'd been holding his breath, willing her to. Now air puffed out of him in a hiss of frustration. He turned to leave.

Her hand caught his sleeve—the first time he'd ever been

touched by a person from another world. "Now wait," she was saying, and William struggled to comprehend her quick, easy speech. "Don't let it get you spazzed. I'll help you out."

William seized with gratitude on the one word he recognized. "Yes, help. Help to go. To *this* place." He showed her the English translation printed above the concept blocks of his own language. "I am *just*."

She scanned the card quickly, then turned to him, plainly guessing. "You don't know where to go?"

"Yes," agreed William fervently. "I'm just."

Sudden understanding so blatant that the Visitor had no trouble seeing it brightened her features. "You're *lost*."

*Lost!* The word linked in his memory, and relief flooded him. William nodded eagerly, putting the cryo unit down. "*Lost!* Yes, lost." He peered at her through his glasses, and for some reason risked the morning glare to take them off so he could see her more clearly. "Thank you . . ." He fumbled to explain. "English . . . not well to me. Learned Arabic . . . for going there."

She nodded sympathetically. "And they screwed up and sent you to L.A.?"

"Yes," agreed William, remembering his entire miserable morning. "Screwed," he repeated, wondering what the new word meant. He felt fairly sure it was a colloquialism. He'd have to ask someone.

"Well, L.A.'s not so bad. Beats Fresno, lemme tell you. What's your name?"

"Ah—" he began, then remembered. "William."

"Well, hi. I'm Harmy." She smiled. "That's short for Harmony . . . can you believe it? I work here." She shifted the tray she was carrying, which was littered with empty paper cups and plates. "Food service, y'know." She scanned the card he held out. "Cryo—Cryogenics Transfer Unit. Well, c'mon, Willy. Let's go find it."

William tried to match her expression to show his gratitude. Smiling wasn't as hard as it looked. They wended their way through the maze of pipes and holding tanks, each with attendants and gauges, until they looked upward at a series of catwalks spanning a huge pressure unit.

William recognized Steven as one of the men standing at the foot of the massive installation.

The officer was shouting, "No, the pressure's still not balanced! Must be the inner seal that's bad. Someone will have to go inside."

Harmy called out, "Is this the Cryogenics Transfer Unit?"

Steven looked over at her. "Yes—" Then his eyes fixed on William, who remembered guiltily that he was *very* late, and he snapped, "William! Where were you?"

He looked over at Harmy, who smiled encouragingly. "Uh . . . I was lost."

Steven shook his head, but obviously held back from any further remarks in the presence of the humans. "Well, get up there." He pointed to the catwalk overhead. "You'll be working with that man."

William looked upward, to see a dark face he remembered, wearing a disgusted expression he knew, looking back at him. The man wearing a hardhat and business suit supplied, "Caleb Taylor is one of our best men. Caleb, meet William."

William was not surprised when Taylor did not speak. He couldn't think of anything to say either.

Juliet Parrish looked up to see Rudolph Metz enter the door of the laboratory, with Ruth only a pace behind him, looking upset. Juliet guessed quickly what the problem was. "Don't tell me they've canceled again!"

Doctor Metz nodded. "Yes. We've been asked to be patient. Their scientists have been too busy setting up the processing at the plants to finish their introductory presentations for us. I just spoke to Vasily Andropov, who was chosen for the Soviet team, and he told me in confidence that their team's visit has been postponed too!"

Juliet was profoundly disappointed, making no attempt to hide it. "But this is the *second* time! When did they say they'd be able to do it?"

Ruth shook her head disgustedly. "They didn't. 'A week or two' was the only thing we could get out of the Visitor who delivered the message. His name was Martin, and he seemed genuinely sorry, but he said Diana had personally given the order to postpone."

"Damn!" Juliet stared morosely at one of the rat cages. "Everybody *else* is going up there! Did you hear that they're even giving kids special visits to the Mother Ships if they join up with this youth organization they're sponsoring? They call it the Visitor Friends."

Doctor Metz nodded heavily. "I heard Kristine Walsh's broadcast earlier. Still, we mustn't be too disappointed. We must remember that the Visitors' primary reason for being here is the production of their chemical. Giving seminars for us is merely a courtesy."

Juliet made a face. "Not the way I heard it that first night. They were going to share 'all the fruits of their knowledge' *in exchange* for our help with processing their chemical."

"You're right," Ruth said. "I remember those were their exact words."

All three scientists turned as Benjamin Taylor poked his head in the door. "Doctor Metz . . . glad I've found you. We've had another requisition from the L.A. Mother Ship for more lab animals."

"But we gave them a shipment just last week!" Doctor Metz exclaimed. "They need *more*? Did they say what for?"

"Of course not," said Ruth sardonically.

"No," admitted Taylor. "They did say, however, that they've been breeding their own, and expect in a month or so to be able to supply their own stock."

"Well, send them what they've asked for, of course," said Metz with a worried frown.

"Of course," mumbled Juliet, so softly that nobody but Ruth heard. "I'm getting curiouser and curiouser to see that Mother Ship."

Robert Maxwell unlocked the door to Arch Quinton's office, then stood in the doorway for a moment, his eyes roving its familiar features. The "current" box was empty. Frowning, he opened several file cabinets, searching with quick, impatient movements, then, frustrated, slammed the gray drawer back into its casing with a bang.

Reaching for the phone, he dialed quickly. "Kathy? Let me talk to Robin for a second."

A pause. "Robin, this is Daddy. Are you sure Doctor Quinton said the stuff he wanted me to look at was in his current files?"

His frown deepened. "Okay. Thanks, hon. See you later."

Almost as soon as he hung up the phone it began to ring.

Maxwell picked it up. "Hello? Doctor Maxwell here. Yes, this is Doctor Quinton's office. I'm one of his associates."

He listened intently for a moment. "No, I've been trying to reach him. Nobody's seen him today. I called his landlady—he didn't come home last night, as far as she knows. He called about midnight last night, and spoke to my daughter. Said he was working late."

Absently, he began searching Quinton's top desk drawer, then lifted the blotter and peered underneath it. "Listen, Officer—Robeson, did you say? Have you checked with the L.A. police? Any sign of his car?"

He paused. "He drove—" He corrected himself quickly, with a grimace of worry, "*drives* a gray Granada. A '78, I think. Yes, it's got a campus parking registry."

His breath hissed sharply. "I'll meet you there. The parking lot behind this building?"

Maxwell was running by the time he erupted into the sunlight. It was Saturday, and this early the parking lot was nearly empty. Quinton's car stood off by itself.

Robert Maxwell felt strangely reluctant to approach the vehicle—somehow it looked abandoned, forlorn. He swallowed, forcing himself to walk numbly toward it.

The door gave easily beneath his hand—not locked. He reached out, past the steering column, then moved away with Quinton's worn leather-tab key ring in his hand. There was an odd smell hanging about the automobile that sickened and repelled Maxwell, making the fear mounting in the back of his throat turn to nausea.

He swallowed again, fighting not to breathe too deeply, turning to look around the interior. Empty. Clean, just as Quinton had always kept it.

His eyes turned to the door. The handle on the driver's side hung askew, and an oily black stain marred the red vinyl. Maxwell realized he was shaking with deep tremors that twisted his gut. His heart seemed to be directly between his ears, throbbing.

Putting out an unsteady hand, Robert touched fingertips to the stain, then sniffed them cautiously. Bile flooded his mouth, and if his stomach hadn't been empty, he'd have vomited. He spat on the cement, then spat again, then leaned back against the Granada's rear door, feeling dizzy, emptied.

Footsteps . . . quick, heavy. The campus cop Robeson. "You Maxwell?"

Robert swallowed, scrubbing the foulness of that oily stain off on the roughness of his jeans. "Yes, I'm Doctor Maxwell."

"This Quinton's car?"

"Yes, it is. I found his keys in the ignition."

Robeson took the key ring with a reproachful *tchh* of his tongue. "Shouldn't have touched it, Doc. There might be fingerprints."

"Sorry." Maxwell's shock was turning to grief now, a paralyzing sense of certainty that he'd never see Arch again. He tried to think rationally, convince himself that Quinton would have called to explain everything by the time he got back inside, called Kathy, but he couldn't.

The cop was inspecting the interior of the car. "Never saw anything quite like this. I'd better call L.A.P.D. right away." He peered at Maxwell. "You gonna be okay, Doc?"

"I'm all right," Maxwell said, untruthfully.

"This is *weird*," Robeson said. "You got any idea what might have happened to him?"

"No." Maxwell found he was shaking again as the breeze brought that smell to his nostrils again. "God, no."

"I'll call L.A.P.D.," Robeson said, then added kindly, "you better sit down, Doc."

The afternoon sun slanted through and spattered itself in a yellow haze against the oyster-white wall of Kristine Walsh's Los Angeles loft apartment. Mike Donovan sat on the sofa, checking and packing his camera equipment. Kristine, in bra and half-slip, was in the other room, putting on her makeup. Her monologue was broken into uneven bursts of speech and pauses as she squinted in the mirror, daubing carefully at her eyes and mouth.

". . . and then Diana said that she was pleased with the progress at the Richland plant. Said it was representative of all the others around the world." She widened her eyes, touching sable mascara to her lashes in quick brushing gestures.

Donovan's voice reached her from the living room. "Did she mention that she'd postponed the seminars for the scientists a second time?"

"Yes. She said they'll be beginning them shortly."

Donovan made a rude noise. "That's what they said the other time."

"But wait, Mike, I haven't told you the best part." Kristine tilted her head, examining her blusher critically. "Then Diana said, 'The other thing I'm pleased with here, Kristine, is *you*.' I didn't know what to say, what she was getting at, you know. Then she explained that of all the journalists they've met since they've been here, the Visitors feel most comfortable with me. She said, 'Our research also shows that your people have a lot of confidence in you. You're trusted and respected . . . attractive—'"

"So is Lassie," snapped Donovan. "What's that got to do with anything?"

"Well, she told me those qualities were essential in the person they selected as the official Visitor spokesperson—and then she offered *me* the job!"

"Huh?"

"Or Press Secretary . . . She said I could call it what I wanted. Which do you like?"

There was a long pause. Donovan's voice, when he finally spoke, sounded tight. "I don't much like the sound of either one."

Kristine gave a final pat to her hair, then pulled on her tan wool skirt and the dark brown striped blouse. "Come on, Mike. You're jealous."

"The hell I am. Don't be a jackass, Kris! I don't understand why you'd even consider it!"

"They want someone the public trusts . . . and *I* think it's an excellent career move." She walked past him into the living room, and, picking up her purse, began checking the contents. Donovan looked over at her. "What about your objectivity?"

"What?" *Notebook*, she thought, *tape recorder . . . lipstick . . . where's my pen?*

Mike's tone was hard, one she'd only heard a few times before—usually when someone asked him a question about his divorce. "Don't you think you're compromising your objectivity by sucking up to those—"

She whirled to face him. "I'm not sucking up to anybody!"

His eyes were troubled. Kristine came over and knelt in front of him so she could look directly at him. "Don't you see?

It's the perfect opportunity to really get the inside stuff! Exclusive stuff . . . material that no one else has access to! I'm sure to get a *book* out of it, at the very least!"

She took his hands in hers. They were limp, unresponsive, and his face still wore that shocked, puzzled expression. She tried to reassure him. "I'm going to stay objective, Mike. After all, I'm one of us, not them."

He looked down, stubbornly refusing to meet her eyes again. Kristine gave his hands a squeeze—then a shake. "Oh, come on, Mike! Any good reporter would be crazy not to jump at this!"

His green eyes, when they met hers again, were full of challenge. Kristine bit her lip. "I'd like to think I had your backing, honey. You know how I respect you." Her hand moved to brush his cheek, lingering for a moment against the freshly shaven smoothness. "More than respect . . ."

Donovan looked down at his hands, slowly extricated them from her fingers. "You'd better put the steaks back in the freezer, Kris."

Her mind flashed back to the conversation with Diana. "Oh yeah. Tonight's a problem—the last thing Diana mentioned was that she'd send a shuttle for me so we could meet. How did *you* know?"

He stared at her for a long moment, and slowly his meaning dawned. Kristine moved blindly to look for her pen, eyes blurring, holding her shoulders stiffly erect. After a second he closed his camera bag, then went back into the bedroom. She heard him packing.

"Damn," she whispered, and was horrified to hear her voice crack. "Damn, damn, damn . . . *damn*!"

She didn't turn around until the apartment door closed behind him.

# Chapter 6

William the Visitor looked out across the cryogenics section to see a familiar blonde head halfway across the compound. He smiled, the expression coming unconsciously now. His bootheels rang on the steel catwalk as he trotted down the stairs and over the pavement. Harmy had apparently seen him coming, and stood waiting, the familiar tray in her hands. William nodded shyly. "Hello."

"Well, hello yourself. How are you doing?"

"Fine, fine." He smiled. "I like to thank you again for your help. Without you, I would have stayed 'just'—probably forever."

She giggled. "Forever, Willy. But listen to you! Only a week here, and your English is better than mine! You guys really learn fast."

William nodded. "We are told to practice all the times. How are you today?"

"Okay—same old, same old. How are you getting along with that guy? He didn't look any too thrilled t'see you, the other day."

William shrugged—another gesture he'd picked up from the humans. "Caleb Taylor is good worker. He knows a lot about refinery equipment. But I don't think he lives us being here."

"Likes. He treating you okay?"

William shrugged. Harmy's face fell. "That's too bad. I

know what it's like t' work with people who are down on you. I had a boss once who—"

An explosion rent the air, and the ground shook beneath their feet. A klaxon screamed. William instinctively jumped between the human and the blast, but they were too far away to be hurt. One quick glance told William that it was his own work area!

He began to run, shoving past panicked workers and Visitors alike. Shouts and screams challenged the alarm klaxon's shriek. He'd been working with Caleb Taylor and Gus Jennings—and they weren't among the crowd!

"Caleb!" he shouted.

White clouds of frozen vapor and supercooled gases poured out of the hatch as William reached the stairway to the catwalk. A shape darkened the opening—Gus Jennings! The burly worker staggered out, his mouth working as though he was screaming, but the whoosh of the gas drowned out even the alarm. Jennings was covered with white frost, clutching his arm above the wrist. Even as William started up the stairs, the human lurched, his hand smashing into one of the steel pipes.

Both William and Jennings stared unbelieving as the impact *shattered* the flesh like so much glass. Jennings was left clutching a bloody stump. William was close enough now to hear his screams.

Even as he reached Jennings, shouting "Caleb?" the man collapsed. Bill Graham, another worker, caught him.

"Caleb's still in there!" He eased Jennings onto the catwalk, shouting down to the men on the ground, "Get an ambulance, for God's sake!" Graham turned back to William. "The liquid nitrogen blew through the inner seal—there's no way anyone can get past it to reach him!"

William stepped over Jennings, heading for the hatch and the billowing frozen gases. Behind him he could hear Graham's shout, "William! Stop! For God's sake!"

William hesitated for a brief second, filling his lungs with a deep breath, then plunged inside.

Graham watched him go, torn between trying to stop the Visitor technician and tending to Jennings. He turned as a hand grabbed his shoulder. "What's happening?"

It was Steven. Graham gestured helplessly. "William went in there after Caleb!"

*"What?"* Steven glanced into the frozen darkness of the hatchway, his features hardening.

Graham stripped off his coat and laid it over Jennings, who was still unconscious, but moaning now. "It's got to be three hundred below zero in there—they're both goners. Nothing human could—" Graham broke off in confusion as he stared into the Visitor officer's eyes. They were flat and cold—shards of ice in that otherwise handsome countenance.

Shouts echoed around them, and both Graham and Steven turned to see what was happening. William emerged from the hatchway, supporting Caleb Taylor. The older man seemed barely conscious, his dark skin and hair frosted white. He twitched uncontrollably as bouts of shivering hit him.

Bill Graham moved quickly to help William lower Caleb to the catwalk. The Visitor technician seemed unharmed, except for his face and hands, which were covered with large, bumpy blisters, whitish in color. Dark cracks seemed to furrow the skin around the raised areas. Graham glanced quickly at Jennings—then at Caleb. Though both men were rimed with frost, their skins roughened by the frostbite, neither displayed those disfiguring blisters.

William, catching Graham's eyes on his face, turned away, ducking his head. Steven leaned over him, blocking Bill's view of the technician.

"The ambulance is coming!" The shout was followed almost immediately by a wail, then the screech of brakes below the catwalk. Graham looked over to see the paramedics pile out. "We'll need three stretchers up here!" he shouted.

"You'd better sit down, William," he said. "The ambulance is here. Are you in much pain?"

The Visitor technician didn't raise his head. His voice sounded even stranger than usual—a high-pitched, muffled tone accompanied the usual reverberation. "No. I am okay."

"I'm taking him back to the shuttle," Steven said. "Our doctors will deal with this."

"Don't you think—" Graham caught the Visitor officer's eye and stopped abruptly. Perhaps it was a blast of the frozen vapor from the open hatchway behind him that made him shudder suddenly, violently.

Doctor Benjamin Taylor sat at a microscope, peering intently into the eyepiece. Ruth Barnes sat across the laboratory from him, labeling specimen dishes. The door banged open to reveal Doctor Metz. "Where are those cultures, Ruth? I can't proceed without them!"

Ben glanced over at the middle-aged woman, saw pain, quickly hidden, shadow her eyes at Metz's brusque tone. "They're not back from pathology, Doctor."

Taylor saw Metz's frown deepen—hastily spoke up in Ruth Barnes' behalf. "They're running way behind there, Doctor Metz."

She nodded. "I heard that two of the top technicians didn't show up for work today. They didn't even call in!" Ruth, who hadn't missed a day of work since Ben had first known her when he was still a med student, sounded scandalized.

Metz pursed his lips. "That's odd. Who are they?"

"Morrow and Prentiss."

"I must say, with their work records, I'd never have expected such a cavalier attitude from them," Metz shook his head.

"Maybe there's a good rea—" The laboratory phone interrupted Ben. He picked it up. "Doctor Taylor here."

He recognized Juliet Parrish's voice, but couldn't recall ever hearing it so strained and anxious. "Ben—get down to the ER, stat. They just brought in your father."

When the three reached the emergency room, Caleb was conscious, barely. Ben clasped his father's hand, shocked at how dreadfully cold it was, while he listened to the ambulance technician summarize the accident at Richland. "How did he get out of there?" Ruth asked.

"One of the Visitor technicians carried him out, apparently," answered the paramedic. "He was damn lucky. Those supercooled gases are kept at temperatures hundreds of degrees below zero. I don't know how the hell the guy managed to get in there and keep moving—he should have been a Popsicle within seconds if he had to pass through blasts of liquid nitrogen."

Ruth leaned forward, peering intently at Caleb's jacket. Whitish flakes adhered to it—*some residue of the chemical?* she wondered, scratching at one cautiously. On impulse she picked up a sterile specimen case and a pair of forceps, and scraped several of the larger flakes into the glass. She'd examine them later, under the microscope.

*They almost look like skin*, she thought, stepping back from the rush of monitors and doctors that surrounded Caleb Taylor. *But not quite . . .*

She remembered the paramedic's statement that it had been one of the Visitors who had rescued Caleb. *Visitor skin?* she thought excitedly. *Rudolph will want to know about this!* She turned to mention her suspicion to him, but he was no longer in the room. On impulse, she decided to analyze and examine the samples herself first, before telling him. No sense in getting him all excited unless she was sure what she had . . .

Caleb moaned, then spoke. "Ben?"

"I'm here, Pop. You're going to be okay."

Quietly, Ruth turned and tiptoed from the room, slipping the sample case into her pocket.

Abraham Bernstein ambled slowly along the street, the afternoon sun baking his shoulders beneath the worn old sweater. His companion was Ruby Engels from across the street. She was a widow, and each day the two walked the two miles to the neighborhood shopping center and back. They rarely bought anything—Social Security checks barely paid for the necessities. But it was a nice walk.

Abraham glanced up as a Visitor squad vehicle cruised by overhead. "More of them every day," he commented.

Ruby nodded. "You get so you don't even notice them on the street anymore. It's like when my husband and I first moved here from Germany. I had never seen a black, and it was all I could do not to stare. Within a couple of months several of the ladies I rode to the market with were black, and I never gave it a second thought."

Abraham shook his head. "It's not the same, though. These people are from a totally different world, one you and I, at least, will probably never live to see. They aren't human." He looked over at two Visitors standing casually on a street corner. "All those uniforms. And more every day. I don't like uniforms."

Ruby took his hand in hers, giving it a little shake. "Abraham, it's been nearly forty years." Her fingers pressed the inside of his forearm, where she knew the faded tattooed numbers were. "This—and everything it represents—belongs to the past. You have to let it go."

Bernstein shrugged. "Maybe you're right, Ruby. Still—I don't like uniforms. And there *are* more of them every day."

With a sigh, Ruby changed the subject. "What is your grandson doing these days?"

"Nice try, Mrs. Engels. But you picked the wrong subject. Daniel . . . Daniel." Abraham kicked desultorily at a pop top on the concrete. "He lost the job at the supermarket. When the register came up short, he thought they were blaming him, so he quit before they could say anything. I've lost count of all the jobs he's quit."

"Abraham." Ruby didn't look at her companion. "Is it possible that Daniel was . . . guilty?"

Instead of the hot denial she expected, Abraham sighed again. "I don't know, Ruby. He's my own flesh and blood, and of course I don't think he'd steal. His father and I have done everything we could to teach him what's right in this world. But—he just never has fit in."

She touched his bent shoulder quickly. "Don't be so hard on him, Abraham! He's only eighteen."

"But he's been this way for years! No good in school . . . hardly any friends . . . can't keep a job, or stick to a task . . ."

"Didn't you tell me that he's gotten involved with this Visitor Friends group?"

Abraham was obviously less than thrilled. "Yes."

"Well, maybe this will be just what he needs. He hasn't found his niche yet. You wait. This may be it."

Abraham Bernstein didn't look reassured. Another squad vehicle whispered by overhead, its shadow blotting out the sun for a second.

Michael Donovan sat in the passenger seat of the Visitor shuttle, looking down on the streets and the people below. He saw an elderly man and woman, then they were gone. He glanced over at a large, imposing house with a beautiful, professionally landscaped garden. Eleanor's house. Another Visitor craft rested on the front lawn.

His pilot, a Visitor officer named Martin, also glanced over at the shuttle. "That's Steven's vehicle below." He adjusted a control without glancing up. "I hear the supervisor visits there a lot."

Donovan smiled wryly. "She *can* be charming." He wasn't sure if Martin knew that Mrs. Dupres was his mother. It was possible—Martin, from Donovan's uneducated reading of his insignia, seemed to have a fairly high rank. If the Visitors were anything like humans, they probably gossiped among themselves.

He busied himself watching the pilot handle the controls. The craft seemed simple to fly. A bar with a handgrip controlled the direction, a lever set within a notched slot regulated the speed. The slot nearest to the pilot was the slowest—cruising speed. Donovan wondered idly what the top acceleration on these babies was . . .

Something shiny behind the pilot's seat caught his eye and he bent over to pick up a small implement. It was about three and a half inches long and perhaps a half inch thick, made from some crystalline substance with what appeared to be a golden metal handle. Small indentations dotted its narrow sides—Donovan had the sudden impression of a key, though why, he couldn't have said.

He straightened, half opening his mouth to speak to Martin, tell the pilot what he'd found—then found himself, instead, putting it in his pocket. *Sean*, he thought. *I don't have anything for him—this will knock him for a loop.*

"Where does your son live?" asked Martin.

"In a small town just ouside of L.A.," Donovan answered.

"Is that your home, also?"

Mike found his mouth tightening, but realized Martin's question was merely polite conversation. "Not anymore," he said, trying not to sound too abrupt. "My wife and I are divorced. My son lives with his mother."

"Where is your home, then, Mike?" Martin asked.

Donovan looked out the window—at his request, Martin had un opaqued the viewports. "I don't really have a permanent base. I follow the stories, I guess you could say. I was staying in downtown L.A. with a . . . friend."

"I see. I have our heading coordinates in view. Where would you like to be set down? At your son's house?"

"No, I want to rent a car. I'm taking Sean camping for a couple of days, and I'll need something to drive." He peered out. "That looks like a car lot down there—" He pointed. "Can you set down in that parking lot?"

"Of course." Donovan watched closely as the pilot maneuvered the craft in for a landing. *Compared to a plane, these things are a snap,* he thought.

They set down with nary a jar. "Thanks a lot, Martin. I appreciate the lift." Donovan hastily gathered up his gear. Martin helped him carry it out, looking curiously at the backpack, the sleeping bag in its nylon covering.

"I was glad to do it, Mike. I wanted to meet you." They shook hands. Donovan was used to the coolness of Visitor flesh now—it barely registered in his mind.

He watched the vehicle lift silently away, before turning around to find the owner of the rental car lot standing behind him, his mouth open. *That's right,* Donovan reminded himself, *most people still haven't seen one this close up. Bet he doesn't have many customers who drop in out of alien spacecraft.*

A few minutes later Donovan turned the little yellow sports car onto a tree shaded avenue. Even as he swung the wheel he heard excited shouts. "Dad! Hey, Dad! Dad!"

Donovan grinned, waving. "Hiya, Sean!" Two boys stood waiting for him, and Mike recognized Josh Brooks, Sean's best friend. "Hi, Josh!" He swung into the curb and parked. He'd barely opened the door when Sean swarmed into his arms. Donovan hugged his son, realizing only when he held him in his arms just how much he'd missed him. He hugged Sean tightly, fiercely, and knew from the boy's grasp that Sean was equally glad to see him.

After long moments he straightened, grinning, to tug at the boy's Dodger cap. "Hiya, kiddo. Who are you today? Fernando Valenzuela or Steve Garvey?"

Sean straightened proudly. "Just Sean Donovan." Then, remembering, he caught his father's arm, pulling him toward the lawn. "Come see what Josh's got!" With barely a break, he demanded, "Hey, did you know how many Visitors it takes to change a lightbulb?"

"No, how many?"

"None. They *like* the lights out."

Donovan grimaced, then laughed. "Right. How are you doing, Josh?"

"Hello, Mr. Donovan."

Josh was about thirteen, a year older than Sean, and half a head taller. They were often mistaken for brothers—both had dark hair and freckles. Sean waved a proud hand at a model of a Visitor shuttle. "See, Dad?" Sean said excitedly. "Check it out! The squad vehicle . . . and the action figures." He picked up two tiny red-garbed and capped figures. "Here's the Supreme Commander, and Diana—"

Mike shook his head, grinning ruefully. "Wonder if they get a royalty?"

Sean carefully tucked the little action figures into the pilot's seats in the squad vehicle. "He's got a Mother Ship at home!"

Josh sounded a bit smug. "I got 'em *all*."

Sean looked up. "Can I get 'em, Dad? Mom said we didn't have the money . . ."

Donovan tried to keep his face from hardening. He hadn't contested his child support or alimony payments, and he'd never been even a day overdue. And any time he'd known that Sean wanted something extra, he'd always seen that the money was there. *Damn Marge*, he thought. *She could have told me— I'd have brought him a set.* He forced a smile. "Well, I'll talk to her about it. But in the meantime," he pulled the little crystal and gold key from his pocket, "this is for you."

Sean took the implement, turning it over wonderingly. "What is it, Dad?"

Mike shrugged. "Just a little something I picked up in a squad vehicle." Behind him he heard the front door open and close, and out of the corner of his eye was aware that Marjorie stood on the steps, watching them. He didn't have to turn to guess her expression—it was always the same.

Sean's eyes widened. "In a *real* squad vehicle?"

"Yeah."

"You mean it came from the Visitors themselves?"

Donovan couldn't help sounding a little smug himself. "That's right."

"Hey! Check it *out!*" Sean held the implement up reverently. Josh leaned forward avidly.

"Wow! Lemme see it, Sean!"

Sean pushed his hand away. "In a minute, Josh."

Donovan heard Marjorie's voice behind them, tight, angry. "Boys, your pizza's ready. Come on in."

Sean stood up. "You coming in, Dad? I've still got some stuff to pack . . ."

"In a second, kiddo. You fellows go ahead." Donovan

followed the boys as they raced up to Marjorie. She was looking good, he thought, seeing that she'd shed a few pounds. Her blonde hair was a little longer than the last time he'd seen her, curling softly about her jaw and neck.

Sean held out the Visitor key to her. "Look, Mom! It's from a squad—"

Her voice splintered like a fallen icicle. "Your dinner's getting cold."

Sean's animation dimmed. He turned and trudged up the steps, looking back once at his father. Mike winked and nodded at him encouragingly.

Marjorie barred his way, and even from the sidewalk Donovan could feel the tightness of her body. He was angry at the way she'd treated Sean. All he'd done was bring his son a little present—you'd think he'd stabbed her, the way she was acting. He tried to control his voice. They couldn't keep tearing at each other like this—it was hell on Sean. "Hi," he said.

She didn't answer, only stood there, arms folded over her breasts. Donovan had a sudden, vivid memory of touching those same breasts but repressed it savagely. *It's over. Over.*

He sighed. "So what's wrong now?"

She gestured helplessly, her voice breaking. "Oh, nothing. It's just that it's a little tough competing with someone who flies around in spaceships."

Donovan felt equally helpless. "Margie, what am I supposed to do? Give up my work?"

Tears glimmered. "And what am *I* supposed to do? Sprout wings and fly him off to never-never land? How else can I compete? With *pizza*, for God's sake?"

Mike was exasperated. The old, old problem—would they ever get past it? "Why compete, Margie?" He'd asked her this same question so many times. He realized he was feeling guilty again, and his anger flared. "It's insane! Why do you always feel diminished if I do something successfully? Why not do something of your own? Something you can feel proud of, someplace where nobody has ever heard of me. What about your college plans? You know I'll lend you the money—hell, I'll *give* it to you! What about—"

She held up her hand, cutting him off. She sounded as weary as Mike felt. "Please. Don't start. Okay?"

Donovan stared at her, words jumbling in his throat. He realized that there was nothing left to say, and that was the most painful thing of all.

Juliet Parrish guided her white Volkswagen convertible to a halt in front of Ruth Barnes' brownstone. Overhead both women could hear the faint whispering passage of a squad vehicle. Julie set the parking brake with an excited jerk. "You're kidding! You really got a Visitor skin sample? *How*?"

Ruth smiled at her eagerness. "When they brought Ben's father in, there were some whitish particles clinging to his shirt and jacket. I just picked them off."

"Did you get a chance to look at them?"

"For just a minute, then Doctor Metz came in with some cultures he wanted mounted on slides immediately. I had a lot of extra work today, since two people didn't show up at the lab."

"*Well?*"

"They didn't look like skin, Julie. Not human skin, anyway. There didn't seem to be any cells—it was all smooth. Too smooth."

"Damn!" Juliet thumped her fist softly against the steering wheel. "Wish I'd known earlier, then I could have had a look! Now I'll have to wait till tomorrow!" She looked over at Ruth and smiled. "Doctor Metz will love you for this, you know."

Ruth's expression froze. "I'd better go. Thanks so much for the ride, Julie."

Juliet put out her hand, catching the older woman's arm. "Ruth . . . what's wrong? It was something I said, wasn't it?" Ruth shook her head, turning her face away. Julie remembered her words, and a sudden flash of insight surfaced. Why hadn't she ever noticed before? "Ruth, it's Doctor Metz, isn't it? You . . . really love him, don't you?"

Ruth bit her lip, managed a wan smile.

"Does he know?" Julie asked.

The lab assistant shook her head. "No, honey. I'm just another piece of lab equipment to him."

Julie patted her sleeve, then slid her hand over the older woman's gently. "Well, starting tomorrow morning, we're going to go to work on him. We'll make him realize that 'Nobel' isn't the only prize he's got."

Ruth smiled gently. *It's been a lot of years since things looked that simple to me, Julie,* she thought, but the younger woman's words awakened a bittersweet optimism nevertheless. She patted the young woman's cheek, remembering when her own skin had felt that smooth, that soft. "You're a darling, Julie. Thanks. Thanks for everything."

Ruth got out of the car, waved Juliet a quick good-bye, heard the VW accelerate away. Fumbling for her keys, she walked slowly up the steps to her home, thinking what a long day it had been. She wished suddenly that she'd remembered to tell Juliet where the skin sample was hidden . . .

The door clicked open beneath her fingers. Ruth Barnes stepped inside, turning to close the door behind her. Her motion brought her face to face with the man who had been standing, hidden, behind the door.

Ruth had barely a moment to take in the fact that he wore a Visitor uniform and cap before her horrified eyes focused on the weapon in his hand. It didn't look much like any gun she'd ever seen before—but she knew, from the way it swung to follow her, what it was.

All the breath seemed to have deserted her lungs. It was like one of those hideous childhood nightmares where you try to scream and can't. Ruth gasped, seeing his finger move—

There was a muffled pulse of high-pitched sound, and a blue light. For a moment Ruth thought he'd missed, for she felt no pain. Then she realized she was falling, falling, twisting in mid-air, uncontrollably—

There came a burst of red-tinged blackness, then nothing. She never felt the impact of her body on the floor.

# Chapter 7

Caleb Taylor hissed with pain as he crossed the threshold of his apartment door and one of his bandaged hands brushed the jamb. "You okay, Pop? A little shaky?" Ben Taylor reached out to steady his father.

Caleb shrugged off his son's ministrations impatiently. "I'll be okay. You let me do it by myself."

Ben Taylor grinned wryly as he watched his father walk carefully into his bedroom. *He may be one terrific father*, he thought, *but he's sure as hell one lousy patient*. From the rustling sounds in the bedroom, he realized Caleb was obeying orders and resting. Ben turned to straighten up the small apartment. Usually his father kept it neat as a pin—a holdover from his dead wife's training—but it was a mess at the moment. That meant Elias had been here. Ben made a face as he tugged a pair of dirty sweat socks from between the couch cushions.

A second later he heard a key in the lock, turned to see his brother bounce into the room, a wide grin on his face. "Say, man! What it is, Ben?"

Ben shook his head. "'What it is' is bad grammar, brother. Elias, when are you going to quit this poor man's Richard Pryor act?"

Elias stared for a second, his smile hardening into a fixed grin. "What you talkin', man? This here ain't no *act*. This here is pure-D *Elias*."

Ben was disgusted and showed it. "It's pure-D *something*, that's for sure. Pure-D shit, if you ask me."

Elias did a mock shuffle, his hard, cocky grin never dimming. "Look here, man, can't all of us be Doctor Kildare, dig?" His voice hardened. "Or *Uncle Tom*."

"Oh, drop that sixties jive, Elias! You can be anything you want, but first you've got to dump that tap dance and two-bit crook routine, and *grow up*."

Ben could tell he'd scored. Elias laughed, a short, forced explosion of sound that sounded anything but amused. "Well, once again we thank you, *Mr. Sidney Poitier*." He turned away angrily. "Hey, Pop!" He headed for the bedroom, his strut plainly put on now. "How you doing?"

Ben watched him go, then resumed his cleaning. He was tired, tired of Elias, tired of work—tired of worrying. His eyes felt as though they were bulging out of his head from eyestrain—he'd had to work on the microscope nearly all day, except when he'd made his rounds. All of them were doing double duty on lab work ever since Ruth had disappeared.

He felt a heaviness inside, remembering that it was now a full three days since anyone had seen her. Doctor Metz was inconsolable, shutting himself up in his office for hours and chain-smoking (he hadn't had a cigarette, Doctor Larraby had told them, since he'd quit in 1963), staring stonily off into space.

*Where did she go?* Ben wondered. *The police conducted an investigation, but I've seen people search for lost dogs with more energy. There have been so many disappearances—what the hell is going on?*

Angrily he slammed half of the mountainous pile of dishes into the sink, ran hot water, rolling up his sleeves. *Damn Elias*, he thought. He remembered what Juliet Parrish had told him: that Ruth had been examining a Visitor skin sample the day she vanished.

He glanced out the window as he scrubbed, saw a portion of the Mother Ship suspended overhead. Wherever you went, it was there, hanging over you. The Visitors had given an "introductory seminar" for some of the scientists, and Ben and Julie had gone. Doctor Metz should have been the representative from their campus, but he hadn't even roused himself to reply to the invitation.

*What a bunch of shit that turned out to be,* Taylor thought, wincing as he stabbed his thumb on something sharp. *They spoon-fed us maybe ten minutes' worth of real information about themselves in half a day's time. The rest of it was either doubletalk or stuff that Kristine Walsh has already released.*

Ben rinsed his bleeding thumb under the cold water and went looking for an adhesive strip.

Night had fallen, carrying just a hint of low-lying mist. Robin Maxwell paced in her yard, talking to her friend Muffy (*née* Abigail) on the cordless phone. From inside she could hear her parents talking quietly as they loaded the dishwasher together. "Oh, it's been grody, Muf, really. My Dad's been so *down* since Professor Quinton left. Or got kidnapped, or whatever. I even had to talk to the police, tell them what he said that night he called, y'know. Yeah, really!"

Her feet slid through the lawn's soft green with a tiny wet swish as she walked back and forth. "But you know about that. I wanted to know if you saw him! Daniel said he was in the neighborhood today . . . What do you mean, who am I talking about? *You* know who! The Visitor Youth Leader!"

"Daniel said he'd be by tonight?" She grinned ecstatically into the phone. "You're kidding! You *saw* him? Isn't he a *hunk*? Just a fox, right. Totally. I knooow . . ."

She sighed, listening so intently to her friend that she was unaware that a uniformed figure was approaching from behind her. "Couldn't you just *die*! Did you see his *eyes*? Gorgeous!"

She nodded vigorously. "Sure I saw them! When I was playing in the band. He looked at me for *quite* a while, for sure. Real meaningful, too, y'know. Like two ships in the night—so romantic . . ." The silent figure was nearly behind her. "I think he really likes me, but is just afraid . . . shy, y'know. Yeah, *totally*."

"Excuse me." Robin whirled, startled, to see the young Visitor she'd just been discussing standing behind her. She moaned softly, then turned away from him for a last agonized whisper:

"My life is *over*, Muf!"

She clicked the phone off, wondering whether to run or just die where she stood. He smiled uncertainly. "Excuse me. Did I startle you?"

"No!" she squeaked, then cleared her throat. "No."

"I'm Brian," he said, holding out his hand. Robin took it, feeling the blood race in her ears. She felt the cool pressure of his fingers for just a second, then dropped her hand. It tingled.

"I'm Robin," she said.

He cleared his throat, the sound very different because of the strange reverberation. "Uh . . . hi. Sorry, I'm a little nervous."

"*You're* nervous?" Robin said blankly.

"Well . . . it's not every day that I meet somebody from another planet."

She relaxed slightly. "Y'know, I never thought of that. It must be just as weird for you. Not that you're weird, I mean, y'know."

Brian smiled again. "Which one is Daniel's house?"

Visibly deflated, Robin pointed. "The one over there, on the right."

"Thanks." He turned away.

"Sure," Robin whispered, watching him leave. *He doesn't care*, she thought. *My life is over.*

He stopped, hesitated, then turned back to face her. "Uh . . . would you like to take a walk?"

Robin hesitated, trying to control the grin surging inside her, threatening to burst onto her face. "Okay," she said, following him.


William threaded his way through hurrying workers, responding to the blast of the noon-time whistle. He could see Harmy's truck standing just ahead of him. As he approached, she looked up, waving. "Hey, hero! Willy!"

William smiled. "Hello, Harmony."

"Everybody's just *raving* about the way you rescued Caleb." William ducked his head, shrugging, unable to think of anything to say. "You seen him yet? Caleb, I mean."

"Yes," William said, "I have seen Caleb. He said he was fun."

"Fine," corrected Harmy automatically. "Did he thank you for saving his life? He ought to, seeing how mean he was acting."

William nodded. "He has been talking to me, since this morning. He shooked my hand."

"Well, that's more like it!" Harmy turned to her lunch wagon. "You want a burger or something? It's lunchtime."

He shook his head. She peered at him intently. "Say, don't you guys ever eat?"

He nodded, feeling uncomfortable, wondering how to change the subject. "Sometimes."

She took a bite of a sandwich, chewed thoughtfully. "You ever go to movies?"

"No, I do not . . ." William said, wondering what "movies" were. Like television, he thought he remembered, only larger. He smiled shyly at her. ". . . Yet."

She chuckled, and after a second, he found himself echoing her. It was his first laugh.


Juliet Parrish was feeding the mice when the announcement came on the television. "We interrupt this program to bring our listeners an urgent special report."

*What now?* she thought. Aloud she called, "Ben? Doctor Metz? There's a bulletin on the television . . ."

She listened to Howard K. Smith explain that this story was being brought by satellite from Belgium. A picture of a distinguished-looking man came on, facing a steel bouquet of microphones. Doctor Metz exclaimed, "That's Leopold Jankowski! What is going on here?"

"He's with the Brussels Biomedical Institute, isn't he?" asked Ben. Metz nodded tensely as the man began to speak.

"I have called this press conference today to reveal a shocking discovery. There exists, in this world, an organized conspiracy of some of our best scientific minds. The aim of this conspiracy is to harm—possibly destroy—the Visitors."

Julie and Ben gasped, their reactions mirrored by the hubbub of reporters' voices in the crowded room. Doctor Metz stared incredulously. "Impossible!" he muttered. "That's insane—has Leopold lost his mind?"

Jankowski was speaking again. "This organized effort to harm the Visitors came to my attention first approximately two weeks ago, when Doctor Rudolph Metz in California called me and asked to speak with me on what he called 'urgent and confidential matters.'"

*"What?!"* Julie grabbed Ben Taylor's arm.

"I did no such thing!" Doctor Metz said, indignantly. "I haven't spoken to Jankowski since—"

"Others of my colleagues here in Belgium have also been approached by scientists," Jankowski continued. "Primarily those scientists in the fields of biomedical studies or anthropology seem to be involved. But we cannot be sure of how far this insidious contagion among some of our best minds has spread."

"*How can he say this?*" Doctor Metz was shaking with rage and hurt. "Jankowski was a good man—I have known him for years. What is he *talking* about?"

Julie patted his arm. "Take it easy, Doctor. Maybe you'd better sit—"

"Scientists of many nations are apparently part of this insidious conspiracy. Their plan, quite simply, is to seize control of several of the Visitors' Mother Ships . . ."

Cries of "Why?", "To what purpose?" rang out from the assembled reporters.

Jankowski shook his head gravely. "They tried to convince me that it was to protect the human race and keep the military from learning advanced Visitor technology secrets. However, I am sure that their true motivation was far more personal than their avowed purpose."

Jankowski ceremoniously lifted a piece of paper. "On this statement I have listed the events exactly as they transpired, and the names of all those who tried to enlist my help in this dreadful conspiracy against those who had proved themselves our friends. I now authenticate this statement with my signature. Copies will be released to the appropriate authorities that they may deal with each of the scientists on this list according to their local laws."

Jankowski solemnly signed the statement. Ben, Julie, and Doctor Metz looked at each other speechlessly.

Within hours, scores of other scientists from around the world had come forward, admitting that they had been approached by representatives of the "conspiracy." Some, like Dr. Jacques Duvivier, a Nobel laureate like Dr. Metz, admitted that they had belonged to it, signing statements similar to Jankowski's.

The entire world scientific community was in an uproar. In

the United States, the FBI began investigating the records of those named by Duvivier, Jankowski, and others, trying to determine whether such a conspiracy indeed existed. They were assisted in their efforts by Visitors, who helpfully chauffeured them from lab to lab, standing by impassively as the record searches implicated scientist after scientist.

Doctor Metz's office was searched the day after Jankowski implicated him in his statement. Juliet Parrish and Ben Taylor stood by helplessly as Doctor Metz, incensed, challenged the FBI representatives to search his files—he had nothing, *nothing* to hide! Search they did—with the result that one of the men discovered a folder taped to a false panel inside the cabinet containing Metz's personnel files. The folder contained notes from meetings, lists of names, coded messages, maps showing the location of the Mother Ships . . .

Metz was dumbfounded, insisting the "evidence" had been planted. The FBI appropriated the files, plus several others they discovered in the office, and told Metz that no policy had yet been determined to deal with those discovered to be conspirators, but that he was not to leave Los Angeles without notifying them. Julie and Ben received several hard looks, but no overt warnings. The FBI representatives left in the squad vehicle their Visitor pilots had landed on the roof.

Kristine Walsh, the Press Secretary for the Visitors, made a sorrowful statement to the effect that, as a result of the conspiracy, the Visitor proposed scientific seminars would have to be postponed.

Many scientists who had been implicated in the conspiracy charges simply vanished, lending credence to the allegations of their guilt. Police departments were flooded with missing persons reports—thousands of them. Law enforcement agencies were at a loss to explain what was happening, much less investigate even a significant percentage of the cases.

Finally, when evidence found in the implicated scientists' files showed that some groups in the secret cabal had even planned violent takeovers of Visitor shuttles and weaponry, John, the Visitor Supreme Commander, officially requested the United Nations to intercede with its member nations to demand that all scientists and their family members register their names and current addresses with local authorities. The information would be verified by computer against local address listings.

When first told about the United Nations' request, most national authorities were reluctant—the President of the United States was openly skeptical of the entire "conspiracy" notion. But within a few weeks, in the face of mounting evidence of a secret scientists' cabal, resistance to the UN and Visitor requests began to crumble. Key people, one by one, began to reverse their stands, almost overnight in some cases.

Finally, by special Act of Congress and the President, the registration commenced.

Abraham Bernstein came out of the house for his daily walk just in time to see his neighbor, Robert Maxwell, walk down to his station wagon. Maxwell carried a sheaf of papers, holding them so tightly they were wrinkled. "Good morning, Mr. Maxwell," called Abraham.

"Not to me, it isn't," Maxwell said grimly, getting into his car. "I've got to take these damned forms down to the post office for this idiotic registration! I *still* don't understand how they got that passed in Congress! And you know something that's *really* weird?"

Abraham shook his head.

"Russia's doing the same thing. Of course it won't be as hard for them, since they kept their scientists pretty much under official Party observation anyway. But they're going to open their files to Visitor observers! I can't believe it!"

Bernstein realized he was trembling as he watched Maxwell start his car and drive away. Ruby Engels came over to him, having caught the end of the conversation. She put a comforting hand on her friend's arm as they started their daily walk. "Abraham, don't get so wound up! Nothing's going to happen. This will all blow over, you just watch."

"Yes, watch," said Abraham through gritted teeth. "Watch while they destroy everything I've come to hold dear."

"Nothing's going to happen," insisted Ruby. "After all, it's not as though you or your family are scientists. You won't be involved with this. And anyway, it's going to pass."

Abraham looked at her for a long moment. "That's what I said in 1938. In Berlin."

Ruby looked upset for a moment. "But this is different!"

"Is it?" Abraham glanced back at the squad vehicle which had just landed in front of his house. Brian, the Visitor Youth

Leader, got out, followed by Daniel. They shook hands. Abraham's grandson wore a brownish-orange coverall, similar in design and cut to the Visitor uniform, a cap, and a wide grin.

Abraham slowly turned to Ruby. "*Is* it?"

She had no answer for him. Fear awakened in her eyes.

Dennis Lowell tried for the fourth time to pull the corkscrew out of the bottle of Liebfraumilch. He tensed his muscles, straining, and slowly . . . slowly . . . the corkscrew came forth—along with nearly half the cork.

"*Shit!*" Lowell slammed the cockscrew down on the kitchen counter, then glanced at the clock. *Forty-five minutes late*, he thought furiously, flicking on the small portable television that sat on the counter. He dug in the drawer for a sharp, thin-bladed knife while he listened.

"In other news, while international police have scoured scientific files for facts on the conspiracy, some startling evidence is being uncovered that many scientists who specialize in medical research in life sciences may have actually had major breakthroughs in research which they've *suppressed*. The Senate Medical Affairs Committee chairman, Raymond Burke, had this to say . . ."

The scene switched to the Senate stairs, where the Senator was surrounded by the press and flashing cameras. Denny dug another piece of cork out of the bottle, watching morosely as Senator Burke spoke.

"Yes, indeed. I do have evidence that new and revolutionary cancer treatments *do* exist, and *have* existed for some time— along with many other breakthroughs of enormous potential benefit to the world. Apparently our scientific friends have seen fit to keep quiet about them."

Shouts of "why?" echoed around him. He shrugged grimly. "Well, I won't speculate, except to say there's a lot of money to be made on research grants." "*Damn*," said Dennis aloud, not sure himself whom he was addressing—or about what. He dug another sliver of cork out of the bottle, then had the dubious pleasure of seeing the remainder of the cork disintegrate into tiny pieces and slither down the neck into the wine.

The scene switched back to the newsroom just as he heard Juliet's key in the apartment door. The newsman looked grave. "A groundswell of resentment has begun to build around the world against the scientific community. In Stockholm, where the Nobel Prizes are awarded each year, a crowd of angry demonstrators—"

"I'm *sorry* I'm late, Den. Everything is a mess!" Julie bustled into the kitchen, hastily pulling off her lab coat. Rain glistened in fine little glimmers on her blonde hair. "Doctor Metz can't seem to pull himself together now that Ruth's gone, and he heard about another associate who's been implicated just as he was, and I—"

Dennis snapped off the television with a final click. "Take your time. They called to cancel dinner."

Juliet looked dismayed. "Oh, Den! You must be disappointed."

"Yes," he agreed, shortly.

"You don't think you'll still get the account." She sounded as though she wished he'd tell her something reassuring. Dennis poured himself a drink, swallowed it in a gulp.

"No, I don't think so. They were *too* polite, y'know."

Juliet hung her lab coat over the back of the kitchen stool. Her fingers smoothed it for a second, then stopped abruptly. "Denny . . . do you think it's *me*? They know I'm a biochemist, and a med student."

Dennis knew he'd waited a second too long to speak. "No. How could it be you?"

She looked at him for long moments. He could feel her eyes on his face, but couldn't raise his own to meet hers. "Now *you* sound a little too polite, Den."

He couldn't think of anything to say. He poured himself another glass of wine, then went into the bedroom, leaving her there, staring at the lab coat.

Mike Donovan watched Tony Leonetti intently as his friend flicked the switch to start the VCR unit. Doctor Leopold Jankowski appeared on the screen, bending to sign his damning statement. "Yeah?" Donovan turned to his partner. "I saw this. I think it's all a load of shit. So?"

"You don't notice anything?" Tony punched up another tape. "When we saw this when it originally aired, it bugged me for *days*—I couldn't figure out what the hell was wrong with the picture. Finally, I woke up the other night with the answer. Look. This is a tape we shot of him last year at that international science fair. You remember when I asked him to autograph that book for my old man?"

The second image appeared beside the first as both signings played simultaneously. Donovan stared, then nodded suddenly. "Yeah!"

"You see it, don't you, Mike? He used his right hand last year—yet when he signed the conspiracy statement, it was with his *left* hand."

Donovan shrugged, his eyes wary. "So? He's ambidextrous."

"No, he's not. And neither is Duvivier. I checked. Both men are now signing their names with their left hands, where before they were righthanded."

Donovan met Tony's eyes, his own speculative. Tony nodded. "Something very strange is going on, Mike. And I'll bet you a steak it's connected with the Visitors somehow. Everything's turned so damned *weird* since those guys showed up."

"Yeah." Donovan frowned. "Somehow we've got to get a look at the Mother Ship, and soon. And not just a guided tour. I mean a look at the whole thing. I'd love to see that area where they're storing the chemicals."

Leonetti nodded. "Just like old times, huh?"

Donovan nodded slowly. "Yeah. But at least the Nam and Cambodia weren't over a mile in the air. We're going to have to be careful."

Tony Leonetti slapped a hand to his forehead, rolling his eyes expressively. "As I live and breathe, the fearless Michael Donovan, the greatest 'cowboy' photographer of all time, is going to be *careful.* These guys got you scared, Mike?"

Donovan's laughter held an edge—he didn't like being reminded of some of his more reckless photographic exploits. Then he sobered, looking back at the stilled images of Jankowski Number 1 and Jankowski Number 2. "Yeah, Tony," he mumbled, his voice so quiet Leonetti had to strain to hear him. "I gotta admit, I have a feeling about this . . . There's not going to be any room for slip-ups this time . . ."

Leonetti forced a grin, jabbing his partner with a muscle punch. "What you're feeling, Mike, is hunger. Been a long time since lunch, old pal. Come on. The steaks are on me."

Donovan turned, punching playfully back at Leonetti, glad his friend had broken the tension. "I'm game. When do you want to do it?"

"Eat? Right now!"

"No, I meant sneak aboard a squad vehicle."

"Tomorrow?"

"Sounds good to me. Think Fran will let you out? The last time we went out together you dropped a bundle at that casino in Atlantic City."

"Now, *that's* where I'll have to be *careful* . . ."

# Chapter 8

Brilliant floods turned the parking lot at the Richland plant into a garish semblance of day. One of the large Visitor shuttles stood, cargo bay doors open, as Tony Leonetti and Mike Donovan crawled carefully through a maze of ground-level piping to crouch, hidden, behind a trash receptacle. Insulated pipes led from the large cryogenic tanks overhead to smaller tanks on board the shuttle craft. Two Visitor technicans stood by, along with two humans wearing hardhats.

"Pretty crowded, Mike," Tony whispered. "Don't you think maybe we ought to call for a squad vehicle and go up like we usually do?"

Donovan shook his head, judging the distance involved to the open cargo bay, hefting the Sony Betacam. It was his smallest and lightest VTR. "This way they won't know we're on board, and we'll have a better chance to find out stuff." He glanced quickly at his partner. "I hope this thing will produce broadcast-quality film. What about the sound?"

Tony shrugged. "It's state-of-the-art, Mike. It'll have to do."

Several Visitors began to uncouple the insulated pipe. Donovan tensed. "Okay, they're finished with the chemical—get ready."

Tony swallowed with an audible gulp, earning him a reproving scowl from Donovan. The human technicians walked away as the two Visitors climbed into the pilot's compartment of the shuttle. "Now!" Donovan hissed.

He climbed out of the piping, dashing forward, leaping over a ground-level pipe hidden by the shadows and the incandescent glare. Tony came after him, but, not seeing the pipe, caught his foot and went sprawling. Donovan, already at the cargo entrance, heard his muffled "Oooof!"

"Damn!" Tony scrambled for the cargo door as its two halves began to rise toward each other. Mike reached out, grabbing for his wrists.

Leonetti leaped gamely. "Can't—get my—leg—up—"

"I've got you—" hissed Donovan, but a second later had to admit defeat as the doors continued to close. He had one last second to see Tony scuttle away from the vehicle before the doors locked together. "Shit!" He crouched behind some containers in the cargo hold, hugging the Betacam. The darkness was complete.

He felt the now-familiar lift and swoop of the craft and knew they were on their way.

The shuttle bay of the Mother Ship was as he'd seen it before. He could hear a woman's voice announcing landings and departures—in English—as the cargo doors began to widen. Donovan scuttled through, almost before the opening would admit him, and in seconds had ensconced himself behind a barricade of the cryo units he'd seen Visitor technicians toting about. He listened to the announcements, wondering suddenly why here, where there were no humans present (except Kristine, probably, he reminded himself bitterly), the Visitors wouldn't use their native language.

"Prepare for venting operation," announced the voice.

*Venting operations?* Donovan frowned. *What the hell is that?*

He peered out cautiously, saw Visitor technicians attaching yet another insulated hose to the chemical storage tank in the shuttle's cargo hold, then screwing the end of it into a nozzle in the floor of the landing bay. Donovan was puzzled—according to the many views he'd had of the landing bay as he'd approached it in the squad vehicles, there were no pipes or storage containers on the outside of the huge Mother Ship. And from this angle, if the nozzle did indeed point straight through the landing bay floor, then there was only empty air outside.

He watched, filming now, as the technicians turned a valve, and there came the whoosh of escaping gases. One of the techs stretched. "This is what the humans would call a royal pain," he commented, the reverberation in his voice echoing throughout the cavernous landing bay. "Dragging this stuff up to the ship, then dumping it out again—what a waste."

"Yeah," his companion agreed. "I can't figure out why we're doing this day and night."

"Who knows why the Leader orders most of the things he orders?" said the first. "But I'm not going to question it; that's too unhealthy."

"You're right," agreed his companion, glancing around to make sure they hadn't been overheard.

Donovan squirmed lower behind the cryo units, his hand grazing an accordion-like structure that looked amazingly like an old-fashioned radiator. The silvery-gray metal quivered under his arm. Donovan glanced at it, then tugged experimentally, and it swung open to reveal a rung ladder leading down to a shadowy catwalk and stairs. *Some kind of service access*, he thought, crawling through, *or that trusty standby of all spies and adventure-bound heroes, a ventilator shaft . . .*

Pulling the strange-looking grille nearly closed behind him, Donovan climbed quickly, one-handed, down the ladder. He found himself in the shadowy walkway. He could almost stand erect, but had to be careful not to bump his head on the piping hanging down.

Light filtered in from grilles set into the walls, and from tiny lights implanted in the walkway floor every couple of feet. Donovan began walking along, feeling a distinct chill. The Visitors must keep parts of their ship colder than human beings would consider comfortable.

Part of the chill came from swiftly circulating air. Donovan grinned wryly as the gust tugged at his hair. *Damn! It is a ventilator shaft!*

He began walking, his soft soles echoing slightly on the metal floor. He wasn't too concerned with noise giving him away; the whoosh of air and the thud of machinery would muffle any sound.

He reached the grille and peered out cautiously, hearing voices. Two Visitors stood by one of the yellow-marked doors he'd seen earlier—the ones Diana had said were inaccessible due to radiation. One of the Visitors produced a crystal-and-gold key like the one Donovan had given to Sean and inserted it into a slot. Light washed outward, illuminating the crystal, then the door slid aside.

*Interesting*, thought Mike. *They weren't wearing any protective suits . . . if there's so much radiation in there, why wouldn't they need them?* He moved onward, then downward as the main duct sloped. He eased the camera along—Tony had said the thing was rugged, but he wasn't taking any chances. Another grating on the other side of the walkway showed him one of the Visitors—a woman, this time—reclining on a bunk, reading something that looked vaguely like a book—if a book were printed on aluminum foil and manuscript-sized paper. She wore a snug-fitting garment that left her arms and legs bare and looked rather like a bathing suit. Donovan, who had been without feminine companionship since he'd left Kristine's apartment nearly a month ago, gave her legs a quick once-over.

*Not bad. A little chunky, but nice . . .*

Silent-footed, he moved on. He was careful to memorize the route as he went—it would never do to be caught in these walkways without being able to get back. *Like a rat in a maze*, he thought, appreciating the analogy grimly as the walkway turned again and he ducked to avoid more overhead piping.

He heard voices ahead—and something about them was familiar. Donovan crept carefully to a larger grille, peering through. Diana walked by, clad in a long red robe open down the throat. Mike's pulse quickened a little at the way the silky garment clung to her breasts and thighs. She was talking to a man Donovan recognized as Steven—the Visitor officer who divided his time between the Richland plant and Eleanor's house.

"You must be pleased, Diana," Steven was saying. "We're well on our way to completely securing most of the continents."

Diana smiled archly. "Well, let's just say that it pleases me to serve Our Leader," her sideways look at Steven was so coy it nearly made Donovan gag, "with whatever minor talents I possess." She walked across the room to a plexiglass cabinet of some sort. In small compartments ranged across the wall, Donovan saw, were a variety of small animals—lab animals, he realized.

Thankful that the Betacam was nearly silent, he began filming the Second-in Command. She reached into one of the compartments and extracted a white mouse. The little rodent squeaked frenziedly as she grasped it, then was still, its beady little eyes glazed in panic.

"The Leader must be very well pleased with your conversion process, Diana," Steven said. Still holding the mouse, Diana turned, walked across the room—and out of camera range. Mike could hear her talking.

"Yes . . . but you know how impatient Our Leader can be." She paused for a long second.

Steven sounded amused. "Even with *you*, Diana? Given the *intimacy* of your relationship, I would think—"

Diana moved abruptly back into camera range, and even from the dimness of the walkway Mike could see her anger. She gestured with both elegantly manicured hands—Donovan wondered briefly where she'd put the mouse. "Be very careful, Steven," she hissed.

Steven spread both hands in a gesture both apologetic and mocking. "It's just that I hate to see you distressed."

Diana sounded frustrated. "He doesn't understand that my conversion process is still limited. It doesn't work the same on every human subject."

"No," Steven agreed, "but when it works—Duvivier, Jankowski and the others—it's remarkable."

"Yes, isn't it?" Diana sounded smug. She reached into one of the other cages, extracted a frog. She smiled brightly at Steven as she walked past him, out of Donovan's line of sight again.

"They actually *believe* that the conspiracy exists—some of them even believe that they were a part of it." Steven walked into Donovan's view, smiling.

"Of course the evidence we planted reinforces their belief," said Diana.

*We've* got *to get this on the air!* thought Donovan excitedly. Briefly he considered leaving, but when Steven came back into his view, heading for the cages on the opposite wall, he decided to see what else the Visitor officer might reveal. He didn't have long to wait. Steven stopped in front of the cages, but Donovan could hear every word.

"The operation's working wonderfully. The scientists are

being ostracized—disorganized world-wide. And *they* pose the greatest threat. Once they're eliminated, or converted . . ." He made a gesture with his fingers as of someone flicking away dust.

Diana sounded a bit rueful. "The problem now is that Our Leader says, why not convert them all? He doesn't understand that human will is much tougher than we bargained for—converting all of them would take forever!"

Steven nodded, still standing with his back to Mike, then reached into one of the small cages, taking out a mouse.

"However, we'll continue to refine the process," Diana said.

"Yes, I'm sure you will," Steven said, holding the mouse up, apparently examining it. As Diana walked toward him, he turned back to her—and only years of training and experience kept Donovan's hands from dropping the camera. The mouse's hindquarters *protruded from the officer's mouth*, and as Donovan watched in horror, Steven jerked his head several times in a bizarre staccato motion. The mouse's wiggling legs and thrashing tail disappeared down his throat with an audible gulp.

Diana's words came in the same matter-of-fact tone. "Well, it's important that we learn the most effective and efficient methods to be used against them." The woman reached into another cage, then grasped a large, fluffy guinea pig. As the terrified creature squeaked and struggled, she opened her mouth—wider, *wider*—her jawbone seemingly dislocated at the last second, and she lowered the frantic animal between her lips.

Donovan clamped his teeth hard on his lower lip, his stomach turning over, as he watched Diana swallow the living animal whole. *Oh, God, what's happening to us? What* are *these things?*

The Second-in-Command's throat bulged outward, rippling with a downward motion. Steven spoke. "Well, I don't think Our Leader could have chosen anyone who could do the job better than you, Diana."

Shaking, Donovan had had enough. Grasping the camera firmly, he turned, making a stumbling progress back along the shadowy walkway. In his mind's eye he saw again the squirming guinea pig—the mouse's tail—and suddenly he turned, braced himself against the wall of the walkway, retching. *Don't puke, you sonofabitch*, he told himself frantically. *You don't want them to know you've been here!*

It took him long seconds to gain control, but finally he was able to grope his way back down the walkway.

He passed the grille closest to Diana's room, which he'd bypassed before, and paused to peer in. A Visitor stood before a washstand of sorts, apparently doing something to his eyes. His pose looked familiar to Donovan, then he remembered. Kristine wore contacts, and from the rear at least, the Visitor's actions seemed to be nearly identical to those of a person removing or inserting contact lenses. In spite of the urgency which drove him, Mike hesitated, watching.

There seemed to be a case of some sort beside the alien. One rounded half-circle with a blue center sat on one of the raised surfaces inside the case. As Donovan watched, the Visitor placed another of the things beside the first. Seeing them together, Mike began filming again. They looked like eyeballs—as though the alien wore human eyes as Kristine wore her contacts. The Visitor turned, and even though Donovan had braced himself, he was unprepared for the shock—the man's eyes were reddish-orange, with black, vertically-slitted pupils!

*And those hideous eyes saw Donovan right through the grille.*

The creature let out a hissing gasp of surprise, then, reaching for the grille, tore the metal frame from the bulkhead with one hand, grabbing for the cameraman with the other. Donovan dodged—but the thing moved with a blurring swiftness that was as inhuman as those eyes. It grabbed Mike, hauling him through the grille opening one-handed, throwing him across the tiny cabin onto the washstand.

Donovan landed badly, grabbing wildly for support. The Visitor advanced on him, his breathing a hissing gasp in the whoosh of air-displacement from the vent opening. Gathering himself, Donovan lashed out with his legs, catching the alien in the midsection, hurling him backwards. The blow would have disabled a man, but the creature recovered immediately, advancing on Mike again—those terrible eyes glaring like bloody pools in the dimness.

It had been a long time since Donovan had been in a fight,

but his early training as a reconnaissance pilot and sometime intelligence photographer had been thorough. He managed to toss his camera onto the bunk as the creature moved toward him, thanking all the gods there were that he'd been using the wide-angle lens to film Diana's chamber. Maybe it would pick up a shot of those eyes—

The Visitor lashed out, hitting Donovan's shoulder, though he managed to duck the worst force of the blow. He slammed a hard left into the Visitor's face, but the blow didn't even faze the creature. They grappled in the tiny cabin, bouncing off the walls, pushing and struggling. Donovan managed to work two hands around the creature's throat, but in turn felt the Visitor's hands groping beneath his chin. Ducking his own chin into his chest as hard as he could, Mike tried to block those squeezing fingers while he tightened his own grip.

The Visitor opened his mouth slightly—Donovan had only a second to realize that the mouth seemed to have *two sets* of teeth—when something lashed out at him. Dry—red—it flew from the creature's mouth, spattering drops of burning liquid— it was a foot long or more—

The tongue lashed again—forked—Mike felt a frenzy of repulsion. His reflexes took over, bringing his knee up in a vicious blow that landed true and hard.

*It didn't faze the thing at all.* Somehow that fact, more than anything else he'd seen yet, brought home the *alienness* of the creature. Panicking, he grabbed madly at the thing's eyes, seeking to blind it. His own vision was beginning to blur as his assailant's fingers groped ever deeper into his throat, nearing his windpipe.

His fingers sank *into* the thing's face. Stunned, Mike looked at the flap of skin that had torn away in his hand, leaving a large, greenish-black oily patch.

As its face began to rip, the creature partly relaxed its grip, half turning away—as though to hide the ripped place. Donovan renewed his efforts, grabbing at the torn place viciously, pulling with both hands.

The rest of the face sheared off in sticky, plastic-stretching strings, like mozzarella cheese off a pizza. Donovan was looking at a reptilian face—the false hair flopping back to reveal a crested head. The thing hissed at him slurringly, the tongue flicking in and out, and, even as he struggled with it,

Mike realized the thing was calling out in its own language. *No wonder the bastards speak English! They can't speak their own language when they're wearing the masks!*

He managed to land two slamming punches to the thing's head, which staggered the Visitor. Donovan grabbed the Betacam from off the bunk in back of him, and, praying it was as tough as Tony had promised, clubbed the creature brutally on the side of its head, then again in the face. It slipped, falling.

Mike didn't wait to see if it got back up. Clutching the camera, he was through the grille before he could even take a decent breath.

Forcing his steps to come quickly, he moved back toward the shuttle bay, feeling blood trickling down his face from a cut above his eye, and, more painful still, the pinpoint smarting from whatever venom the thing had spit at him. It burned sharply, but luckily, he thought, feeling his head, it seemed mostly to have landed in his hair, missing his eyes.

He crawled back through the grille into the shuttle bay, only to see a craft being readied for immediate liftoff. Several Visitor technicians stood by the cargo doors. Somewhere overhead a pulsing sound began to reverberate through the landing bay.

"Emergency," said the announcer. "Emergency on level seventy-three. Emergency. Intruder alert on level seventy-three." The cargo bay doors began to rise as two of the Visitor technicians hastened away.

*Oh, shit,* thought Donovan, eyeing the slowly closing doors to freedom.

One of the Visitor pilots turned to the other. "I'm so tired of all these drills. Let's go, before we have to sit here and wait through another one." His companion nodded agreement, and they climbed into the pilot's compartment—leaving the bay, for the moment at least, deserted.

Mike crouched frozen for a precious second, unable to believe his good luck, then, diving forward, raced for the cargo doors. There were perhaps two and a half feet—no more—separating the moving sheets of metal. Donovan leaped, flattening his body in mid-air, launching outward in an impromptu racing dive.

One of the doors struck his shin with paralyzing force, then he was through, inside, hugging his shin, and blinking away tears of pain or thanksgiving—Mike wasn't sure which.

He felt the familiar lift of the shuttle, and hastily, dragging his leg, crawled behind the cargo tank. He crouched in the darkness, rubbing his shin, breathing deeply, trying to slow the blood racing in his veins. He was trembling violently from adrenaline overload . . .

*Don't kid yourself, Mike,* he told himself cynically, *adrenaline overload in this case is just another word for* fear, *and you're goddamned* scared, *admit it . . .*

"Okay, I'm scared," he mumbled, laying his head against the coolness of the Betacam resting on his pulled-up knees. *What the hell is going to happen to us? What have we gotten ourselves into?*

The shuttle tilted slightly as it landed. Favoring his leg, Mike crawled to the doors, peering out. He watched the two Visitor pilots walk away from the shuttle, then, when the area seemed deserted, limped out.

He'd barely reached the other side of the parking lot when a dark shape rose from a sitting position by a dumpster. Donovan tensed, ready to swing the Betacam again.

"Mike!" Tony sounded horrified. "What the *hell* happened to you, man?" Hastily he took the camera out of Donovan's lax fingers. "You look like hell!"

"Feel like it too," Donovan admitted, staggering a bit with relief. "I'm glad to see you, buddy. Let's get over to the station. I've gotta see what I got on the tape."

"What—"

Mike shook his head. "If I try and tell you, you'll think I'm crazy. Or drunk. I hardly believe it myself. We've got to see this tape."

Reaching Tony's car, they climbed in. Donovan looked at the lighted digital clock on the dash, then, with a muffled exclamation, peered at his watch, wiping the blood off his eye with a curse. "Is this thing *right?* Can't be!"

Leonetti started the car. "What?"

"You mean I was only up there *twenty-five minutes?*!"

Tony checked his watch before putting the Toyota in gear. "Yep. Seem longer?"

Donovan leaned back against the seat cushions, letting his breath out in a long, long sigh. "Yeah. Forever longer."

Amazingly enough, he dozed off during the twenty-minute drive to the television station. When Tony stopped the car in the parking lot, he roused, sitting up with a jerk. "Wha—"

"Take it easy, Mike. We're here."

As he climbed out of the small car, Donovan groaned, feeling the stiffness of bruised muscles, and a dull ache in his back where the Visitor had thrown him against the washstand. He almost welcomed the pain as proof that he hadn't dreamed the whole thing.

They went in the back way, straight to the network president's office. It was after nine, and he had gone home, but the evening director was there, preparing for the eleven o'clock news broadcast. Leaving Donovan, Tony went over to speak to the man, a heavy-set bald fellow. Mike remembered having met him a time or two before. Sitting down gingerly on the edge of one of the newsroom desks, Donovan tried to recall his name. *Martini? Gibson? Some kind of drink*, he thought fuzzily. The back of his neck was killing him.

Leonetti came back with the bald man. "Mike, this is Paul Madeira. He's willing to put on a special bulletin, if your tape warrants it. Are you willing to do a live interview to accompany it?"

For all his years behind the camera, Donovan had never had one focus on *him*, except for the press that had gathered around following their first visit to the Mother Ship. He hesitated. "Okay. Just so long as you don't expect Barbara Walters' brand of poise out of me."

They went into one of the rear screening rooms, while Tony readied the tape. Donovan sat in the darkened room, his pulses racing, as the images began to unroll.

First the loading dock. "What's 'venting operations'?" Madeira wanted to know.

"They're evidently taking some of those chemicals up there, then dumping them into the atmosphere," Donovan said. "The chemical story may be just a cover-up."

"But why would they do that? Why present such an elaborate hoax?" Tony asked.

Mike shrugged, wincing as his back protested. "Don't know, buddy. But I doubt they're going to all this trouble just for a social call."

The shadowy walkway came next. "Cut that when we

broadcast," Donovan suggested. "It doesn't show up well, and nothing happened there."

Then they heard distant voices. Donovan tensed as the scene with Diana and Steven replayed. When Diana reached into the chamber holding the mouse, Donovan gulped audibly, for the first time realizing what was happening to the creatures off-camera.

"Get set," he whispered quietly to Madeira and Leonetti. "This next part's a doozy. Hope you guys have strong stomachs."

"What?" said Madeira—then the big man froze as Steven gulped down the mouse.

"Holy *shit*!" Tony hissed.

Donovan swallowed. "The best is yet to come, boys and girls." He watched Diana raise the guinea pig, her jaw expanding—

Then, almost without realizing he'd moved, he found himself leaning over the trash can, vomiting. Tony stopped the machine with a curse, then turned on the light. "Mike—"

Donovan waved him away, then heaved again. "No—okay—I'm . . . okay." He straightened, gasping, then rinsed his mouth with the cup of water Madeira handed him. "Thanks. I feel like an asshole—I suppose better here than there, where they might've heard me."

"Believe it," said Tony. "I nearly whoopsed just watching the tape. What *are* those things?"

Donovan looked at him. "You'll see—at least, I hope you will."

"Start it up again, Tony," said Madeira.

Donovan could have kissed the Betacam. The tough little camera had landed on the bunk, making the picture sideways, but by craning their necks, they could see most of the fight. One or two closeups of the alien, his human mask dangling off the side of his face, made both Madeira and Tony gasp.

Lights back on, the three looked at each other. "Reptiles of some kind," said Madeira. "It was like seeing a science fiction movie come to life. The things are evidently very strong, Donovan. You're lucky you're not hurt worse."

"Yeah," echoed Tony

"Let's get that bulletin on the air," said Donovan.

Minutes later, Donovan sat with the station's anchorman for

the eleven o'clock news, listening to the calls throughout the studio.

"Lights! Give me lights, dammit. *Now!*"

"We're feeding bars and tone right now."

"Dan, check your patching."

"Get lavs on them. I want them double-miked." A technician came up and fitted them with small mikes. She offered to dab some antiseptic on Donovan's blistered and battered face, but he waved her away, seeing the director give the signal to begin.

Mike heard an off-camera voice: "We interrupt this program for a special bulletin live from our newsroom in Los Angeles."

Madeira's voice reached Donovan. "Stand by, one—take one. Cue, Charles."

The anchorman across the table from Donovan looked up: "An astonishing occurrence just took place aboard the Mother Ship. With us tonight is—"

"Hey! What the hell!" Madeira's voice interrupted. "Hang on, Chuck, we've just lost our line—"

The assistant director, a young black woman with long, dark hair, looked up in amazement. "We've lost our line. We've lost Ma Bell."

"*What?!*" Madeira looked frazzled. The studio lights glistened on his bald head.

"Somebody's pulled AT&T right out from under us! The whole damn network's off the air!"

"So are both the others!" shouted the technical director.

"And now I've lost New York," said the young woman in a hopeless tone.

The monitor flickered above Mike's head. "There's something!" shouted Madeira.

The screen filled with the Visitors' symbol.

# Chapter 9

"Damn," Donovan mumbled, looking up at the monitors on the newsroom wall. The screens flickered, then filled with Kristine Walsh's familiar features.

"This is Kristine Walsh. The Visitors' Supreme Commander, John, is here to make a statement."

Mike sighed, slumping on his spine behind the broadcast desk. *We were too late . . . too damn late, and now we're shit outa luck.* He didn't look up as John spoke:

"My friends throughout the world. First, I must thank the leaders of each of your countries, who have graciously and in the interests of peace, turned over all their broadcasting facilities to us to help avoid confusion in this crisis." Donovan heard the ripple of disbelief and growing anger as the broadcast room reacted to the Visitor leader's lie.

"I am sad to say that there has been a carefully coordinated, and quite violent attempt by the conspiracy of scientists to commandeer control of our facilities at many key locations around the world." Shots of several refineries in flames filled the monitors. "These scenes came from Rio de Janeiro, Tokyo, and Cairo, where our plants came under furious attack by terrorists—at least two dozen other places suffered similar attempted assaults, but managed to partially or completely repel them."

Shots of ambulances and stretcher-bearing paramedics appeared against a backdrop of flaming chemical tanks and guerilla-style warfare. The victims wore human clothing as well as Visitor uniforms. John's words voiced-over the scenes: "The loss of life has been enormous—both to your people and ours. In addition, thousands have been wounded—and we're fearful there will be more attacks."

John's image filled the screens again. "The outbreak is so widespread and so dangerous that most civilian members of your governments have asked us to extend them protection—which, of course, we were happy to provide. They're safe aboard our ships, and we'll take good care of them."

"I'll bet, you lying sonofabitch!" the assistant director snarled. Donovan looked over at Madeira, who appeared to be in shock.

John sighed, looking regretful. "I'm also sorry to report that this man—a person in whom we placed considerable trust—" a photo appeared on the screens, and with weary expectation, Mike looked up to see his own face, "Michael Donovan, of the United States, has proved to be the biggest traitor to the peace and well-being of the world. He is one of the leaders of the conspiracy, and is responsible for engineering the violent attacks conducted today."

"Too bad they didn't get one of your best side, Mike," said a disgusted voice, and Donovan looked down to see Tony Leonetti crouched by his side. "Come on, you'd better get out of here. This'll be the first place they'll look."

Donovan followed his partner to the video-tape room. "Did you get a chance to copy my tape?"

"Setting up to do it now. Man, we're in trouble."

"Tell me about it," said Donovan bitterly, hearing the last words of John's statement: "Any person who gives information leading to Donovan's capture will be handsomely rewarded by the UN General Assembly and the government of the United States.

"If you see this man, do not—I repeat, do *not* attempt to apprehend or speak to him. He should be considered armed and dangerous."

"*What?!*" Donovan turned to Leonetti. He'd never thought they'd go this far. It was like something out of the Middle Ages.

A scream broke from the newsroom, then the place seemed to erupt with the sounds of booted feet and strange, whining pulses of sounds. "They're here, Mike!" shouted Tony.

The locked door burst inward, and beyond it Donovan could see Visitors wearing strange protective helmets and carrying heavy-duty weapons. He yanked open the other door, just as Tony tossed him his tape. "Here!" Leonetti overturned a rack of video components in the path of the Visitors—effectively cutting off his own escape route. Donovan had no choice—it was run or be gunned down where he stood.

He bolted out the door, dashed across the corridor, hit the fire exit door with his shoulder, and, accompanied by the shriek of the alarm, hurtled out into the night. The stair railing caught him across the waist, as, unable to stop, he careened over it and down to the parking lot. It was a short drop—only four or five feet—but Donovan landed badly, knocking his wind out.

Bad landing or not, the fall saved his life. Almost before he'd landed, a bolt of energy cut the air above the railing like a lash, leaving a singed, ozone smell. Scrambling to his feet, Donovan stuffed the precious tape inside his jacket pocket and raced down the alley toward where he thought the parking lot lay.

He rounded a corner, running full-tilt into another trooper—a California highway patrolman, this time. The man reeled back, then, seeing Donovan's face, made a grab for his sidearm. Mike's foot lashed out, and the weapon went spiraling away.

Panicked by this new evidence that his own people believed the Visitor report and would treat him like a criminal, Donovan raced on farther into the alley. With a sick feeling he realized he'd lost his sense of direction—instead of the parking lot ahead, there was nothing but a high wall.

Behind him came the beat of booted footsteps, then that strange whining pulse as the shock troopers fired their alien weapons. Realizing he had no choice, Donovan lengthened his strides, then, when he was only feet away from squashing himself on the bricks like a bug, leaped, arms over his head. His groping fingers closed over the top of the wall, and he hung there, feet kicking wildly, trying to get a toehold that would allow him to swing up—

A bolt singed the wall beside him, and Donovan felt sudden heat in his right buttock. As though the blast had been a whip to encourage a balky horse, Mike pulled himself up, his leg swinging up to hook over the wall. He hesitated for just a second, then another pulse nearly singed his hair, and he jumped outward, into the darkness below.

Daniel Bernstein sat up excitedly as the Visitor leader, John, described the violent attempt to take over the chemical plants. "I wonder if they got Richland," Stanley Bernstein murmured. Abraham sat across the room, very still, only his eyes moving.

"Oh, God, Stanley!" Lynn whimpered. "Look at all those people they injured! What's going to happen to us?"

"Nothing, honey, nothing." Bernstein patted his wife's shoulders encouragingly.

"Quiet, Dad!" Daniel turned around. "This is important!" John had just finished describing the manhunt going on for the photographer, Michael Donovan. Daniel's lip curled, watching the picture. *After all these guys are doing for us, this sonofabitch tries to screw it up? He'd better not get in my path . . ."*

John smiled reassuringly from the television screen, and Daniel smiled back automatically. John would handle everything.

"Your national leaders have suggested that a state of martial law will be most helpful at this time, and we agree. Police at local levels will be working with our Visitor patrols—and we'll also ask the help of all our Visitor Friends units everywhere . . ."

"All *right*!!" Daniel sat up, squaring his shoulders, tugging at his uniform to straighten it.

"We anticipate that this crisis will pass relatively quickly. In the meantime, friends, I and my fellow Visitors will do our best to see you through it and help you maintain control. There will be more announcements later, giving you specific rules to follow during the crisis."

The television screen went black. Daniel stood up, his head held proudly. "Gotta go, Mom and Dad! You heard the Supreme Commander!"

He left, hearing his mother behind him. "Stanley, oh, my God . . ."

Then his father's reassurance. "It'll pass—you heard what John said. Right, Dad?"

But Abraham said nothing at all.

# Chapter 10

Mike Donovan lay on his belly on a windswept hillside, sighting through the telephoto lens of his 35-millimeter reflex camera at what lay below: Davis Air Force Base—Strategic Air Command Headquarters for Southern California. He snapped off several shots of the Visitor sentries patrolling the entrances and perimeters of the base. Suddenly a puff of dust rose in the distance, and Donovan focused on a long black limousine approaching.

As the car came closer, he could see several high-ranking military officers in the vehicle's passenger seats, and—he narrowed his eyes to read the stripes—a captain was driving.

He swung the camera back, focusing on the base again, then saw something interesting—the Visitor shock troopers scattered, moving quickly inside the building, and suddenly several MP's clad in standard-issue uniforms appeared, taking up positions at the entrance gate. Donovan glanced back at the limo, frowning helplessly. The gate was too far away for those in the car to have seen what was happening.

The Lincoln pulled up in front of the gate, and the Lieutenant Colonel got out, gesturing at the inside of the car. Mike squinted again at the older man inside. He was a General.

Sick, he watched. The sentries stood helplessly as the Visitor troopers emerged from the building, heavy-duty weapons at ready. They ordered everyone out of the car, and when the Lieutenant Colonel made a move toward his sidearm, shot him without hesitation. The General, the Colonel, and the Captain were led away under guard, while the MP's, under direction of one of the Visitor troopers, picked up the Lieutenant Colonel's body and carried it away.

Donovan recorded the entire incident on film, wondering, as he'd wondered so often these past two weeks, if anyone would ever see this record he was collecting of the Visitor occupation. He changed film, stowing the record of the slaying safely in his jacket. His pockets bulged with film and the VTR tape—he'd have to try and get copies made and the pictures developed soon, but wasn't sure just how he was going to manage that. He fingered his week-old beard . . . Not really enough yet to cover his features.

He wished his beard grew faster, or that he hadn't worked so hard, that entire first week, to shave each day. It hadn't been easy—sleeping in flophouses, all-night movies, one night at the "Y." He rolled over onto his back, letting the sun play on the now-gaunt planes of his face, appreciating its warmth. He'd had only fifteen bucks on him the night of his foray into the Mother Ship, and the money had soon run out. For the past two days he'd eaten at missions and soup kitchens—when he'd eaten. His thinking was a little fuzzy from hunger, he suspected.

Four days ago he'd picked up ten dollars from a woman living near Eleanor when he'd knocked on her door, asking for work. His nose wrinkled. The only job she'd been able to offer him was cleaning stalls in her backyard stable. He'd taken it—but if he didn't get his clothes washed soon, he didn't know what he'd do . . . There were always coin-op laundromats, but when he only had the one set of clothes . . . He pictured himself sitting buck naked on a wooden bench, watching his clothes spin, and found himself chuckling. The laughter had a desperate, zero-hour quality.

He wondered bleakly if Tony Leonetti had managed to get away. He hadn't seen a soul he knew, but he'd have to try and make some contacts. He couldn't go on like this much longer.

He scratched suddenly at his shin, then felt something nip his thigh. He'd been fleabitten before, when he'd been caught and interned briefly in Laos, but he'd hardly noticed then—fleas, compared to dysentery, lice, and torture, paled a bit. Now the little buggers were driving him crazy.

He'd have to take the risk of trying to phone Tony, he decided. He hadn't heard any news reports given by anyone but Kristine lately—he didn't think any of the networks were doing their own news anymore—but the situation was terrible, and getting worse. Visitor troopers were stationed on nearly every street corner. Others spent their time, along with the Visitor Friends, putting up propaganda posters showing Visitors hugging old folks, or toting babies on their shoulders. Prices had risen astronomically, and the curfew was still in effect. Donovan had overheard gossip in the flophouses that the police force was acting only on the written orders of the Mayor—that the man hadn't actually been seen for more than a week. Donovan wondered bleakly which hand the Mayor had used to write those orders commanding the police to cooperate in every way with the Visitor troops . . .

Wearily he climbed to his feet, stowing his camera in a battered plastic shopping bag. The camera represented his one foray to gain help—he'd broken into Eleanor's house one night, while she and Arthur were in the living room with Steven, talking. He'd left the camera there the night the Richland plant began producing the Visitors' "life-sustaining" chemical. The camera and some of the rolls of film—now used—were all he'd had a chance to grab.

Arthur, hearing a noise in the back, had come in just as Mike had put a leg over the sill in the spare bedroom and was climbing out. Eleanor's husband had stood in the doorway, his gaze locked with Donovan's, for seemingly endless seconds. Then Donovan had forced himself to move, waiting all the time for the shout that would bring Steven and the other Visitors down on him. But the man hadn't raised the alarm.

With a sigh, Donovan began the long walk back to the main highway. If he was lucky—and he admitted, fleas or not, he was incredibly lucky still to be free and in one piece—he'd be able to thumb a ride back to L.A. by late afternoon. Then he'd try and scrounge a few bucks, and maybe by night he could risk calling Tony . . .

His head filled with planning another night as a fugitive—plans that had become second-nature since he'd been on the run—Mike Donovan walked on . . .

* * *

Tight-lipped, Juliet Parrish folded a blouse and tossed it into the open suitcase on the bed. Denny sat across the room from her, not meeting her eyes. "You going to stay with your folks in Manhattan?"

She swallowed, keeping her voice even with an effort that hurt. "No, I can't get through to them. You need a special permit for long distance now, and anyone in the life sciences doesn't have a prayer of getting one. It's better not to even ask." She picked up her hairbrush mechanically and put it into the suitcase. "Besides—maybe it's better if you don't know where I'm going. I'll get the rest of my things—I don't know . . . sometime later." She took a deep breath, forcing herself to breathe out through her mouth slowly, but not letting Denny see her effort.

Denny made a small gesture as he picked up a bag of Hershey bars—Juliet's chocolate addiction was one of the first things he'd discovered when she moved in—and handed it to her. "Here. You'd better take these. I'll never eat them, and they say it's getting hard to find stuff in the stores."

Blindly she took the plastic bag, careful not to touch his fingers. He shifted on the bed, still not looking directly at her. "I still think you're overreacting."

She shook her head, folding a skirt. "No. I don't want you losing any more accounts because of me."

"But Julie, we don't know that's it for sure."

She stopped, sobs rising, looking directly at his dark, handsome features. "No, that's the really nasty part. They're always *so* damn polite!" She slammed the skirt into the suitcase without looking at it. "But we know, don't we? We know . . ."

He didn't argue, and after a second Julie realized she was waiting for him to. She shook her head and walked over to get her jacket out of the closet. Making an attempt to change the subject, she told him the news she'd learned that morning. "Anyway, another biochemist—Phyllis, you remember? Well, she didn't show today, either. And no one's heard from her. Just like Ruth and all the others. Classes in the medical school are still suspended until the 'resolution of the current crisis.' If I'm going to go, I'd better make it now."

"Maybe Phyllis just went away," said Denny, not looking up. Juliet stared down at his bent head, resisting an urge to touch his wavy hair just once more . . .

She felt absurdly protective of him in his self-enforced blindness. "Denny. Have you ever thought that maybe she—and Ruth—were *taken* away?"

Denny looked uncomfortable, but still stubborn. "There's nothing to those rumors, Julie!"

She snapped the suitcase with a final click. "You think not? Shall I stay, then?"

The seconds dragged by, then she heard his voice, so low she had to strain to pick up the words. "I think . . . you should do . . . whatever makes you happy . . ." His voice died away.

"No, Den," she said, picking up the suitcase. "Sometimes you can't do the things that make you happy. Sometimes . . ." she bit her lip, ". . . you have to do the things that make you *un*happy—because they're the things you *must* do." She turned away, the suitcase thudding against her blue jeaned leg. "I'll see you, Denny," she whispered, and left.

Daniel Bernstein proudly polished his Visitor sidearm, then took a swig from a glass of burgundy as he inspected the results. The bottle, half-full, sat beside him on the carpet. He looked up with interest as his father turned on the television set and Kristine Walsh's voice filled the room:

". . . and there were even fewer incidents of violence today. It seems that people everywhere are starting to report in to the authorities when they suspect someone might be involved with the conspiracy. This early warning will save countless lives, and the Supreme Commander urges—"

"Dammit!" Stanley angrily switched off the television set. "I'm so *tired* of her face, and only hearing *one* side of what's going on!"

Daniel didn't understand why his father was upset. Carefully he holstered his sidearm, and then poured himself more of the wine. "The truth's the truth, isn't it?"

"Then why not let some others say it?" Stanley peered at the level of wine in the bottle with some disbelief. "Don't you think you've had enough of that, Daniel?"

Daniel looked at the bottle as though he expected it to answer for him. "No," he said finally.

"Well, *I* do." His father reached out suddenly and snatched both the bottle and the glass away from Daniel, who glowered at him sullenly.

"You know, Stanley, there *is* the newspaper," said Lynn Bernstein placatingly.

The elder Bernstein gave his wife a disgusted look. "Yeah. It says exactly the same thing *she* says—sometimes word-for-word! And not just that! It's everything! Look at these bills!" He grabbed a handful of the bills Lynn was working on, shaking them at her. "The price is up on everything! Can't make a long-distance phone call without a permit—and when you get the permit, most times you can't get through!"

He paced angrily back and forth, ignoring Daniel, who watched him, narrow-eyed. "It's not even safe on our own block anymore! Dad told me that the Maxwell's kid, Polly, got beat up at school when her project won the science fair! That's crazy! And last night, when that carload of drunks rode by, yelling—well, they didn't just make noise over there. They smashed in their bay window. Dad told me Kathleen said she was scared to death. Crazy! That's what it is!"

"But Stanley, you know Robert is . . ." She trailed off apologetically.

"A scientist? That what you were about to say? Well, so what if he is? We've lived across the street from them for ten years now, and you couldn't ask for a nicer guy—the idea of Bob being involved with a conspiracy is ludicrous! This whole thing is nuts!" Stanley paused, breathing hard.

"You always said this would pass." Lynn frowned up at him, peering over the top of her reading glasses.

"Yeah." Stanley sighed. "Well, it'd better hurry up and pass before we sink. I want things back the way they were."

Lynn glanced around. "Where's Daniel?"

Berstein made a face. "Well, he's not out looking for a job, that's for sure."

His wife lowered her voice. "Stanley, you have to be more careful what you say in front of him."

"*What?* In my own house?"

"But *he* lives here too, and you know how involved he is with . . . them."

He made an impatient, yet conciliatory gesture. "All right, all right . . . I know. But he shouldn't have the right to—"

Lynn watched the light flash on her wedding band. Her voice was soft as she interrupted, "I've heard stories . . ."

"Rumors, you mean."

"*Stories*, Stanley, that a member of his group had actually . . ." She twisted the ring, swallowing.

"Actually what? Informed, you mean?"

She nodded. "On his own parents—and then they disappeared."

Bernstein rubbed the back of his neck roughly, then dropped into a seat beside her. "Well, Lynn, I hardly think that *Daniel*—"

She shivered. "I don't think so either, but . . ."

"I mean, what's to inform on?" He tried to sound casual, but even to his own ears the words sounded unconvincing. "*We're* not scientists, and it's not like I said anything . . ." He frowned, trying to recall exactly what he *had* said. His mouth was suddenly dry.

"You were very critical. Of her—Kristine Walsh. Of them. The papers. Of him, also."

"Well, I don't think he ought to drink that much. Seems like every time I turn around, the liquor's disappearing faster than I can replace it! And with the prices so bad!"

"But that's not all that you said."

"Look, all I said was that I was tired of hearing—"

"One side of the news. *Their* side."

"Well, I meant . . . hearing only one opinion. No, I meant . . ." he trailed off, his eyes flicking around the comfortable room as though it were a place he'd never seen before. "You don't think he'd call them, do you?"

They both stared at the telephone. There were three additional extensions in the house—one in Abraham's room, next door, which they would have heard—but the other two were in the kitchen and their bedroom. On the other side of the house. Bernstein tried to think, to calm himself. In the middle of his effort, Daniel came back into the living room.

Lynn spoke with a pathetic attempt at normalcy. "Danny, honey, where have you been?"

Daniel sat down on the couch with the paper, not looking up. "To the bathroom."

Stanley turned to his wife, and moved his lips exaggeratedly, while barely breathing the words: "Do you think he's lying?"

She stared for a second at Daniel, then looked back at her husband and shrugged.

Bernstein leaned back in his chair, fighting back fear. *This is terrible. What am I going to do? Why is this happening to me?*

* * *

Robin Maxwell trudged slowly up the street, her arms filled with books. Usually she only did her homework to keep her parents from bugging her, but lately, the way things were going, even her textbooks had begun to feel more friendly than the school and the neighborhood.

The only boy she knew who wasn't acting like she had the plague or something was Daniel. Robin's pretty mouth thinned—she was angry at Daniel Bernstein. He'd managed to mention, in front of Brian, that Robin's dad was an anthropologist. She hadn't seen Brian in several weeks now.

Robin shook back her dark hair, and her indigo eyes were stormy. *Damn you, Daniel Bernstein!* The grody little creep must've thought that if he turned Brian off her, that she, Robin, would have no one to turn to but *him*. Well, she'd teach him to think again, that was for sure . . .

If it hadn't been for Brian's absence, Robin would have felt worse about the situation at school—but even the pain of having kids she'd known all her life treat her like crap was nothing to the ache she felt whenever she thought of Brian. Thoughts of the handsome Visitor tormented her dreams at night, and filled her mind's eye by day. Every time she looked at that great Mother Ship hanging in the sky—and you couldn't go anywhere without seeing it—Robin thought of him.

She was so deeply engrossed in her current visions of him that Robin almost walked by her house. Her father's voice jolted her out of a daydream where Brian was there, everywhere, his arms around her, smiling down at her— "Robin, get in the car!"

She looked up to see the family station wagon loaded down with clothing, camping gear, and valuables. Her father was lashing a large bundle to the luggage rack on top of the vehicle. "What?" Robin said blankly. "Where are we going, Dad?"

"To the mountain cabin, honey." Maxwell gave a final tug at the knots, then fumbled in his jacket for the keys. Robin looked beyond him to the cardboard-covered hole that had been their bay window.

"For the weekend?" Robin asked, somehow knowing the answer would be negative.

"Maybe, honey. But more probably we'll be staying there awhile. Your Mom and I packed for you. Hop in, unless you have to make a bathroom run."

"No," responded Robin, feeling something shatter inside her. *If I leave, I'll never see him again. I'll die.* She moved a few steps toward the car door, then suddenly balked. "But I don't *want* to go up to the mountains. Please, Dad. I hate our place up there. It's *boring!*"

Her father's mouth thinned, and Robin took an involuntary step back. But his voice was even. "Get in the car, Robin."

Her mother opened the car door and came around, the expression in her green eyes gentle, but unyielding. "Please, Robin, try to understand. Too many things are happening. A scientist your father works with was arrested for conspiracy this morning."

Polly poked her head out the open car window. "I think we ought to stay and fight, Dad! You haven't done anything wrong!"

Kathleen bit her lip in silent anguish, looking back at her home, then her chin came up. "It's not that simple, Poll."

"But Daddy's no conspirator!" Robin wailed. "Those others—"

Robert gave her a look. "They weren't either, Robin. Get in the car."

"But all my friends are *here!*"

"Yeah." Polly's voice dripped sarcasm. "Especially the one in the red uniform . . ."

Robin whirled on her sister. "Shut *up*, Polly!" She turned back to her father. "Please, Dad. I could stay with Karen and her—"

"*Robin.*" The girl had never heard that tone from her father before. "*Now.*"

Robin clenched her fists helplessly against her textbooks as she stalked around the car and jerked the door open. She climbed in, ignoring both Polly, who stuck her tongue out at her older sister, and Katie, who wanted to "sit in Binna's lap, Mommy!"

Robert put the car in gear and backed it out. His tension was reflected in the squeal of the tires as he gunned the motor. Kathleen recognized a figure watching them from across the street, leaning on a rake, and waved sadly. The man waved back. Robert glanced over at her. "Who was that?"

"Sancho Gomez. He came around a couple of months ago looking for gardening work, and I hired him for a couple of hours a week, on Fridays. He worked for a couple of families on this street . . . did a really good job with the roses . . ."

Robert frowned. "But I was just noticing that our roses really needed cutting back."

"They do . . . did." Kathleen brushed distractedly at her hair. "Sancho told me a couple of weeks ago that he couldn't work for me anymore—that his other customers, among them Eleanor Dupres, had told him if he kept working for us, he couldn't work for them anymore. What could he do? The guy's got a wife and kids . . ."

Maxwell nodded tightly. They drove in silence for nearly twenty minutes, until they reached the outskirts of L.A., and topped a small hill. Suddenly Polly pointed. "Look, Dad! It's a police roadblock!"

Kathleen made a tiny sound in her throat as she stared down the street to the Visitor squad vehicle that had landed across the highway, blocking all but one lane. A line of traffic sat waiting, bumper-to-bumper. Two police black-and-whites sat on the side of the road, lights flashing red-blue-red-blue-red . . . A helmeted Visitor shock trooper stood by the nose of the squad vehicle, his stun rifle carried muzzle-up. His helmet swung back and forth as he watched the L.A.P.D. officers check cars, two at a time.

Maxwell's fingers tightened on the wheel of his car, and he didn't dare look at his family, afraid they'd see the naked fear in his eyes. Without a word he swung the station wagon off the road, put on his blinker, then, as other oncoming vehicles slowed to take in the scene below, swung the wheel savagely in a U-turn.

*They can't have blocked* every *road*, his mind argued against his growing panic. *One of the smaller secondary ones* . . .

Ten minutes later they pulled over to the side of the road, staring in dismay at the roadblock ahead of them. "Another one," Kathleen said tightly.

"Daddy, why don't you just drive through?" Robin asked. "You haven't done anything—"

Polly gave her sister a withering look. "Boy, Robin, you sure are *stupid*. Were you born that way, or did you have to study?"

Robin stared at her sister in shock, then flared angrily. "God, Polly, how can you be so *totally*—"

"Shut up," Robert commanded without raising his voice. "I have to think."

"How come they want to keep us in the city, Mom?" Polly asked.

"Makes it easier to find us," Kathleen said.

"Why do they want to be able to find us—and people like us?"

"We don't know, Poll." Kathleen cast a quick, frightened look at Robert.

Shouts broke the silence, and they watched a man leap out of the back of one of the cars stopped at the roadblock, running frantically down the road toward them. Horrified, they watched as the Visitor trooper sighted carefully at the fleeing man's back, then fired. A pulse of sound filled the air with a brief flash of blue electricity, then the smell of ozone. The man staggered on a few steps, then fell against Robert's door, his anguished face pressing briefly against the glass, then slid bonelessly down to the road, leaving a trail of saliva and mucus on the window.

The Maxwells sat frozen with shock, unable to move or think, as the Visitor shock trooper and the two police officers ran up to the fallen man. The Visitor got there first. Without a glance at the horrified Maxwells, he pushed the man's face brutally against the pavement. The first cop came up with the handcuffs. They heard the man whimper as they dragged his arms behind him, wrenching his back where a black burn showed the impact of the alien weapon.

Sickened, Maxwell recognized that oily blackness of charred cloth and singed meat—and knew, with a terrible certainty, what had happened to Arch Quinton. The other police officer approached, stood looking down at the injured man, his face expressionless, but something flickering in his eyes that might have been pity. "Another scientist?" he asked.

"No," answered the officer with the handcuffs. "He was *helping* one try and run the roadblock. So that makes him one of 'em, in my book. On your feet, pal!" He dragged brutally at the now sobbing man.

"Easy, Bob—" the first officer remonstrated. "He's wounded."

"That's his fault, Randy. He wants to break the new laws, he's gotta take the consequences."

Randy gave a quick glance over at the Visitor trooper, who was walking back toward the squad vehicle, to make sure the alien was out of earshot. "Come on, Bob! This is different!"

"No it ain't!" The man glared at his partner. "A crook's a crook, and don't you forget it. Ain't nothing different except the guys who give the orders."

Without a backward glance, he dragged the barely conscious man away. The officer named Randy looked after him, then back at the Maxwells, obviously troubled. "You folks coming down the road?" he asked, indicating the roadblock.

"Uh . . . no," answered Robert, thinking fast, pasting a fatuous grin on his face. "The . . . uh . . . little woman forgot her grocery list, can you believe it? We're gonna have to go back and get it." Heart threatening to erupt from his chest, he put the car in reverse.

The officer looked at him a moment, then nodded sadly. "Yeah, okay. Prices what they are today, you can't shop without a list, all right." He glanced back at the roadblock, then at Maxwell. "You all take care, now."

Robert backed up and turned the car around, and they started back toward town. Kathleen gave a choked, hysterical laugh. "Little woman! Oh, God, Bob, what are we—"

"Don't start, Kathy! Or we'll all be doing it!" Maxwell swallowed.

"Where're we going to go? Who's going to help us?" Robin wailed plaintively. Maxwell felt a strong urge to spank—or slap—her, but repressed it. *It's not her fault—this whole thing is as far outside her experience as it is yours*, he thought.

"I don't know, Binna," he said as gently as he could.

Kathleen suddenly straightened beside him. "*I* do. Head back for the house, Robert."

He looked curiously at her, but obeyed, turning on the blinker and swinging the car back onto the crosstown freeway, toward the house that, until this morning, had been his home.

## Chapter 11

Juliet Parrish peered carefully through a crack in the venetian blinds. A few blocks away, a police siren shrieked, but as Julie listened and watched, the sound began to diminish. She dropped the slat back into place with a sigh of relief. "It's all right, I think."

The others in the dry-cleaning shop also relaxed perceptibly. Ben Taylor, sitting beside a steam-pressing machine, made an exaggerated gesture of wiping his forehead, producing a few wry grins. Then, sobering, he began to speak. "All right. We know what's happening: censorship, suppression of the truth— the whole United States ruled by a totalitarian dictatorship under martial law. The military are apparently under arrest, or else they've made them disappear—"

"Talk about paranoia," a dark-haired woman in her forties broke in, "all the scientists I know are scared to death. With good reason."

"Yeah, they're still disappearing," said Brad, a young police officer with curly brown hair and worried eyes. "Like my partner and all the other cops who wouldn't go along with their 'requests'—that's how they phrase it. A real joke, huh?"

Nobody laughed. The dark-haired woman—Julie couldn't remember her name—twisted her hands together. "Yesterday they took another family from my building. He was a doctor . . ."

Ben Taylor looked over at Juliet. "Why do you think they're

so hot to arrest scientists? Especially life science researchers, anthropologists, and physicians? They haven't paid nearly the same kind of attention to theoretical physicists, for example, or astronomers."

Julie nodded agreement, thinking. "They must think we're a threat. That people with expertise in the life sciences might . . . find out something about them—" She shrugged, her mind groping for an answer.

"Like maybe how to stop them?" Ben asked.

Juliet chuckled dryly. "I only hope we turn out to be as big a threat as they seem to worry we'll be!"

One of the women, a black receptionist who had announced that she worked for the telephone company, shook her head. "There's no way we're going to stop them . . . There's too many of 'em."

"No!" Ben glared at her. "There *has* to be a way!"

"There is." Juliet tried to sound positive. Her bluff was called when they all turned to her, their eyes hopeful. She thought faster than she ever had in her life. "We . . . organize," she said, feeling her way into the idea as she talked. "Look, any complex biological structure—our bodies, for instance—starts with individual cells. The cells will reproduce—expand themselves—join with others—"

Brad snorted. "That's great for a biology lesson, Julie, but—"

Juliet whirled on him. "*Listen*, Brad—" She took a deep breath, then started over. "Sorry. Look, I know we're embryonic. There are only a handful of us here in this shop. But you can be sure we're not the only ones who are meeting in darkened rooms at this moment! We can't be the only ones who have come up with the idea of fighting this thing!"

Mumbled agreements came from all quarters. Juliet nodded. "Now what we've got to do is *find* those others, and still more after that. Then we'll need equipment—"

"Weapons," said Brad.

"Supplies," said the dark-haired woman.

"A headquarters," said Ben.

"Yes," Julie agreed. "We're going to need all those things. But I was especially thinking about laboratory equipment and medicines—microscopes, culture dishes—all scientific stuff. That way we can work on trying to figure out why the Visitors want to eliminate the scientists first. We're a threat to them, and we've got to discover that threat!"

"Right!" "Yeah!" "Good thinking, Julie!" they all chorused. The former med student paused, waiting for some of the others to make contributions, but nothing was forthcoming. She began thinking fast again. "We ought to also figure out who is closest to the Visitors, and try to see if they'll join us. That way we'd be able to keep an eye on their actions."

The black woman nodded. "Like that reporter—what's her name? Kristine—"

"Walsh," Ben supplied. "Sure as hell, she's on the inside."

"Maybe too much on the inside," Brad said glumly. "Think we could trust *her*? Maybe she's a hundred percent in favor of what they're doing."

"How could she be?" Ben asked grimly. "If she is, she's the worst traitor since—I dunno—"

"Judas?" suggested the dark-haired woman.

"I agree with Ben," said Juliet. "We ought to at least watch her, see if she seems like the sort of person we should risk contacting. Then, if the group agrees that she's okay, we'll ask her for her help."

She waited, but nobody volunteered. Julie decided that leadership definitely wasn't all it was cracked up to be, and stood up. "I'll find her, and watch her. See if she's someone we can trust. Why don't we meet back here . . . uh . . . Thursday night. Eight sharp?"

"Okay by me," said Brad, who was the only one in the group assigned to work nights. The rest agreed.

"And everybody has to bring at least—" Juliet thought rapidly, "four other people with them. How about that? Agreed?"

"Agreed," they echoed.

"Good," Juliet said. "Guess that's it for now."

She stood in the dimness, the smell of cleaning fluid and steam all around her, watching them file out of the shop and into the alley, warily, one-by-one, exhibiting a caution none of them (with the possible exception of Brad) had ever needed before—and tears filled Julie's eyes. *It's not fair*, she thought. *We shouldn't have to do this. It's not fair at all . . .*

* * *

Mike Donovan dropped coins into the slot of a pay phone, then dialed the number scrawled on the back of a crumpled dollar bill. He counted rings, then, when it was picked up on the twelfth, sighed with relief. Anything but the twelfth ring, and he wouldn't have spoken. "Hello?" said Tony's voice. "Is that you, Uncle Pedro?"

"Uncle Pedro?" Donovan frowned, trying to remember if this was one of their old code responses. He didn't recognize it.

"Ah, it *is* you, Uncle Pedro! *Buenas noches!*"

"Tony, cut the—" Donovan stopped suddenly as another thought occurred to him.

"We've been having trouble with the phone. You comprende? *Uncle Pedro*? Trouble with the phone."

"Yeah?" said Donovan heavily. "*Pobrecito . . .* you must be all tapped out, eh?"

He could almost see Tony's careful nod. "You got it, Uncle. The 'repairmen' even came to check things out—a lot of 'em— and they smelled your cooking all around here. Boy, they sure would like to get their hands on *your* burrito—"

"Yeah, I'm sure they would."

"But I like *Italian* food even better than your Mexican cooking, Uncle . . . remember?"

Donovan grinned. "Yeah, I remember. You still owe me a steak, do you remember? A *twelve ounce* one. Pay up amigo."

"Right, Uncle. Well, don't let me keep you standing there— I know you have to run. Good luck . . ." The phone clicked off.

Donovan started to hang up when suddenly, with no warning siren, a police car skidded around the corner, two wheels on the sidewalk, heading straight for him.

Mike took off, heading down the opposite street—but a squad vehicle swooped down, firing! Donovan zigged, and the powerful electric blasts rocked a nearby car. Donovan threw himself away from it just in time—it exploded, spraying deadly edged metal all over the street!

Donovan dashed down the nearest alley, one too narrow for the squad vehicle to enter. More and more sirens sounded like they were converging on the area. At the end of the alley was a board fence. *This is getting monotonous*, Mike thought, leaping to scramble over it. *I haven't had to get over so many obstacles since Basic—*

He hit the ground on the other side, and dashed away, grinning. At least he'd been able to reach Tony . . . the first thing he was going to do following their twelve o'clock meeting tomorrow was buy some new clothes and a bath—then for a real meal . . .

His mind filled with visions of steak, Donovan crouched behind a garbage-filled dumpster, waiting for the onset of darkness, and safety.

Shadows lengthened on the lawn of the Bernsteins' house, but there was still a good hour of daylight left. Not that you could tell here in the pool house, Kathleen thought. Off to her right a broken barbecue leaned drunkenly against a wall, and the place was filled with old lawn furniture.

Abraham Bernstein nodded at her reassuringly "Lynn and Stanley never use this old cabana—it's just for storage. Nobody comes here. You will be safe."

Kathleen smiled gratefully at him. "Thank you, Abraham. We can never repay you for this."

The old man smiled, waving aside her gratitude. "I will bring supplies, when everyone is asleep. Sheets, and soap, towels. There is a bathroom in there, used only when they have pool parties. And with this curfew . . . there are no more parties."

Kathleen had a sudden, vivid memory of Eleanor's party the night she'd first seen the Visitors, and sighed. Robin blundered into a cobweb and jumped back with a little shriek. "Daddy!" She lowered her voice, but Kathleen knew Abraham's hearing was excellent. "It's grody! Gross! We can't *live* here . . . It's filthy!"

"We'll clean it up," Kathleen said. "It will be fine."

"But there's no way it's ever gonna look decent—"

"Robin! That's enough!" Robert snapped, then turned to Abraham. "I apologize, Abraham. My daughter isn't usually so rude. It's just that . . ."

"It's all right, I understand," Abraham said graciously.

"I'm afraid *I* don't," said Stanley Bernstein, peering in. "Father, can I talk with you? Outside?"

They walked a few paces away from the cabana, but Kathleen could still hear the conversation, Abraham's low, accented tones contrasting with Stanley's shriller, accusing ones.

"I really don't believe you brought them here, Father!"

"They have nowhere to go. Their home is being watched, to see if they try to return there."

"But so is ours! Daniel's here whenever he isn't off with his alien buddies! Tell the Maxwells we're sorry . . ."

"Stanley, son, you don't understand. They have to stay. They need a place to hide, and we are the only place—"

"But Robert Maxwell is a *scientist*, and therefore suspect! And now he's a *fugitive scientist*! That makes him doubly dangerous."

Abraham's voice held a dogged, quiet persistence. "They have to stay."

"And I am telling you to get them out of here before—"

"I won't!"

Stanley turned back to the pool house. "Then *I* will!"

Abraham exploded. "*No, you won't!*"

Kathleen had never heard kindly little Mr. Bernstein use that tone before. She flinched back involuntarily from the fury in it—even though it wasn't directed at her. Stanley Bernstein stared at his father in shock.

Abraham began to speak in a monotone that was all the more passionate for its very lack of expression. "We had to put you in a *suitcase*. In a *suitcase*! An eight-month-old baby. And that's how the underground smuggled you out. But they couldn't help the rest of us . . ."

Stanley made an uncomfortable movement. "I know this story, Father."

"*No, you don't!*" His voice returned to a low monotone. "You don't, Stanley. Your mother . . . *auv shalom* . . . your mother didn't have a heart attack while we were in the boxcar. No. She made it to the camp with me. I can still see her . . . standing naked in the freezing cold, ice on the ground . . ."

He took a deep breath. "Her beautiful black hair was gone. They'd shaved her head. I can see her . . . waving to me, as they marched her with the others—all those people—to the showers. The showers with no water, you understand."

The old man's eyes were focused only on the past. "And perhaps . . . if somebody had given *us* a place to hide . . . she could still be alive today." He looked back at Stanley. "They have to stay, you see? Or else we haven't learned a thing . . ."

Stanley Bernstein rubbed wearily at his face, then made an inarticulate little sound in the back of his throat, nodding. He blinked, his lips moving, but there was no sound. Abraham nodded past him, reassuringly, toward the cabana. Kathleen smiled back, clutching Robert's hand, trying to blink away the tears in her eyes.

"But Elias, we really need your help!" Benjamin Taylor said, lengthening his strides to keep pace with his brother.

Music, remotely of Hispanic origin, blared from loudspeakers along the row of shopfronts. The Visitors were sponsoring an International Day in the shopping district—festivities (food, dancing, and exhibits) were going on around the corner. Ben had noted grimly that the proportion of Visitor attendees to human was almost two to one.

Elias gave a shudder of mock shock and surprise. "What? The great big doctor needs *my* help? How come it is, Ben my man?"

Ben swallowed, realizing Elias was baiting him. " 'Cause you've got contacts here on the street."

His brother's lips drew back in a wolfish grin. "Damn right I do! But listen, brother Benjamin, ain't you the one who is always putting down my 'street contacts' and how I come by them?"

"Yeah. Look, Eli, the times have changed." Ben tried to look as humble as he could, despite the anger bubbling inside him. Elias' help in this could make all the difference.

"Well, the streets ain't changed. There's just a different man to be The Man. Fact is, the streets is doin' fine right now, better than before. Man can make a whole lotta money out here right about now."

Ben nodded grimly. "Black market."

"You should pardon the expression, Ben," Elias said. "You know how much fresh fruit is goin' for? And beef?" He laughed shortly. "I make more sellin' hamburger these days than I do pushin' reefer!"

"Well, you can keep on doing all of that you want, Elias, but there's a group of us who're trying to fight this thing—"

Elias broke in. "That's no never mind to me, man. Why fight it? It don't affect me none—'cept to line my pockets."

Ben put a hand on his arm, swinging Elias around to face

him. "Eli—what is happening to this country . . . this world . . . is wrong."

"Says who?"

"We *need* your help."

Elias glared a him, dropping the street jive in his intensity. "Where were you when I needed yours?"

"Elias, I was always there for you!"

"But just a *little* unapproachable . . . Golden Boy."

"That's only in your head, man!"

"Shit!" Elias' dark eyes flashed. "I heard once I musta heard a thousand times, 'Why can't you be like Brother Benjamin, da Doctuh?'" He took a fierce step forward and Ben stepped backward in reflex. "*Huh*? And now *you* need *my* help?!"

Ben nodded, his voice low. "That's right."

Elias took a quick little shuffling step sideways, away from his brother, his "jivin' mask" dropping over his features again. "Well, gee man, I'd sure like to help you out, but I gots to go up to the *medical libraree*—study mah *anatomee* . . ." He turned away. "Catch you *later*, Bro!"

Ben watched his forced, jaunty walk, feeling tired, guilty, and sad. He'd never realized before the depth of his brother's jealousy and anger.

Mike Donovan hesitated in the darkness, looking up at the balcony of Kristine's loft apartment. A vaguely human shape crossed the frosted glass of the window, deciding him. His meeting today with Tony had been unsuccessful—Leonetti had walked down the street toward their favorite Italian place just at noon, right enough, but as Mike loitered on the street corner, then shuffled toward him, Tony's almond-shaped eyes had flicked quickly to the side, his lips forming a silent "no." Then Mike saw the shock troopers patrolling behind Tony—just before they'd seen him. He'd managed to elude them (thank goodness the layouts of human cities seemed to baffle them still), but at this point he was so famished that he knew another day without food would make him easy prey.

The rungs of the fire escape quivered beneath his weight as he climbed, the metal harsh and cold beneath his hands. Thunder muttered overhead, and then a quick flash of lightning showed him he was almost to the fourth floor. He reached the balcony, swung over the rail, then crouched for long seconds in the gathering threat of the storm. The shape silhouetted by the light moved again, within, and Donovan reached out and tested the balcony door. Locked—of course. He crouched, then sprang, putting his weight against the bolt, and the French doors sprang inward.

Mike went through them with a rush, hearing a horrified gasp—a woman's voice, thank God, and human. Then, blinded by the sudden light, he fell over a row of potted plants sitting before the doors.

He looked up, heard Kristine's voice. "Mike! My God, you scared the hell out of me!" She bent down to help him up, and as his eyes adjusted to the sudden light, he realized she was damp and wearing only a pale green towel, held loosely across her breasts. As tense as the moment was, Donovan couldn't help noticing that the view was impressive.

"What are you doing here?" she asked.

"I'd like to say it's just to take another shower with you, but I need help. You got any money? Please, Kris I haven't eaten in two days."

"Jesus, you look it." She turned, went to her purse, and bent over, fumbling in it. The towel slipped further. She came back and handed him a wad of cash, which he stuffed in his filthy jeans. Her nose wrinkled.

Donovan grinned. "A mess, aren't I?"

"Yes," she agreed frankly, grinning, "but I'm so glad to see you I don't care." She leaned toward him and their lips met in a long, warm kiss. Donovan touched her shoulder, pulling her to him, and her arms went around him. With one part of his mind, Mike realized that the closeness of their bodies was all that was keeping the towel up at all. He checked the slippage factor again, his fingers gentle on her skin.

But even in his rising excitement, the reactions of a fugitive were still with him—his eyes roamed around the room behind her head, noting the furniture, the television set, the peacefulness, and he listened . . .

Sensing his distraction, she stepped back, grabbing quickly for the towel. "I've been so worried for you!"

Mike smiled grimly. "I've been worried for me too."

"Why are they so hot to capture you?"

He stared directly into her green eyes—oddly, they were

almost the exact shade of his own. "Because I've seen their faces."

"What? What faces? What do you mean?"

"They aren't human, Kris. I shot a VTR of them eating small animals *whole*—alive. Then, while I was trying to get off the Mother Ship, one of 'em spotted me—their real eyes must be able to see farther into the infrared than we do—or maybe they just have better night vision—but this guy saw me, dragged me through a ventilation grille *one-handed*, and did his damnedest to kill me. During the fight I tore at his face— and the mask came off. They're reptiles of some sort, Kris." He shivered at the memory. "I got it on film. Greenish-black skins, and red-orange eyes. Tongues this long—" he measured off a space with his hands, "that spray some kind of venom."

She was shaking her head. "Mike, honey—"

"You don't believe me, do you?"

"Well, it's so incredible . . . *reptilian*? With tongues that—I want to believe you, but—"

"It's all true! I've seen it, Kris!"

"I really do believe you *think* you've seen it—"

"*Think* I've— Damn it, Kris!"

They glared at each other, and the sound of their breathing was loud in the quiet room. "Mike, I work so closely with these people, every day . . . It's hard to—" She hesitated.

"Be objective?" he said sarcastically.

For long moments they stared at each other, then he turned back to the window. "I guess this was just a waste of time. Thanks for the loan. I'll get it back to you someday—with interest."

She came after him, grabbing him by the arm. "No, don't leave yet, Mike."

"Why?" He turned back to her.

"If I could see the tape you shot . . ."

"It's hidden."

She moved closer to him, her hand sliding up his arm to his shoulder. "Listen, Mike. It's possible you're right. I may have gotten closer to them than I should." She grimaced wryly. "It's funny, *you're* the one I always wanted to get closer to . . ."

Her open admission took him a little off-guard. "You've got a funny way of showing it, Kris," he said.

"I'd really like another chance," she said, then laughed self-deprecatingly. "That seems to be my favorite line."

She kissed him again, and again Mike wanted to lose himself in the kiss—in her warmth—and again, that sentry inside him wouldn't sleep. He opened his eyes mid-kiss, seeing the darkened glass of Kristine's television set. And in it—the reflection of a uniformed shock trooper crouched on the balcony. The alien was taking aim with a stun rifle.

Donovan swung around, pushing Kristine away so roughly that her towel fell completely off. Donovan was too busy to look; grabbing a barstool, he swung it viciously at the French doors and they exploded outward, showering the Visitor with glass.

Simultaneously the apartment door resounded with a crescendo of thuds and reverberating demands to open up. Donovan gave Kristine a disgusted glance, wondering if she had set him up. "Thanks," he said, his voice harsh.

He headed for the shock trooper who was struggling to his feet on the balcony.

"Mike!" she called.

Donovan ignored her. Grabbing the still-dazed alien's weapon, he headed for the fire escape—when suddenly he felt arms grasp him from behind. Whirling, he brought the butt of the alien weapon up, chopping hard at the trooper's head. The alien went staggering backwards, hit the balcony rail, and went over.

Donovan felt vaguely sick, but had no time to spare. He swarmed down the ladder, hearing the ruckus in Kristine's apartment above him.

A shot from a stun rifle struck barely two feet from him, flaming and slagging the ground where it hit. Donovan looked up, saw a figure momentarily outlined by a sullen flare of lightning, stationed on the roof of the opposite building, then awkwardly tried to aim the weapon he held. He pressed a stud, saw a flare of blue from the muzzle, smelled the ozone. A clean miss—but the bolt sheared off a metal air duct on the roof, which fell, striking the Visitor on its way down. Mike heard the creature give a peculiar ululating cry as it staggered, lost its balance—then the thud as the trooper hit.

Donovan raced for the gate of the apartment complex, still clutching the Visitor's gun, as several shots resounded from

Kristine's balcony. Reaching the gate, he bolted through, turning and twisting to avoid the shots—but the aliens were losing his range. His breath choking in his throat, Donovan forced himself to keep running, and soon even the faint echoes of his footsteps were gone.

A dark-garbed figure wih a gleam of blonde hair rose from the bushes beside Kristine's building, slipped through the gate, then closed it behind her.

Juliet Parrish darted off into the night, hearing the pulse of a stun gun behind her. Looking back, she saw the latch on the gate sizzle and flame brightly. One of the Visitors was taking out his anger at missing his quarry on the wrought-iron fence. Juliet shook her head. She'd recognized the man who had darted away from Kristine Walsh's balcony—his picture had been flashed on wanted bulletins often enough lately. Mike Donovan.

Why had he climbed the ladder to Kristine Walsh's balcony? Juliet grinned sourly to herself. She was fairly sure his actions weren't attributable to a romantic interlude—Donovan was hard to cast as Romeo, the balcony to the contrary. No, Donovan must have gone to Kristine Walsh for help. The man had been a fugitive for several weeks now—he must need money, a place to hide . . .

She wondered what had really happened up there. The two silhouettes against the French doors had merged into one—and then the troopers had arrived. Of course it was possible that Kristine was completely innocent, that the Visitors had staked out her place without her knowledge, figuring Donovan would go there. But it was equally possible that Kristine Walsh had betrayed Mike Donovan, almost to his death.

Juliet gave a small, dismissing shrug. Whatever had happened up there (and they'd probably never know) was academic. The point of the matter was that they couldn't risk betrayal by contacting Kristine Walsh . . .

A sudden, brutal gust of wind whipped Juliet's hair off her forehead, and as she hurried on into the night, the storm broke, soaking her within moments.

Daniel Bernstein fumbled with his key, missing the lock several times before he managed to insert it and open the door. He stumbled into the hall, lit only by the watery glare from the backyard security light, a bit unsteady on his feet. He saw a figure standing by the French doors leading out to the backyard and the pool. He peered blurrily. It was Robin! Robin Maxwell!

Funny. Daniel frowned, trying to think clearly, without a great deal of success. He'd thought the Maxwell family had run away. What was Robin doing here? The lightning from the storm outside silvered her features as she looked out the doors, turning her hair into a dark cloud. She looked awfully good to Daniel. He smiled at her, said "Hi."

She turned with a start, then giggled nervously when she recognized him. "Oh, hi, Danny. You startled me."

"What are you doing here?" He went over to her, enjoying the way the security light shadowed the full, rounded curves of her breasts. She was wearing those tight designer jeans, the ones he'd always liked, that her mother had raised such a fuss about her buying.

She sighed. "I know I'm not supposed to be here, but I just couldn't stand it in your pool house for another minute." She smiled at him. "So I took a walk."

Daniel focused slowly on her words. "Our pool house? What are you doing there?"

"Living there—if you can call that living." She made a face. "It's too small for *one* of us, let alone *five*! It's totally outrageous . . ." She sniffed audibly. "Oh, hey Danny. You've been drinking."

He shrugged. "Yeah."

A touch of eagerness entered her voice. "With Brian?"

"He wasn't there. He doesn't drink," Daniel told her. "I don't think he can hold it." He snickered.

"Did he ask about me?"

"No." Daniel frowned. "Why should he?"

She shrugged. "I just thought he might, that's all . . ."

Daniel dismissed Brian with a gesture. "Well, not tonight he didn't. I'm real glad to see you. You look real pretty in that sweater . . . and those jeans. I always liked them."

Hesitantly, he touched her arm. She didn't appear to notice. "Other nights, though?" she asked.

Daniel looked blank. "What?"

"He asks about me other nights, then?"

"Who?"

"Brian, Danny! You really *have* had too much to drink!"

He stroked her arm, but still she didn't seem aware of his fingers, only watched his face avidly, waiting for him to answer her. He summoned words, almost at random. "Well . . . sometimes . . . yeah . . . I guess he does. He wondered where you went. We both did." He gave her his most meaningful look. "Me especially. Until I found out you were in my pool house, that is."

She turned back, staring out the window at the rain turning the pool into a multitude of silver ripples. Daniel continued to stroke her arm. " 'Member that day when the Visitor ships first came? When we didn't know yet they were going to be our friends?"

"Hmmmm?"

"You said that day that you didn't want to die without having made love. You still feel that, Robin?" The curve of her breast beneath her sweater was so close to his fingers that he felt dizzy just looking at her.

"Sure," she said, still not turning around. Daniel leaned closer, his lips readying for the kiss, then she spoke again. "Is he a virgin, do you think?"

"Who?"

"Brian."

He looked at her abstracted face and dropped his hand from her arm. She didn't even notice . . .

# Chapter 12

Doctor Benjamin Taylor pushed a linen cart heaped with dirty sheets and towels along the loading dock of the Stamos Pharmaceutical Company. With quick, nervous movements, he swung the cart sharply into the back of a waiting industrial-sized van, then gave it a sharp push. Juliet, waiting in the back of the van beside several similar carts, darted forward to catch it. "Terrific—with all this stuff we should be able to set up a lab that can do just about anything. Including finding out enough about those guys to uncover some weaknesses." She picked up a pile of linen, peering underneath it. "Good! You managed to snatch that high-powered microscope!"

Ben looked around nervously. "Yeah. We better get a move on. I'm not sure they bought my act completely. There was one guy looked kinda suspicious."

She nodded, heading for the driver's side of the van. Brad McIntyre, the cop, was waiting in the passenger seat, wearing, like Julie and Ben, a delivery coverall. Climbing in, Juliet started the van, listening for the sound of Ben shutting the rear doors. The sound came—but at the same moment, they heard running feet. Brad and Julie looked out to see several Visitor shock troopers burst through the doors onto the loading dock!

Ben pounded the rear of the van. "Go! Go GO *GO!!*"

She looked back to protest, saw Ben running away from the

129

truck, drawing the Visitors' fire. "*Go, Julie!*" screamed Brad. "*We've* got *to save this gear!*"

Juliet gave a cry of protest, but rammed the truck into gear, popping the clutch so hard the big van fairly leaped forward. She hit second with a squeal of rubber, then drove swiftly down the long service drive, past the ramps of the enclosed parking lot next to the warehouse. A few troopers fired at them, but none of their shots even came close.

Juliet drove for several minutes, snaking the big truck through a complicated series of turns and double-backs, until Brad announced that he thought they'd shaken off any possible pursuit. Julie nodded numbly, turning back toward their headquarters. Brad, looking over at her, saw tears streaking her face, but she made no sound.

Finally she pulled the truck to a stop beside her little white VW convertible, then set the parking brake with a jerk. Brad looked over at her as she swung the door open. "What are you doing, Julie? You don't need your car now!"

She looked up at him, then at her watch. "It's been ten minutes—with any luck they still haven't caught Ben. I'm going back for him. I have to."

"*Julie!*" But she was gone. Cursing, Brad slid into the driver's seat as she swung the little car in front of the truck and shot back down the street in the direction from which they'd come. Slamming both hands into the steering wheel in frustration, Brad watched her go. Then, reluctantly, he drove away in the opposite direction.

Juliet turned back onto the driveway leading up to the loading dock, her blue eyes scanning desperately for a running figure in a navy blue coverall . . .

She gunned the VW up the driveway, then saw movement on the top deck of the huge parking garage, three stories above the driveway. She squinted against the sun—it was Ben!

Julie beeped the horn to attract his attention, saw that he was running, aiming for a service ladder running down the rainspouts along one of the massive concrete pillars supporting the outside wall of the garage. But even as he leaped to grab the ladder, a blue bolt struck him from the side, spinning him around and over the edge of the three-story drop.

"*BEN!!!*" Julie slewed the car into a seemingly impossible U-turn, tires protesting, then braked beside her friend's crumpled body. He'd fallen into a heap of rubbish beside the driveway. There was blood everywhere.

She heard the pulsing sound of another stun rifle as she jumped out of the car, ran around it, jerking the passenger door open. Then a distant voice shouted, "Capture them! Diana wants some of them alive to question!" The sound of distant booted feet began to echo inside the garage.

"Ben, Ben!" Julie knelt by the young doctor, her med school training demanding that the man not be moved—but she had to, there was no alternative. She tried not to see the blood, the white shard of bone peeping out of the arm of the torn blue coverall. Grasping her friend around the chest, she began dragging him backward, toward the car.

The movement roused Taylor slightly, and he tried to speak. "Julie?"

"Easy, Ben," Julie panted. It was taking every ounce of her strength to drag him—she didn't want to think how she'd manage to boost him into the VW.

"No, Julie. Go on . . . no use . . ." Juliet could barely hear him over the drum of the approaching booted feet.

"God, please . . ." she sobbed, heaving the injured man halfway up, bracing his body on the running board as she took a second, lower grip to complete the job.

Something struck her right hip, and suddenly Juliet found herself lying on the road beside Ben's legs—smelling charred meat. Then the pain connected in her stunned brain, and she gasped and choked in agony—searing flames seemed to be devouring her right side!

With what seemed like agonizing slowness, she managed to get her hands under her body, levering herself up. The pain flooded back in a wave of black flame, and she forced herself to breathe deeply, closing her eyes. *Please, God . . . please. Help me . . .*

With an effort that left her coverall soaking with sweat, Juliet climbed to her feet, then, with a strength she'd never known she possessed, dragged Ben the rest of the way into the seat. Hobbling, she staggered around the car to the driver's side, leaning one hand on the metal for support.

"Hey! She's getting away!" exclaimed a surprised voice, and there came another stun bolt behind her. Starting the car and putting it into gear brought more waves of agony, but she managed it. The little white car roared down the driveway—as a Visitor trooper appeared in the middle of it, having leaped the barrier wall from inside the garage.

With more hatred than she'd ever known, Juliet aimed the VW at the alien, flooring the accelerator. The Visitor jumped wildly aside, dropping his stun rifle, and Juliet felt the thud as the bumper struck his leg. Then she was past, turning the wheel, driving away.

She slowed slightly after the first block or two, wondering where to take Ben. The hospital? Out of the question—there were sure to be troops stationed on every floor and at every entrance and exit. Besides, she didn't know if there were any doctors left. She heard a groan, turned to see Ben's eyes open. She pulled the car over into a parking space, fumbling in her glove compartment for the little first aid kit she carried.

Tenderly Juliet wiped the blood off the young man's face, feeling the curly softness of his short beard. The touch of her hands seemed to revive him somewhat. "Julie . . ."

"Ben, I don't know where to take you. Can you think of a place where I can get you some help?"

"No . . . good, honey," he said, closing his eyes as though it took too much strength to keep them open and talk at the same time. "I've had it . . . can tell . . ."

"*No*," Juliet said, refusing to believe him. She checked his arm—compound fracture of the radius, but, thank God, the artery wasn't involved. "Your arm is broken, Ben. Are you in much pain?"

"None," he said clearly, then opened his eyes to see Juliet's startled surprise at his answer. "Julie . . . honey . . . my back . . . it's also broken . . . Can't feel . . . anything . . . neck down . . ."

Juliet bit her lip, fighting back sobs—she'd suspected it, from the way his body had hung in her arms, but hadn't wanted to acknowledge the probable truth. "God . . . God, please, Ben—"

"Don't . . ." His eyes closed. "Not . . . much time . . . Want to see my Dad . . . Elias . . ."

"Okay, Ben." Juliet controlled her sobs, feeling the stab of agony in her hip as she restarted the car. "I'll get you there, I promise."

He nodded, then coughed—only his head moved. Flecks of

red sprayed onto his face. Juliet wiped them away as she drove, then used the bloody rag to wipe her eyes—tears kept welling up to blind her, and she needed clear sight. She pulled up to a stoplight, taking time during the red to tilt Ben's seat back so it reclined somewhat—she suspected a punctured lung, for his breathing was becoming hoarse and labored. A passerby looked over at them as they idled waiting for the line of traffic to move. She saw the woman's eyes widen, then she looked straight ahead again, walking faster. The shadow of a squad vehicle eveloped them, and the craft passed by.

Five minutes later—it seemed like five years—Julie swung the VW around to the back of Caleb's house, to the garage. Loud rock music blared, so she knew that Elias, at least, was home.

He sat outside with his portable radio, carefully inspecting eggs, then placing them into cartons. He looked up, grinning, as Juliet swung the VW up beside him. "Hey, Julie! Looka-here! Six bucks for a dozen clucks—ain't they beauti—" His voice died as he looked at his brother, sprawled bonelessly in the passenger seat.

"Is Caleb here?" Juliet looked around frantically. "Ben's hurt."

Elias came over to the car, shaking his head in response to her question. Ben's breathing, without the sound of the engine to mask it, was loud, rasping. "What happened, Mama?"

"We . . . we were trying to steal some equipment for a lab." Juliet bit her lip as she turned to check Ben's pulse. Her own wound throbbed with ever-increasing pain. She could feel cold sweat starting out on her forehead—clinically, she recognized the symptoms of shock. Ben's pulse was thready and irregular beneath her fingertips. "They shot him."

Elias shook his head, refusing to believe what his eyes told him. Not an uncommon reaction, she remembered, in the relatives of accident victims. "What?" he gave a nervous laugh. "The doctor? Stealin' stuff?" He shook his head in mock disapproval. Julie could hear the horror underlying his tones—in a minute or two, it would break through into his conscious mind, and he'd fall apart. Elias' voice cracked. "Whoa, brother! You shoulda come to me. Elias would have taught you how to do it *right*, man!"

A wave of pain from her own injury wrenched a whimper from between Juliet's clenched teeth. Elias glanced at her. "They got *you*, too?"

Ben coughed again, weakly, and Julie dabbed thin reddish foam off his mouth. Elias backed away, his dark eyes frightened—the horror was very close to the surface now. "Hey, Julie. I think I ought to call an ambulance . . ."

Ben's eyes opened. "No . . . ambulance . . . Made our prognosis, right . . . Doctor?" Juliet grasped the limp fingers.

"But, man—" Elias paced alongside the car, gesturing. "I just don't *get* it, man! What you wanta try pullin' a heist without your little brother?" The unceasing beat of the rock music gave a ghastly mock party effect to the scene.

Ben smiled faintly. "We did it . . . though." His eyes shifted to Juliet's, and, realizing he couldn't feel her holding his hand, she caressed the side of his face. "The truck . . ." he coughed. "Truck . . . got away?"

She nodded emphatically. "Yes, Ben. It's safe."

"But *look* at you, man!" Elias' voice broke. "You a *wreck*, man!"

"Is . . . Papa . . . home?" Ben's voice was very weak. Juliet was about to tell Elias to turn down the radio, then heard the sound in Ben's throat . . . she held him, awkwardly, through the final spasms as Elias paced up and down, talking, talking—never looking at them.

"Ben, you listen here. Do I try doctoring? Course not. An' the next time you got to boost some stuff, you gonna come to me, you got that, Bro? Elias will show you how to do it right. You dig? Like liftin' these eggs this mornin' . . . shoot. Never broke a one, that's how you gotta do it. Smooth, you see. Shoot. I sound like Papa, don't I?"

Juliet lifted her tear-stained face, then, very carefully, lowered Ben's head so it rested against the seat again. Automatically she closed the staring dark eyes. "Elias," she said quietly, but Ben's brother was pacing even faster, in rhythm to the music, never lifting his eyes from the ground.

"*Anyway*—you gonna come to me, and then we'll take 'em *all* on together . . . you an' me . . . the Taylor brothers . . . Man, we'll whomp them upside the head, those jokers."

"Elias . . ." Julie closed her eyes against the darkness that was hovering at the fringes of her vision.

Elias shook his head angrily, never looking at her. "*Man*— I'll teach you how to do it *right*. You won't get messed up again—"

He paced, every stride like a piston striking, his voice rising into one hoarse prolonged cry: "We'll show 'em, won't we, Ben? And they'll say 'Woooo! What blew through here?' An' we say, the Taylor brothers! *Yeah*! The doctor and . . . the other one . . . the other one . . . whatshisname . . ."

Julie put out a hand toward him. "Elias—"

"*No!*" Whirling, Elias smashed the radio across the garage. Suddenly all was silent. "The 'other one' . . . can die . . . but not the doctor. Doctor can't die . . . not Ben . . . make it be the other . . . but not . . . not Ben . . ." He was sobbing now, the painful, chest-tearing sobs of one who never weeps aloud. "No . . . no. Dammit, Ben!"

He embraced his brother's body frantically, rocking back and forth. Julie reached through the haze of her own tears to take his hand. His returning grasp at her fingers was the grip of a man who has lost everything else to cling to . . .

Abraham and Ruby were walking slowly toward the shopping center when they saw the children grouped by the Visitor propaganda posters. One of the boys held a large can of red spray paint, and was busily drawing a moustache and beard on the aggressively handsome features of the Visitor—Abraham thought distractedly that the posters looked as though Brian, Daniel's friend, had posed for them. The gang giggled, and one of them said, "Do it again, Kenny! Those creeps look better that way!"

Without thinking what he was doing, Abraham reached out and grasped the boy's wrist. "No!" The group moved back, half-fearfully, half-aggressively, in the face of adult authority.

Abraham summoned words. "If you are going to defy them, then do it right. You need a symbol . . . we all need one. We used to use this one." Carefully he sprayed a large red "V" over the poster. "Only we did it with our fingers . . . a long time ago. For Victory—you understand?"

Hesitantly they nodded. Abraham handed the can back to Kenny. "Go tell your friends."

Nodding to Ruby, Abraham turned away. Hearing the hiss of the spray paint behind him, he turned, saw another dripping "V" spread across a smiling Visitor. Smiling for the first time in a long while, Abraham and Ruby walked on.

# Chapter 13

Mike Donovan drove the small yellow sports model quickly, efficiently, swinging off the freeway into a lesser highway, then, after several miles, onto a two-lane street that led into San Pedro, where Sean lived. He drove automatically, mechanically, his mind busy trying to figure his next move. He'd get the key from Sean, try to talk Margie into loaning him a few bucks—*fat chance*, he thought cynically—then try again with Tony at the Italian restaurant . . .

He slowed the car down, really *looking* at the street for the first time, then stopped with a jerk, staring. Smashed windows marred the storefronts of the ice cream parlor and hairdresser's shop . . . A pickup truck and a sedan were overturned, partially blocking the street . . . The row of houses on the right had suffered damage that looked like burns—even the grass underfoot extending onward to the park where Sean played was singed and blackened.

Grabbing the alien stun rifle from the back of the car, Donovan scanned the area, his heart beating so loud it was hard to hear anything else—he forced himself to take deep, slow breaths—then listened . .

Silence. Utter and total. It was an ugly sound, Donovan discovered. He forced himself to listen until he was sure there was nobody in the immediate area but himself. The alien rifle propped beside him, he drove slowly toward Margie's house. He parked, got out, rifle held ready (he'd practiced using it out

137

in the fields—it was a snap to aim and fire), then began to walk toward the house. "Sean? Marjorie! Sean? Hello, anybody!"

Silence . . . silence. Donovan was trembling. He wanted to smash something—scream "Why?"—but only stood . . . silence—

A tiny scrape of leather on concrete, then a muffled sob!!

Donovan dropped and spun, crouching, his finger nearly tightening on the firing button—then heard a voice. "*No!* Don't shoot me, Mr. Donovan!"

Mike stood up, to see Josh Brooks, Sean's thirteen-year-old friend, peering around the side of the house. The boy walked toward him, and Donovan could see that his clothes were rumpled and dirty, his face tear-stained. His eyes were glassy with shock—Mike had seen eyes like that on children in Laos, the Nam, and Beirut . . .

He made his voice gentle as the boy, like a frightened deer, walked toward him. "Josh . . . I'm glad to see you. Where is everybody?"

"I dunno." His voice, which had already been changing, was high-pitched with fear, cracking on his words. "They're gone . . . all gone . . ."

As he approached, Mike put an arm around his shoulders, hugging him reassuringly. Josh clung to him, his thin body trembling. Donovan held him for a few minutes. "How long ago?" he asked finally.

"Three days."

"You've been all alone in this town for three days?" Josh nodded, trembling.

"Well, you're not alone anymore, Josh. I've got you, and I'll take care of you." He gave him another reassuring hug, trying to keep from rushing the terrified youngster. "What happened here, son?"

Josh looked down at the ground, then his legs seemed to give out, and he sat down on the curb. Donovan sat beside him, still keeping his arm around him. "Lots of people were getting tired of what the Visitors were doing. So Sunday a bunch of ranch hands in the area—you know the kind of guys—they drove into town and threw a homemade bomb right underneath a squad vehicle. Blew it up. The local supervisor guy was inside."

Josh trembled at the memory. "They blew it up and killed him."

Donovan glanced at the charred ground inquiringly. Josh nodded confirmation. "Then a lot of folks started shouting, stuff about this was America, and we weren't gonna put up with these goddamn Visitors anymore—" He blushed, looked up. "My Mom doesn't let me say things like that, but I'm just telling you what *they* said, you understand . . ."

"Sure," said Mike reassuringly. "Go on, Josh."

"Then everyone was clapping and cheering. Suddenly the lights went out. All at once. Then everyone got scared, and ran." He shuddered again. "Then there were lights in the sky, so bright you couldn't see where you were going. Roaring toward us. They were troop transports, I recognized 'em when they landed. People screamed and ran. Some shot guns at the Visitors—but the shots didn't seem to hurt 'em much. I lost my Mom and Dad. Then your wife." He hesitated. "Sean's mom, she grabbed me and Sean and pulled us into her house. She slammed the door, but they were everywhere—the lights came through the windows—"

He nearly gagged. "I backed up, toward the kitchen—then somebody grabbed at me from behind, and I turned. I could see a Shock Trooper in the lights, but his helmet shield was up and I could see his eyes—" He covered his own eyes at the memory. "It was awful! Those awful eyes! They were like—"

"Easy, Josh. I know what they look like. You're all right now. Then what happened?"

"I twisted loose and ran. Just then the front door broke down and they came in and took 'em."

Donovan jerked as though he'd been hit, then, pulling Josh up beside him, walked across the street and into the house. As the boy had said, the front door was a battered wreck. The inside of the house had obviously been the scene of a violent struggle. Donovan walked over to the shattered remains of a vase and picked Sean's Dodger cap out of the middle of it, remembering with a tightness in his throat how his son was forever hanging his cap on Marjorie's best vase—much to her displeasure. Josh's voice came from the doorway, choked with sobs. "He fought real hard and kicked at them to leave his mom alone. He fought and fought—told 'em his dad would come and get 'em."

Mike folded the small cap and thrust it into his pocket, not looking up. "He was really brave, Mr. Donovan. But me . . ." he choked again. "I just . . . I . . . I'm a . . . I hid. In the back of the closet. I was scared, Mr. Donovan. I'm sorry. I should of helped . . . I'm a . . . chick—"

"No, you're not!" Donovan shook his head fiercely. "Don't beat yourself up about this, Josh! There was nothing you could have done. Those guys are tough bastards. I'm not looking forward to tangling with 'em again. Finish telling me what happened."

"They took everybody to the square near the park. I could hear shouts and crying. Then the lights were gone, and so was everybody. Everybody but me."

Josh stopped, drained, and wiped at his nose with the back of his sleeve.

Donovan sighed and said, "'. . . I only have escaped alone to tell thee . . .'"

There was a long pause while Mike tried to think what to do. Josh looked up finally. "Mr. Donovan . . . will . . . will I ever see my Dad and Mom again?"

Mike's throat tightened again, then he looked squarely at the boy. "You bet. If I have anything to do about it." He thought suddenly of his original purpose for the visit. "Josh, the last time I came here, I brought Sean something—do you know where he kept it?"

Josh nodded and went over to the mantel. A picture of Donovan and Sean, glass now cracked, lay on its side atop it. Josh reached behind it, then pulled the golden key out of the small crack between the mantel and the wall. "Here it is. What is it, sir?"

"A key," Donovan said, hefting it and staring at it thoughtfully.

"To get into where?"

"The belly of the leviathan . . ." He stood thinking for another long moment, then nodded. "C'mon, Josh. You look like you could use a square meal."

The boy nodded. "Thanks, Mr. Donovan."

The two walked back out into the lonely streets and the overwhelming silence.

\* \* \*

The cork slid from the champagne bottle with a satisfying pop. Daniel Bernstein smiled. The young man continued to grin as he poured the foaming wine into Lynn, Stanley, and Abraham's glasses, then into his own. "Pretty classy, eh? Champagne for breakfast?"

Stanley didn't pick up his wine glass. "Where'd you get it, Daniel?"

"From a local merchant. One who knows the value of having friends, especially Visitor Friends." He held up his glass. "And now a toast—to my engagement!"

"What?" Lynn said blankly. "To whom?"

Daniel grinned crookedly. "To Robin Maxwell."

The adults glanced at each other furtively as he drank. Finally Lynn ventured, "But she's gone away, Danny."

Daniel smiled winningly. "Oh . . . not *that* far away, hmmmm?"

They glanced at each other again. "How does Robin feel about this, Daniel?" Stanley asked.

His son's fatuous grin widened. "She doesn't know about it. But I want her . . . so I'll get her. Just the way I wanted this champagne . . . and I got it." He sipped his wine. "Or else I'll turn her whole damn family in."

He set his empty glass down, smiling brightly at his family. Slowly his grandfather raised his glass, his dark eyes holding Daniel's eyes, so like his own . . . then the old man threw the wine directly into his grandson's face. Daniel choked and sputtered furiously, momentarily blinded. Abraham got up and left the room, heading for the pool house.

A moment later Daniel shoved Abraham out of the way, slamming through the door. "Oh, God!" Lynn cried as the rest of the Bernstein family followed.

They rounded the corner to the pool house to see Daniel, his hand clamped brutally around Robin's wrist, dragging her out of the pool house. His face was twisted into that of a stranger. "Come *on*, you dumb little bitch! I'll teach you what Brian couldn't do on a bet!"

"Let me go! *Danny!* You're crazy!" She struggled harder, hearing the frightened wails of Katie behind her, her father's startled questions. "Stop it! Daniel! I'm not going anywhere with you, you freak!"

He continued to pull her along as her father and mother

stormed out of the pool house. There was blood in Robert's eye. As much to save his son as Robin, Stanley grabbed him, spinning him around, then pushed him into the swimming pool. "Cool off, you idiot!" he shouted.

Daniel came up out of the water, eyes deadly, his Visitor sidearm in his hand. *"Daniel! No!"* Lynn shrieked, interposing herself between her husband and her son.

He hesitated, then the muzzle of the gun dropped. Furiously Daniel sloshed out of the pool, heading inside. They all stood frozen, until Kathleen Maxwell's voice broke their paralysis. "We've got to get out of here, Bob. He'll call his friends."

"He wouldn't—" protested Stanley, then Lynn put a hand on his arm.

"You saw his face. Yes, I think you'd better get out of here. We'll help—what can we do?"

Sancho Gomez frowned as he maneuvered his ancient blue pickup around the corner. Looking both ways, he pulled out slowly, in marked contrast to his usual cheerfully slapdash style of driving. His eye fell on a package of silver-wrapped teardrop shapes on the seat next to him, and he cursed softly. Finding a parking spot, he pulled over, then sauntered casually toward the back of the truck, carrying the Hershey kisses. He opened the tailgate and made a show of checking the ropes holding his lawnmower and some shrubbery to be transplanted, while whispering, "You all right?"

Robert Maxwell and his family lay squashed together beneath the false bottom of Gomez's truck, gasping greedily at the fresh air. "Fine," whispered Maxwell, and was immediately contradicted by Katie's whimpering. "How are we doing?"

"Okay so far—but the roadblock is close now."

Katie whimpered again, and Kathleen shushed her. Robin grimaced as she squirmed to give her little sister more room. "We're never gonna make it if she doesn't stop crying, Mom!"

"Yeah, I almos' forgot." Sancho handed down the Hershey kisses. "These ought to help."

"You've thought of everything!" Robert Maxwell sounded surprised.

Sancho grinned, looking off across the roof of the truck at the distant clouds. "Well, I've had some experience at this . . ."

For a second he looked down, winked, then walked back
and climbed into the driver's seat. As he put the pickup in gear,
Eleanor Dupres came out of her house on the opposite side of
the street, her car keys in her hand. She looked thoughtfully at
the truck as Sancho tipped his hat to her. He began to sweat
when he heard the little girl whimper, then a muffled wail as he
pulled away from the curb. He glanced quickly in the rearview
mirror at Mrs. Dupres, to find her staring after him speculatively.

A few minutes later the roadblock loomed dead ahead.
Sancho grimaced slightly as he took a large onion from the
dash and bit into it, chewing vigorously, then forced himself to
take another bite.

He put the truck in gear, and, still chewing, headed for the
two cops manning the roadblock. But his eyes kept traveling
back to the silent shock trooper standing guard.

One of the officers approached the cab as Sancho pulled up,
waving at the other man. "Check out the back, Randy." The
other man nodded, walking to the back of the truck.

Sancho smiled brightly at the policeman and leaned toward
him. "Hello, officer! How are you?" The man recoiled visibly
from Gomez's killer breath.

"You're headed where?"

"El Tepeyac, just outside of town. Best food north of
Ensenada." Sancho glanced in the rearview mirror, seeing the
officer called Randy inspecting the back of the vehicle. The
gardener's sensitive ears picked up a fretful whimper from the
rear of the truck—he saw Randy tense, knew he'd also heard
it. *Keep the kid quiet, Maxwell, or we've all had it*, Sancho
thought fervently.

"El Tepeyac? Never heard of it," the cop was saying,
examining Sancho's driver's license. He turned back to his
partner. "So what's the story back there, Randy?"

The man shook his head, and Sancho closed his eyes
momentarily in relief. "No story, Bob. It's okay."

"All right." Officer Bob stepped back, relieved to be out of
range of Sancho's breath, waving the truck through. "Move it
out, then, Pedro."

"*Sancho, senor.*" He put the truck in gear, glancing in the
rearview mirror as he did so, found Randy watching him.
Sancho smiled, nodding pleasantly. "Thank you, *senor.*"

* * *

Juliet Parrish looked out across the enormous culvert to the ramshackle building that had once contained offices and machinery for part of the L.A. wastewater processing system. Elias took her arm. "Now you be careful, Julie. Kinda steep here."

Awkwardly Juliet made her way down the slope, bracing herself on her cane. Brad followed them. It had been a week since Ben's death—his funeral had been the day before yesterday. Caleb was now, along with Elias, a confirmed member of their steadily growing underground. Juliet hissed with pain as a rock turned under her foot, jarring her hip. She wasn't sure if the nerve damage there would prove permanent—the burning jolt of electricity from the alien weapon had certainly left a hideous, disfiguring scar on her right hip.

When she'd unwrapped the bandages this morning, Ruby Engels helping her, Juliet had winced, and tears had filled the older woman's eyes as they surveyed the still-livid weals. Julie smiled wanly. "Good thing bikinis were never my style . . ."

Remembering that scene now, Juliet grimaced. She wasn't thrilled about the prospect of permanent disfigurement, but at the moment, her lack of mobility was more worrisome. How could she lead this group if she couldn't get around? And nobody else appeared willing to assume that responsibility. (If anyone did, she'd gladly renounce it.)

With a final skid that made her bite her lip, they were down, walking across the massive concrete flooring, looking into the dark mouth of the runoff tunnel. It was a good twenty feet high at this point. Elias indicated it. "The tunnel runs down underneath the city. Connects up to some nifty places. It ain't the Beverly Hills Hotel inside, you dig? Spiders an' rats is probably the nicest critters we're gonna have to persuade to relocate. But there's a lotta space down underneath . . . even an old train station at the end of one of the tunnels. Bums sleep in there, sometimes."

"We'll need every hand we can get," Julie said, looking around. "Think they'll help us?"

"I'll talk to 'em." He looked back at the building. "Course the electricity don't work."

"I'll take care of that," Brad said.

Elias looked back at Julie. "Then it's okay? Course, bein'

near the hills like this, we're all gonna have to drive to get here—"

"It's *perfect*, Elias," Juliet said warmly. "Completely hidden from overhead surveillance—which is why we've got to relocate from the mountain camp. And I have hopes of converting the tunnel into living quarters, so we won't have to travel—we'll be able to live here full time. We've got a lot to do!"

"Dynamite." Elias looked relieved. "Now while you get the stuff moved in, I'm gonna counsel with the Angels. This here's part of their turf."

"The street gang?" Juliet thought rapidly. She didn't know how they'd respond to the idea of a woman as leader, but they'd make good scouts.

"Sure. They hate the Visitors as much as we do—they've never taken kindly to bein' leaned on."

"You really think you can talk them into helping us?"

Elias shifted rapidly into his jive act. "You kiddin', mama? You is talkin' to de Henry Kissinger of East L.A. I'll catch you-all *later*."

He strutted off, then turned back as Juliet spoke. "Elias . . ."

As he looked, she smiled, nodding wordless thanks. He flashed her a "V" sign, and left, whistling "We Are Family."

Daniel Bernstein unlocked his front door, then heard the telephone ringing. He sprinted across the room and caught it on the fifth ring. "Hello?" As he spoke, he reached for a glass from the bar to his right, pouring a stiff shot of Scotch. "Yes, this is his son, Daniel. No, my Dad hasn't been here. They *what*? Took him? When? But they probably just wanted to give him a ride home . . . They *said* 'arrested'?" He hesitated for a second then hung up without saying good-bye.

Punching buttons with quick stabs, he made another call. "Hello . . . may I speak with Mrs. Bernstein, please." He hesitated. "She what? Lunch? But that was *four hours* ago! What time did she *go* to lunch? No, she's not at home! *I'm* at home, alone . . ." The reality hit him then, and he hung up the phone, looking around at the silent television set, the locked doors . . .

Maybe it was time for Grandpa's walk, that must be

it . . . He wandered from room to room, sipping uneasily at the Scotch. Two hours later, he realized, drunkenly, that they weren't coming bck.

Sancho Gomez smiled tentatively at the same two police officers as he pulled up before the roadblock on his way back into the city. Neither smiled back. The officer called Bob and a Visitor guard walked to the rear of the truck, jerked the tailgate open. "That report from Mrs. Dupres was right—he *was* smuggling someone in here—but it's empty now," he called. "You sure missed it this time, Randy!"

The policeman next to Sancho raised his gun sadly. "Get out of the truck . . . slowly."

Sancho looked around to see four Shock Troopers with stun rifles centered on him. Shrugging, he got out of the pickup.

Mike Donovan and Josh Brooks paused across the street from Vitello's. The Italian restaurant's sign illuminated a van parked in front of it. "Right on time," Donovan said, taking Josh's arm. They crossed the street, scrambled into the van. Tony and Fran Leonetti nodded, then the vehicle began to move. Tony threaded through the dark streets for several minutes before stopping.

"We ought to be safe here . . . at least for a couple of minutes," he said. "How you doin', Mike?"

Donovan quickly introduced his companion and recounted the main events of the past weeks since his foray into the Visitor ship, concluding with what he'd found in the deserted town of San Pedro. Tony and Fran both shook their heads, looking sympathetically over at Josh. "Josh needs to stay with Fran for a while," Donovan said. "Are you still at home?"

"Not much," she answered. "Most of the time I'm helping out with the underground." She turned to Josh. "You like spaghetti?"

The boy nodded. "Sure."

She smiled back at him. "My name's not Leonetti for nothing. We'll get along fine."

"Where's this underground camp?" Donovan asked.

"Several around the city, Mike," Tony said. "One is in the mountains, a decent drive away, but recently they've found another location . . . an abandoned wastewater plant on the verge of the foothills.''

Donovan grinned. "The mountains? Like in El Salvador?"

Tony chuckled. "Yeah. I also hear that there's another place downtown somewhere, but I don't know which building.''

"We ought to find out," Donovan mused. "But the first thing I want to do is see what this unlocks." He held up the alien key. "They must have some Achilles heel . . . some chink—"

Tony wagged a warning finger. "Watch it there, pal . . ."

Mike laughed. "Some *flaw* in their armor. *Something* we can use against them. And we need to find out where they're taking the people who've disappeared.''

"Okay, you've convinced me." Tony restarted the van. "So let's get going.''

"You guys be careful, okay?" Fran said, looking from one to the other. Her hand came out to clasp Tony's as he drove. "I couldn't do without either of you.''

"Where are you going, Mr. Donovan?" Josh wanted to know.

Mike jerked his thumb straight up. Josh's eyes widened, then clouded with worry. As the van threaded its way through the streets, he leaned back against the seat, looking out the window, up at the enormous ship hovering over the city.

Daniel Bernstein sat at the head of the dining-room table, a bottle in front of him. The burgundy was two-thirds gone. The remains of a TV dinner littered the kitchen, but out of force of habit, Daniel had cleared the table. Now he sat, pouring another glass of wine, trying not to let his gaze shift from one empty chair to another. A knock on the hall door made him look up hopefully, but his face fell when he saw Brian. Daniel looked down at his glass, not asking the Visitor Friends' leader to sit down.

Brian sighed. "Daniel, I apologize. I know you must be very disappointed with me. I promised your parents amnesty, but . . . my superiors overruled me and ordered your family taken in for questioning. But they'll be back home soon, I promise.''

Daniel looked up. "They will?''

"You have my word." Brian's tone was very reassuring.

"Did you manage to capture the scientist I told you about?"

"No . . . I'm afraid by the time we got here, they'd disappeared. We'll get them, though, don't worry. Who are they, anyway?"

"Just a scientist and his family . . ." Daniel took a sip of wine. "You sure my folks will be all right? How about my grandfather? He's kind of old . . ."

Brian looked uncomfortable for a second, then his smooth tones resumed. "He isn't well, Daniel."

"But he was fine this morning!"

"Well, you know how old people are. Excitement isn't good for them. But our doctors are taking care of him . . . They're very, very good. They hope to get him feeling better right away. How about you? Are you feeling better now?"

"I guess so . . ." Daniel mumbled, his eyes on the table.

Brian dropped into a seat beside him, and put a comforting hand on the younger man's shoulder. "Well, I've some other news that ought to help. You're getting a promotion."

Daniel looked up. "Huh?"

"To my second-in-command."

"What?!" A light began to dance in Daniel's dark eyes.

"Congratulations!" The Visitor reached over and grabbed Daniel's hand, shaking it vigorously, then patted him on the back.

"Well. I . . ." Daniel stammered, grinning.

"That's not all. When I informed Diana of your loyalty, she gave me this for you." Brian took out a lucite case, handed it to Daniel. He opened it, to see a man's gold ring, set with a large diamond.

"Brian! Wow!" He tried it on. It fit perfectly.

"Glad you like it. And, again, I'm proud to have you in my unit." He held out his hand, and this time Daniel took it enthusiastically, pumping it up and down, smiling gratefully at his friend.

## Chapter 14

Dark waves sloshed, grabbing at Mike Donovan's sneakers as he and Tony Leonetti crept along the base of the Richland refinery seawall. To their left, a high stone wall butted up from the rocks, with a narrow service ladder leading upward from a ledge midway up. Donovan paused, his stun rifle slung over his shoulder, looking up. "We're gonna have to get up there," he whispered, his mouth nearly touching his friend's ear. "Can you boost me?"

Leonetti grimaced. Donovan was nearly six inches higher and forty pounds heavier than Tony was—but his reach and strength were also greater. Tony nodded. "Yeah—but be quick about it!"

Donovan nodded, handing Tony his gun. Leonetti slung it over his shoulder, cupped his hands, then braced his back. "One. Two. Three . . . Allez-oop!" As Tony hoisted, every muscle protesting, Donovan sprang upward. Finally his groping fingers caught on the ledge, and grunting, he drew himself up, his feet scraping softly as he found a tochold on the wall.

Once up, he rested for a long second, then cautiously climbed a few rungs up the ladder. He scuttled down more quickly than he'd gone up. "Sentry posted," he hissed down into the darkness where his partner waited. "They're not taking any chances on any more unauthorized joyrides like I took . . . Toss the gun up."

A moment later his groping fingers caught the sling of the

149

alien weapon, then he leaned over, extending one hand. "Jump high, Tony!" With the other hand he gripped the ladder behind him. A grunt of exertion—then a muffled curse and a splash. "You okay?"

"Yeah."

"You're gonna have to jump higher than that, pal."

"Damn you, Mike!" But this time Tony's grasp met his. Donovan braced himself, pulling slowly, and in a minute Leonetti was crouched beside him.

The Asian fingered the alien gun. "You know how to use this thing?"

"It's pretty easy. This thing controls the intensity—how strong a jolt it shoots . . . the higher the notch, the stronger the intensity. You prime it here, and this is the firing button."

"Did it come with extra batteries?"

Donovan chuckled. "I figure they're rechargeable. If I just could figure how to hook it into an outlet, I'd have it made."

Tony's hushed whisper held amusement. "Clever guys, these Japanese. Think of everything . . ."

"Look out!" Donovan ducked as a searchlight beam swung out over the water.

"Shit! That was close!"

"Irregular cycle," Donovan hissed, looking up at the tower built near the refinery. "Or else it's hand-operated."

"How are we gonna get by him?" Tony jerked his head at the sentry. From this angle they could barely see the top of his helmet every so often as he paced his beat.

"How about the direct approach?"

"You mean like that time in Cambodia?"

"Yeah."

"And I get to be the pigeon again, I suppose." Tony sounded disgusted.

Donovan hefted the gun. "I'm the one with the firepower."

"Okay," Tony sighed. "You're also the one that'll have to explain it to my widow."

He scuttled up the ladder, rubber soles making almost no sound, then swung over the wall. Donovan swarmed up behind him. As he got to the top, he saw the back of the sentry ahead of him, rifle pointed at Tony, who stood, hands over his head, talking rapidly. "Uh, hi. My name's Tony, you see, and, uh, my shrimp boat had a flat on the way from Korea, and I've been walkin' across this water for so long that—'' Donovan swung the butt of his rifle, hard, and the sentry went down and lay still.

Tony scooped up the Visitor's weapon. "Took you *forever*, Donovan. You're losing the old touch."

"C'mon."

A few minutes later, within the refinery grounds, they heard a cry from the seawall and knew that the sentry had been discovered.

"We should have heaved him over the wall," Donovan said, annoyed that he hadn't thought of it at the time. "Would have bought us a few more minutes while they looked for him." He squirmed between two huge pipes, ducking to avoid a third in the maze that surrounded them as they worked their way toward the parking lot.

"Hindsight is always twenty-twenty," Tony grunted, dropping to hands and knees to follow him, "but somehow I'd hate to think we've sunk to the level of cold-blooded murder. Even if they are a bunch of lizards under those pretty faces."

Several minutes of squirming through the piping brought them within sight of a Visitor shuttle, cargo bay doors open. But this time there were no workers connecting hoses to transport chemicals. The tanks inside were gone, and before the doors, hands atop their heads, stood *people*.

Donovan and Leonetti crouched, watching, as the Visitor shock troopers roughly pushed and shoved the prisoners into the shuttle. Men. Women. Little children, some of whom sobbed brokenly, others who stood glassy-eyed with shock. One little girl clutched a ragged teddy bear. There were bruises on her face. There was a mother with an infant. A young woman swollen and awkward with the last stages of pregnancy. A boy Sean's age wearing a baseball cap . . .

"Jesus, Mike!" Tony turned horrified dark eyes to his friend. "What the hell is going on?"

Donovan shook his head. "I don't know. But we've got to find out." He looked around, forcing himself to study the people they were taking. They seemed a cross-section. He noticed one man, wearing a battered cowboy hat and work shirt, with dark eyes and Hispanic features. Blood oozed from a cut over his eye, but he stood defiantly, unbowed.

"Okay, Tony. Same drill." Donovan readied himself as the cargo bay doors began to close, and the pilots stepped inside.

"Right. This time, I ain't gonna trip . . ."

They gathered themselves, moving forward—but suddenly, a burst of alien gunfire surrounded them! Looking up, they saw shock troopers on the catwalks above them, shooting! Donovan fired back, but another burst nearly caught both of them. They ducked back, away from the shuttle, realizing they were caught in crossfire. Donovan took aim at the power cables overhead running to the spotlights in the parking lot. "The cables, Tony! Shoot the cables!"

"I can't make the damn thing work!" Donovan reached over to Tony's weapon. A burst of blue electricity filled the air with the smell of ozone barely two feet from his head. Mike flipped a switch. "The safety! Now try!"

Tony raised his weapon, aimed, and a burst of blue fire ruptured one of the cables. The lights flickered, and several went out. A swinging cable fell, showering a golden spray of sparks, to strike one of the shock troopers. The creature gave the peculiar ululating cry Donovan had heard earlier as it died.

Donovan shoved his partner. "Up to the catwalk! We can move faster there! Go! I'll cover you!"

Tony sprang for the stairs and pounded up them. At the top, he turned the corner onto the catwalk, only to find another Visitor facing him. Almost without thinking, Leonetti swung his weapon, striking the guard in the face. The creature staggered back, catching hold of the railing on the way over, and Tony raised his gun to hit it again—just as it turned its face.

Its true face—Tony's blow had knocked its mask off. Leonetti shrank back for a second from those reptilian features, and the creature hissed and spat at him. A cloud of venom surrounded the Asian's face. He staggered back, hands to his eyes, which felt as if they'd been seared with hot needles. "Mike! My eyes!"

A bolt from Donovan's gun pulsed in front of Tony, then the Oriental heard the thud of a heavy body. He clawed at his eyes as he heard his friend run toward him. There were sounds of a struggle, then another alien death cry—then the pulse of a rifle, followed by a human gasp. Something fell at Tony's feet.

"Mike?" Tony dropped to his hands and knees, feeling the suede of Donovan's jacket beneath his groping fingers.

"Mike—oh, God, are you okay?" He crouched over his partner, trying to feel—

A step behind him. Tony began to turn, just as something hard connected with the back of his head. He pitched forward over his friend's body, and lay still.

# Chapter 15

Daylight was only a distant glow behind Robert Maxwell as he hefted the box of bottled chemical reagents, then ducked under a sagging beam. Cautious in the dimness, he picked his way along the old sewer tunnel. The soil beneath his feet was dry, but his nose wrinkled at some of the scents the dust brought to life as he walked. Robin, picking her way behind him, sniffed audibly. "Stinks down here, Daddy."

"What did you expect, Binna? It's an abandoned sewer network."

"Why couldn't we get to this building on top of the ground?" Robin whined. "It's been a week already. I'm sure they're not looking for us anymore!"

"Don't bet on it," Maxwell said. "The reports in the mountain camp were that Sancho got picked up on his way back into the city . . . poor guy. If there were only something I could do to help him . . ." He ducked to avoid a cobweb, seeing a distant glow ahead. "We're coming to the end, Binna."

"Terrific." Robin was completely unimpressed. Maxwell frowned, fighting to keep his temper. Their week in the mountain camp had been hellish, thanks to his eldest daughter's endless whining and complaining. Several times Maxwell had to turn away to keep from shaking her physically. *Why are teenagers so damn selfish?* he wondered. *Is it just my daughter, or are all of them like this? God knows, Polly's got more spunk than Robin's ever shown, and she's only twelve . . .*

He immediately felt ashamed of his thoughts. Polly had always been his favorite of his three daughters, and Maxwell felt guilty every time he acknowledged this fact to himself. It was partly this guilt that had led him to bring Robin with him this morning—along with the realization that if he didn't distract her, she might try something harebrained. Robin had never been very good at visualizing the consequences of her actions—a fault that drove Maxwell particularly crazy because it was also one of *his* faults.

The two Maxwells emerged from the tunnel, picking their way across the rock-strewn culvert, then approached the headquarters' main door. A sentry looked them over pleasantly, but her hand rested on the butt of the police .38 she wore at her hip. "Robert Maxwell and my daughter, Robin. From the mountain camp."

"Hi, Doctor Maxwell. They told me you were coming. Password, please?"

Robert grinned. "I wish I knew who comes up with these things. 'Jabba the Hutt eats Visitors . . .'"

She laughed. "Yeah, I'd like to know too. Must be Robin's generation. They had to explain the reference to me."

Robin stared stonily ahead. The guard glanced at her, raised an inquiring eyebrow in Maxwell's direction, who shrugged helplessly. "Well, now that I'm here, I'd like to talk to whoever's in charge. See what I can do to help."

"Ever do any carpentry?"

"I got pretty good at banging my thumb," Maxwell said.

"See Juliet Parrish, she's upstairs. Short, blonde. Walks with a cane."

"Okay, see you." Beckoning to Robin, Maxwell headed for the stairs.

At the top of the stairs, he saw a woman walking away from him, leaning on a cane. "Juliet Parrish?" Maxwell called hesitantly. She turned at the sound of his voice. "Ms. Parrish?" he repeated, putting down the carton of chemicals he was carrying. "Robert Maxwell, anthropologist. My daughter, Robin." The young woman turned to smile at Robin. Maxwell was surprised at her youth; she seemed about the same age as his grad assistants, twenty-three or -four. No makeup, blonde hair caught back off her shoulders, a button-down shirt and brown sweater. Only her blue eyes, shadowed with weariness, betrayed an age beyond years.

"Glad to have you with us, Mr. Maxwell, Robin," she said with a smile.

"Robert, please. Mr. Maxwell is my father," Maxwell said, looking around. "They said you were organizing things up here."

She laughed. "They did, huh? Shows you they're easily fooled. But I'm trying. C'mon, let me show you around."

They followed her through the crumbling, dusty interior of the old wastewater plant. Maxwell saw the red "V" symbol sprayed on several of the broken-plastered walls. The sounds of hammering and sawing reached Robert's ears, and they came upon several people mending holes in the walls and floors. Juliet spoke above the noise. "We're trying to get this place ready so we can bring down all of our people and equipment from the mountain camp. We're trying to make it livable—" She ducked a shower of plaster from overhead, where a lightbulb hung nakedly through a hole in the ceiling. "Or at least safe."

Robert sighed. "I don't think any place is safe anymore."

"You're right," she agreed.

A woman with tousled brown hair stuck her head out of one of the rooms. "Hey, Julie! Where's the water cutoff valve?"

Juliet made a hand-spreading gesture, sounding a bit frazzled. "I don't know, Louise. Try in there . . ." She pointed across the hall and turned back to the Maxwells. "The toilets, by the way, are out through that hall . . . They're *very* picturesque." She grinned wryly, brushing a strand of hair out of her eyes with a grimy hand.

Robin rolled her eyes. "I'll bet."

They passed a room holding a microcomputer and a bank of radio equipment. Juliet gestured at it as they passed. "There's our poor man's BBC. The kitchen's over there. We try to keep snacks, as well as mealtime stuff. Be careful, Robin—" The girl had wandered close to the elevator shaft. "The holes—"

"Yeah," said Robin, "I see the holes." Her voice also said she'd noticed the dirt, the cobwebs, and the roaches. Juliet looked over at Robert.

"One can ascertain that she's *not* thrilled to be here."

He nodded. "Yeah. It's not the Galleria, is it? I brought her here because I thought she'd *really* go crazy up at the mountain camp."

"Poor thing." Juliet looked at Robin's back as the girl hesitantly peered into the kitchen. "There aren't many others her age around here."

Robert had poked his head into the laboratory. "I see you're getting things under control here . . . There's quite a bit of stuff left up at the mountain camp, you know. I was impressed. An electron microscope! How'd you manage *that*?"

Juliet smiled and shrugged. "We've . . . paid for everything we've gotten. One way or another." She looked at Maxwell. "We can't leave the more sophisticated, hard-to-replace gear up there much longer. We've got to get it down here. Every day I worry that they'll fly over the camp and suddenly tumble that it's no longer a summer resort for rich brats." She smiled at him. "Which reminds me, this is where those chemicals belong. Mind bringing them in?"

"Of course not," said Maxwell. "I'll get them immediately."

The box of chemicals in his arms, Maxwell followed Juliet into the laboratory. "You can put them over there, please." She pointed to a scarred old laboratory table next to a sink. Two other people bustled around the room. One, a young black man, looked up at Juliet. "Julie—where'd you say you wanted this Bunsen burner set up?"

"Over there, Elias." She pointed to the corner of the table. "Did you manage to find some bottled gas?"

"No problem." He jerked his chin at a bottle in the corner. The other young man, white, with curly brown hair and glasses, looked up.

"Hey, boss. Where'd you say you wanted the sterilizer?"

"Over there, under the cabinets." She turned back to Maxwell. "Robert Maxwell, I'd like you to meet Elias and Brad. Doctor Maxwell is an anthropologist."

They nodded pleasantly. Maxwell looked around the lab, seeing with a wry, pleased grin that it was by far the cleanest room he'd seen in the complex. Juliet Parrish, it seemed, had her priorities straight.

Louise, her hair festooned with a cobweb, entered the room. "Julie, I *can't* find that water cutoff valve!"

Juliet nodded at Maxwell with a "what can you do?" expression. "I'll get it, Louise."

Outside the lab, Juliet saw Robin Maxwell standing in the corner, looking up at the sun shafting in from one of the boarded-up windows. Something about the girl's expression reminded Julie of Algernon's wistful expression just before feeding time. She bit her lip. She'd deliberately avoided thinking about the college, or Doctor Metz, or Ruth . . . or Ben . . . or Denny. Juliet tried to swallow the tightness in her throat as she looked for a wrench before heading into the storeroom where she'd seen some piping. Sure enough, both the hot water pipe and its cutoff valve were there.

Julie began tightening the cutoff valve with the wrench. Suddenly the pipe over her head began to spray rusty water as the pressure caused an ancient seal to blow. Juliet gasped, choking on the dirty water, feeling it spray her hair and clothing—she'd need to take another bath when she was done, and their current water supplies were so limited! Frustrated, she fitted the wrench back onto the lug, tightening it with quick, furious jerks, but the water made it slippery—the wrench loosened and slipped off, banging her knuckles so hard Julie saw stars.

Her breath coming in angry sobs, Julie tried again—only to have the consarned thing peel back the skin from the already-sore knuckles! Juliet yelped and threw the wrench down, cradling her bruised hand. "Julie, honey . . . are you okay?"

It was Ruby Engels. The older woman peered in the doorway, then, seeing Juliet dissolve in angry tears, she came in, closing the door behind her. "I'm okay, Ruby," Julie said, gesturing at the spewing water pipe and shaking her head.

"Sure you're okay, Julie," Ruby said, coming over to put her arms around her. "But you shouldn't be struggling with the plumbing with your hip still injured! I'll get somebody to help."

Juliet hugged her, breaking down completely at the sound of a sympathetic voice. "Oh, Ruby! I can't handle this! Most of the time when something has to be done there *isn't* anyone else willing or able to do it! Look at me!" She pushed her dripping hair back from her face. "I'll have to take another bath . . ." She wrung the hem of her wet sweater ineffectually. "I'm supposed to be a *scientist*, Ruby! A doctor—maybe someday a biochemical researcher! Not a plumber! Or—or some kind of rebel guerilla leader!" She sniffled, swiping at her nose with her soaked sleeve. "You all look at me like I know what to do, but—"

"Yeah." Ruby hugged her again, patting her back. "I know. You're just as scared and lost feeling as everyone else."

Juliet hiccuped slightly as her sobs abated. "More."

Ruby stroked the wet hair gently. " 'These are the times that try men's souls . . .' and women's too. I'll tell you why we all look to you. You're a natural for the job, and we see it, even if you don't. A natural leader."

"I don't feel like it," Julie said, raising her head.

"You don't have to. All you have to do is trust your instincts, and your fine mind. Trust yourself as much as everybody else trusts you."

Julie took a deep, hesitant breath. "And if I can't manage to feel that kind of trust in myself?"

Ruby shrugged, assuming her "Yiddish momma" manner. "So then you fake it. We won't know the difference."

Juliet began to laugh, her first genuine laugh since Ben's death. Ruby grinned back at her.

Later that evening, Juliet heard Elias' triumphant voice call her name. "Julie! Hey, Julie! Special delivery! Specimen time!"

She hobbled out of the tiny room she was using as an office/bedroom, leaning on her cane. Elias was coming down the hall, accompanied by his friends, the Angels. The street gang members were carrying something long, bulky, and red—after a second, Juliet realized their burden was a Visitor trooper with a trashcan over his head. Brad and Robert Maxwell joined them.

The booted legs kicked as they put the alien on his feet, then, with a "Ta-da!" from Elias, jerked the trashcan off.

"Be careful of his gun!" Julie cried, and Brad hastily grabbed the alien sidearm as it skidded to the floor. The Visitor staggered, raising a hand to his thick brown hair, turning to inspect the varied range of weapons leveled or pointed at him. Juliet gasped sharply in recognition. It was Mike Donovan, the cameraman!

"Goddamn it, you bozos!" Stunned, he pulled his fingers

away from the spot where the garbage can had landed, then, seeing the red smear his hand, his mouth twisted sardonically. "Anybody got a Band-aid?"

"Doesn't sound like one of them," commented Robert Maxwell, baseball bat still poised.

"He's not," Julie said. "But he may be a sympathizer. Where did you find him, Elias?"

"In an alley, couple of blocks from here. He was wanderin' around, lookin' lonely, so me and the Angels here decided he'd make a perfect specimen for your lab. You hardly ever see them out, 'cept in pairs."

Juliet's words had apparently penetrated Donovan's mind, and he whirled on her so rapidly he staggered again. "*Sympathizer?* Where do you come off with a load of shit like that?"

Julie addressed the group rather than him directly. "He knows Kristine Walsh. We'll have to be careful of him. It could be a setup." She turned back to the stunned Donovan, who rallied after a moment.

"I don't have to stand here and take this! Who's in charge here, anyway?"

Brad shrugged, the muzzle of his rifle never leaving Donovan's midsection. "Guess you could say she is." He jerked his chin at Juliet, who, dressed in a faded red sweatshirt, her hair still draggled from her battle with the plumbing, looked even younger than usual.

"Who? *Her?*" Donovan barked a short, incredulous laugh. "That *kid?*"

Maxwell grinned and winked at Juliet. "One smart kid, I'd say." She returned his grin with a wan smile, before turning back to the indignant Donovan.

"Would you like that bandage now, Mr. Donovan? Or would you prefer to go on bleeding?"

Brushing coffee grounds from the stained shoulders of the Visitor uniform, Donovan followed her into the lab. She motioned to a stool as she washed her hands, then, when he sat down, she limped over with some disinfectant. He eyed her warily. "You walk with a cane?"

"Yes," she said, parting his hair with quick, competent fingers, and inspecting the wound.

"You get hurt too?"

"Yes . . ." She moistened a cotton ball with disinfectant. "How'd you get the uniform?"

"They had a sale." She dabbed at the wound. "Owww!! You did that on purpose!"

"Of course I didn't," Juliet said coolly, dabbing again. "Hold still."

"You a doctor?"

"More or less," she answered, dabbing again, holding him with a hand clenched in his hair as he jerked, breath hissing through his teeth.

"How comforting—ouch! Don't you have any Novacaine?"

"Yes, but I have to save it. If you'd hold still—" Julie said, inspecting the lump, then dabbing at it again. "How'd you get the uniform?"

"On the Mother Ship. My partner and I—ouch, dammit!— Tony and I were going up for a little reconnaissance, and they knocked us over with those stun guns. When I came to, two of the Visitors helped me escape. One was a guy I'd met before, named Martin—the other was a woman named Barbara. They gave me the uniform, told me when a shuttle was coming down. I climbed aboard, and then, when I got down here, I stole a truck and crashed out through the fence. Things got a kind of sticky for a while, but I managed to ditch the rig outside of town. I was wandering around, looking for a headquarters I'd heard of downtown . . ."

"In that uniform? That was very foolish, Mr. Donovan. Elias and the Angels might have killed you if they'd been in a different mood." She dabbed at his cut again, thoughtfully. "Your escape sounds like maybe it was a setup, to me."

"I don't think so—damn! When are you gonna be done?"

"Why don't you think so?"

"Because . . . they sounded so damn sincere, talking about some kind of organized Fifth Column within the Visitors . . . said there weren't nearly enough of 'em, but that not all of 'em agreed with their leader's plans for us— ow!"

He twisted away. "That's enough! Dammit, you're torturing me as bad as Diana is torturing our people up on that Mother Ship!"

"Is she?" Juliet wasn't particularly surprised.

"Yeah. Apparently the bitch gets some of her kicks that way." He felt his head gingerly.

"Sneaking aboard that Mother Ship was no easy job," Juliet observed. "What made you try it?"

"I'm highly motivated." He glared at her.

"Why did you do it?" Her questions were gentle, but inexorable.

With a muttered curse he swung on her. "Because, kid, my son Sean is aboard that Mother Ship, along with my ex-wife and my partner, and God knows what's happening to them! Or to the rest of San Pedro—they just scooped up the whole goddamn *town* and transported 'em all to the L.A. Mother Ship!"

"I suppose I should believe you?" Juliet said quietly, staring at him. "After all, *you* sound so damn sincere . . ."

"That's it!" With a short, bitten-off laugh, Mike Donovan threw his hands up. "I'm leaving!"

He turned to do just that, but even as he stepped out of the lab door, Brad cocked his rifle ostentatiously, and the air was filled with the snick of switchblades and the hiss of chains. Mike Donovan hesitated, crouching low, his hands poised to slash. Juliet stepped up behind him. "I wouldn't, Mr. Donovan. We're also short on bandages."

She paused for a long moment, then, as Mike slowly straightened, continued, "You have to understand our point of view, Mr. Donovan. You were among the first to go aboard their ship; you worked in close proximity with them for quite some time; several nights ago you met with Kristine Walsh—".

Donovan turned, his surprise plain. She nodded. "And now you show up here, escaped from someplace no one ever escaped from before . . . wearing that—"

"*Goddamn it!!* I know what I'm wearing! How'd you know about Kristine?"

" 'Cause I was there. Outside. Watching."

"Listen, kid, you want to talk about *setups*—"

She nodded. "Yes, I saw it."

"Then why the hell didn't you let out a yell and warn me?"

"I wasn't sure who was setting who up—or which side you're really on."

Mike looked at her, his green eyes very serious. "I'm on the right side, kid. Believe me."

There was a long pause, then finally Juliet nodded. "Well. Why don't you tell us what you know?"

The group gathered in the conference area, and Donovan faced them, looking out across the expanse of still-suspicious faces. "Did any of you see the interrupted broadcast the night the Visitors declared martial law?"

A general murmur of assent followed.

"Well, indirectly, I suppose I'm responsible for that move on their part . . . though I'm pretty sure they would've done it eventually. That evening I got aboard the Mother Ship. I filmed Diana and Steven, one of her lieutenants, eating animals as large as guinea pigs *whole*. They're not humanoid at all. They're reptiles of some sort, wearing very clever masks to hide their alien features. Up till tonight, I thought they were all just as ugly on the inside . . . as evil . . . as they appeared to my eyes on the outside. But tonight, two of them, Martin and Barbara, risked their lives to get me off the Mother Ship and back here—so I guess looks really aren't everything. That's it, in a nutshell."

An excited babble—mixed equally of belief and skepticism—swelled after Donovan finished speaking. Elias waved an excited hand. "Reptiles? You *sure*, man? What did they look like?"

Donovan grimaced. "I'm no artist, guys."

"But Roger is!" a young black woman pushed a dark-haired man forward. "Go on, Rog!"

Taking a piece of charcoal from someone, Roger, in response to Donovan's description, began to sketch on the concrete wall. Mike watched in admiration—and with a shudder of recognition—as the reptilian features he'd glimpsed twice now (the second time had been just prior to his capture at Richland) took shape as a result of his words. As Roger drew, Donovan continued to give a detailed summary of the Visitors' behavior.

"How's that?" Roger asked, stepping back.

"Yeah." Donovan gave him a respectful nod. "I'd have to get my tape to check every detail, but that's pretty close."

"Where is that tape, Mr. Donovan?" Juliet asked. "We could use it in our studies. We really need to recruit a herpetologist. Does anybody know one?"

"Herpetologist!" Elias rolled his eyes in mock horror. "Julie, don't tell me you is *diseased*, mama!"

Amid general laughter, Robert Maxwell admitted that he'd minored in paleontology, so had some background in animal biology. "But, *reptiles* flying around in spaceships?" Brad asked. "That's crazy! Lizards are stupid—I used to have a chameleon for a pet, and they make a cat look like a genius by comparison."

"Cats are smart!" flared Louise, who had adopted a stray tabby within days of their move into the ancient building.

"It's really not crazy, Brad," explained Maxwell. "It could have happened here on Earth."

"What?" Donovan said.

"Up till about sixty-five million years ago—the end of the Cretaceous period—reptiles ruled this planet. They had been evolving and changing for *millions* of years . . . far longer than man has been around. Who knows what they might have evolved into? But then, the geologic evidence shows, a meteor—a really *big* one—impacted with the Earth, probably landing somewhere in the ocean. Its impact messed up the environment—probably screwed up the food chain, by first raising temperatures, then by creating so much dust the whole planet was dark for a couple of years. Nobody knows definitively whether this raised temperatures—via the greenhouse effect—or lowered them, by blocking out the sun's rays. But either way, the impact probably contributed to wiping out most of the reptile population—allowing the mammals—us— to gain the ascendancy."

"Wai-i-it a minute, Doc!" Elias shook his head. "How the hell you know all this if it happened so long ago?"

"Iridium," said Julie.

"Right, iridium. It's a common substance in asteroids, comparatively rare here on Earth. Sediment layers around the Earth show marked increases in iridium in the soil layer sixty-five million years ago. The asteroid impact has been pretty well accepted as an actual occurrence—what they're still arguing about is how it affected the ecology of that time . . ."

Elias looked impressed in spite of himself. "So you're sayin' that maybe this meteor heated up the place, and those reptiles couldn't handle it?"

"Reptiles here on Earth are cold-blooded, Elias," Juliet said. "Their internal metabolism can't adjust to handle wide temperature variations as well as the metabolism of mammals."

"Hey!" Elias snapped his fingers. "So all we got to do is heat up all our outdoor barbecues at once and—boom! Kentucky-fried horny toad!"

Everyone laughed. Maxwell shook his head, grinning. "It's not that simple, I'm afraid. Wish it were. Extreme heat *would* probably drive them away—only problem is, with their technology, we'd have to get the whole planet so hot *we'd* probably fry too. Besides, to generate that much heat quickly would take something on the order of a nuclear holocaust."

"Forget that, then," Brad said. "Killing off the human race just to get rid of the Visitors is definitely cutting off your noses, so to speak."

"What about cold?" asked Louise. "Reptiles here on Earth can't handle cold."

"Those suckers sure can," said Caleb Taylor. "The one who rescued me took over two hundred degrees below zero."

"Those fake skins may act as insulation," Donovan volunteered. "Besides, I'm sweating wearing this uniform. This fabric is super-insulated. Maybe that accounts for how he did it." He thought for a moment. "They keep their Mother Ship so dimly lighted . . . maybe bright lights would blind them?"

Juliet nodded. "That may be a very practical suggestion— the most practical offered so far. But even though it may be a partial strategy, we're going to need more effective and longer-lasting means than that."

Everyone murmured agreement. Juliet rested her chin on her hand, thinking. "The eating Mr. Donovan described seems consistent with the biochemistry of reptiles as we know them. I wonder if there's a way to get at their main food source . . . poison it, somehow. If we could identify where they keep it."

"Yeah," said Robert Maxwell. "But we'd have to develop a poison that wouldn't kill the host animal. Reptiles prefer live— or freshly killed—animals."

"What about that poison spray I described?" Donovan asked. "I thought snakes had to bite you—these guys don't have fangs to inject venom."

"It's fairly common for reptiles here on Earth to spray their venom," Maxwell answered. "Besides, it's probably a sort of vestigial trait they've retained from earlier times."

"It's pretty deadly," Mike said, thinking of how Tony had been blinded. "Can you make an antidote?"

Juliet shrugged. "Possible. Procedures for creating an antivenin are pretty standard—but we'd need a quantity of venom."

"Good," said Robert sardonically. "Let's add that to the old shopping list. We've *got* to get one of those guys for Julie to examine!"

"Yeah . . ." Juliet sighed. "If wishes were horses . . ." She exchanged a quick glance with Ruby, then straightened in sudden decision. "You know what we ought to do? Define our overall plan of resistance."

"Good idea," Robert said.

"How about this," she began, ticking points off on her fingers. "First of all, to undermine all Visitor activity in every way we can. That means by direct methods as well as more passive resistance . . . work slowdowns at the factories, stuff like that. For the more direct means, well, they can't have an unlimited supply of vehicles. Those things sit on street corners unattended . . . sometimes for hours. We ought to be able to bollix 'em somehow." A general murmur of agreement filled the room.

"Then, secondly, I think we've got to find out what their hidden goals are," Juliet continued.

"Hidden?" asked Brad.

"Sure," Donovan said. "They've lied to us about every-thing so far. They're dumping that supposedly life-saving chemical out into the atmosphere—at least, here in L.A. they are."

"And they've brainwashed so many people with that conversion process of theirs," Juliet said. "We need to find out more about it. And more about who they may have gotten to in that way."

Donovan waved his hand for attention. "When I was captive up there, Diana told them to take me to what she called the 'Final Area'—whatever that is. To forestall that, the Visitor who helped me out, Martin, asked her why she didn't convert me. He made it sound like a challenge. First Diana said that converting me would take too long . . . ." He looked slightly sheepish. "There seems to be a popular misconception that I'm stubborn and rather pig-headed."

"Oh, I can't *imagine* that!" said Juliet, with a twinkle. Laughter echoed around the room.

"Yeah . . . Well, anyway, after Martin kinda threw down the glove to her, Diana changed her mind, and told him to lock me up—which was how he was able to break me out of there later. So the success of their conversion process is dependent on the individual involved. Martin told me that if Diana just needs information, she'll go for it in much more ordinary ways . . . like torture. They were strapping one poor little SOB into a chair, and preparing to use something like a miniature blowtorch on him . . ."

Murmurs of unsurprised outrage filled the room. Donovan shrugged. "I guess the message is, don't fall into their hands if you can possibly help it. They're not playing for small change. We also ought to consider whether we can get in touch with other Visitors themselves who are like Martin—opposed to their leader's scheme—whatever it may be—here on this planet."

"Yeah," agreed Robert Maxwell. "And third in our plan of attack should be to analyze them physically. Which brings us back to the fact that we need a specimen."

"We've also got to spread the word about their reptilian nature," Julie said. "Most people are repulsed by snakes and lizards anyway—unfair as that may be to the creatures here on Earth, it will probably work in our favor. For that, we're going to need Mr. Donovan's tape."

"Agreed," said Mike.

Ruby Engels spoke up for the first time. "We should also circulate the word about them abducting whole towns of people, and torturing them. Most people still think that if they're not scientists, they have nothing to fear!"

"Yeah," said Elias, pain flitting briefly across his dark features, "that sort of thinking is easy to fall back on. We got to let folks know the truth!"

"And, lastly," Julie said, "and most importantly, we have to establish contact with other groups in other cities . . . around the world."

"Right," said Donovan. "They're sure as hell out there.

We're gonna have to bypass ordinary means of communication—we know they've got AT&T in their pockets."

"Right. And once we figure out a way to talk to each other, we've got to organize coordinated plans to get rid of them. That's our only chance at winning."

Everyone nodded, and murmurs of agreement filled the room.

"Now . . ." Juliet said. "Let's make a list of targets locally. We'll make our first overt move tomorrow."

# Chapter 16

"What sort of thing did you have in mind for tomorrow, Julie?" Caleb Taylor asked.

Juliet sighed. "We need weapons. Much as I hate the idea of violence, Mr. Donovan's story about San Pedro pretty well confirms that if we're going to stand against them, we've got to be armed. Our information confirms they've set up an armory here in the city to equip all their roadblocks and the Visitor Friends units. How about it?"

Taut faces nodded silent agreement. Robert Maxwell felt something squeeze his insides at the idea of going up against the Shock Troopers he'd seen—he'd never had any military experience. Too young for Korea and too old for Vietnam . . . He straightened, deciding that he'd send Robin back to the mountain camp and her mother, tonight, to wait until the attack was over.

Maxwell looked around the assembled group. His daughter wasn't there . . . No great surprise, but he realized suddenly he hadn't seen her since before Donovan had arrived—several hours, now. Leaving the group to plan the logistics of the raid, he searched the headquarters quickly. No Robin.

Venturing outside, he looked around. There was a half-moon, masked occasionally by scudding clouds, but Maxwell could see well enough to tell she wasn't in the culvert. He wandered around the side of the building. "Robin?"

His soft call frightened some tiny creature in the underbrush, but otherwise brought no response. "Binna? It's Dad." In the distance, a police siren shrieked.

Maxwell's heart was hammering by now, the blood thudding so emphatically in his ears that it was hard to listen. He checked his watch—eight-thirty. After curfew. If Robin was outside, on the streets that lay just over the hillside and down the road, then she would be fair game for the nightly Visitor patrols. Maxwell hurried through the gap in the battered chain-link fence, his steps coming rapidly.

Once on the streets, he ducked his head into his collar, shuffling along like a man who has had one drink too many and has only just realized the time. He kept his head low, but beneath his brows his eyes were busy, roving every intersection, every alley. His fear was so tangible that he fancied it followed him like a cloud—like that little guy with the unpronounceable name in the Li'l Abner comics. Every time he glimpsed a red uniform he was afraid there would be a familiar figure in a white blouse and gray jeans with it.

Nearly an hour passed and there was still no Robin.

Maxwell thought of turning back. His prepared excuse of having had one drink too many was now very thin, it was so late. Maybe Julie could send Elias and the Angels out after her . . . Robert bit his lip. Those young punks in the gang had looked pretty tough . . . *What am I going to do?* Maxwell wondered.

He decided he'd turn back after one more corner.

Robert Maxwell rounded the corner, only to find himself facing a squad vehicle. He stopped, half-turned, then heard a hard, reverberating voice: "Stand right there! You're breaking curfew—let me see your identification!"

*Oh, damn. Damndamn DAMN!!* Maxwell halted, though his anguished mind wanted only to run.

"Against the wall."

Robert, moving like an old, old man, walked over to the cement-block side of the building. "Sorry," he said, slurring his words. "Got to drinkin' with a . . . lady friend. You know how it gets . . . forgot the time, I'm sorry . . . m'wife's gonna be *pissed* at me . . ."

He heard footsteps behind him, but realized that the first trooper had not left his original post—so there were two of them. Harsh fingers grabbed his hands, placing them on the gritty surface, then, moving with unpleasant, impersonal familiarity, grabbed his legs at the thigh, first right, then left, so he stood spread-eagled in the position television police dramas had made so familiar. Now he really understood why they did it this way—it was impossible for him to move easily, since all his weight rested on his hands and his toes. It would take him two moves, instead of just one, to free himself and run.

The hands ran over his body, digging hard into pockets, beneath his arms, at his sides, finishing with his thighs. "He's unarmed," said a second Visitor voice. The trooper removed Robert's wallet. "You can turn around now."

Maxwell turned around, so frightened that he was afraid he'd disgrace himself—his stomach heaved and he had a sudden, terrible need to urinate. He took deep breaths, forcing himself to study the man who was going through his billfold.

A black—or, he amended to himself in the face of Donovan's revelation, this one wore the mask of a black man in his late thirties. Maxwell found himself experiencing a strange double-vision effect, picturing the reptilian features underlying the ones he could see with his eyes. He thought of long, flicking tongues and venom within that grim-jawed mouth, and felt his stomach flip-flop again.

The trooper looked up from his prisoner's driver's license. "Another Maxwell. Now isn't that interesting?"

Robert looked up at him, his eyes widening. "*Another* Maxwell? What do you mean?" But, sickened, he knew already.

"Just that we picked up a young lady late this afternoon with the same address as yours. Her name was Robin. Your daughter?" The Visitor's deep voice was almost sympathetic beneath its alien overtone.

"Yes," said Robert numbly. There didn't seem to be any point in denying it. *Oh, God, Binna! Where are you? What's happening to you? Are you all right?*

"I've got to report this to headquarters," the Visitor said, turning his head to address the guard. "Bring him over beside the hatch."

Maxwell, under the guard's direction, re-assumed his spread-eagled position against the side of the squad vehicle, while the black leader went inside. Maxwell turned to the guard. "Please . . . tell me where my daughter is."

The Visitor just smiled. Robert swung the other way at the sound of booted feet on the ramp. "My daughter? You have her? Where is she?"

The Visitor's deep voice still held that touch of sympathy. "She's our prisoner."

Maxwell made a quick lunge toward the interior of the craft. The leader stopped him with a hard hand on his arm. "Not in there. She's been taken to the Mother Ship."

"Is she all right?"

The Visitor looked at him levelly, unblinking. "I'm told that will depend on you, Mr. Maxwell."

Robert looked down, biting his lip. *Oh, God, don't let this happen to me . . . please, no . . .* "What do you mean?" he asked.

"We need some information," the leader said. "We think perhaps you can help us."

Maxwell looked directly at him. "I don't know anything that could help you . . . believe me."

The Visitor went on dispassionately, as though Robert hadn't spoken. "Information about a camp in the mountains."

"No—" Robert tried to keep his voice steady; to his horror it broke. "I never heard anything about a camp . . ."

"We know it exists," the squad leader said, inexorably, gently, "but we need to know its location."

*God help me! Help Binna, please!* thought Maxwell, keeping his eyes steady on the Visitor's ebony features. "I can't help you. I don't know anything about a mountain camp. Really!" He put every bit of sincerity he could muster into his voice.

"Hmmmm." The dark eyes in the dark face were sad. "That's too bad. I'm very sorry . . . for your daughter, Robin." He turned to climb back up the ramp.

One step . . . two . . . "No, wait!" Maxwell yelped, thinking fast. "Wait! You don't understand!" Tears blurred his vision, but he could see the Visitor turn back to look at him. "My wife—my other daughters . . . they're all up there. I can't choose between them—I can't! No matter how much I want to tell you!"

"In the mountain camp?" The deep, sympathetic note was back.

Robert nodded, closing his eyes, trying to think. The night breeze made trickles of coldness as the tears broke free and ran down his face. "Yes . . . in the camp. I can't . . . you can't expect me to . . . God, please . . ."

"Come over here, Mr. Maxwell." The Visitor's hand was on Robert's arm, pulling him a few paces away from the sentry. His voice was low, conspiratorial. "I understand your anguish. Your daughter's position has placed you in a terrible dilemma . . ."

Robert nodded wordlessly.

The leader hesitated for a long moment, then glanced quickly over his shoulder at the sentry, who was looking the other way, paying no attention. "I understand, because, you see, I have children too . . ."

Maxwell looked at him. From some insane corner of his mind that still remained a scientist he wanted to ask if the Visitor young were live births or eggs. He waited.

"Suppose," the leader said, still in that quiet, gentle tone, "that I could guarantee that the mountain camp would not be taken until a certain time, so that you could get your wife and daughters out beforehand. What would you say to that?"

"You'd do that?" Maxwell said, wanting to believe. "But what about Robin?"

"After the camp is no longer a problem, then I could slip her aboard my vehicle and bring her back. Turn her loose, with your message as to how to contact you. She's only a young girl. Nobody will look for her."

"No. Believe me, she doesn't know anything! She's only a kid!"

"I could see that when we found her today. Frankly, I hated to even pick her up, but unfortunately, the others saw her too. So I had to. But she hasn't been harmed, and she won't be—if you help me."

"I—"

"If you warn the others before we arrive, Diana will question Robin. Do you understand what I'm trying to say?"

Maxwell closed his eyes, thinking of Donovan's words. Thinking of Robin's smooth, pretty skin . . . thinking of small blowtorches. "Yes. Yes, I understand. I won't warn them—" *There are only a few still up there,* he thought. *Just a couple left . . . and fewer still tomorrow, because of the attack on the armory. Maybe only one or two . . .* "But they're my friends. Can your people take the camp without—without—"

"Yes," said the squad leader forcefully, his hands gripping Robert's shoulders. "It can be done quite easily, with no harm to anybody. And we won't get there until . . . what? Four o'clock tomorrow afternoon? Does that give you enough time?"

Maxwell nodded. He was so exhausted he felt as though he could lie down and sleep right here. The Visitor shook him a little. "All right. Here's the map. Point to the location."

Numbly, Maxwell did so. "Tell Robin to come to the elementary school playground. I'll meet her there tomorrow evening."

"All right. Four o'clock. You have my word . . . as a father." He extended his hand.

Maxwell looked at the hand for a long moment, then slowly put his own into the other's cool, firm grasp. They shook, then the Visitor said, more loudly, "All right then, but don't let me catch you violating curfew again. Do your drinking at home from now on!"

He gave Maxwell a rough shove back toward the street. "Hurry up—and remember what I said!"

"I'll remember," said Robert fervently. "Thanks, officer!"

He turned, his feet taking him automatically back toward the underground headquarters. He couldn't get back to the mountain camp tonight—but tomorrow. Tomorrow.

Clinging to his numbed exhaustion as a shield against thought, he kept walking, faster . . . faster. Within a street or two, reaction set in and he ran, mindlessly, scurrying through the empty streets like a frightened animal.

Diana glared at Martin. "Escaped? How?"

Martin took a deep breath. "I'm not sure. I left him in a holding cell, and later sent Barbara to bring him to me so I could begin preliminary injections. When I realized she was late, I went to the cell to see what had happened. Barbara was unconscious, victim of a short-range stun. Her gun and uniform were gone."

"*Shit!*" Diana said explosively. Martin wondered fleetingly where she'd learned the obscenity. She stalked back and forth along the wall of her private office/lab, sending the lab animals into a flurry of hysterical motion each time she approached. Martin waited, tensely, for her fury to abate.

"All right." Calm once more, she turned back to him. "We have to assume the worst—that he's escaped aboard one of the shuttles. Alert all units to report any unauthorized crewmembers. We're going to have to institute some kind of security clearance procedure for all incoming personnel. I'll have to consider what would be most efficient."

"At once, Diana," Martin said, turning away. He was two steps from the door when her voice stopped him. "And, Martin?"

He was almost afraid to turn—afraid that, even with his contacts covering his eyes, she'd discern his fear—but he forced himself to look back at her, showing merely a junior's deference to a superior officer. "Yes, Diana?"

"Send Brian to me."

"At once, Diana."

He left the room fighting the urge to run.

When Brian arrived, Diana nodded pleasantly to him. "Ah, Brian. Thank you for coming so promptly. I need your help."

Brian was puzzled, but tried to remain calm. He'd done his job perfectly so far—he had nothing to worry about. At least he hoped so. "Of course, Diana. Whatever I can."

Her long red lounging robe shimmered around her as she turned to eye him speculatively. "It's come to my attention that you have developed a relationship of sorts with this young lady." She pressed a button, and a screen on the wall awakened to show a girl crouched in one of the holding cells, makeup and tears streaking her rounded young face.

"Robin Maxwell!" Brian exclaimed. "But I thought she and her family had escaped!"

"Not this one." Diana looked at the girl's image reflectively for a long moment. Robin sat quietly, only raising her hand now and then to wipe at the tears which continued to well and drip down her cheeks. "So, you *do* know her?"

"Well . . . Yes, I know her," stammered Brian, wondering if Diana had somehow been told about the times he'd taken a little time off and gone to the video arcade with the girl—but he'd only done it a few times, and mostly to case the place for potential Visitor Friends recruits.

"Is she attractive to you?" Diana's dark blue eyes were very intent.

Brian shrugged. The thought had never occurred to him. He looked directly at his leader, deciding honesty might be the best move in this case. "Not like you are."

She smiled, pleased. "Ah. I see now how you've managed to rise through the ranks so quickly."

"I'm quite serious," Brian said, moving closer to her, his eyes holding hers.

"That's very interesting," Diana conceded. "Because I've had my eye on you for quite some time."

Brian smiled at her. "Of course I'm at your service." His eyes traveled down the length of the red robe, his mind filled with images of Diana in her true form—no wonder even the Leader had found her irresistible. "In any way you require service . . ."

She smiled, glancing sideways at him. "Perhaps presently. At the moment, I want your help with an experiment. A medical experiment. Involving you and . . ." her gaze flicked to the image, ". . . her."

Brian was a little taken aback. "Are you suggesting what you seem to be? For what purpose? I'm not sure it's even possible."

She smiled, showing her false human teeth. "Oh, I'm sure you can manage. My reports indicate you're very . . . flexible. And the girl has been very sheltered, with little basis for comparison." She nodded. "Will you help me?"

"Will it be . . . painful?" Brian glanced at the girl again.

"We'll have to spend a little time in the science lab first. While I work, I'll brief you on your role. I can't promise complete freedom from discomfort, but most of the action will take place on an inter-cellular level. And the actual experiment *could* even prove . . . pleasurable."

Brian remained doubtful, but tried not to let it show. "If it's important to you, Diana, then of course I'm willing."

She smiled. "You won't regret your loyalty to me, Brian."

Together they left the room, heading for the lab on the other side of the giant ship.

\* \* \*

Robin Maxwell crouched on the strange, shelf-like bunk, sniffling, wishing she had a tissue. It had been hours since she'd been brought aboard the Mother Ship. She was beginning to feel hungry and thirsty.

When she'd first been brought aboard, she'd been handed over to a Visitor woman who had taken her to a strange, laboratory-looking place, then told the girl to remove her clothing. When Robin had indignantly refused, she'd drawn her sidearm and, still smiling politely, had suggested she think again. Robin had taken off her clothes.

Then the woman had made her lie on some kind of couch and passed an alien instrument slowly over her entire body, then a different one over her midsection. It hadn't hurt, but Robin had felt humiliated. The woman wouldn't answer her questions—had only finished whatever it was she was doing, returned the girl's clothing, then, when she was again dressed, gave her a sandwich and a carton of milk—afterwards taking her to a remarkably normal-looking bathroom. Since then, she'd been locked here, in this horrible cell.

The tears started again. Robin shivered as she slumped backward and her spine touched the cold metal of the bulkhead. She buried her face in her arms, wondering if she'd ever see her father and mother again. She was only a kid. What could they possibly want with her?

A sound came from the door—a soft hiss. Crouching, she trembled, then, moved by the thought that she'd rather face whatever was coming standing up, she climbed to her feet, hugging herself protectively.

The door slid open, and Robin's eyes widened ecstatically. "Brian! Brian, Brian!" She rushed toward him, filled with relief at the sight of his familiar, handsome features. "Oh, thank God!"

Even as she reached him he stepped forward, and—wonder of wonders—put his arms around her, tenderly, protectively. "Robin . . . just take it easy. You're okay. You're safe now. I won't let anyone hurt you."

She sobbed, half in relief, half in joy. "Oh, Brian! I missed you! I thought I'd never see you again!"

"I'm here now. I'll protect you. I'll get you out of here." He gathered her even closer, and she felt the cool hardness of his muscled body. Tentatively, Robin slipped her arms around him in return, her mind whirling chaotically. Her knees felt rubbery, and she leaned against him. He supported her weight without effort, and his hand came up to caress her thick, tumbled hair. "Robin . . . I missed you."

"Brian . . ." She touched his cheek hesitantly, hoping her eyes weren't red and that her makeup hadn't run—she still couldn't believe he was here, holding her. It was like a wonderful dream, the kind that she woke from at night, her heart beating so hard it seemed it would break out of her body, and then she sobbed to realize it *was* just a dream—that *he*—the wonderful, godlike *he* who lived only in dreams—was gone.

*It's* real *this time*, she told herself fiercely. *He's here. He's holding you in his arms. I think—I think he even wants to kiss you* . . .

He did. His mouth touched Robin's, brushing quickly, exploringly, then returning to press harder. She closed her eyes, feeling faint, her hands clutching at him frenziedly. *Brian, I love you*, she thought, feeling his hand touch her breast, at first hesitantly, then returning to cup it firmly. He slid his hand beneath her sweater.

"No . . ." she said dreamily, as his mouth traveled down her cheek, settling on the tiny pulse in her throat. His hand was pulling at her sweater. "No . . . yes . . . Brian . . ."

Her eyes closed and she swayed dizzily. She was scarcely aware when he lowered her to the bunk. She had one more sharp, insistent return to clarity when she realized her jeans were open, but by then his weight was holding her down. He was heavy; she couldn't get up.

*No*, she wanted to say. *Stop, this is* too *real* . . .

But it was also too late.

# Chapter 17

Juliet Parrish woke just before the windup alarm clock rang at six o'clock. She rolled over and shut it off quickly, before it could jangle; she'd always hated being jarred awake by alarms. She lay back in her narrow, lumpy cot for a moment, thinking that as soon as she moved, swung her legs out, reached for her jeans, she'd be committed to this day and what it could hold. *Please, God, don't let anybody die. Don't let anybody get hurt. Please.*

She closed her eyes, feeling sleep nibble at the edges of her body, wanting to suck her back down into its warm depths. With a quick jerk that stabbed her hip, Juliet sat up, reaching for her clothes.

Clad in old jeans and a red sweater, she coiled up her shoulder-length hair, pinning it into a bun. Then, picking up her cane, she limped out into the hall. The first person she saw was Robert Maxwell—from the haunted look in his brown eyes and the darkness beneath them, Julie gathered that he'd slept even less than she had. "You okay, Robert?" she asked.

"Yeah," he mumbled, not meeting her eyes.

"Is anything wrong?"

He shook his head. "No . . . no. Just nerves, I guess."

"Tell me about it."

Elias came out of the room they'd outfitted as a men's dorm, his usual jauntiness noticeably subdued. "Hi, Julie," he said.

"Sleep okay, Elias?" she asked.

181

"Oh, sure," he said bleakly. "Like a baby—one with the colic."

By now the main hall was filled with people. Julie turned, addressing them. "Everybody try to eat something, okay? I know you're nervous, but it's going to be a long day. Can't have anyone passing out from hunger in the middle of this."

Turning, she limped into the laboratory. She was washing her face in a pan of cold water when she heard a step. Mike Donovan lounged in the doorway. "Morning, Doc," he said.

"Good morning, Mr. Donovan," Juliet said primly—she wasn't sure why she treated him with such arms'-length formality, but there was something about his cocky grin that irritated her.

"Caleb's scrambled up a pan of eggs," Mike said, nodding in the direction of the big meeting room. "Aren't you gonna take your own advice?"

Juliet smiled wanly. "I'm afraid it's a case of 'do as I say, not as I do . . .' Quite frankly, I don't think my stomach would cooperate with anything more than a cup of orange juice."

"That bad, eh?" He watched her dry her face with a ragged old towel. Juliet, conscious of his scrutiny, made an effort to keep her hands steady as she emptied the pan into the sink, but, to her dismay, water slopped onto the floor. Donovan continued as if he hadn't noticed. "I gotta hand it to you, Doc—you've really pulled this bunch together. Juiced 'em up. They're ready to go out and fight tigers this morning."

She looked over at him as he continued. "But I'll tell you something: keep a little of that juice for yourself. Don't give it all away, 'cause you're gonna need it. You've cut yourself a big piece of pie with this raid, Doc."

Julie smiled wryly at him. "So, it's 'Doc' now, Mr. Donovan? What happened to 'kid'?"

He ducked his head for a moment, then met her eyes again, his own slightly sheepish. "Yeah . . . well . . . you're older than I thought."

"Thanks," said Juliet, grinning. "I think."

"You know what I mean." He gestured.

"Hey, Julie." Elias stuck his head in the door. "I got juice and a doughnut out here for you. A *chocolate* iced one."

"Thanks, Elias." Taking her cane, she went out into the hall. There she sipped her juice and managed to nibble at the pastry, studying her people. There were more of them than yesterday—many members of the new resistance group still lived at home, especially those employed in non-science-related fields. The rebels talked loudly, laughed uproariously, their movements quick and abrupt . . . all except for a few, like Robert Maxwell, who sat silently, stilly, pulled deep within themselves.

*Better give them something to do, quick*, Julie thought. *They're really wired.* "Everybody?" she called out, and at the sound of her voice, they all turned to watch her. "Okay, one last time. Everyone clear on his or her assignment?"

A general murmur of agreement accompanied the nodding heads. "Diversionary actions begin at one o'clock. Right, Caleb, Ruby, the rest of you?"

Caleb, dressed for work at the Richland plant, his friend Bill Graham beside him, nodded. "They'll know we're alive and well at the plant, all right."

"And downtown," Ruby said. "Especially at the police stations."

"Good," Julie said. "Our main assault at the armory will begin just before two, when they should be at the most disorganized."

"*Two?*" Robert Maxwell said, paling. "I—"

"Yes," said Julie. "You missed the end of the meeting last night. You're coming with us to the armory, all right?"

"Uh . . . yeah, okay," Maxwell said. A pulse jumped beneath his eye. Julie frowned. "By the way, I haven't seen Robin. Did you send her back to the mountain camp, so she'd be safe?"

Maxwell nodded without speaking, not looking up. Studying his pallor, Julie was tempted to tell him to go back to the camp himself—it was obvious the man was terrified. But they needed every hand they could get.

While she was considering, Maxwell looked up, saw her concerned gaze, and smiled weakly. "I'm okay, really. Just a little nervous . . ."

"All right, Robert," Julie said doubtfully. "Now, those of you who will be in on the raid on the armory. We've got to keep in mind our primary objective—"

"To grab as many high-powered weapons as we can get our

little patty paws on, without gettin' ourselves wasted," Elias supplied.

"Right." Julie nodded emphatically. "It's critical for all our future operations that we be able to defend ourselves. For that we'll need arms. Then we'll be able to protect all our equipment when we bring it down from the mountains."

Mike Donovan stirred restlessly. "Listen, gang, while you guys are stirring up a ruckus down here, I think I'm gonna try to infiltrate the Mother Ship again. I want to—"

"Find your family?" Julie interrupted, remembering Donovan's single-minded outburst of the previous evening.

"Yeah, that too. I won't deny it. But I also have an idea on how to get into a place where I'll be able to find out just what their real plans are. With the uniform, I should be able to get in and get back out."

Ruby turned to look at him. Her expression said plainly that she thought he was crazy. "That sounds really suicidal to me."

"Yeah," Donovan shrugged. "Maybe I was a kamikaze pilot in a previous incarnation. That's what my partner, Tony, always says. Don't forget, he's still up there. I won't sleep nights until I find out what's happened to him—to all of 'em."

"In that case, you'd better tell us where you hid that tape," Julie said. "As a precautionary measure."

He grinned crookedly. "And I thought you loved me for my mind. It's in a locker at the bus terminal." He dug in his pants pocket, handed Juliet a key. "A kid I know named Josh has been paying the rental each day."

"Good enough," Julie said, her eyes on his, her fingers gripping the key. "Take care, Mr. Donovan. We'd hate to lose you."

"I'd hate to lose me, too."

"Good luck," Juliet said, still looking at him, then added abruptly, turning away, "To all of us."

Caleb's deep tones cut through the other murmurs. "Hey, Julie . . . how 'bout a prayer? One for the road, so to speak."

The young woman nodded. "Go on, Caleb."

"Me?" He glanced around, then composed himself for a second. "Well, Lord. We sure do need your help on this one. Please help every one of us to do our best, 'cause a lot of folks are counting on us. Give us wisdom and strength and courage, if that be your will. Thanks, Lord. Amen."

Julie was surprised to hear Donovan's voice mixed with the others as they echoed Caleb's "amen." She faced them, taking a deep breath. "Let's do it."

Harmony Moore hastened toward the commissary, carrying a tray of refilled salt, pepper, and sugar containers. It was a nice day, she thought, looking around her at the blue sky, the gently scudding clouds. Her eyes were so accustomed to the huge Visitor ship hanging over the city that she didn't even notice it consciously anymore.

As she walked along, her eyes turned upward, wondering if it would rain by evening, her foot jerked as her shoe stuck to something on the concrete. "Huh?" Harmy stopped, put the tray down, and lifted her foot. Tendrils of bright pink chewing gum clutched her shoe lovingly. Harmy made an exasperated sound.

As she attempted to scrape the mess off her shoe, she braced her hand against one of the massive pipes thrusting outward from a huge refinery tank. Her fingers brushed something yielding at the same moment as she heard the ticking sound. Harmy looked up at her hand. Attached to one of the pipes was a wad of grayish-white goop, with a small black box attached. There was a clockface on the box. A red pointer showed one o'clock, while the time read twelve forty-five.

*What the heck is that?* Harmy wondered, staring at it. *It almost looks like . . . like . . .*

Swallowing, forgetting the tray, she backed away, jerking her foot free of the gum with a sudden panicky yank. She wondered what the range of the thing was . . . if there were others planted to go off. She ran the little distance to the parking lot, and her truck, her mind racing. *The resistance! This must be something they're doing. What should I do?*

Harmony had watched Kristine Walsh's reports on the television, listened to the radio—and wondered what the real truth was. Her father had died in Korea, her brother in Vietnam—she'd been a pacifist since high school. She didn't like seeing armed Shock Troopers on the streets of her city. But setting bombs where they might hurt or injure people, destroy property, was something else.

Harmy bit her lip as she sat on the tailgate of her truck, the minutes ticking by in her head, on her watch. There was nobody else in sight. Maybe she ought to call the cops. But from the rumors she'd heard, that could result in reprisals from the Visitor troops. She'd even heard a rumor that they'd apprehended a whole town that tried to rally against them. One of Harmy's best friends, an X-ray technician, had disappeared over a month ago. She missed Betty horribly—they'd been so close.

Harmy checked her watch again. Twelve fifty-eight and thirty-three seconds.

She looked back up. A figure in a red uniform was walking around the tank, a clipboard in his hand.

"*Willy!*" Harmy shrieked. Without thinking, she jumped up and ran toward him. "*No!! Get away!!*" Racing over to him, she grabbed his arm and dragged him toward the parking lot.

The blast knocked both of them off their feet. Wild-eyed, they stared at each other. Then they heard the other blasts. The alarms shrieked. Harmy climbed to her feet and offered a hand to William. "Harmy?" he shouted as he stood up. "What's coming on?"

"*Going on,*" she corrected automatically. "I think it's the resistance people."

"You saved my life," William said, still clutching her hand. "I am thankful to you always."

In the midst of the chaos of running feet and shrieking sirens, she smiled at him. "You saved Caleb. It was the least I could do."


Mike Donovan hesitated for a second before the yellow door, feeling in his pocket for the gold and crystal key he'd given to Sean so long ago. It slipped into his hand, cool and smooth. Glancing quickly down the shadowy corridor of the Mother Ship to make sure he was unobserved, he pushed the key into the slot. With a tiny hydraulic hum, the door slid aside. Donovan pulled the key out and stepped through.

*So far, so good,* he thought. He hesitated for a second, blinking to accustom his eyes to the even dimmer light within. A dark corridor stretched ahead. Behind him, the door slid shut, making him jump.

He hadn't had any trouble getting aboard the Mother Ship—

it had simply been a matter of keeping his dark glasses on and
lingering near a shuttle until it was ready for departure, then
scramming aboard at the last moment. Under his pulled-down
Visitor cap, the dark glasses masking his features even further,
he'd been just another anonymous figure in uniform.

Just as the shuttle had landed, an announcement had echoed
through the docking bay that the Richland plant was under
attack. In the resulting confusion of troops and departing squad
vehicles, he'd slipped away into the bowels of the alien ship.

Donovan moved forward, trying to keep the heavy uniform
boots from echoing on the metal-gridded floor of the corridor.
He passed no one. Finally his way opened out into a huge
central room, so large that even the echoes of his footsteps
were lost and muffled. The cavernous room was filled, floor to
ceiling, with huge tanks—but not the heavy-duty refinery tanks
that he'd seen at Richland. These tanks—he tapped one to be
sure—were thin-walled and bore no pressure gauges or
instruments to indicate the condition of their contents.

A valve lead out of one of the tanks. Donovan twisted it. A
stream of clear liquid trickled out. Bending over, Mike eyed it,
then, frowning, put out a finger. The cold liquid felt familiar on
his skin. Donovan sniffed it, then cautiously tasted.

"Jesus, it's *water.* In all these tanks?" Turning the valve
wider, Donovan took a few swallows; he was thirsty. Then he
roamed through the huge room, trying valves at random. After
the first ten or so confirmed that each tank had the same
contents, Donovan stood, trying to count them. He lost track
after five hundred, but there were more than that, many more.
How many millions of gallons did they represent? And were
there similar holds with the same cargo on the other ships?

Mike rubbed the back of his neck as he stood in the dim
coolness of the hold, puzzling. There was something going on
that he didn't understand here, and that he *ought* to. Com-
prehension niggled at the fringes of his mind, tantalizing him,
but staying just out of his reach.

When he stepped out of the corridor, he went looking for
another of the yellow doors. He found it, inserted his key, and
stepped in. As he moved along the corridor, he heard footsteps
approaching. Quickly, he flattened himself into a darkened
alcove, seeing a technician pass. Donovan heard the yellow
door hiss, then peered out cautiously. He jerked back quickly at

the sound of more footsteps, then cocked one eye around the edge of the alcove. *Martin!*

As the Visitor officer walked by, Donovan reached out and grabbed him. He felt the false, cool flesh of the alien's nose and mouth beneath his stifling hand, saw the contact-covered eyes widen as they recognized him. Cautiously, Donovan removed his hand.

"Donovan!"

"Yeah." Mike regarded him grimly. "I want to know what's going on. I just got back from the hold where the tanks are. The *water* tanks. I asked you before about the real reason for your little visit to our small planet here, and you said there wasn't enough time if I was going to escape. But right now I've got all the time in the world, and I want you to level with me."

Martin looked at the floor for a long moment, then sighed. "All right. Yes, the tanks are full of water, there's no chemical."

"Then you *are* dumping the chemical out into the atmosphere?"

"Yes."

"*Why?*" Mike shook the Visitor's shoulders a little in frustration. Then his eyes widened as it hit him. "Ohmygod— I've been an idiot. The *water.* You're stealing the water. The chemical is just a smoke screen. All the water that gets pumped into the plants to supposedly process the chemical is actually taken up here. But why?"

"Pure liquid H-2-O is the rarest and most valuable commodity you can imagine. It's one of the first resources any industrial society destroys and pollutes. You've already started here, so you should know. Unlike most planets, ours included, your world has a lot more water than it has land area. We need water desperately—for sustenance, industry . . . everything."

"But we would have shared it—"

"Some of us proposed the idea of telling you the truth, asking you to do just that. But Our Leader wants it *all.* Now that Earth is regarded as more or less secured, other ships from our home are already on their way. The whole plan will take a generation—our lifespans approximate yours—but in the end, we'll have it all, if the Leader has his way."

"Earth will be a desert," Mike said hollowly. "Humanity . . . all of us . . . will die without water."

Martin sighed. "There won't be any people left when we leave."

Mike looked at him.

The Visitor officer nodded. "There's something else I have to show you."

With a terrible sense of foreboding, Mike Donovan followed Martin along the corridor. Like the other one, it opened out into a huge room, but this one contained smaller, cylindrical chambers, each about three feet by seven. The hair prickling on the back of his neck, Donovan looked around. "What the hell are these for?"

Martin gestured wearily. "See for yourself."

Stiffly, Mike walked the short distance to the nearest cylinder. It was filled with some kind of gelatinous, gray-colored substance that flowed and eddied within the container. As Donovan peered into it, the thick gray gel swirled and thinned, and, abruptly, a face drifted into view. It was an older man, with a thick moustache. His eyes stared, vacant; his mouth hung open. He was naked.

Martin's voice came from behind Mike. "They're your people. The ones who disappeared."

Mike whirled to face him, his mouth so dry he had trouble speaking. One name burned in his mind—*Sean*. He choked on the question. "Dead?"

"No. Not dead." Donovan closed his eyes in momentary relief, then forced himself to listen. "Metabolism slowed extraordinarily, perfectly preserved—they can be revived in a matter of minutes. Diana developed the technique."

Mike looked out at the thousands upon thousands of cocoons, then, turning, directly at Martin. "My son is here. Someplace."

"He was taken?"

"Along with the rest of San Pedro. I have to find him."

Martin rubbed wearily at his forehead with a very human gesture of frustration. "Mike, there's no way, short of looking him up in the central computer—and I have only limited access to it. We don't even know for sure he's on *this* ship. He could be on the San Francisco ship. Or the Seattle one. I'm sorry."

Donovan gestured at the cocoons. "There's a way of finding

him—there's *got* to be. But Martin, *why*? Why are they being taken—stored—like this? Because they're troublemakers, or scientists who'd like to do tests on you, reveal your true faces?" Martin gave him a quick glance, then looked away. Mike grinned ironically. "You know I've seen 'em. It's weird to stand here talking to you as though you're human like I am, and know you're not. Really weird."

"Yes, I know about your fight with Jerome. He said you're—what's the term? A mean customer?"

"I do my best," Donovan said absently. "But if that's so, why not kill 'em? Why keep them here?"

"The Leader wants them living. Some of them will be conscripted into fighting his battles. I think the term is 'cannon fodder.'"

"How did somebody like that get into power anyway?"

Martin looked grim. "Charisma. Circumstances. Promises. Financial backing. A doctrine that appealed to the unthinking—assurances that he, as their leader, would bring them to greatness. Not enough of us spoke out to question him—or even took him seriously—until it was too late. It's happened here on your planet, hasn't it?"

"Yeah. It has." Mike remembered something abruptly. "I've been meaning to ask about Barbara. She ordered me to shoot her—told me they'd never believe I overpowered her and stole the uniform, otherwise. Is she okay?"

"She's recovering."

"Good. I want to thank her someday." He looked back at the cocoons. "So many. There must be thousands of 'em."

"Yes."

Mike looked at him. "*Some* of them, you said, would be used for troops in your leader's army. What about the rest?"

Martin looked off across the chamber, refusing to meet the human's eyes. "In addition to water, there's another basic shortage on our planet."

Donovan felt the blood drain out of his face, leaving his features stiff. His lips moved silently. "Food?" But even though he hadn't spoken aloud, Martin, who was watching him again, nodded.

"Yes."

Shaking violently, Donovan put a hand to his face. "Oh, God. Should'a known. I think . . . gonna be—" He swallowed gulpingly, trying to control his nausea, rubbing furiously at his mouth as though Martin's revelation had left a bad taste on his lips—a foulness that could be wiped away.

"Take it easy, Mike," Martin said. "We don't have time for that."

"I know." Still trembling, Donovan forced himself to take deep, slow breaths. "God. I should have guessed. You could . . . do that? To a kid like Sean?" He looked over at another container where a young woman's face floated. "To her?"

Martin shook his head. "Don't. I feel terrible about it. Making both us sick isn't going to help. I'm not going to say that I'm a vegetarian—that's not our way. But intelligent species? No. When this expedition was first mounted, we were told the inhabitants of this world were . . . like cattle. Not intelligent. Then, when we came here, there were those who protested when they saw the truth. They were . . . disposed of."

"Yeah? Iguana burgers?"

"What?"

"Never mind. Bad taste." Mike spat into a dark corner. "We'd better get out of here."

As they walked back toward the door onto the main corridor, he whispered, "Just promise me something, Martin."

"What?"

"If you can, find out where my son is. Sean Donovan. And his mother too. Her name is Marjorie."

Martin nodded bleakly. "If I can. It won't be easy. I have to be very cautious."

As they reached the door, Donovan put a hand on the Visitor officer's arm. "Now for Tony. I want you to take me to him."

The alien hesitated for a long moment. "I know which holding cell he was in, but Diana said she was going to question him personally. I didn't hear anything else."

"Let's go there, then."

Martin was obviously frightened. "That's a well-trafficked area, with a lot of security. If I'm seen with you, I'll never be able to explain it away."

"You're not taking nearly the chance I am. Let's go."

The Visitor hesitated as though he would argue further, then stopped when his eyes met Mike's. "All right," he said reluctantly.

They walked quickly, purposefully, Donovan with his cap pulled down and his dark glasses on. It made seeing difficult—the ship itself was already dim for human vision. But he had little choice.

Finally they reached the detention area. Martin checked door numbers, then inserted his key. "I must warn you, Mike, this will be unpleasant."

Donovan nodded. "Okay."

They stepped inside. The room was cool and still and smelled of blood and excrement. In its center was a draped gurney. Martin stepped over to the drape, picked up the edge, and looked beneath it. As Mike stepped over to join him he turned and nodded wordlessly.

Mike's breath caught in his chest. "Tony," he said softly, knowing his friend could not hear. Gently he pushed Martin aside and picked up the sheet.

Tony Leonetti's face was composed, serene. Someone had closed his eyes. There were no bruises on the features. Looking for the cause of death, Mike raised the sheet higher, scanning the body. The cause of death was obvious. Someone had cut Tony open, someone with consummate surgical skill and technique—but they'd neglected to sew him back up. The gurney on which he lay was slightly hollowed, and he was inches deep in blood.

Donovan choked, then gently touched his friend's face. "Tony . . . God, I'm sorry, buddy. I'm so sorry . . ." He lowered the shroud back over the still, pale features. "Diana?" he said, keeping his voice steady with an effort.

"Yes." Martin sounded nearly as anguished as Donovan felt. "She's authorized some . . . medical experiments. She occasionally demonstrates surgical techniques for her staff . . ."

"I want to kill her," Mike said, his voice hard and brittle.

Martin's voice was weary. "You'd have to stand in line."

A groan from the corner made both of them start and turn. A figure in a blue work shirt lay curled in the dark, on the cold floor. Donovan hastened to turn the injured man over, gently. He'd obviously been beaten by someone who was obsessed with doing a thorough job—his features were bruised so badly that it was difficult to get any idea of his age or normal appearance. His left eye was swollen so badly it made a hideous reddish-blue bulge on the side of his head.

Battered, cracked lips moved, and Donovan made out a hoarse whisper. "Who . . . who are you?"

"A friend."

"You're . . . not . . . one of them?"

"No."

The man tried to smile, weakly. Mike realized from his dark hair, the intonations of his speech, that he was Mexican. "They tried to make me talk . . . I told them nothing." He grinned, the expression hideous. "Do you have . . . any water? I used . . . the last of mine . . . to spit at Diana."

"Here," said Martin, holding a cup to the man's lips. He swallowed with an effort, but managed to drink the whole cup, seeming the better for it. Martin came back with some medical supplies. While Donovan cleaned and medicated the man's face, Martin bound his ribs to support them, and gave the man several injections.

At Donovan's inquiring look, he explained, "To prevent infection. Antibiotics, mostly, but the second one should get him on his feet. I assume you're going to want to take him back with you?"

Donovan hadn't actually thought about it until Martin spoke, but at the Visitor officer's words, he nodded. "Yeah. Think we can smuggle him into a squad vehicle?"

"I'll scout ahead, see what I can turn up. There's someone else you ought to take with you. They picked up a young girl yesterday, and I understand she's being used as a hostage to make her father betray one of the underground bases. Diana seemed particularly interested in her, so you'd better get her out of here. She's only a kid."

"Okay, I'm game. I'll take care of him while you go check on the kid. I'll meet you in the docking bay in . . . ten minutes?"

Martin checked his chronometer. "Make it fifteen. See you, Mike."

When he'd gone, Donovan got his patient another cup of water. "Think you can stand now?" he asked, when the man had finished it. "We're gonna try and get off this crate. You up for that?"

"Believe it, *amigo*," the man said.

"Good. My name's Mike Donovan, by the way." They shook.

"Sancho Gomez."

"Nice to meet you, Sancho. Too bad it couldn't have been under better circumstances."

When his chrono indicated that it was time to move, Donovan took Sancho's arm, unstrapped his Visitor sidearm, then put his hand on its butt. "Just a little prisoner transfer to another cellblock," he said, "that's all we are. Try and look scared of me, Sancho."

*"Comprende."*

They reached a hiding place just inside the docking bay without incident. A few minutes later, Martin entered, holding the arm of a terrified-looking teenage girl, her face dirty, tear-stained, smeared with eye makeup.

Glancing quickly around, Martin motioned to the girl to climb into one of the small squad vehicles. Even as he turned back, Donovan and Sancho were beside him. They climbed into the Visitor craft. Martin nodded, preparing to climb in also. "Let's go."

"You're coming too?" Mike was surprised.

"I have to. It's silly to think that nobody saw me with you or Robin. It'll be dangerous for me here now."

"You ought to stay here, Martin." Donovan leaned out of the craft, his green eyes very intent.

"What? Why?"

"We need somebody up here on our side. You'll be invaluable to the underground."

"But, Mike—" Martin looked frankly scared. "I've got to fly this thing for you."

"Shit on that. I can fly it. You stay here, Martin."

"You can't fly this thing!"

"Wanna bet? I'm a good pilot, and I spent every trip we made together watching everything you did. I can fly it, I know I can."

"But listen—"

"Dammit, Martin, admit it!" Mike leaned close to the Visitor, his eyes holding the alien's. "You're scared, right?"

"I—" Martin's shoulders sagged and he glanced behind him. "It's going to be very dangerous for me."

"You'll make it." Mike clasped his shoulder. "Nobody even gave Sancho and me a glance. Nobody will connect this little caper with you. Just duck outa sight, so I can get out of here."

Martin still hesitated. Donovan shook his shoulder roughly. "Dammit, Martin! Dangerous for you? It's dangerous for all of us! I've lost a son, and my partner. And what about Barbara? She was willing to risk me shooting her to help! What does Sancho look like, a day at Disneyland? Hell, we're all damn scared, Martin, but each of us has got to help in the best way we can." He hesitated for a long moment, seeing Martin's quick glance at Sancho. "How about it, man, you game?"

Martin nodded suddenly. "All right." He pointed to the controls. "You'll have a tendency to overcompensate, Mike. It's very sensitive."

"Which one controls direction?" Martin showed him. "Good. Speed?" He watched and nodded.

"And that one over there is your altitude gauge. It's fully fueled. Good luck, Mike."

"I hope so." Mike hesitantly started the craft. It whined into immediate life. "You ought to sell these babies in New England," he mumbled. "Make a fortune." As Martin turned to leave, Donovan caught his arm.

"Hey . . . Martin. Thanks. I'm proud to have you as a friend. Our side is lucky you're around."

Martin nodded. "I'm glad to have *you* as a friend. Now, if you don't get this thing out of here, we won't live to be old friends—which would be the best of all. So, 'scram' is the word, I believe."

"Right." Martin hurried away as Donovan closed the hatch. "Strap in, everyone." Just as the newsman began to ease the lever forward, there came a shout. "Damn! We've been spotted! Hang on!"

He goosed the squad vehicle, which leaped forward with a rush, heading for the landing bay doors. They began to close as the fugitives neared them, and Donovan had to make a quick swerve. The craft bounced slightly as they struck the opposite door—then they were away.

They soared out into the open blueness of the upper atmosphere. As Donovan eased the lever forward, trying to get the feel of the craft, they were abruptly aimed at the roiling blue-green of the Pacific. The girl sitting next to Donovan gasped shrilly as the vehicle dived, "Pull it up!"

"I'm *trying*!" Donovan snapped, pulling back on the lever, fighting panic as the ocean grew in the windscreen. The nose of the craft came up . . . up . . .

With nearly equal suddenness, the three humans found themselves upside down as the Visitor craft looped violently. The girl screamed. "Shut up, you idiot!" Donovan shouted, fighting the controls. Finally, by using only the lightest of touches, he was able to right the craft and fly in a fairly straight path. He banked into a long, gradual turn that would lead him out to sea. Martin was right—the thing nearly flew itself. But he wanted to practice awhile before attempting a landing.

"Where are you going, *amigo*?" asked Sancho, who was sitting in the rear of the craft.

"Out to sea, so I can try this baby out without being hassled by any other air traffic," Mike said. "I want to practice before I have to even *think* about any fancy moves or trying a landing. Out here I'll have a little peace and quiet."

"Uh, I hate to tell you this, *Senor* Donovan, but I'm afraid we're being hassled."

"Huh?"

"There are two other craft like this one chasing us, and—"

Sancho was interrupted by something striking the squad vehicle, making it shudder.

"What was that?" yelped the girl.

". . . and shooting at us," finished Sancho. "I think we're in trouble."

# Chapter 18

Ruby Engels dragged her ancient shopping cart behind her as she walked slowly up the familiar sidewalk. She checked her watch for the twentieth time—twelve-forty. Only a few minutes to go. She took a deep, shivering breath, hoping that God would give her the strength to do what had to be done. In spite of her bravado of that morning, Ruby was scared. All her life she'd been a law-abiding person, and it was hard to change at her age.

As she walked along, she saw two familiar figures just ahead—people she'd never expected to see again. Quickening her pace, she smiled and waved. "Stanley! Lynn! You're back!"

Stanley and Lynn Bernstein were standing in their backyard, out near the pool house. They both looked up at Ruby's hail. "Ruby!"

Leaving her cart at the corner of the driveway, Ruby hastened toward them. "I'm so glad to see you! I thought maybe you wouldn't be coming back!"

Stanley's arm was bandaged from the elbow down—he held it stiffly, as though the slightest jar would bring agony. Lynn appeared uninjured, but her blue eyes looked changed—as though they'd beheld the worst she could have imagined, and was only now beginning to realize it hadn't destroyed her. She reached out to embrace the older woman, her arms shaking. "Ruby, it's so good to be back!"

"Where's Abraham?"

The Bernsteins looked at each other. "We never saw him," Stanley said dully. "When we got home, we saw Daniel." He said the name as if it hurt him. "He hadn't seen him either. He promised to ask his leader, Brian, where Father is, but—" he swallowed. "I'm afraid it's better not to know."

Lynn put her face in her hands, shaking. "Daniel said he . . . was sorry . . . that we'd been—"

"Take it easy, Lynn," Stanley said, putting his good arm around his wife.

"I understand," said Ruby clearly. "Please, Stanley, take care of yourself. Lynn, I'll see you later. Try to get some rest." She patted the younger woman on her bowed shoulder, then walked quickly away.

She refused to think. Her legs moved mechanically, one-two, one-two, as she reclaimed her shopping cart and followed the path she and her friend had walked so many times. At the first corner, one of *their* vehicles was parked, hatch open, next to two police cars.

Ruby stopped. Halfway down the side block, several shock troopers, accompanied by two policemen, were searching some tough-looking youths in front of Visitor posters festooned with the "V" symbol. Cans of red spray paint bore mute witness to the kids' crime. Quickly, Ruby took one of the Molotov cocktails out of its concealment in her shopping cart, then pulled her Zippo lighter out of her pocket. Holding the gasoline-filled bottle concealed beneath her huge purse, she lit the rag fuse as she passed the open hatch. Nobody was watching—the troopers were concentrating on the kids.

With a quick, sure gesture, Ruby tossed the cocktail into the open shuttle. "This one's for Abraham," she muttered, giving a defiant glance at the Visitors' backs. Then she trotted on, the cart bumping.

The first, small explosion was joined a second later by a much bigger one. Ruby cast a quick, satisfied glance back to see the shuttle in flames; one of the police cars had also caught. The Visitors and cops were staring at the flames; the kids were only flying, distant figures. She smiled tautly, before she noticed that one of the policemen was watching her over his shoulder.

Ruby's back stiffened—then she saw his grin, quickly

stifled, and the "V" sign he made behind his back for her benefit.

Ruby Engels walked on down the street, her eyes scanning for another target.

# Chapter 19

As the delivery truck lurched around a corner, Elias' hands slipped on the steering wheel. "Sorry 'bout that," he said, wiping first his right, then his left palm on the thigh of his jeans. "Hands are sweaty." The sound of another explosion echoed in the distance. "You scared too?" He checked the rearview mirror; the garbage truck was still back there.

Juliet, sitting beside him, looked tensely through the window at the hulk of a burning police car. "Yeah. I just hope nobody gets hurt. I would hate to lose one of us."

Robert Maxwell, sitting beside Juliet on the swaying seat of the fast-moving truck, was thinking fast. He stole a quick look at his watch, which showed one forty-seven. *Two hours to go. I'll have to break free during the attack and steal some transportation so I can get Kathy and the girls out.* He thought of the people in the mountain camp, imagined Juliet's face if she knew how he was betraying them, then resolutely pushed such thoughts out of his mind. *Robin. Think of Robin, up there in that damn hulking ship . . .*

The truck turned another corner. Directly ahead of them was a huge concrete and brick building, enclosed within a twelve-foot chain-link fence. Two shock troopers stood guard at the gate. Inside the fence they could see army vehicles parked.

"There. There's the loading dock, Elias." Julie pointed.

"I see it. Hang on!" The truck accelerated toward the

gate. With a huge lurch it struck the chain-link and burst through.

"Look out for the two on the roof!" Julie shouted. They slewed around, bouncing off a parked troop carrier, then backed up to the loading dock.

The garbage truck trundled in through the wreckage of the gate and its back door began to open as the pulsing whine of Visitor weapons filled the parking lot. Armed resistance fighters jumped out and began firing at the Visitors. Several fighters produced large framed mirrors, using them to flash the bright sunlight in the faces of the roof guards.

Juliet jumped out of the delivery truck and ran around to the back, her hip stabbing with pain—she barely felt it. "Open it up! Let's get it loaded! Fast!"

The rear door of the truck opened and more resistance fighters tumbled out onto the loading dock. They raced inside the armory with Julie, the sounds of the battle outside following them. Elias came up beside Julie as she grabbed several guns. "Whoo! Lookit all this hardware!"

"No time to pick and choose," she snapped. "Load 'em on." Quickly they formed a chain, passing weapons from hand to hand into the truck. Elias and Brad raced around, handing machine guns, a bazooka and ammunition, then a rocket launcher and rockets to the chain. Julie looked up at a shout to see one fighter dragged in by another, then Robert, who half-carried a moaning woman. "Oh, no!" She hastened over to the wounded. "We've got to get them into the truck!"

Robert's eyes were wild, his mouth anguished. "I've got to get out of here, warn the mountain camp! They're going to be raided this afternoon!"

*"What?!"*

"Robin is a prisoner—I was only trying to protect her! But there are too many lives at stake—I can't keep quiet and let them be taken!"

Without waiting for a response, he turned and dashed out of the armory, located a parked jeep, scanned to see if the keys were in the ignition, then climbed in. Juliet hesitated, but there was nothing she could do. Robert started the jeep, gunned the motor, and, crouching low over the wheel, roared away.

"Elias!" Juliet called. "Help me get these people into the truck!"

As they carried the wounded man and woman out, she

shouted to the other rebels: "The truck's getting full—pass the word. Get ready to haul it out of here! We've got to head straight for the mountain camp—they're going to be raided!"

The next few minutes passed in a blur, a hideous one. Several more wounded were slung hurriedly into the truck, and Julie saw that at least one of them wouldn't make it as far as the mountain camp. Elias and Brad oversaw the retreat, while Juliet remained in the rear of the delivery truck with the wounded.

When she peered out to see how the courtyard fighting was going, Juliet saw many red-clad bodies. All of the alien vehicles were in flames. Even as she watched, the fire spread toward the munitions storage. "Elias!" she shrieked. "Get us *out* of here!"

Brad leaped into the rear of the truck just as the engine rumbled to life. "Did everyone else make it into the trash truck?" Julie asked.

"Yeah." Brad looked around at the jumbled stacks of weapons. "We did okay, looks like."

"If you can call five wounded, one probably critically, okay then you're right. Come over here." When he reached her side, she continued, "Okay, hold this rag here, until the bleeding stops. How much first aid did they give you as a cop?"

"I've delivered a baby," he said. "But mostly it was just basic wait-for-the-ambulance stuff."

"That's better than most people. At least you don't upchuck at the sight of blood."

"What were you yelling about the mountain camp?"

"Robert got away just after telling me that the Visitors captured his daughter, Robin, and forced him to give the location of the mountain camp. They're going to raid it. We've got to get our equipment out of there!"

"Oh, shit! That sonofabitch!"

"Brad, are you crazy? What do you expect the poor guy to do, just throw away his own daughter's life? I just hope that somehow we can manage to get her back. Maybe this 'Martin' Donovan spoke of can help."

"Damn. Somebody better."

By the time the truck left the city behind, they had done all they could for the wounded. Juliet sat on the swaying floor, her back against a pile of army rifles, Lenore's head in her lap. Her hand held the young black woman's, partly for comfort, partly to check her thready, erratic pulse. Brad looked over at them. "She gonna make it?"

Juliet looked at him soberly and shook her head from side to side. She didn't want to speak aloud because it was barely possible that Lenore could still hear, even though she seemed to be unconscious. Hearing, she knew, was one of the last senses to go.

"We must be nearly there by now," Brad said, checking his watch. Julie nodded, looking down at Lenore. The pulse beneath her fingers fluttered, throbbed, fluttered as the woman twitched and gasped. Then it stopped.

"She's gone," Juliet said. She noticed that her hip ached terribly and that she was crying. Neither fact seemed very important.

Brad looked closely at her face in the dimness of the wan overhead light, then scuttled across the floor. "Hey, Julie. Hey . . ." Awkwardly he put his arm around her. Juliet leaned against him for a long time.

The truck banked into a sharp turn. Lenore slid bonelessly out of Juliet's lap. "That's the turn onto the mountain road," Julie said. They could feel the alteration in the truck's engine now as it strained to take the incline. "Just a little way to go now. What time is it, Brad?"

She could see the tiny glow of his watch. "Two-fifty."

"You mean it only took a half-hour in the armory?"

"Less," Brad said. "It's weird, isn't it? We used to notice that in Nam. We'd be in a raid, or pinned down somewhere under fire, and time would get real short—or sometimes real long."

Juliet stiffened. "I hear shots!"

A moment later, the pulse of Visitor weapons was plainly audible, as well as screams. "They're attacking the camp!" Juliet jumped up and pounded on the wall separating the truck from the cab. "Hurry *up*, Elias!"

"He can't hear you, Julie!" Brad said. They braced themselves against the rear door, waiting, holding guns ready to toss out to the fighters.

The truck's brakes squealed, then it jolted to a halt. Immediately Brad pulled the rear door open. "Here! Guns!" Pulses from the Visitor weapons resounded, and as Juliet watched, a squad vehicle swooped down to strafe the center of the camp. Blue fire blazed from its weapons, exploding on impact with the ground, the tents, the people. Juliet handed out arms, hardly daring to watch. She felt light-headed with horror.

Brad and Elias dragged the bazooka out of the truck and hastily set it up. Juliet grabbed the nearest gun and clumsily crawled out of the truck, grabbing the arm of a man she recognized as Terry. "There are wounded in the truck with the guns! Get some people and get them both out! If they shoot the gas tank, they're dead and we're unarmed!"

"Right!" he shouted, turning away. Julie stayed for a moment, then heard one of the craft coming in again.

"Get him, Brad!" Elias yelled, and the ex-cop fired the bazooka at the craft sweeping at them head-on. A brilliant burst of light impacted against the Visitor craft, which spun away, out of control, arcing beyond the trees. A second later they heard the explosion, saw the ball of greasy orange flame reach greedily for the sky.

Julie gave a wordless yell of encouragement at the two, who hurriedly reloaded the bazooka. One of the other craft—they moved so fast it was hard to tell how many there were—bore down on the camp. It fired a burst just as a brown-haired woman dashed from a burning tent. She crumpled with a shriek of pain. A boy of about thirteen raced out behind her. He wasn't strong enough to lift her. "Help!" he shouted, but none of the panicking figures seemed to hear. Juliet grabbed a weapon and started across the campground toward him. "I can't lift her!" he yelled.

Julie's hip stabbed as she moved, and it seemed to take an eternity for her to reach the boy. She took the woman's arm in her right hand and, together with the boy, began to drag her toward the cinderblock building housing the scientific equipment. Ahead of her, she saw another group setting up the rocket launcher.

*Hurry . . . hurryhurry . . . Faster!!* Julie's mind screamed. Dimly, from the stabbing pains in her hip, she realized she was running. But her movements felt thick, gluey, as though she were trapped in an eternal nightmare. Out of the corner of her eye, she saw the largest of the Visitor craft diving directly at them. Dropping the woman's arm, she turned, the weapon she'd grabbed in her hand.

It was a .45 automatic. She recognized it from Brad's lessons. Her mind screamed that it was crazy—a handgun against an aircraft—but, possessed by the unreality that was surrounding her, Juliet took the stance Brad had shown her, the gun braced carefully in both hands, aiming. It was the first time she'd ever fired at anything but a straw target.

The gun bucked in her hand as she squeezed off several rounds. Would the bullets even penetrate the skin of the craft? It swooped by, its weapons firing, and she recognized one of the occupants.

*Diana.* That dark, beautiful countenance had been on too many magazine covers for her to be mistaken. Juliet's finger squeezed the trigger again, and this time she *saw* the spark of impact on the alien craft.

The squad vehicle sailed by, unharmed. Elias and Brad fired the bazooka at it, but missed. Juliet turned to grab the fallen woman's arm again. "Come on!" she screamed at the boy.

She heard the craft zooming in again for another strafing pass, and knew, with a terrible certainty, that this time the pilot had their range—he wouldn't miss. She waved frantically at the boy. "Get out of here! I'll get her!"

He stubbornly shook his head. They began dragging the fallen woman again. Juliet fixed her eyes on the building facing them, refusing to look elsewhere. She couldn't stop her ears, though, and she could hear the pulsing whine of the Visitor weapon coming closer . . . closer . . .

Suddenly she heard the whoosh of another squad vehicle, then the pulse of its weapons. "Look!" the boy yelled, pointing.

Diana's craft spun crazily, plainly hit, while the new vehicle swooped toward them—heading for the fighter that had been strafing the other side of the camp. Diana's craft recovered, then flew slowly, awkwardly, back in the direction of the city and the Mother Ship, escorted by the other alien ship. As Juliet and the others watched, the newcomer tailed them almost out of sight, firing steadily, then, turning, came back to the camp.

It landed clumsily, throwing up clouds of dust. The hatch opened, and a face they all recognized emerged. "Hi, there."

"Mike!" the boy beside Juliet shouted, jumping up and down ecstatically. "How'd you get the ship?"

"Trading stamps," answered Donovan. Juliet felt a hand on

her arm, pushing her gently aside, then realized Louise and Bill were picking up the woman, who was still unconscious, but groaning now.

Limping, Juliet started toward the alien craft, conscious again of that odd arms-length impulse. "Mr. Donovan," she said coolly, "it's good to see you. You have a knack for knowing when to drop in." Other fighters were collecting around them.

"Yeah," Donovan said. "You're lucky Sancho managed to figure out where the firing button was in that baby." Elias and Brad were lifting a nearly unconscious man out of the craft. His battered face managed a grin as Donovan gave him a "V" sign. Robin Maxwell climbed out of the passenger seat, looking considerably more chastened than the last time Juliet had seen her.

"Ms. Parrish, have you seen my Dad and Mom?"

"No," Julie said. "Has anyone seen Robert Maxwell?"

"I saw him," one of the men said. "He drove in here just before you folks did. He was heading for the dorm."

Robert Maxwell stumbled past the flaming chaos of the dorm, calling his wife's name. The building sent out waves of heat that did nothing to still his trembling. If Kathy had been in there . . .

Refusing to continue the thought, he walked on. "Kathy?" Dimly, he was aware that the Visitor craft were gone—he didn't even wonder where, or why. "Polly? Kathy! God, answer me, please!"

In front of him was a small shed that held canned goods and other supplies. Maxwell rubbed blearily at his eyes, trying to focus. There was a splotch of blue draped on a picnic table under the overhang of the shed. *Blue*, Robert thought fuzzily. *My favorite color.* He remembered Kathleen complaining once, because every birthday he gave her a sweater, always a blue one . . .

His vision sharpened as he rubbed, enough so he could see that the pretty expanse of blue was marred by red—

"Kathy!" The scream clawed his throat. "No!" He ran toward his wife.

She lay sprawled across the picnic table, legs dangling. Dark blood pooled on the table, oozed down her thighs from the gaping maw that had been her stomach. Her face was streaked with crimson, but her green eyes opened as he lifted her. "Kathy? Where are the girls? Are they okay?"

Her head moved with the tiniest of shakes, back and forth.

He put his face against her forehead, feeling the spattered silk of her hair. "Oh, God, Kathy! This wasn't supposed to happen." Sobbing, Maxwell cradled her head against him, rocking back and forth. "No . . . no . . ."

Time slowed, stopped, narrowed to this one moment, the urge to shelter his wife, hold her against the inevitable. It didn't take long. He knew immediately when it was finally over; her body was heavy in his arms . . . so heavy.

When he finally released her, staring into her empty, fixed, and huge pupils was like looking down into an eternity of darkness. He reached out and closed her eyes quickly, unable to stand looking at that loneliness. Carefully he lowered her body to the table, then took off his jacket, placing it gently over her face. Something bumped his side, and he looked down to see the pistol in its holster. It seemed an eternity since he'd buckled it on in preparation for the raid this morning.

*My fault*, he thought, looking at his wife's covered form, then at the desolate camp. *All mine. Kathy's dead. My little girls . . . the people who trusted me . . .* He thought of Robin, helpless in that damned ship, and cursed himself with a bitterness that seared his entire being. *I cannot live like this*, he thought. *I just can't.*

The gun slid into his hand, cool, heavy, and comforting. Absently he clicked the safety off, staring into the little round darkness at the end of the muzzle, the darkness that promised relief from this guilt, this pain, then his finger found the trigger.

"Daddy! *Daddy!*"

Maxwell turned, the gun slipping from his hand, to see Polly running awkwardly toward him, carrying Katie. Both girls were sobbing, but obviously unhurt. "Katie! Polly! Oh, God!" He raced toward them, caught them in his arms. They cried together, clutching each other, and then, miracle of miracles, Robin was somehow there too.

Mike Donovan stared incredulously at Juliet Parrish. "What do you *mean*, 'it sounds like we'd better focus our attention on destroying as many of the Mother Ships as we can . . .' Are you *crazy*, Doc? Haven't you been listening to what I just told you? They've got thousands . . . *thousands* . . . of our people on board! People they've kidnapped! Destroy the Mother Ships, and they go with 'em!"

"Yes, I understand," Juliet said, not looking at him. She was watching the camp evacuation that was under way. "Elias! Get those trucks out! The ammunition ones go *first*! And, Mr. Donovan, we'll try, of course, to find a way to get them off the ships, but—"

"*Try?*" He reached out and grabbed her arm, swung her to face him. She saw he was wearing a baseball cap that was ridiculously small for him, perched on top of his thick shock of brown hair.

Juliet nodded, her eyes holding his. "Yes, *try*. Mr. Donovan, you have to understand that we may have to sacrifice those thousands."

"*Sacrifice?*" He was so angry his voice broke on the word.

"To save *millions*—even billions—that are still here on Earth. I don't like it either, not a bit—but we may not have a choice!" She gestured to someone behind Mike, shouting, "*Now* the lab equipment." "And get started on the wounded!"

Mike stood in the center of the compound, watching her limp away, conscious of a strong feeling of *deja vu* that he couldn't quite identify. His gaze wandered past her to a group of stretchers waiting to be loaded into a truck, and, seeing a familiar brown head among the wounded, he sprinted over.

"Fran! What happened?"

Fran Leonetti looked pale, her arm and side swathed in bandages, but she turned her head as Donovan ran up. Josh stood by her side. "Hi, Mike," she said. "I got hit during the attack, but Juliet Parrish and Josh toted me off the battlefield before anything more permanent happened. Where's Tony?"

Mike felt a pang of guilt, realizing he'd completely forgotten Tony Leonetti's death during the rush to reach the camp. Looking down at Fran, he knew suddenly that he'd hesitated a moment too long. Her brown eyes were slightly fogged, probably by painkillers, but they didn't leave his face. "Bad news?" she asked in a small voice. "Mike? Tell me."

Donovan swallowed, then picked up her unbandaged hand and held it gently. "I'm sorry, Fran. They'd beefed up their security patrols, and they nailed us. Knocked me out. When I woke up, a couple of 'em helped me get off the ship, but said they couldn't get to Tony. When I could, I sneaked back aboard to find him, but it was . . . too late.''

"Dead," she stated, not wanting to believe it. "You're telling me Tony's dead?"

"Yeah. God, I'm sorry, Fran. I can't ever say how much." The grief that he'd repressed threatened to overwhelm him now. He swallowed heavily, trying to keep his breathing steady. If he gave way an inch, he had a feeling he'd be unable to stop—and Fran needed him. He held her hand in both of his, wishing he could put his arms around her, but the bandages forestalled him.

"It hurts . . ." Fran sounded as much surprised as grief-stricken. "God, Mike, it's making a real pain inside me. Now I know why they talk about heartache . . . broken hearts . . . Oh, it hurts!" Tears were running down her face, but she didn't seem to realize it. "He was only twenty-eight . . . three years younger than I am. Things were going so well. Did you know we were talking about starting a family? I didn't want to be pregnant in the summer, so we were gonna wait a couple of months . . ."

"Fran," came another voice. "We're going to lift you now."

Looking up, Donovan saw Elias and Brad. "Is there room for me to ride with her? I had to give her some really bad news about her husband . . . I want to stay with her."

"What about the lizard go-cart over there?" Brad asked, jerking his chin at the Visitor squad vehicle. "Juliet said we should move it down and hide it in the woods near headquarters. You're the only one can fly that thing."

"Yeah," Donovan said. "I guess you're right. Fran?" He brushed her hair back from her wet face. "I'm going to have to go. But I'll see you down at the other camp, okay?"

"Okay," she whispered.

Josh looked up. "I'll ride with you, Fran, if they don't mind. I'm awfully sorry to hear about your husband . . ."

"Yeah, I think we can scrunch you in," Elias said.

Mike got up and walked toward the squad vehicle, through the carnage of the wrecked camp. *We won this one*, he thought, *they didn't get the lab equipment, and we've got weapons. But it's only starting, and already the price has been so high . . .*

* * *

Stanley and Lynn Bernstein looked up from their dinner at the knock on their back door. Favoring his bandaged arm, Stanley went over to peek out the window, then opened the door hastily. "Robert!"

Robert Maxwell stepped in soundlessly, then pointed to a picture of Daniel on the counter with a questioning look. "He's gone for now," said Stanley. "He's out with Brian."

"Why have you come here, Robert?" Lynn twisted her napkin worriedly, her expression verging on hostility.

"Please. I have to talk to you."

She shook her head wildly, a feral, frightened light in her eyes. "You have to leave! Our son might come home any moment! Don't forget, he's the one who—"

"I remember," Robert said. "But the resistance needs your help."

"What?" Lynn said blankly, then turned to her husband in bewilderment.

"We want this to be known as a 'safe' house—a place where some of us can hide if we're in the neighborhood and get into trouble."

"Are you out of your mind?" Lynn was on her feet now. "Robert, I don't like what's happening either, but we've been arrested once already. Look at him." She indicated her husband. "He's the one who has really suffered. They tortured him! He didn't know anything that could have helped them—but they did it anyway! The only reason they let us go was that our son—*my son*—is an informer. They wanted to stay on *his* good side. We meant nothing to them!"

"That's part of our reasoning. They know that you know nothing, so they won't try here again. It's like lightning—they won't strike the same place twice."

"The only reason they let us go was so we could tell others what happened—how they could be tortured if they don't cooperate fully. If they took us again, we'd be killed!"

Robert looked at her for a long, long moment. When he spoke, his voice broke hoarsely. "Lynn, three days ago they killed Kathleen. My little girls have no mother anymore. If I die, my kids will have nobody. But I've decided that even so, it won't be so bad to have to die myself if that means others . . . thousands, maybe millions of others . . . can be saved. Some fights are worth even terrible personal loss and risk, and *this is one of them!*'' He looked back at her, his dark eyes very serious. "Please, Lynn . . . reconsider."

Lynn slumped back into her seat, her eyes filling as she took in his news. "Kathleen? Oh, Robert, I'm so sorry. Truly sorry. But—" she looked over at her husband protectively, "we can't. We simply *can't.*"

Stanley Bernstein moved for the first time since Maxwell had entered, heading for a chest that stood in the dining room. He was back in a second, carrying a piece of paper, which he handed to his wife.

"What's this?"

"Father left it for us. It's dated the morning they took us . . . he must've figured they would. Read it, Lynn. Aloud, so Robert can hear."

Automatically, Lynn began to read:

"My dear family. It's painful knowing I won't share the days ahead with you. I pray that I am the only one who will be taken today. It hurts to know that I'll not see your faces anymore. Already I am missing you . . . Stanley, my son . . . Lynn, who is as dear to me as the daughter I never had, and Daniel, for whom I worry the most. But I am too old to run away this time. What I must do is to stay instead, to show I have faith in what is right.

You may think that an old man wouldn't be afraid to die, but this old man is very frightened. I keep hoping that I'll find a little of my wife's dignity and strength, but so far I am as frightened as a child who fears the dark. Yet I am determined.

We must fight this darkness that is threatening to engulf us. Each of us must be a ray of hope. We must each do our part, and join with all the others until each ray joins together to become a blinding light, triumphant over the dark. Until that task is accomplished, life here on Earth will have no purpose, no meaning. We cannot live as helpless victims.

More than anything we must always remember which side we're on . . . and be willing to fight for it.

Your mother and I will march beside you . . . holding hands again. We'll sing your song of victory—you'll feel us in your hearts. Our spirits will be—"

Choked by sobs, Lynn stopped, but Stanley quoted the last line from memory. "Our spirits will be with you always . . . and our love."

He looked at his wife. "Don't you see, Lynn? We *have* to help . . . or else we won't have learned a thing."

# Book Two

## Four Months Later . . .

# Chapter 20

The four months following the Visitor raid on the mountain camp were full ones. Mike Donovan continued to meet with Martin, exchanging information and encouragement with the alien officer, who was busy organizing and expanding the fifth column growing amidst the Visitor ranks. Directed by a woman named Jennifer on the New York ship, a quiet cadre of dissenters aided the human resistance movement whenever possible. But their help was limited; Visitor security was at an all-time high since Donovan's theft of the squad vehicle. In spite of his best efforts, Martin had made little headway toward discovering Sean Donovan's whereabouts.

If Martin was unhappy with his progress, Diana and John were pleased with theirs. Development of an improved Visitor head and chest armor rendered Visitor guards and shock troopers nearly immune to most small-arms fire. Even machine guns only knocked down the wearer. Resistance members painfully learned to shoot for vital points, but their lessons cost dearly. The armor, coupled with the Visitors' own naturally thick hides, plus their human-seeming body suits, defeated several resistance raids on plants where Visitors "processed" humans, rounding them up under one pretext or another, gassing them unconscious, then entombing them in the glass canisters Donovan had seen aboard the Mother Ship.

Abandoning the desalinization plants for the moment, the Visitors, now in complete control of human society, began tapping freshwater reservoirs. Soon "conservation" entreaties (supposedly necessary because purification plants were being attacked by terrorists from the scientists' conspiracy) filled the news—water supplies for large cities were growing extremely low.

Diana continued her attempted conversion of world leaders—including the President of the United States and the Secretary of Defense. It might have been simpler to eliminate these leaders altogether, but explanations for their disappearances would have been awkward, particularly with Kristine Walsh requesting interviews with them continually.

Kristine continued her association with the Visitors, but her own doubts as to their good intentions were growing. On one occasion, Corley Walker, a distinguished physician and Nobel laureate whom Kristine had met at Gerald Ford's house, publicly denounced her for serving as the Visitor Press Secretary, telling her that she was no longer a newswoman, but merely the minister of propaganda for a fascist regime. Kristine was stunned and humiliated by the man's open hostility and contempt.

A few weeks later, she was summoned to Diana's office/lab just prior to her regular evening broadcast, to meet a "special guest"—and was introduced, by a smiling Diana, to Corley Walker. A very changed Corley Walker, who shook hands pleasantly and babbled about their bridge game with the Fords when they'd met in Palm Springs—a man with none of his previous hostility. As she smiled, Kristine struggled to hide her shock, frightened that Diana would see her reaction. Questions she'd repressed since her last meeting with Donovan awoke, and this time would not rest. She remembered the things Donovan had told her, and wished she could talk with him—but with Donovan on the Visitors' most-wanted list, such a meeting was too dangerous even to consider.

Donovan himself was extremely busy, recruiting new fighters into the resistance and teaching selected recruits to pilot the Visitor craft. His relationship with Juliet Parrish was still strained—Donovan had never been a joiner, and chafed under the restrictions of his new, underground life. It might not have been so bad if it hadn't been for the dreams . . . At least once a week Mike would dream of Sean—frantic, futile nightmares in which he saw his son die, over and over, while he stood by—helpless to prevent it.

All the resistance fighters felt the strain. Elias had managed to get a job at the hospital, which proved extremely useful in supplying the rebels with laboratory equipment and drugs. In addition, he continued his "dealing"—with one difference. Now his supplies of pot, cocaine, uppers, and downers went to members of Visitor Friends groups, including Daniel Bernstein, who now held a security rating and was the human head of all Visitor Youth activities in the Los Angeles area. As Daniel's "dealer," Elias occasionally garnered snippets of information while providing free samples to the young man and his friends—including several Visitors, who discovered that a number of the drugs gave them a high.

Caleb Taylor took a dim view of his son's dealing, even though he knew that Elias was using the drugs to undermine Visitor discipline and obtain information. It was hard for him to shake his distaste for Elias as a pusher. His son sensed his feelings. Relations between father and son were strained.

The Visitor headquarters just outside the city acquired a cleaning lady. Everyone agreed she dressed like a refugee from a bag lady convention, but did good work. Actually, Ruby Engels found she rather enjoyed her cloak-and-daggerish existence. It was surprising the juicy tidbits of intelligence one could glean from emptying trash cans. Years ago she'd spent several years as an actress in little theatre and off-Broadway productions, and her ability to play different roles convincingly stood her in good stead.

Over the months, the resistance had added a few core members: Cal Robinson, a young biochemist who had, like Juliet, started out in med school; Maggie Blodgett, a young woman who, with her now-deceased husband, had run an air transport company; and Father Andrew, a Catholic priest who proved that he'd learned more than a little about military strategy during the time he found himself embroiled in a guerilla war in South Africa.

In addition, the actual resistance developed a network of contacts who, like Stanley and Lynn Bernstein, furnished them with information and aid, while continuing to live and work as they always had. Fred King always worried that he would be caught. He was an intern at Los Angeles Medical Center, where Elias worked, and had taken several classes with Juliet. Julie, fully conscious of their desperate need for a full-fledged physician, begged him to join them, but King was adamant—he was a doctor, not a fighter. Even his half-hearted assistance was invaluable. It was Fred who told Juliet about the gala celebration planned to coincide with John's highly secret visit to the hospital. The Supreme Commander, it was rumored, was going to announce some kind of medical breakthrough the Visitors intended to bestow on humanity. Extensive media coverage would be part of the presentation ceremony. But Fred didn't know exactly when—or wouldn't tell.

Juliet had been waiting for just this kind of event. The fighters had suffered too many defeats in the past months (with full Visitor-sponsored news coverage of each) to overlook a chance to publicly unmask the Visitors and demonstrate that resistance to the aliens' domination was possible.

Juliet discussed the possibilities with Robert Maxwell, who, with his daughters, now lived in the headquarters. After Kathleen Maxwell's death the family had grown closer, and the four of them had informally adopted young Josh Brooks. Even Robin's tearful announcement of her pregnancy hadn't shaken Maxwell's new-found patience. He'd been shocked at first, but rallied quickly, even accepting Robin's decision not to reveal the identity of the father. Privately, seeing the shadowed look about his daughter's eyes, he agonized that she might have been raped by one of the other prisoners while interned aboard the Visitor ship.

Robin's decision not to reveal that Brian was responsible for her pregnancy stemmed from her own discomfort. Inexperienced as she was, she knew instinctively that there had been something *wrong* about his lovemaking—something inhuman. Her infatuation with the handsome young Visitor had evolved into something akin to hatred. She couldn't forget the way he'd pinned her down, forced her, during those last terrified moments.

She endured her pregnancy uneasily, with a deep-seated fear that she kept to herself. In the beginning, Robert had asked her if she wanted an abortion, but her own belief, sparked by her Catholic upbringing, held that abortion was wrong, sinful, so she'd refused. Now, well into her fifth month, she was frightened enough to wish she'd accepted. The baby seemed to be growing faster than Robin's limited knowledge said it should. Her body felt strange . . . One night she'd stumbled sleepily out to the refrigerator in the headquarters and, without thinking, began eating a handful of raw hamburger. It had tasted wonderful—until she woke up fully and realized what she was doing. Shortly afterward, while washing her face one morning, she'd noticed a small, greenish patch of skin on her neck. It looked like an old bruise.

Terrified, she had tried to scrub it off, but the strange-colored band remained, spreading. Juliet tried to reassure the girl, telling her that odd pigmentations are common during pregnancy. But Robin realized bitterly that the bizarre patch baffled Juliet also—heightening her own concern.

The more frightened Robin grew, the more doggedly she clung to her denial of the true nature of the Visitors. She refused to view Donovan's tape, saying privately to Polly that Mike and Julie had faked it to help the resistance recruitment program. When her sister tried to convince her, Robin slapped the younger girl, then burst into tears, begging her forgiveness. After talking with Polly, Maxwell concluded that Robin's experience aboard the Mother Ship had caused such anxiety that she was intentionally blocking out the truth, not wanting to believe she'd ever been imprisoned by creatures as alien as they now knew the Visitors to be. Nobody in her family raised the subject to her again, and Robin became adroit at not hearing references to the Visitors' reptilian nature dropped by the other fighters.

It was Elias who managed to confirm that John would be speaking at the hospital, though he couldn't discover the actual date. Fred King produced the hospital layout plans, while Ruby Engels began to find out about the security. Steven, the Visitor officer who continued to pay court to Eleanor Dupres, was now in charge of security, and it was *tight*. Special one-time-only passes to the gala event would be issued to those on a preferred list of celebrities and Visitor sympathizers. Eleanor was Honorary Chairwoman of the conference, and would be one of the speakers, along with Doctor Corley Walker. There was talk that the President of the United States might attend, and many governors were on the guest list.

During Donovan's next shadowy rendezvous with Martin, the Visitor officer promised him a supply of uniforms.

Weapons were out of the question, though, Martin said. But he had managed to call up Sean Donovan's name on the computer, discovering that the boy was in Section 34 of the Los Angeles ship. The Visitor officer asked Mike for a picture to aid him in identifying the boy. Donovan promised to get one.

Mike Donovan wanted to go aboard the Mother Ship immediately to search for his son, but realized that to risk capture before the hospital raid was to court disaster for the entire resistance effort—by now he definitely knew too much. For Martin's own protection, he told him nothing of their plans, but he did request two Visitor communications experts to assist the underground. Mike wanted to prevent the Visitor censors from blanking the disrupted presentation ceremony off the air.

As he left Martin to return to resistance headquarters, Mike promised himself—and Sean—that as soon as he could get away after the raid, he'd find him.

Back at headquarters, Donovan found Juliet, Maggie Blodgett, Robert Maxwell, Elias, Brad, and Ruby Engels gathered in front of the television set, watching Kristine Walsh's evening broadcast. Sitting next to Kristine was his mother, Eleanor, fairly oozing charm. New diamonds glittered at her throat and ears, and on one perfectly manicured finger she sported a rock the size of a human incisor. Kristine was saying, "John, the Supreme Commander, has chosen the Los Angeles Medical Center to make an announcement described to me as, and I quote, 'An answer to a question that has baffled your world and that will relieve untold suffering.' Ladies and gentlemen, this could be a pivotal moment in history, and it is characteristic of this extraordinarily modest man to choose this modest forum to reveal what promises to be one of the most important announcements of all times and the answer to a monumental riddle."

"Yeah," Brad drawled. "How to get rid of the Visitors."

Everyone laughed. The screen focused on Eleanor, and Donovan, with a grimace, moved abruptly to click off the set. Everyone looked up. "How did it go?" Robert Maxwell asked.

"One out of two ain't bad. Uniforms, yes, weapons, no. Apparently this security kick they're on includes a careful daily accounting of the number of weapons."

"Damn," Juliet said, then glanced around guiltily to see if

Father Andrew was in earshot—he wasn't. "Ruby, what's the word on the passes?"

"They're not being issued until the last moment. They'll be special ones, difficult to duplicate, if not impossible."

"Can you get hold of one for us?" Juliet asked.

"I don't think so. Cleaning ladies can empty trash and listen to what's going on, but I have no excuse to go into their documents-and-printing section."

"Are they using their materials or ours?" Donovan wanted to know.

"Ours."

"Then they can be duplicated," Donovan said.

"Not easily." Brad frowned, thinking.

"What's easy?" Donovan looked up at him. "This whole movement's one giant can of worms. Brad, you're a cop—"

"*Ex*-cop."

"And, Elias, you're a hood."

Elias grinned wolfishly. "*Ex*-hood."

"Together you should be able to come up with the name of the best counterfeiter around."

"Pascal," said Brad immediately. "Dan Pascal."

Elias grimaced. "If he ain't dead. Lotta underground figures were almost as fast to disappear as the scientists."

"Find out," Donovan said shortly.

Robert Maxwell picked up the binoculars and moved to the window of the rented room. Standing sideways so his body was hidden by the cheap drapes, he scanned the newly installed security wall that surrounded the Los Angeles Medical Center. A gate in the wall was manned by armed shock troopers. As Maxwell watched, a figure emerged from the guard box and examined the identification of a Lincoln that pulled up before the security checkpoint. Maxwell recognized his erstwhile neighbor, Daniel Bernstein. After careful scrutiny, he waved the car through.

"Officious little bastard," Robert mumbled, watching Daniel strut over to the shock troopers, obviously giving them orders.

The door into the room opened and closed, and he turned to see Ruby Engels, dressed in her cleaning lady getup. Wearily she pulled off her bandanna, the frowsy platinum wig coming with it. "We got problems."

"What's up?" asked Mike Donovan, who was sitting on the bed, a notepad in hand. "What kind of problems?"

"There's no way we can get those tickets. And they say they can't be counterfeited."

"Everything can be counterfeited." Donovan stretched lazily. "Some things take more doing than others."

"Is there *any* way you can get hold of one?" Robert asked.

She made a disgusted face under her near-mask of caked and excessive makeup. "Couldn't even get close. And not only that, they have an exact count. If *one* pass turns up missing, they're going to change the whole system and redo it."

Robert sat down heavily on the bed. "You mean we have to steal one, counterfeit it, and put it back, *before* they know it's missing?"

"That's right." She slumped into a chair, putting her feet up on the cheap desk. "Houdini couldn't pull that off."

"But *I* might be able to," Donovan said, sitting up straight, a gleam in his eyes.

"How?" Robert wanted to know.

He grinned unpleasantly. "My dear mother."

Juliet Parrish was pacing up and down in the common room at headquarters, thinking over the plan Mike Donovan had presented to her for counterfeiting one of the special passes. She didn't like it. It was too risky. She'd said so to the ex-newsman, and he'd agreed with her. Then, fixing her with his frank green stare, he had inquired innocently if she had a better idea.

"Shit!" Juliet said, then looked around guiltily—even though Father Andrew had undoubtedly heard worse, she'd been brought up by parents who held that cussing in front of a man of God was a sin tantamount to murder, if not worse. She wondered briefly how her folks were doing—then shook her head, dismissing that particular concern. She couldn't contact them, now that the Visitors controlled the long-distance lines, and in the past few months she'd learned to worry only about things she could affect.

Elias entered the room. "We got a lizard and his human girlfriend on ice. You want him filleted or fricasseed?"

"You captured one? Oh, good!" Julie's face broke into a radiant smile. "Great! Now I can start some of those experiments!"

"If you still got a live one to play with, Doc."

"What do you mean?"

"Couple of our people got themselves a nasty blood lust."

"Oh, God. I'd better put a stop to that!"

"Figured you'd want him still kicking."

Hastily Juliet followed Elias to the laboratory, where Ruby, Robert, Brad, and Caleb were confronting a mournful-faced Visitor who sat huddled in the corner of the lab. A frightened looking blonde woman stood between him and the resistance members, clearly protecting the alien.

"Stop it, Robert!" Ruby was saying as Elias and Juliet entered the room. "You're behaving as if *you* were one of them!"

"He killed my wife," Maxwell said. Juliet had never heard that note in the anthropologist's voice before.

"And my partner," Brad said. He tried to circle around the woman, and Juliet saw the gleam of steel in his hand.

The blonde woman stood her ground. "William didn't kill anyone! He's not a shock trooper—he's just a technician!"

"Yeah?" Brad was openly skeptical. "How do we know that's true?"

"Because I say it is," Caleb Taylor said in his deep, resounding tones. "He worked at the plant where I did. He may be one of them, but he saved my life once. Harmony's right. William's no fighter."

"We need information," Brad said, his eyes shining behind his glasses. "And he's going to give it to us. Aren't you, snake-eyes?"

"Stop it!" Juliet yelled. "This isn't the way!"

"What are you talking about, Julie?" Brad asked. "Here's your lab animal. Do you worry about how mice and guinea pigs feel?"

"As a matter of fact, I do," Juliet said coolly. "And I care about what happens to all of us. We can't let personal tragedies make us treat the Visitors as ruthlessly as some of them have treated us."

Father Andrew poked his head in the door, then, as Juliet beckoned to him, came into the laboratory.

"That's right, Julie," Ruby said. "Don't let them."

"Easy for you to say, Ruby. You haven't lost anyone to them," Maxwell said bleakly.

"Abraham Bernstein and I were friends for seventeen years, Robert," Ruby snapped. "You're calling his loss nothing?"

Father Andrew stepped forward. "Nothing rational can be decided in this kind of atmosphere. I suggest we all calm down."

"Good thinking, Padre," Elias said.

A small van drifted down the street, lights out, toward the Dupres house, which shone like a beacon, nearly every window aglow. Dozens of parked cars lined both sides of the street, and Donovan, Dan Pascal, Elias, Brad, and Juliet could hear the laughter of the partygoers halfway down the block. Brad, who was driving, looked over his shoulder at the others, who sat huddled amidst a forest of cameras, chemical analyzers, microscopes, paper and ink samples, color wheels—in short, a counterfeiter's paradise.

Dan Pascal, a lanky man who looked permanently tired, peered at Elias, Donovan, and Juliet, who were dressed in black commando outfits. "A cop, a crook, and several commandos all cozy in the same place. The world makes no sense anymore."

Brad grunted as he maneuvered the van over the curb into the leafy concealment of a eucalyptus. "You mean an ex-cop, *two* crooks, and commandos."

Elias winced. Pascal indicated Brad. "First he busts me, then he recruits me. How did a nice hood like you get mixed up with a bunch like this?"

"War is hell." Donovan grinned sardonically. "You set, Pascal?"

"Yeah."

Elias put a hand on the counterfeiter's shoulder. "Dan, my man, nothin' less than your best this time, or we're dead. D-E-A-D, as in permanently *de*-ceased."

"Nobody told Picasso how to paint, Taylor," Pascal said. "Get moving."

"Be careful," Juliet whispered.

Elias and Donovan left the van, and the three remaining sat

in silence for long minutes. Finally they heard a soft sound,
then Elias reappeared.

"Did you get it?" Julie cried.

"Yeah. Mike knew right where to look. In a third-floor safe.
But that house is swarmin' with lizards, so we've got to
hurry." Quickly he handed over a rectangular piece of plastic.
"Looks like a damn credit card," Elias commented. "And the
ceremony's in nine days. The date's on it." Pascal took the
card and began working.

"Where's Donovan?" Juliet said nervously.

"He stayed up there, so we wouldn't have to chance
throwing the rope up to the third-floor balcony again. He said
he was gonna lock up the safe again and hide till I come back."

Pascal analyzed the pass under red light, then under a
spectroscope. With agonizing slowness he took a minuscule
piece (too small for the naked eye to discern) off the magnetic
strip and examined it under a high-powered microscope, while
the computer decoded the markings on the strip itself. Elias
checked his watch, his breath coming in a frustrated hiss.
"Picasso, I hate to rush you—"

The counterfeiter turned, pointed a finger at him. No words
were necessary. Elias subsided into the corner.

Now it was Juliet who fidgeted. "The bitch *would* pick
tonight to throw her damn party!"

"Yeah." Elias squirmed again, looking at the third floor.
"Lotta lizards in there . . ."

"What could she feed them with her human guests at the
same table?" Brad asked.

"The human guests," Julie said, eliciting a muffled, nervous
laugh.

"Shhh," Pascal said, and they all quieted once more.

The Kaypro purred once, then beeped, and a computation
appeared on the screen. "Good," Pascal breathed, bending
over a square of plastic. He typed in a command, and, seconds
later, inserted the counterfeit card, with its magnetic strip.
Then he gave another command, and the word "match"
appeared on the screen. "That's it!" he said, handing the
original card to Elias, who was quivering like a racehorse in
the starting gate.

Elias grabbed the card and vanished into the night.

*    *    *

Donovan, upstairs in Eleanor Dupres' sumptuous bedroom, paced back and forth near the drapes, not getting more than a foot or so from them, in case he had to hide. "C'mon," he muttered. "*C'mon!*"

He could hear the sounds of the party downstairs, but he forced himself to ignore the murmur of conversation and the high ripples of laughter. His ears strained for any sound of footsteps on the carpeted steps. He'd already obtained his personal prize—a photograph of Sean now resided in his pocket. Eleanor had so many that he didn't think she'd miss this one. He glanced nervously out the balcony window.

*Dammit, where are you?* He was too tense. *Calm down, asshole. You can't lose it in a clutch like this. You used to be better at this . . .*

*Yeah,* he agreed with himself, *but there's never been this much riding on me . . . If we screw this up, the whole resistance is apt to go down the tubes . . .*

"Hssst—" It was barely audible, but Mike jumped as if he'd been goosed.

Hastily he moved onto the balcony, pulled up the thin rope with the card knotted into it. Waving Elias away, he went back into the room.

He'd opened the safe, stashed the card safely away, and was on his way toward the balcony again when the hall door opened and his mother stepped through.

Her mouth opened, but instead of screaming, she moved with a blurring quickness to her jewelry box, pulling out a small .22 automatic. "Stop right there, Michael."

With an almost palpable effort, Donovan kept his eyes fixed on her face, not allowing himself to look at the spot in the rug that hid the floor safe. "Here's a nice portrait for the family album, Mother," he said. "Allow me to compliment you on your gown. And those diamonds. Steven's gifts?"

"What are you doing here?" she snapped.

"I came to ask you if you knew that the Visitors have kidnapped Sean. He's a prisoner aboard the L.A. Mother Ship. Does that mean anything to you anymore?"

He saw her face flicker at the mention of her grandson. "You're lying."

"I wouldn't lie about something like that. Furthermore, if you don't help me get him out—use your influence with Steven and Diana—he's going to end up on their dinner table one day . . . raw, in pieces."

"What?" The gun wavered slightly, then steadied.

"It's true. The Visitors are *reptiles*, Mother. They want our planet's water, and they want all the living things on it . . . including us. For *food*."

Eleanor laughed. "*Really*, Michael, next you'll ask me to believe you have telepathy or something. That's outrageous . . . science fiction!"

"You—" He glared at her. "Listen! Whether you believe what I've told you or not, the truth is that your grandson and ten thousand other people are already prisoners aboard your friends' ships! Good God—don't try and tell me that you haven't seen what's been going on around this city, and all over the world!"

"Of course I know." Her hazel eyes were cold, contemptuous. "I'm not a fool—I'm a survivor. Otherwise I never would have gotten out of that Louisiana hick town where I started. Never would have made it through your father's alcoholism . . ."

"Did you ever think about *why* he drank? Why Arthur's turning into a lush? He's basically a decent guy . . . weak, but so was Dad. You wouldn't marry a man you couldn't run roughshod over, would you?"

She ignored his last remark. "And because I'm a survivor, I know how to take care of myself. And you'd better too. Steven has told me they'd give a lot for your willing cooperation."

"Yeah?" His mouth curled sardonically. "Sorry, I never cared that much for diamonds."

"Michael!" She looked at him with a trace of appeal on her cold, patrician face. "I know the Visitors aren't saints. But they *are* power. You and I are in unique positions, don't you see that? Why not take advantage of that?"

"Because I can't *survive* at the expense of other people. That's not living, that's battening on blood, like a leech. It's not right!" He paused, then continued in a softer tone, "Y'know . . . there was a woman when I was a kid who taught me what was right, and what was wrong. I wonder what the hell ever became of her?"

Eleanor's eyes hardened. "Empty your pockets."

He did, and something fell out, drifted to the floor. "What's that?"

Donovan held it out to her. "Just a picture of Sean. Silly, I suppose . . . sentimental."

She gestured with the .22. "What were you doing here tonight?"

Mike shrugged. "I needed money. I thought you might have a few bucks in your purse. I hated to do it this way, but the only time I tried to call, you sicced your lizard buddies on me."

"Put your hands back up!"

He did, eyeing her nervously. The way she held the gun made it clear she knew how to use it, and she'd flicked the safety off. "Look at us, Mother. This is crazy!" Slowly, he began to lower his hands.

"Put them back up!"

His hands continued their slow descent. "We said it could never happen here. But it did. One morning we woke up and this country was a fascist state on a planet that's becoming a prison."

Eleanor's chin came up, and her eyes were like bronze. "Those of us who respect law and order are still free. It's the criminals like you who are screaming 'fascist!' "

"No, Mother." He began drifting toward the window by slow inches, barely moving his feet. "You're only as free as the leash they've put you on. You pull too hard, and they'll hang you with it."

He reached the French window and began to move through it. Her voice was like shattering crystal. "Stop. I'll shoot!"

Donovan looked at her, his green eyes level. "Kill your only child? Even you're not that corrupt, Mother. Good-bye. I feel sorry for you."

He vanished onto the balcony. Eleanor's finger tightened on the trigger, but she couldn't quite force herself to shoot him. Instead she lowered the gun, shaking with frustration and anger, thinking she had to cover herself in case someone saw him. With quick, decisive fingers, she ripped at the bodice of her gown, tearing it. She dragged her fingers through her perfectly coiffed hair. Then, taking a deep breath, she screamed and fired two shots into the wall.

# Chapter 21

Juliet Parrish carefully dropped a large spot of green-ish-yellow blood onto a sterile slide. Carefully covering it with a clean top slide, she prepared to fix it in place on the electron microscope platform. She worked doggedly, refusing to give in to her worry. The door to the lab opened; Juliet looked up hopefully, but her face fell when she saw Father Andrew framed in the entrance. "Is he back?"

"Not yet," the priest answered. "Don't worry, Julie. Mike Donovan can take care of himself."

"Elias and Brad wanted to stay and wait for him. I was the one who told them to leave." Juliet bit her lip, fighting tears.

"And quite rightly too. Donovan would strangle you if you'd been stupid enough to risk that counterfeit pass just to wait for him. You did what you had to. You couldn't risk the whole mission."

She rubbed her eyes fiercely. "I can't handle many more of these decisions. They tear me up so I can hardly stand to look at myself in the mirror each morning."

"They get easier."

"I doubt that."

Father Andrew sighed. "In Africa, there was a war going on all around us. A soldier came into the church. I'd hidden a family who had come to me for help. He told me he was looking for suspected guerillas." He shook his head. "Guerillas. An eleven-year-old boy and his twelve-year-old sister, and

231

their mother. He found them there where I'd hidden them, and was going to shoot them." He ran a hand through his hair with a gesture of finality. "I had to decide if I would let him do that."

"You killed him," Juliet said, her eyes intent. It was not a question.

"Right in my own church. Maybe they were guerillas—it's happened before. But I didn't think so, and I had to act on my own judgment. You did the same thing tonight."

They both turned as the door opened again, to reveal a breathless and grinning Mike Donovan. "Hi, folks! Anyone miss me?"

Juliet rushed over and hugged him, hard. Donovan looked momentarily surprised, then his arms tightened around her. Juliet looked up at him. "I'm sorry, Donovan. We didn't want to leave, but—"

"Hey—hey, kid." He smoothed back her tumbled hair. "I'd have kicked your butt if you'd done anything else." Their eyes met for a long second, then Juliet stepped back, laughing a little self-consciously.

"See, Father?" She grinned at Donovan, her blue eyes dancing. "I told you he was too mean to die."

"Just a bad penny, that's me," Mike agreed.

Elias Taylor popped his head in. "Hey, Mike! Your old lady ask you to stay to dinner, man?"

Donovan grinned. "She *insisted*. Such a bore, these social obligations."

They all laughed, except for William the Visitor, sitting behind the plexiglass containment of the sterilization chamber. Donovan glanced over at the Visitor. "So that's what our new arrival looks like. He done any talking?"

"A little. I've been taking samples. You should see this blood!"

"Yeah?" He followed her to the microscope. Juliet motioned to the priest. "Father, can you ask Robert to come in here? He should see this too."

"Sure," he said and left.

Donovan goggled at the greenish-yellow blood sample. "Weird. Of course, I'm sure human blood would look almost as strange to an amateur like me. Elias told me a woman was with him when they picked him up. What happened to her?"

"She's still here. Her name's Harmony Moore, and she ran the concession wagon down at Richland. We couldn't let her leave, now that she knows where we're located."

"Think we can recruit her?"

"She says she's a pacifist, but we may be able to use her in another way. She's been studying nursing in night school."

"What was she doing with him?" Donovan asked.

"I think they were out on a date," Julie said.

"You're kidding!" He glanced at William. "Does she know what they're really like?"

"I don't think so. She—"

"What have we got, Julie?" Robert Maxwell said from the door. His eyes flicked coldly over William.

"A blood sample. Take a look," Julie said, moving aside.

"Hey     " Maxwell breathed, forgetting his antagonism in his fascination. "Look at that! A totally different kind of hemoglobin!"

"Yes," Juliet agreed. "But I've found out a few other surprises. His internal arrangement isn't as different as you might think. The X-rays show a heart, lungs, kidneys—all in about the same places as ours. The shapes were a little different, of course."

Maxwell jerked a thumb at William. "He cooperate with all this?"

"Perfectly," Julie said. "He seems to understand what the resistance is all about—why we're fighting back. When I asked him what he'd been told before coming here—" She grinned. "It was funny. He's got some problems with our language. I asked him if he knew that we were intelligent beings before they came to Earth, and he told me, 'No. They told us that you were all brats.'" She chuckled again at Maxwell's uncomprehending expression. "The woman who was with him, Harmy, said, 'Not *brats*, William. You mean *rats*.'"

Robert's dour expression did not change. Julie tapped his shoulder. "Come on, Bob. William is just what he said he is, a technician. He's not a shock trooper. He didn't kill Kathleen!"

"But he's one of them—that makes him responsible."

"The hell it does," Mike Donovan said roughly. "That's like blaming all the Germans for Dachau, or all the Japanese for Pearl Harbor."

"Or all the Americans for Hiroshima," Juliet said, nodding.

"Remember, if it weren't for Martin, you wouldn't have seen Robin again."

Maxwell sighed. "Maybe you're right. But I still don't like having one of them under the same roof with me."

A week before the raid planned on the Los Angeles Medical Center, Mike Donovan went grocery shopping in a local Safeway. He wore his Visitor uniform, complete with dark glasses, cap, and sidearm. Proclamations spread across the front of the supermarket advertised the fact that the Visitors had upped the individual ration allotment.

He entered the store, hand on the butt of his sidearm, then casually took up the parade-rest stance he'd seen Visitor guards assume. His eyes roved quickly behind the dark glasses, scanning the aisles and shoppers.

Perhaps five minutes had passed when Kristine Walsh, wearing dark glasses, a beat-up sweatshirt, and blue jeans, her hair bundled up in an old red bandanna, entered the store. She glanced quickly around, then headed purposefully for the meat counter.

Donovan caught up to her near the hamburger. "Kris . . ." he said.

She half turned, then recognized him. "You! But I thought Arthur Dupres—"

"Keep your voice down. Look at the meat. Move toward the chickens—the mirrors are angled better there."

He took up his stance beside the butcher's doors, feeling the cold leak onto his neck. Kristine sauntered down the aisle after him, occasionally picking up a tray of meat, examining it, then putting it in her cart. As she approached, he nodded, then, barely moving his lips, said, "That's better. By the way, you used to call me Mike."

"I wondered why your stepfather wanted to talk to me on the q.t. This was a lousy trick to play on me. If they find out I'm talking to you—"

"I wasn't sure you'd come if you knew who it really was."

"I sure as hell wouldn't have! You're at the top of their most-wanted list! They'll kill you on sight!"

"Keep your voice down!"

"What do you want, Mike?"

"They have Sean, my son. I want him back."

"Sean?"

"Yeah, they took the whole damn town of San Pedro."

Kristine was silent for a long moment.

"Maybe they're dead," she said finally.

"Not quite. They're packed away somewhere on *your* ship."

"What are you talking about?"

His eyes met hers in the mirror. "People are packed in cocoons for shipping, in suspended animation . . . just this side of death. But they can be revived."

"Why are they doing this?"

"Food."

Her mouth dropped open, and only his warning hiss kept her from reacting loudly. "No! I don't believe it!"

"Wise up, Kris! You didn't used to be so stupid! Why do you think they increased the daily ration? To fatten us up. They intend to take all the living creatures on this planet for food, except maybe for the fish. Starting with us. Once we're out of the way, the rest of the planet will be a snap. What I told you before . . . what you undoubtedly have seen in our underground bulletins . . . is true. They're reptiles. They eat freshly killed prey. Including us."

He fumbled one of the copies he'd had made of his son's photo out of his pocket, handing it to her. "This is a picture of Sean. Take it!" Then he handed her the alien key. "And this. He's in what they call Section 34." His voice dropped to a lower whisper. "Please."

Her fingers closed on the photo and the key. "I'll do what I can, Mike. But you stay out of sight. I'm not kidding—they'll do anything to get you. If I'm successful, I'll get word to you."

"There's an officer called Martin. Know him?"

"Yes. He's one of Diana's aides."

"That's him. He knows how to reach me. You can trust him."

"All right." Her voice hardened. "I'm doing this for *you*, Mike. I'm no ally of your resistance—I'm too closely watched. I'm in too deep to get out now."

Without another word, she turned and pushed her cart away.

Donovan waited for her to get out of the store and out of the area, then "patrolled" the aisles, gradually inching closer to the exit. He'd just stepped out into the parking lot when a Visitor spoke to him. "Hello, there. New, aren't you? Which section are you from?"

Turning his head slightly, he saw a large black "man" wearing a shock trooper's helmet and chest armor. The Visitor's eyes were wary beneath the shaded plastic of his helmet. Donovan hesitated, then nodded pleasantly, holding up two fingers. The man studied him consideringly. "I see. Well, nice meeting you. I'll say good-bye now, and *you do the same.*"

Donovan wet his lips, looking terribly trapped and frightened, even as he drew and shot the alien. Blue fire and ozone pulsed, and the black trooper dropped with that drawn-out, ululating shriek, fumbling for his sidearm even as he died.

Mike was already running, passing cars inching out of the parking lot, bolting directly across the road without looking. He heard brakes shriek, then the *wham-bam!* of a crash. He reached the woods on the other side of the road and kept running, cursing the damned Visitor boots. *No wonder the Germans lost the war,* he thought. *Bastards couldn't concentrate on anything except how much their feet hurt.*

It took him several hours to reach one of the safe houses in a nearby suburb. There Donovan changed clothes, and the owner drove him to headquarters. When he picked his way down the culvert to the plant, Juliet was there inside the door, pale and furious. "Can I speak to you for a moment, Donovan?"

Wondering angrily why he was doing so, he obediently followed her to one of the sleeping dorms, deserted now in the daytime. Quietly she closed the door. Donovan told himself that he was an adult now, at least ten years older than this young woman; but it did no good. The solid thump of the closing door had taken him straight back to his eighth-grade sojourn in the principal's office.

Juliet stared at him for long moments, her blue eyes sparkling, whether from angry tears or sheer rage, Mike couldn't guess. Finally she spoke, the calmness in her voice belying her expression. "How did you ever get to be such an asshole, Donovan?"

Mike marveled anew at the efficiency of the grapevine. He couldn't keep himself from bristling. "Now, wait a minute, Doc! I had a good reason for doing what I did!"

"Sure you did. You want your son, and you're willing to

cozy up to anyone you think will help you. Even the worst traitor the human race has ever known—dammit, Donovan!"

"I don't think Kris is helping them willingly anymore! And even if she is, she'll help me get Sean. She said so, and I believe her." He looked at her for a long moment. "Julie, he's my *son*. How can I not do everything in my power to get him back safely?"

"Oh, I've no doubt that your motives were totally admirable, Donovan, but any personal motives are also *totally unjustified* when you consider the circumstances we find ourselves in at the moment!"

Juliet turned back to the door, her hand raised, he thought, to open it. Instead she balled her fist and thumped it loudly into the doorframe. "Dammit, Donovan! *How* could you *do* this to us?"

"Kristine's going to try and find Sean. What the hell am I supposed to do, forget I have a son? That he's up there, on that goddamned ship? They could be serving him up for breakfast! I can't totally submerge my personal concerns in the goals of this resistance movement—I'm not built that way!"

"Then maybe you don't belong here with us." Her voice was deadly quiet again. He saw her cheekbones come up beneath her skin as she set her jaw. "You can't ever do anything like this again. You know too much. You risked all of us, Donovan."

"But—"

She raised a hand to stem his argument. "Don't say anything more. Just *think* about what I'm saying. I expect everyone here to do that. Think of *us* before their own comfort or safety. It won't work any other way. You've got to *care*, Mike. You don't care about us."

Donovan had known he was taking an unconscionable risk in contacting Kristine, but hadn't allowed himself to think about it. Juliet's words lanced into his own guilt, releasing it in a torrent of bitter regret. He swallowed painfully, feeling tears well up—and turned away quickly so she wouldn't see them. "That's not true. I care." He bit his lip, running a hand through his hair distractedly.

Juliet looked at him, her blue eyes somber. "Mike, we need you. *I* need you. But if you can't give us your best, you should go—get totally away from here. Before you really hurt us."

Donovan didn't trust his voice to answer her.

She turned back toward the door. Her next words reached him softly. "We're a unit, and we're at war. We can't afford a maverick who is only committed when it suits his own personal goals."

Harmony Moore walked quietly down the corridor toward the storeroom where they had Willie. Behind her she could hear Maggie's footsteps and knew the other woman was following her. Harmy kept her hands out and away from her body. She'd seen the efficient way Maggie handled her rifle, and she was never without it.

The man named Brad was standing guard in front of the storeroom, also armed. He looked up suspiciously. "Yeah?"

Harmy faced him, frightened but determined. "Have they done anything to Willie?"

"Just some blood tests." He glared at her. "*Humane* ones. More than the sucker deserves."

"You're wrong about him. He'd never hurt anybody. He's nice," Harmy said angrily.

"Sure," said Brad sarcastically. "Nice, if you like reptiles. You must have some weird tastes, lady."

"That's not true, either! I don't believe those stories!"

"You've never seen the tape Donovan shot up there on the Mother Ship?"

"I've seen it. Kristine Walsh did a whole special report. The terrorists did it with makeup—like they do in horror movies."

He laughed shortly. "Think so? C'mere!" He grabbed Harmy's wrist with one hand, then motioned to Maggie to unlock the storeroom door. "Keep him covered, Mag."

William sat in the corner, on the floor. His face was expressionless, but Harmy could sense his fear as he saw Brad. Then his gaze fixed on Harmy, and his whole demeanor changed to glad recognition. "Harmony! They have not hurted you?"

She smiled at him reassuringly. Brad jerked her over to stand beside him. "I hope you've got a strong stomach, lady," he said, then reached down to grab Willie's hand. The Visitor tried to pull it away, but stopped as Maggie Blodgett cocked her rifle ostentatiously in the doorway. Using his fingernails, Brad began to dig viciously at William's hand.

"Stop it!" Harmy cried. "What are you doing?"

She stared in horror as the skin of her friend's hand peeled back to reveal greenish scales, then five too-slender, overly jointed fingers, tipped with short, stubby claws. "Look!" Bard snarled, gripping William's wrist despite his attempt to draw away. "Now ask him if those movies are faked! Ask him why they've come here!"

Harmy put out a finger as though to touch that scaled skin, but instead backed away, shivering. "Is it true?" she asked, looking not at Brad but at Willie.

William hung his head, covering his ripped fingers with his other hand. Brad shook his wrist. "The lady asked you a question!"

"It's true," Willie said. "I'm sorry, Harmony."

Harmy backed to the door, then, blindly, turned and stumbled away.

# Chapter 22

Kristine Walsh stared wide-eyed at the sleeping/dead face of Sean Donovan. The boy floated, naked, inside the glass cocoon, lapped in translucent, gelatinous fluid. He was surrounded by other children—this entire row of canisters contained children. Enough to populate a school, at least. Kristine swallowed, digging her fingers into her palms, wondering if she'd faint.

Hastily she sat down on the metal-grid flooring, burying her head between her knees until the buzzing in her ears died, and she could look at the world again without dizziness. *What can I do?* she wondered. *I'm only one person in the face of this hideousness—is there anything I can do, realistically?* She thought that there probably wasn't—and that was the worst of all. *To live with this horror, and be helpless . . .*

Clutching the key Mike Donovan had given her, she took careful note of the row and location of his son's canister, then headed back. As she walked down the shadowy corridor of Section 34, she decided that it would be best to wait until after the hospital broadcast to contact Martin and release Donovan's son. Diana and Steven had been even more security-conscious than usual in anticipation of the gala presentation of John's "gift." Her mouth twisted in a bitter smile, thinking how impressed she'd been with John, how she'd allowed herself to be dazzled by the Supreme Commander's charm . . .

*Even if I can get Sean out,* she thought desperately, *what about all the others?* Tears flooded her eyes as she stepped cautiously through the hatch, leaning against it for a moment to collect herself, assume the professional demeanor that had become her protective coloration.

Hearing footsteps, she moved away from the hatch, slipping the key into her pocket. Steven rounded the corner with two Visitor guards. He looked at her, his suspicion plain.

"What are you doing here, Kristine?"

She smiled ingenuously at him. "I took a wrong turn. I swear, if I stay on this ship five years instead of five months, I'll never learn my way around."

He looked at her coldly. "This is a restricted area, as you know. We'll have to discuss this incident with Diana."

He beckoned to the guards and they closed in on either side, escorting her to Diana's lab/office. Kristine waited alone, watching Diana and Steven through the transparent partition, trying to read their expressions as they talked. Finally Diana came in. The animals in the cages squeaked and chittered, then froze, as the Visitor walked by. Kristine felt pretty much the same way as Diana stopped before her, her expression forbidding.

"What were you doing in a restricted area, Kristine?"

"I took a wrong turn. I was on my way to the landing bay to get some of my equipment out of my personal shuttle, and— I swear, Diana, I think you people built these ships as mazes, I really do!" She managed a laugh.

Steven entered the room, walking over to Kristine, then, in a darting motion that was much faster than human, his fingers pulled the key from Kristine's pocket. "Interesting," he commented. "I wonder, did you use it? Were you looking for someone in Section 34? A relative, perhaps?"

"I don't know what you're talking about," Kristine said firmly. "I found that instrument in the door and was going to turn it in to security."

Diana and Steven exchanged glances. Diana sighed. "Kristine, I have too much respect for you to mince words. You have a choice to make now. We want you working with us. You're of enormous value to both our peoples. *I* need you."

"I'm honored, I suppose," Kristine said carefully. "What is this choice you're talking about?"

"You see," Steven said, "we want very much for you to

continue working with us, as our spokesperson. You can either do that willingly, or . . ." he trailed off, smiling, and suddenly Kristine had no trouble at all visualizing him as a reptile.

She took a deep breath. "You have ways of seeing that I . . . cooperate, I suppose. Like Corley Walker."

Diana nodded. "Exactly. Unfortunately, the conversion process, which worked so well on Mr. Walker, is unpredictable. It can be extremely dangerous to the subject. I don't want to expose you to those . . . risks." She reached over to put a hand on Kristine's shoulder, looking directly into her eyes. "I'd hate to lose you, Kristine. I like you for yourself, and I value you for the service you do us. I hope you value yourself as much as I do. Please, think about it."

With a final look, she turned and left, Steven behind her. Kristine sat silently in the room, her only company the caged animals.

Juliet Parrish pricked carefully at William's scaled back with a sterile needle. "Only a few more in this series," she said, referring to the allergy tests. "I know it must hurt when I do this—it's hard to avoid, because your skin is so much tougher than ours."

"I understand," Willie said, his alien voice muffled as well as reverberating. He lay on his stomach on the examining table, a large section of his back exposed. He'd shown Juliet how the plastic substance could be peeled back, then repaired. Both hands were once more covered with the artificial skin. He hadn't seen Harmony Moore since Brad's revelation of the night before—but every time he closed his eyes he relived that moment when she'd looked at him with such horror in her eyes.

Juliet looked over at Sancho Gomez, who was serving as her assistant that day. "Martin says they've been immunized against all known Earth diseases. And so far, Willie doesn't seem to exhibit any allergic reactions at all."

"Willie," she said, "during your time on Earth, have *any* substances made you feel ill, or uncomfortable? Exhaust fumes from cars? Vegetables? Anything?"

"No," William said quietly. "The only thing that has made

me uncomfortable is realizing that the human run is as intelligent as we are—"

"The human *race*, Willie," Juliet interrupted, smiling.

"Yes, thank you," he continued, "And that I like some humans better than I like some of my own people. I feel bad about what is happening. You must do what you have to do to save yourselves. Just as we must."

Juliet worked quietly, considering. "But surely there must be some other way to save yourselves than by destroying the life on this planet."

"I don't know," William said miserably. "Before we came I never thought you would be so much like us. Except for the way you look."

"But now that you know, doesn't it make a difference?"

"Yes. To me it does. I cannot speak for all the others. Our planet's life depends on us, on the success of our mission. Or that is what the Leader tells everyone. But now I feel we should try and find another way."

The half-open door swung inward and Juliet looked up. Harmony Moore, who had evidently been standing outside and listening, moved out of the way to let Robin Maxwell enter. The girl carried a first-aid kit in her hands. "Julie, Polly has a splinter. Could you help me with—"

Her words broke off in a gasp as she took in William's exposed back, the greenish-patterned scales shining in the overhead light. Her eyes bulged, and her hand flew to the patch on her throat. The first-aid kit crashed to the floor, its contents scattering. Robin staggered backward, gasping.

"Robin! What—" Juliet started toward the girl just as she turned and bolted from the room. From the corridor they heard the screaming begin.

"Sancho! Stay with Willie!" Juliet snapped, running after Robin.

When she reached the shrieking girl, the corridor was filled with people—Robert Maxwell, Mike Donovan, Caleb and Elias, Ruby, Cal, and Robin's sisters. Julie grabbed Robin's hands as they tore at her throat, raking hysterically at the strange marking. "Robin! What is it? Answer me!"

She thought for a moment that she'd have to slap the frantic girl, but suddenly Robin's shrieks turned into words. "No! No! I can't have it! I want an abortion!"

Robert Maxwell tried to take his daughter in his arms, but she pushed him away, panting and wild-eyed. "You've *got* to do it, Julie! Right now! I've got to have an abortion!"

Juliet forced herself to calmness. "It's okay, Robin. Let's talk about it."

"But, Binna," Robert Maxwell was puzzled, "you said you didn't want an abortion. I asked you months ago, when it would have been safe—"

"I want one *now*!"

"The important thing is to calm down, Robin," Juliet said.

"Not until you get rid of . . . *it*!" Robin sobbed. "You've got to, Julie. You've got to!" She raised her eyes, still wild and swollen now with tears. "It's one of *them*—a reptile!"

The crowd froze. Finally Robert reached out, pulling the sobbing girl into his arms. Everyone looked at one another blankly.

"Robin," Maxwell said, "what are you trying to say?"

"The father is one of *them*!" Robin sniffled, and someone handed her a tissue.

"You mean a Visitor?" Juliet said. "Robin, that's impossible, honey. Maybe you were tricked into—"

Polly stepped closer, glaring at her older sister. "It was *Brian*, wasn't it?"

"Yes!" Robin shrieked.

"I don't believe it," Elias said blankly. "Julie, I don't have much schooling, but I remember in biology class they told us that two different species can't interbreed. Even with horses and donkeys, close as they are, the offspring are sterile. Now she wants me to believe that a *human* and a lizard—a reptile that didn't even evolve on *this* planet—can make a baby? That's gotta be a boatload of fertilizer!"

"Quiet, Elias," Juliet said. "We don't know what happened to Robin up on the ship. She could've been drugged, knocked out, almost anything—"

"No!" Robin shook her head wildly. "I'm *not* imagining this or making it up! It was Brian—he was the only one I ever slept with. While I was locked up, he said he'd get me free . . . I thought I *loved* him! Oh, God!" She pulled at her dark hair frenziedly, as though only the pain could keep her from flying apart in the face of her horror. "How could I have been so stupid? It's *his* baby, and I want an abortion *now*!"

Juliet shushed her, holding the sobbing girl close. "I think we'd better discuss this in more depth . . . just Robin, her father, Cal, and me. We'll talk later about what's to be done. Okay, everybody?"

A mutter of agreement filled the air, and slowly the group dissipated. Juliet nodded to Cal, and the three adults and Robin went quietly into the laboratory. Willie sat behind the plexiglass door again, regarding them sadly. Juliet began, "Now, Robin, I think you'd better tell us about what happened to you up on the Mother Ship. Be as specific as you can. Remember, it's not only your life we're dealing with here."

"Okay, Julie." Robin looked up, her blue-green eyes awash, then haltingly began to tell of her imprisonment. When she described the medical examination she'd been given, Juliet and Cal made her recount every detail.

"It could be anything," Julie mused. "But the few others who've managed to get off the Mother Ship were never put through anything like that. This sounds like one of Diana's experiments. Go on, Robin."

Her eyes on the floor, Robin told the rest of her story in halting phrases. Robert Maxwell was breathing hard by the time she finished, his hands clenching and unclenching.

"Well," said Juliet, after she'd sent Robin back to her room to wash her face and brush her hair, "it certainly seems as though the intercourse actually took place."

"The bastard raped her," Robert said. "When I think of my little girl treated like that—"

"Stop it, Robert," Cal said, not unkindly. "That kind of talk won't get us anywhere, and it's certainly not going to help Robin."

"But even if intercourse took place, how does that explain a conception?" Juliet shook her head. "Elias is correct—by rights there can be no interspecial conception!"

"You're forgetting that the Visitors are more advanced scientifically than we are," Cal pointed out. "And even we've made some strides in that direction. Did you ever hear of the sunbean plant?"

Slowly remembering, Juliet nodded. Cal explained for Maxwell's benefit. "Cross-species genetic combination has been done since 1981. They call it gene splicing. Geneticists from the USDA and the University of Wisconsin succeeded in moving genetic material from a sunflower plant into a bean plant—or vice versa, I don't remember at the moment. Anyway, it created a new species that was a combination of both. They used a bacterium as the vehicle to transport the genetic material. If this *was* one of Diana's experiments, she could have exposed Brian to radiation, or used chemicals, or surgery. Or maybe a combination of more than one technique, or possibly they've developed entirely new techniques we haven't even imagined. It's not impossible that Robin is carrying a child fathered by Brian." He sighed. "Unlikely, but not impossible."

William tapped on the plexiglass for attention. The three scientists looked over at him, startled, then Juliet got up to unlock the door.

"What is it, William?"

"I must tell you," Willie looked down at the floor, then back up at Juliet. "Among the females of my species, the sign of carrying young is that the skin around the throat changes color. This band is visible very soon after conception, and grows around the neck as the pregnancy advances. I noticed it on Robin."

Very quietly, Juliet thanked him. The three scientists sat in silence until Robin came back into the room. The girl had regained some of her poise. "Julie? Can we do the abortion today?"

Juliet shrugged. "I don't know, Robin. We'll have to do some tests." Taking Robin by the arm, she headed for the corridor. "I'll have to talk to Fred, see if he can get a room at the hospital . . ."

The other resistance members, hearing footsteps, came back out into the corridor. Juliet hesitated. "Robin, I can't lie to you. This could well be dangerous. There's so much we don't know. There's never been a pregnancy like this before."

"I don't care," Robin said quietly, but her voice was hard. "I'd rather die than have this . . . *thing*."

"Abortion is murder, Robin!" said Father Andrew pleadingly.

Elias glared at the priest. "Not in this case. How would you like to give birth to a lizard, Padre?"

"We don't know that it'll be reptilian," Caleb said. "We have no idea what it'll be, right, Julie?"

Juliet shrugged and nodded wearily.

"Which is why I'm against abortion," Father Andrew said. "This child, if it lives, could be a bridge between the two races."

"The world is full of monsters," Brad said, averting his eyes from Robin. "Why create a new breed?"

"They're not all monsters," Sancho said. "They're intelligent creatures. One of them even saved my life."

Robert Maxwell put a protective arm around his daughter. "Look, this discussion is irrelevant. It's nobody's business. Robin's *my* daughter—not the subject of a lab experiment!"

Father Andrew said gently, looking at Robin, "This is the first mating between our species and a race from another world. I think it's too important a decision to leave to a seventeen-year-old—or her distraught father."

"Nobody's going to experiment on my daughter, Father!"

"Stop it!" Robin shouted. "This is hard enough without all this—this—" She struggled to control her sobs.

"Yes, stop it," Mike Donovan said, speaking for the first time. "We've heard these arguments before, about life being so precious that nothing should interfere with it. It's an old argument on an old issue. But this is *different*."

"The principle is the same," the priest said.

"No, it's not. Robin may give birth to a completely new species. You're dealing with more than a curiosity here—you're dealing with a potential threat."

"The scientific and moral implications of this pregnancy are inescapable! This is a unique—"

"So are the dangers," Donovan interrupted the priest coldly. "It's a big responsibility. It's Robin's body. It should be her decision."

Robin looked gratefully at the ex-newsman, then, after long seconds of silence, turned to her father. "I want it gone. I want the abortion."

Elias Taylor, dressed in a hospital maintenance uniform, peered cautiously out the door of the Proctology Section, his sidearm concealed behind his body. He sighed with relief and turned back to Brad as the sound of footsteps receded. "Just a nurse," he whispered, closing the door. Hastily the two men finished taping the cracks so no betraying chinks of light would show. They'd barely finished when more footsteps resounded, causing them to stiffen once more, weapons ready.

These footsteps, like the others, continued on down the corridor. Brad swiped at the thin sheen of sweat on his forehead. "I can't take much more of this," he said, slumping into a seat. "This is crazy! What if someone comes in here?"

Elias grinned. "Oh, I think we're pretty safe. It's three A.M.—whoever heard of a hemorrhoid emergency at this hour?"

Brad looked disgusted at his companion's wit. They sat in silence for long moments, then Brad turned to look at the inner door of the small room. "I wonder what's happening in there?"

"Dunno," Elias answered helpfully. "But I'll tell you one thing. I wouldn't be in that girl's shoes for *anything*. Imagine havin' one of those snakes *inside* you . . ." He sat down, cradling his gun, his eyes on the door leading to the operating room.

As it happened, Robin wasn't wearing shoes at the moment. She was wearing only a hospital gown, and lying flat on her back, her legs up in stirrups. They'd rigged a sheet to hang below her chest, obscuring her view of the operating area. Juliet approached with a hypodermic needle. "Just a blood test, Robin. Won't hurt a bit."

Robin stared stonily at the ceiling, holding her father's hand fiercely. "I don't care how much it hurts, Julie, just as long as it's over."

Nodding, Juliet wrapped a piece of elastic around the girl's bicep and stroked her inner forearm. A vein obligingly popped up, and Julie carefully inserted the needle. Orange-colored blood rushed into the syringe. Julie looked quickly at Robin and her father to see if they'd noticed the strange color of the blood, but both were looking away. Quickly, Julie withdrew the needle and swabbed off the puncture mark.

She carried the syringe quickly into the adjoining lab, where Fred King and Cal waited. "Look at this," she said, keeping her voice down. "I nearly dropped the syringe. Have you ever seen anything like it before?"

They examined the sample under the microscope, then Fred looked up. "This sample has some of the same characteristics as the alien sample you showed me—waste products from the fetus must be causing this."

Leaving Cal to make further tests in the lab, Fred and Juliet came back into the operating room. "Robin, have you ever had a pelvic examination?" Fred asked gently.

"Once," admitted Robin. "It was kinda embarrassing, but it didn't hurt."

"Well, I'm going to do one now, with Julie to help me. Also some palpations of your tummy. Don't worry, it's not going to hurt."

"Okay."

The young doctor worked in silence for a little while, giving the girl a brief pelvic examination, then spending a much longer time touching and palpating her belly. "How far along did you say she is?" he asked Juliet, not looking up.

"She doesn't remember the exact date of her last period, but she's between five and five and a half months along," Julie answered.

"Feel this," he commanded, indicating a spot on the girl's abdomen. "I've got a head here, just where it should be—but the uterus is *large* for the end of the second trimester. For a moment it seemed like an awful lot of movement in there too. Feel anything?"

"No," Juliet said, concentrating. "Have you located a heartbeat?"

"Yeah, I've got one—but it sounds kind of blurred, and a bit slow." He sighed. "I don't know. I wish I had more experience at this. I've only served one tour in obstetrics—I'm due for the next in the fall."

"What do you think we ought to do?"

"I'd recommend taking a look-see before initiating the abortion. So we'll have a better idea of what's in there."

"A laparoscopy?"

"Yeah. I'll tell Cal to get the instruments set up."

"Okay. I'll talk to Robin and her father."

Juliet stepped around the sheet to where Robin lay. "Honey, we want to make a small incision in your abdomen and take a look at how things are situated inside you. It won't hurt—you won't even have to be knocked out. I'm going to give you fifty milligrams of Demerol before we begin, and I'd like to try using acupuncture as an analgesic. I studied the technique in

China, and it's amazing—you won't feel any pain, and we won't have to cope with getting a groggy patient out of here."

"Aren't you just going to do a regular abortion?" Robin asked.

"You have to remember, Robin, that you're at least twenty weeks pregnant, maybe as many as twenty-four. We can't do any of the simpler kinds of abortions, such as the D&E or D&C. Looking inside you will help us decide whether to use one of the induction methods, or do a hysterotomy—which is kind of like a mini-caesarean—it's *not* the same thing as a hysterectomy."

Robin nodded. "I understand, Julie. I know you'll do the best thing. I . . . I want you to know I understand the risk you're taking, for me. Thanks."

"Of course we want to help, honey." She left them for a moment, then came back with a hypodermic. "Here's the Demerol."

A few minutes later, when the drug had had time to take effect, she came back with several slender needles. "This won't hurt, Robin. You'll feel a little pressure, but that should be all. It won't bleed, or cause a scar."

"Okay, Julie," Robin said, her eyes closed. The Demerol had made her sleepy.

Minutes later Robin lay quietly as Juliet checked the positioning of the needles in each forearm. Then Julie carefully inserted two more needles into the teenager's ears, then another near her collarbone. "She's a good subject for this. In about fifteen minutes we can begin."

By the time Cal had the results of several blood tests, Juliet had checked Robin's reactions, finding them satisfactory. At her nod, Fred carefully made a small incision in Robin's abdomen. "Easy . . . okay, Julie, sponge, I'm going to look first, then you can go ahead. Okay?"

"You're the doctor," Juliet said wryly.

A few minutes later, Juliet slipped on the head apparatus that allowed her to see the images the tiny camera was picking up inside their patient. "I can see what you mean, Fred," she said quietly. "Strands of wispy fibers threaded throughout the abdominal cavity." Cautiously, she moved the tiny camera of the laparoscope. "I can see them . . ." Suddenly she looked up at him in concern. "My God, Fred, they're growing right through the uterine wall! Looks like they're tapping into the liver and the bladder!''

Fred nodded soberly. "That's what I thought I saw. This is *weird*." He kept his voice low, so neither Robert nor Robin could hear. "Let me try and get a look at the fetus."

Juliet assisted as he peered into the headpiece, moving the tiny laparoscope. "Can you see it?" she asked.

"Sort of . . ." he mumbled. "Never seen anything like this before, either. The sac is opaque. Gelatinous. All the tiny fibers seem to be running out of the sac, threading through the abdominal cavity. Like hundreds of tiny umbilical cords. I'm going to try cutting one."

He shifted his weight, staring fixedly into the projection before his eyes, as he extended a tiny filament of cutting surface into the incision. Suddenly Robert's voice reached them, sounding panicky, "Julie! What's going on? She's lost consciousness! Her temperature's dropped four degrees and her heart rate's up to one-thirty!"

Carefully Fred retracted the tiny probe. Robert sounded relieved. "That's better. She's stabilizing."

Fred slipped out of the apparatus, his soft brown eyes meeting Julie's over the green of his operating-room mask. "Keep me posted on the slightest change, Robert," he directed, then slowly began to probe again with the minuscule scalpel.

"Slipping again," came Robert's tense whisper almost immediately.

Fred sighed. "That's it, Julie. It'll kill her before it lets us get to it."

Her own eyes over the green mask were anxious as she remembered Robin's hysterical pleas for the abortion. "How about the salting-out process? If we introduce the saline solution maybe it would kill the fetus before—"

"You want to risk that?" He shook his head. "We don't know enough about the Visitors' metabolism. One of *their* babies might think a saline bath was the best thing since sliced bread. Face it, Julie, we're dealing with something here that's beyond our know-how. Maybe Diana could figure out how to abort this thing—*we* can't."

Juliet nodded, suddenly feeling the exhaustion hit her—her

feet felt as flat as her spirits. Leaving Fred to close the incision, she walked over to Robert, beckoning him aside. Shaking her head, she indicated the bulge beneath the sterile drapes. "We can't do it, Robert. I'm sorry. The fetus has linked into her vital organs, and if we try to take it out, she'll die. We're going to have to let this thing run its course—whatever that turns out to be."

Late as it was, Juliet found Mike Donovan waiting up for them in the common room when they came back from the hospital. Robert took Robin off to get her settled in bed, with a tranquilizer Fred had prescribed, and Elias and Brad relieved Maggie on security patrol. Cal, giving a huge yawn, headed for the dorm. Juliet hesitated in the doorway, leaning against the jamb, so tired she thought she might flow down it like honey and lie in a puddle on the floor. Mike looked at her exhausted face. "Not good, eh?"

Wearily Julie shook her head. "No go. The fetus has tapped into Robin's vital organs. It most emphatically doesn't want to be evicted."

"That's too bad," Donovan said. "That poor kid."

"Yeah," Julie said. All she could feel was numb. She turned away, toward her tiny cot down the hall, but Donovan was beside her before she'd taken more than a few steps.

"I'm heading to the kitchen for a nightcap. I'll walk you to your room."

She didn't look up. "I think you'd better excuse me, Donovan."

"Pretty bad, huh? Want to talk about it?"

She knew Donovan was referring to her own mental and emotional state, rather than Robin's operation. Juliet heard her own voice, as though someone else were talking—she seemed to be floating somewhere. "I'm sick and tired of it, Donovan. Tired of trying to be some kind of guerilla leader. Of trying to hold everybody together. Of passing myself off as a doctor, because there's nobody else most of the time. Dear God, it's all such a joke! I just can't handle it anymore . . . Let somebody else do it for a while."

He looked sideways at her, thoughtfully, then spoke quietly. "You're pretty much it, Doc. There ain't anybody else. You're doing it, because you're the only one who *can* do it. I know

I couldn't do what you're doing—plan this raid, organize this bunch, assign everyone the tasks he or she can best handle . . ."

Juliet was dimly surprised to hear Donovan, usually so brash and self-assured, admit that he couldn't do something. But her mind was still occupied with Robin's plight. "That girl could die because I made the wrong decision tonight. Because I don't know enough."

"Know everything, you mean?"

"Yes!" She put her hands to her face, ashamed to be crumbling in front of Donovan, of all people, but unable to stop herself. She was shaking with exhaustion.

His arm was warm and hard as he put it around her shoulders, supporting her as she stumbled. He gave her a little shake. "*Nobody* expects you to know everything—except *you*. You're too damn hard on yourself, Doc. Ease up."

Juliet laughed a little shakily. "I guess that *is* pretty arrogant, huh?"

He grinned wryly. "I wouldn't know. I'm too busy being self-centered to worry about your arrogance. Remember?"

She looked at him, wondering if he was laughing at her, and realized suddenly that he wasn't. He was coming as close to apologizing for his escapade the other day as he could. She smiled back, nodding, and together they continued down the hall.

When Julie reached her door, she looked up at him. "Thanks, Donovan."

He nodded. "G'night, Doc."

Juliet stumbled inside, flopped onto her cot, her hip stabbing her for the first time in weeks. She thought foggily that she ought to take off her shoes and turn out the light, then she was asleep.

On his way back from the kitchen with a beer, Donovan saw her light burning through the partly open door and tapped softly on it, to see if Julie were still awake. When there was no response, he peered inside.

He smiled, a much different expression than his usual ironic grin, staring at the small blonde woman sound asleep on the cot. Setting down his Coors, he tiptoed into the tiny room. Moving quietly and efficiently, he took off Juliet's shoes, then covered her with a blanket. As he moved to turn out the light still burning over her desk, he noticed the calendar hanging over it. Big blue X's marked off the days to go until the hospital raid, which was circled in red.

*Only three days left,* he thought. *Then the fun* really *begins* . . .

# Chapter 23

The limousine, driven by Cal Robinson, deftly threaded its way through the downtown traffic toward the Medical Center. Juliet Parrish and Robert Maxwell sat in the back, going over the final plans for the raid.

"You're sure Martin understands that he and Lorraine are supposed to patch in the broadcast from the Mother Ship when they try and cut it off at this end?" Maxwell asked nervously, tugging at his tie.

"I'm sure," Juliet said, leaning forward to adjust his black bow tie one more time. "Now leave that thing alone. It's perfect now, so don't touch it."

"Haven't worn a tux in *years*," Robert grumbled. "Now I remember why, too. Damned monkey suits." He smoothed the material across his shoulders, then checked the gun resting in an underarm holster, making sure he could get to it when necessary. "God, I feel silly," he mumbled. "What the hell is a forty-three-year-old professor doing making like James Bond?"

"I think you look very distinguished, Robert," Juliet said, smiling at him. "Do I look okay?"

"You look great," he said huskily, stung suddenly by the remembrance of the last time a woman had asked him that question.

"Thanks," she said nervously. "And thanks for having Lynn find me an evening wrap. I totally forgot about needing one."

"That's all right," he said, looking out the window as the limo rolled majestically through the night. He didn't tell her the shawl from Pakistan had been Kathy's—there was no need to remind Julie of his own loss. "You look good in that color."

"It's my favorite," she admitted. "Thank God, Maggie was able to help me with this dress. I was always better at sewing up people than clothes. The design is really clever."

Juliet's gown was a shimmering red with a hint of gold thread running through the fabric. The low, blouson top displayed her lovely shoulders, and the luxuriant draping of the bodice concealed the gun, held under her arm with surgical tape. Strapped to the inside of her lower thigh was another gun. Robert smiled at her. "You look more like a model than a walking arsenal."

She grinned ruefully. "This whole thing is so crazy. Maggie and I designed this dress so that when I need to, I can loop the skirt up and run in it. Cached among our weapons are my Adidas, if I make it to the rendezvous point. I had a whole list of things I checked over today—while I was sitting under the hair dryer! The whole time Maggie was combing me out and putting the final touches on my coiffure, we discussed our plans for turning the Visitors' security system against them."

"Okay, you beautiful people," Cal said from the front seat, "we're almost there. Good luck."

"Thanks, Cal," Juliet said, drawing her shawl around her shoulders and clutching her evening bag, which contained nothing more sinister than handkerchiefs and perfume.

As the car pulled up before the hospital security entrance, Cal, dressed in a very proper chauffeur's uniform, raced around to open the door for Juliet and Robert. They stood on the sidewalk, their special—counterfeit—passes in hand. In the crowd ahead of them, Maxwell recognized Kristine Walsh, interviewing many of the guests waiting their turn to go through the security check.

Even as they watched, the special machine designed to screen each pass lit up with a red "reject," and a siren sounded. Instantly, Steven and several shock troopers converged on a hapless young couple and bore them away. The lighthearted aura of the event darkened a bit. Robert took a deep breath. "They're not fooling around, are they? This could get nasty."

Juliet held his arm, her smile unwavering. "It'll get nastier if these passes don't work." She watched Kristine Walsh and her television crew narrowly. "Avoid the camera, Robert. She's looking for someone to interview about that incident."

As they waited in the crowd, they could make out, farther back along the lines, Elias in evening clothes, then behind him, in Visitor uniforms, Maggie and Caleb. Farther back in the crowd was Brad, also dressed as a Visitor. Maxwell saw a flash of white on black and recognized Father Andrew in his clerical collar, and with him Ruby, who wore an evening dress and ropes of pearls. She was sitting in a wheelchair, a heavy shawl across her lap. The crowd parted respectfully to allow the priest and the handicapped woman through.

Juliet stepped up to the machine, her pass in her hand. With fingers that only determination kept steady, she pushed the piece of plastic into the slot. After a second that seemed like forever, the machine beeped quietly, and lighted up, in green, the word "pass." Juliet walked on, smiling genuinely this time.

Once inside the huge lobby of the hospital, Robert and Juliet spent several minutes just mingling with the other guests, to allow all the resistance fighters time to reach their assigned positions. High above the glittering crowd milling around with canapes and drinks, a podium was set up, thrusting out into the room with typical Visitor arrogance. Maxwell spotted Arthur and Eleanor Dupres, and made sure he and Juliet stayed far out of their sight.

Juliet touched his arm, indicating an area before the podium that had been roped off with heavy velvet. "That's where he's bound to come out. He must be backstage, waiting for the big moment."

Maxwell nodded, looking longingly over at the bar. "Are you sure we don't have time for even *one* drink?"

Juliet gave him a mock-disgusted look. "You're an incurable lush, Robert. One little commando raid, with a whopping twelve percent chance of success, and you need liquid courage."

Maxwell grinned at her. "Even 007 gets to drink on the job." He sobered after a moment, checking his watch. "They should all be inside by now. When are they going to start this shindig?"

"It's fashionable to be late in Visitor circles too, I guess."

The minutes dragged by as Robert and Juliet smiled and nodded, trying not to let the tension they felt show on their faces. Across the room they could see Father Andrew and Ruby, both holding glasses. "Club soda, I hope," Julie whispered.

Finally Kristine Walsh appeared with the camera crew focusing on her. They realized the presentation was about to begin. Behind the draperies Maxwell saw a flash of red, then recognized Diana's dark hair. A fanfare blared without warning, making both Robert and Juliet jump.

The dark curtains swirled, and then the Supreme Commander, in a glare of flashbulbs, emerged, smiling and waving. Applause thundered through the lobby. Maxwell, relieved to have something to do, clapped till his hands stung.

John mounted the steps to the podium, then stood waiting for silence. As the crowd milled, quieting, Robert took Julie's arm, and they joined the press of people moving closer. By judicious use of elbows and apologies, they ended up just a few feet from the velvet rope, directly opposite the steps to the podium.

John's warm, reverberating tones filled the lobby. "Good evening to all of you. We Visitors are particularly proud of tonight's ceremony, since it gives us a chance to repay the wonderful hospitality the people of Earth have shown us ever since we arrived here. You have all done everything you can to help us collect the resources we need to save the people of our planet; it seems only fair that we reciprocate."

Robert and Juliet edged closer to the velvet rope. A quick look around the lobby showed Maxwell that Sancho Gomez and Elias were positioned close to a couple of the guards, as was Father Andrew. Carefully he selected a target for himself, a guard standing in back of the podium. The man wore a standard Visitor uniform and cap, not the shock trooper armor. Maxwell was pleased—he'd been practicing, but it was nice to have more and bigger target areas.

John's voice continued, nearly overhead. "Thus I am honored to announce that, beginning tomorrow, the doors will be open at this hospital—and within weeks at hospitals around the world—to dispense a proven, safe, and painless vaccine for a disease which afflicts millions of people . . . cancer."

A shot rang out, then another. People screamed and tried to run. Robert's gun was in his hand, and he aimed carefully as the guard behind the podium raced forward. The .357 Magnum bucked in his hand, and the guard dropped, clawing at his throat.

In each corridor leading into the lobby, they could hear the drumming of feet as the Visitor security squads headed for the lobby—only to be thwarted as heavy steel doors thudded down, sealing off the presentation hall. Robert turned to Juliet. "Brad and Caleb made it, I see!"

Another shot rang out, and as he moved forward, gun in hand, Maxwell saw Father Andrew holding a gun to a guard's throat. Ruby was grinning like a little girl at the circus.

Robert and Juliet reached the steps of the podium together, their guns out and ready. Robert saw a flash of red at the back of the steps, and lunged. It was Diana—she'd managed to grab a weapon from a hiding place in back of the podium. With a savagery that he'd never know he possessed, Maxwell swung the muzzle of the heavy handgun across her fingers, sending the Visitor sidearm spinning away. Then he grabbed her, holding her despite her struggles—she was far stronger than most men her size—and brought the Magnum up to her throat. "Hold it, lizard!"

Juliet darted over and retrieved the Visitor weapon. Maxwell turned, his gun digging into the Visitor officer's neck. He wished violently that he could shoot her for what she'd done to his daughter, but at the moment, it was the danger to Diana that was keeping John at bay.

"Freeze!" he shouted loudly. "Nobody moves! I mean nobody!" *Christ*, he thought, *I haven't heard dialogue like that since old Cagney movies* . . .

Juliet scrambled past him, the alien weapon in her hand. "Do we need to persuade the camera crew?" Robert asked her.

"No," she said, climbing the stairs to the podium. "Kristine Walsh waved to them to keep filming—I saw her."

The Supreme Commander was turned toward the back of the platform as Julie approached, the laser weapon in her hand contrasting weirdly with her dress and coiffure. "Face front!" she ordered loudly, gesturing with the weapon.

For long seconds John didn't respond, then, as Juliet raised the weapon, aiming for his heart, he slowly obeyed. Holding the gun at ready, Juliet stepped forward. Dragging Diana with him, Maxwell stepped around the side of the podium to see Kristine Walsh gesture her camera crew to a closeup of Juliet. Directional mikes swung in her direction.

"Listen to me, everyone!" Juliet's voice rang out through the lobby. "The Visitors are *not* our friends. They've come to rape our planet, and kill all of us! They're *not* human, as they pretend to be!"

Reaching out quickly, she pulled sharply at the side of John's face, ripping his human mask away with one quick jerk. Maxwell could feel Diana stiffen in his hold as gasps of horror ran around the packed lobby. Diana's voice rang out, despite the jab of the gun. "Stop this transmission! Control room! Blackout!"

"Shut up, you bitch!' Maxwell jabbed the gun brutally beneath her jaw, saw it tear her mask. The shining blackish-green scales showed through the hole. "I'd love to kill you!" *I hope Martin and Lorraine cut in those transmitters on the Mother Ship*, he thought, looking back up at the podium.

"Look at him," Juliet was saying, turning John's head to the side, so the audience could see his features in profile. "They're stealing our water! They're taking our people prisoner aboard their ships! The resistance is fighting them. We need your help!"

The banging at the door near Father Andrew increased suddenly, then the door shivered visibly. As they watched, it jumped upward, disgorging Steven, the Visitor Security Officer, and a horde of shock troopers.

Even as they tumbled through the opening, Ruby, still in her wheelchair, whipped away the shawl from her lap, and began blasting away with a submachine gun. Slugs ripped into the Visitors and the metal door, and many fell. After a second, the Visitors pulled back, and Ruby, leaping from her wheelchair, raced away.

Hastily Maxwell clubbed Diana, thrusting her out of his way, just as Juliet, kicking off her high heels, leaped off the podium. Sancho caught her. As he darted after them, Maxwell was nearly knocked down by the flying figure of John, who raced backstage, vainly trying to shield his reptilian features from the cameras. Maxwell heard Kristine Walsh's voice call out, "Don't miss any of this!"

Then he was with the others, sprinting for his assigned exit route.


"Keep filming!" Kristine shouted at her crew. "This is great!" The resistance fighters were racing for the doors, then out of the lobby. Someone grabbed her arm. It was Diana, one hand covering the ripped place in her human skin as she gave a terse order.

"Get on the air and assure the viewers that what they've just seen was a terrorist hoax."

Kristine stood staring at her, fascinated by the greenish-black spot of reptilian scales she could see beneath Second-in-Command's masking hand. Diana reached out and slapped the human woman's face, her movement blurringly fast. "*Now*, Kristine!"

Obediently Kristine Walsh beckoned to her cameras and mikes. "Ladies and gentlemen, you have just seen a terrorist attack on this hospital . . ." She hesitated for a long moment.

"At least that is what the Visitors *ordered* me to tell you. But what we all saw just now was the truth! Resistance fighters trying to reclaim our planet from these aliens, who have lied to us, cheated us, and now strive to *kill* all of us. They're *monsters*, ladies and gentlemen, who are trying to steal our planet from us. You saw them just now the way they really are!"

Out of the corner of her eye, Kristine saw Diana race across the lobby to a guard, jerking his sidearm out of his hand. She spoke faster. "They *must* be fought, ladies and gentlemen! They must be defeated, or they will totally exterminate us! Join those who are resisting and—"

The blast of the laser pistol caught Kristine Walsh full in the chest, flinging her backwards like a boneless doll. As she fell, Kristine experienced a brief, intense satisfaction, then she felt nothing at all.


Mike Donovan was the first one out of the air-conditioning duct onto the roof, and found himself staring directly into the muzzle of a Visitor rifle. A squad vehicle was parked on the top of the Medical Center, and several shock troopers stood by as the other fighters climbed out onto the roof, putting their hands in the air. Suddenly more troopers erupted onto the roof from the stairs, Steven in the lead, stopping as they saw that the fighters had been captured.

The helmeted pilot leaned out of the squad vehicle and waved to Steven. "Report to Diana that the rebels have been captured and that I'm taking them to the Mother Ship." There was considerable pride in the alien reverberation.

Steven was obviously chagrined at not having made the capture personally, but finally waved for the shock troopers to load the prisoners aboard. "Inform the Mother Ship that we'll need another shuttle on the roof so we can smuggle the Supreme Commander out without anyone seeing him."

"Acknowledged, sir," the pilot said.

The shock troopers herded the resistance fighters aboard. They went quietly, all the fight seemingly gone out of them. The squad vehicle took off—and promptly executed a triumphant barrel roll.

Whoops of exultation filled the Visitor craft. The "shock troopers" pulled off their helmets, to reveal Bill Graham, Cal Robinson, and several other resistance fighters. The pilot of the craft was Maggie. William sat beside her, grinning.

"Slick, real slick!" Caleb crowed. "William, old son, I owe you another one!"

"He deserves an Oscar," Maggie said, "for sounding so calm when I was sitting here with a bead drawn on his head."

Willie looked hurt. "I *wanted* to help," he said plaintively.

"Well, you sure did!" Brad whooped. "Did you *see* Steven's face?"

The laughter, shouted congratulations, and back-patting went on as the craft swooped and banked to head for headquarters. Donovan had to shout to make himself heard over the din. "Shut *up*!" He glanced at all the inquiring faces. "*Where's Julie?*"

The celebration was over almost before it started.

# Chapter 24

The enormous lobby of the Medical Center was filled with glittering formal gowns and the flashbulbs of the press as John, the Visitor Supreme Commander, smiled warmly at his attentive, grateful audience. His words echoed throughout the hall, picked up by the reporters' mikes clustered around the podium. ". . . a proven, safe, and painless vaccine for a disease which afflicts millions of people . . . cancer."

Thunderous applause rocked the lobby. Lights dazzled as photographers captured the moment. John smiled, a humble, dedicated smile of good will and sincerity. "Thank you, ladies and gentlemen. Thank you. Thank you."

As the applause increased to deafening proportions, the Supreme Commander nodded graciously and descended the stairs at the side of the podium.

"Cut!" shouted a reverberating voice. "Applause off!"

The thunderous clapping halted with a click.

"Good," Diana nodded. "Where's Eleanor Dupres? It's time for her spot."

"I'm here, Diana."

Carefully the dark-haired woman arranged herself in front of the cameras as makeup technicians gave her a last once-over. "Ready?" Eleanor nodded. "All right, lights. Three . . . two . . . one . . . do it!"

Eleanor Dupres smiled graciously into the camera. "Ladies and gentlemen, what you have just seen was the *real* broadcast

265

given by John, the Supreme Commander, at last night's gala here at the Los Angeles Medical Center. Tragically, terrorists, rewarding generosity with contempt and hatred, cut in a faked broadcast, using materials stolen from several local television stations. Michael Donovan, the former newsman, was one of those responsible."

Eleanor's gracious smiled faltered, and her face assumed lines of well-controlled but nevertheless poignant grief. "One of the most tragic aspects of last night's hoax was the slaying of Kristine Walsh, the Visitor spokesperson. Terrorists cold-bloodedly kidnapped the newswoman and filmed her *actual* murder, making it appear that the Visitors were responsible."

She hesitated, then continued gravely, "I'm sure I speak for all the peace-loving people on this planet when I say that the Visitors have given *to* us, far more than they have ever asked *from* us. And I'm sure you'll join all of us in our grief at the unconscionable slaying of a talented professional like Kristine Walsh—mercilessly killed by the terrorists we must uncover and stamp out, if our planet is ever to know peace again." She hesitated for a dramatic beat. "This is Eleanor Dupres, from the Los Angeles Medical Center. Good night."

"Cut!"

Eleanor smiled tentatively as Diana and Steven approached her. "How was that?"

"Perfect," Diana said warmly. "Excellent, Eleanor."

"As long as you're pleased," Eleanor said, watching the groups of Visitors dressed as human guests. From where she was standing she could see clearly the dark marks of the Visitor weapons scoring the lobby walls. Debris lay everywhere, except where it had been cleared away to do this broadcast. Eleanor smiled over at Steven as Diana walked over to direct the cleanup operation. "Do you think the audience of television viewers will . . . accept this broadcast?"

"We've had a lot of experience in this sort of thing already," Steven said, not looking at her. "Humans tend to believe the things that they *want* to believe, and it's certainly more pleasant to accept the version of the evening that we taped tonight, wouldn't you agree?"

"Of course," Eleanor said, looking at him. She had seen Diana's anger at what she had termed Steven's "inexcusably lax" security, and knew that today might not be the best time to approach the Visitor. But with his new duties, Steven had had less time for social visits. She'd better speak with him now, while he was here, Eleanor decided.

"There's something I've been wanting to ask you about," she said, looking up at him with a warm smile.

"What's that?" Steven said, trying for his usual gallantry, but falling a little short.

"Actually, two things." She hesitated. "Two favors."

"You have only to ask, Eleanor," he said, doing better with his smile this time.

Eleanor reached into her evening bag. "This is a photograph of my grandson. I'd like him back. He's been . . . detained. I understand he's aboard your L.A. ship."

She handed him the picture. Steven took it, studied it, nodded. "That's very easy. I'll have it seen to."

"Thank you, Steven." Eleanor looked back up at him, her eyes very direct. "And, secondly, I feel I've made a rather . . . sizable contribution to your . . . movement."

"If it's a question of more money—"

"No, no, not the money. She picked her words with obvious care. "I'd like to serve in a more fulfilling capacity, so to speak."

"You want position."

Eleanor was taken aback by his candor. Trying to recover herself, she nodded. "Well, yes, in a sense, that's it, I guess."

He was all business. "Certainly. Would 'World Spokesperson' suit you?"

"Kristine Walsh's position?"

"Yes."

"Well, yes. That would be—"

"Done. It's yours. Now I must go. There's a security operation I must oversee." He took her hand, formally bowing over it. "Good day, Eleanor."

"Good day, Steven."

Daniel Bernstein watched Steven walk across the room, not missing Diana's glare at the Security Officer's back. He grinned at the tall, attractive young woman in the nurse's uniform who stood beside him. "Diana's really pissed at Steven—I heard John tell Diana that if it weren't for her brainstorm to shoot this broadcast today, the underground could actually pose a real threat to their mission."

"John?" she said, looking up at him in a way that made Daniel feel about six inches taller. "You don't mean—"

"Sure," he said offhandedly. "The Supreme Commander. I met him this morning. He congratulated me for capturing the rebel leader."

"You did *what*?" she moved closer, avidly hanging on his words.

"*I* was the one that shot the tires out of the ambulance that Juliet Parrish was trying to escape in last night. Diana said her capture alone almost made up for the nuisance of having to reshoot the presentation ceremony so it can be shown tonight."

"Juliet Parrish? The leader of the terrorists was a woman?"

"Yeah. A little blonde thing. Not my type, really. I like 'em more like . . ." He grinned widely at her. "Actually, more like *you*, darlin' . . ."

She lowered her long, dark eyelashes before his gaze, blushing slightly. "Geez, a real hero. You really captured some terrorists singlehanded?"

"Yeah. Had to kill one of 'em—they said he was an intern here. King was his name. But I got the leader without hurting her." He shook his head, remembering. "She might have been luckier if she hadn't been taken alive. Diana was *really* torqued about the raid. Juliet Parrish is in deep shit."

"Where is she?" She glanced around the lobby, eyes wide.

"Oh, they took her up to the Mother Ship last night."

"What are they going to do with her?"

"Dunno. If I was Diana, I'd make her admit that the live broadcast the people saw last night was a hoax."

"It was?"

"Sure, baby. You're not dumb enough to *believe* all that stuff, are you?"

She was indignant. "Of course not. But it did look so *real*."

*It was, you dumb bitch*, Daniel thought, looking speculatively down the neck of her uniform. *Nice set you got there* . . .

She looked around at the shock troopers assembling in one of the halls. "What's going on now?"

"Security stuff." Daniel smiled tolerantly. "So, how about your giving me your phone number, honey? I'd like to take you someplace nice for dinner tonight."

"Really?" Her face fell. "But I don't get off duty till almost curfew time. Maybe on my day off . . . ."

"Hey," he grinned. "Don't worry your pretty head about the curfew. The curfew is for civilians—you're gonna be goin' out with the Second-in-Command of Visitor Youth Activities *worldwide*."

"Really?" Daniel saw admiration in her eyes, although she was trying to play it cool. "Well, Daniel, if you're talking about a date, I'm interested. If you've got something more horizontal in mind, I'm warning you that I'm not *that* kind of girl."

*Wanna bet, sweet?* Daniel thought cynically, smiling down at her.

"I know you're not, Margaret," he protested, looking hurt. "Don't tell me you're one of those men-haters, who think a guy is only out for one thing."

"Well . . . nooo . . ." She glanced at him sideways, trying to hide her smile. "I just thought I'd get a few things straight before we went out."

*You've got me straighter than a ruler, baby.* Daniel smiled. "Okay, Margaret. I've got the picture. Tonight, all right?"

"Okay," she capitulated with a grin. "And call me Maggie. I hate Margaret."

"Sure, Maggie."

Brad McIntyre peered through his binoculars. The gray-haired man squatting in the shadow of some bushes halfway down the hill was surveying their resistance headquarters through *his* binoculars. "Take a look at this, Sancho," he said, indicating the man. "He sure doesn't look like a Visitor, but I'd almost rather find one of *them* spying on us. That guy looks *mean*."

"What do you think we should do with him?" Sancho asked. "Where do you think he came from?"

"Dunno," Brad said. "We can't let him just walk away. Do you suppose he's somebody wanting to join us?"

"Somehow he doesn't look like a recruit," Sancho said, frowning. "He looks like one of the foremen I used to have when I worked as a picker. He broke a kid's jaw one day, when the boy talked back to him."

"Well . . . this guy's not armed, at least as far as I can tell."

Sancho clicked on his walkie-talkie. "Hill patrol here. Do you read me?"

"HQ here. We read you," said Caleb's voice. "Commence identification sequence."

"Three-four-two-nine, SB."

"Go ahead."

"We've got a guy down the hillside who's observing the plant through binoculars. This place is getting too crowded for comfort, no?"

"We're packing as fast as we can." Caleb's voice assumed a more personal note. "But you'll never convince me that they'll get anything out of Juliet."

"Hey, man." Sancho shook his head. "Don't talk until you've been there. Those snakes can be very persuasive."

"I don't want to think about it," said Caleb. "What about your target? You goin' to capture that Joe and bring him in for interrogation?"

"Yeah, I think we'd better," Sancho replied. "Have a little welcoming committee ready, okay?"

"Roger and wilco. HQ out."

Sancho turned off the walkie-talkie with a sigh. Brad grinned at his expression. "Caleb's been watching those Audie Murphy jungle epics again."

"Yeah." Sancho's gaze shifted to the silent figure downhill from them. "I'll go first. You back me up."

Climbing to his feet, he picked up his shotgun and started down the hill, making little noise on the tough brownish grass. As he neared the silent observer, he stepped even more carefully, so that he made no sound at all. Finally, standing just behind the spy, his shotgun pointed at the man's head, he said pleasantly, "Hey, my friend, you looking for something?"

The man's steel-colored head did not even turn to look into the double barrels. Sancho heard Brad coming up behind him. Then the ex-cop stepped in front of the binoculars, blocking the man's view. The man casually reached out and pushed McIntyre aside as though he were a sunbather and Brad were blocking the rays. His voice had all the warmth of a file dragged over rusty metal. "Do yourself a favor and tell the greaser back there to take that twelve-gauge away from my head before I make him swallow it."

Brad stared incredulously down at the man. "You got a nasty mouth, pal."

Sancho gestured with the shotgun. "Why don't you stand

up, *amigo,* and we'll take a little walk, okay? Move *mucho* quiet, or this greaser would love to unload both these barrels into your *muy poco* brain."

"In about five seconds you're going to be cloud dancing, slick."

Sancho, furious, was about to grab the man when something cold and hard was gently inserted into his left ear. He stiffened, then heard a voice say, "Drop it."

Sancho carefully lowered the shotgun, then let it drop to the hillside. "You there," the voice said, addressing Brad. "Hand over that Smith and Wesson, real slow."

With exaggerated care, Brad handed his gun, butt first, to the man on the ground, who took it without even putting the binoculars down. "Look at them, Chris," he said disdainfully. "Bottlenecked both front and back. They're in a tomb, not a camp. What a bunch of yo-yo's. Jeezus." He replaced the binoculars in the case hanging around his neck, retrieved the shotgun from the grass beside him, and stood up.

He was of medium height, his features bony and undistinguished save for his eyes, which were a very light, bright blue. They were nonreflecting eyes, taking in everything and letting nothing back out. "Okay, slick. You and macho man here can take us to your leader."

Caleb and several others were waiting in the entrance for them. When they saw the gun muzzle pressed to Sancho's temple, they slowly moved out of the way, allowing the four men to enter. The gray-haired man spoke to Sancho as they stood in the hallway. "You got a war room?"

Sancho found his voice, sullenly. "I'm telling you nothing."

"Chris," said the man. The gun moved near Sancho's ear as the man cocked it.

"I'll show you where it is," Brad said hastily. "Not that it'll do you creeps any good. If you haven't noticed, you're badly outnumbered." Keeping his hands up, he started up the stairs, then down the hall. Sancho followed, feeling the gun hovering near his hairline. Behind him he could hear Caleb, Elias, and the others. Brad paused in the doorway of the main conference room. "Here."

Mike Donovan was sitting at one of the tables, writing in a notebook. He looked up as Brad spoke, then his gaze went to the gray-haired man holding the shotgun. The cameraman's eyes narrowed. "Well, well, well. I wondered when you'd crawl out from under a munitions dump."

The two intruders lowered their weapons. Sancho turned to look at his captor. Chris was young, compactly built, and had all the friendly presence of a a wolverine.

"Hey, Gooder," the gray-haired man said. "Long time no see."

"Short for 'do-gooder.' That's his little nickname for me," Donovan explained to the resistance fighters who were assembled in the corridor, watching uncertainly. "He blows it up, I film it, and the folks back home hate him for it. We met in Laos, El Salvador—you name it. Meet Ham Tyler, master of covert operations, communications, and bad relations. If the world weren't sick, he'd starve to death."

"If the world weren't sick, all you'd have to cover is rose festivals, Gooder," Tyler said, with what he evidently considered a smile. It lacked charm. "This is my associate, Chris Faber." He paused for a beat. "And you people are doomed."

He beckoned to the rest of the resistance fighters. "C'mon in, folks. We're gonna have a little talk."

Caleb, Elias, Robert Maxwell, and the rest came into the room, edging cautiously past Chris Faber, who still held the .357 Magnum, though it was now pointed at the floor.

Ham Tyler sat down on one of the battered old chairs and looked around the room with a contemptuous smile. He shook his head, sighed, then spoke. "Gooder here's got you believing you're gonna pull down the baddies with a little muscle and God on your side. That's gonna get you nothing but dead. It's time you left it to the professionals."

Donovan leaned back in his seat, his voice heavy with sarcasm. "Now that's got a familiar ring. If the world were to have an epitaph, that should be it."

"I'm not here to fence with you, Donovan," Tyler snapped. "We don't have the time. I'm telling you that we've got a world network going, and from now on, you guys are going to do what you're told."

"Shit!" Brad exploded. "Who the *hell* do you think you are?"

"Shut up!" Ham glared at him, and Brad glared back, then subsided. "You people got lucky last night and pulled off a nice little stunt. But without professional leadership, you're just meat on the hoof, waitin' for the barbecue. We're organized and we've got a plan. *Plus* new ammo that will cut the goddamn lizards in two. It's up to you: stay independent and get wiped out, or join our network and help hammerpunch those scaly bastards right off this planet."

A babble of voices filled the room as everyone began talking at once. Tyler sat silently until Brad, with a contemptuous glance, managed the last word. "I think we ought to kick him out on his ass with a set of bruises to remind him to be more polite to the next joker he talks to. You heard Donovan—this guy's a warmonger. Getting people killed turns him on. How do we know he's not working for Diana?"

With the motion of a striking leopard, Tyler was out of his seat and had Brad by the throat. Faber cocked his gun, still leaning negligently against the doorframe. "You bastard!" Tyler said, his face nearly touching Brad's. "Don't you ever say that again!"

"Stop that, Ham!" Donovan said, then, as the other returned to his seat, shook his head at Brad. "He's a creep, but he's a *human* creep. Believe me, he's too mean and perverted for Diana to convert."

Tyler nodded, his teeth showing in what passed for a smile. "He's right. Listen to me. Donovan may hate my guts, but he'll tell you I know what I'm doing."

"What I'll tell *you*, Tyler, is this." Mike crossed the room and stood over the other man, his expression stony. "And you'd better get it straight, or I'll explain it in terms even you can't miss." His green eyes held the pale blue ones determinedly. "Keep your damn hands off us. Don't *ever* touch one of us again. These people aren't trained killers like you and your apple-pie boy over there, but they . . . *we* . . . have done more to monkey-wrench the Visitors than any other group around. We may not be professional guerillas, but we're a unit, and we've been making a bigger noise than *you* have, so far."

Tyler nodded grudgingly. "Yeah. That was a decent little piece of business you folks pulled off at the hospital."

"They know *we're* here, man. Where's *your* so-called network been?" Elias challenged.

"You're damn right they know where you are. Matter of fact, they're planning a raid on this dump right now," said Ham, but he was obviously backing off slightly.

Donovan turned to face the others. "Okay. So he's a professional killer. But he's right about organizing. We've been looking for a chance to get together with the other resistance groups, join up with the network. I say if he gives us what we want, we should agree to help him out."

"What would that be, Gooder?"

Donovan turned back to him. "Juliet Parrish, our leader, was captured last night during the raid. We want her back. We *need* her back."

Ham nodded. "Deal. The network will do everything we can to spring her."

He offered his hand to Donovan, who hesitated. Flying footsteps sounded outside in the hall. Father Andrew slung himself through the door, panting. "Ruby just called the Bernstein house from work and Stanley came to warn us! The lizards are on their way! We've got to get out of here!"

"Told you so," said Ham calmly. "We'll talk over the details of our association later. Right now you folks had better beat it. As a gesture of good faith, Chris and I will cover your retreat. I've got a couple of ideas for a little party in this dump."

"Okay! Get the stuff and load it in the trucks! Ten minutes, no more! *Move it!*" Donovan shouted. The room emptied.

"What've you got in the way of explosives?" Ham asked.

Donovan thought for a moment. "Not a lot. Some grenades, some dynamite. We're out of plastic explosives at the moment."

"Blasting caps?"

"Yeah."

"Okay, bring 'em here. Chris and I have some stuff stashed outside—"

"Where is he?"

"Gone to get it, along with our heavier artillery."

"Right." Mike was already moving for the door.

A minute later he was back, carrying a wooden box piled helter-skelter with explosives. "This is all we've got."

"Okay, Gooder, get your people out of here."

Setting the box down, Donovan nodded and vanished. Tyler and Faber could hear him directing the removal of the laboratory equipment. Ham nodded at Chris. "Okay, sounds like he's handling that end. You set the charges—I'll cover you." He hefted the automatic machine pistol Faber held out to him. "You got Teflon loads in this?"

"You bet."

"All right. Let's go."

"I checked with Sam while I was back at the car. Ten minutes isn't going to be enough," Faber said, stacking grenades methodically into a cardboard container.

"I'll tell 'em."

In the hall Tyler found Donovan at the upstairs window watching the van, camouflage net and branches still attached, pull away. "There goes the lab equipment," he said.

"Chris checked the status of the snake patrol. You gotta get out *now*."

Donovan gave the older man a harried glance. "Great." Raising his hands and his voice, he waved for attention. "Calm down everybody! Listen!"

Obediently, the frantic rush slowed. Tyler spoke to them. "You got one escape route through the sewer system tunnel. Bad planning, folks—but you'll learn. Take it *now*, with what you can carry."

"Okay, you heard him! Get moving!" Donovan shouted.

"Have we got all your munitions?" Ham asked a few minutes later as they stood in the doorway with Faber, watching the fighters scatter down the culvert.

"Those who have flashlights stay with those who don't!" shouted Donovan, before he turned back to Tyler. "There's the bazooka—it's in the room upstairs, next to the one we were in. Also a small rocket launcher. I think it's got a shell or two left."

"All right, Gooder. We'll handle it from here. Get your tail out of here. Your people are gonna need you. Have you got a hidey hole picked?"

"Yeah."

"One this Juliet Parrish doesn't know about?"

Pain shadowed Donovan's eyes for a second. "As a matter of fact, yes, we picked it this morning, figuring we'd move just to be safe. But Julie didn't talk—"

"Sure, right. Get your ass in gear, Gooder."

Donovan turned, flashlight in hand, and raced for the culvert.

Tyler turned to Faber. "Remember what we pulled at that armory in Afghanistan?"

Faber nodded.

"Same drill."

"You got it."

Several minutes later they heard the squad vehicles outside, and Ham, sneaking a peek out the window, saw several SWAT team uniforms mixed in with the red ones. "You set?" he asked Faber, who was checking the walls of the main second-story corridor, a box of grenades in his hands. Feet rumbled downstairs.

Chris nodded, carefully setting down the grenades. "Here's the spot."

"Take some of the grenades with you in case they've blocked the rear windows, and clear out."

Nodding, Faber took his grenades and disappeared into the shadowed corridor. Tyler set up the bazooka, positioning it carefully, making sure it was just far enough from the grenades. Quickly, he dragged mattresses out of the dorm and set them up in a screen behind the bazooka, taking up his position at the weapon.

Seconds later, the far end of the corridor filled with Visitor shock troopers. Sighting carefully, Tyler fired at the grenades, then threw himself behind his shield. There was a huge *kathump*, then a searing whoosh of displaced air as the box of grenades, placed under the main support beams for that side of the structure, went off. The entire western end of the ancient plant buckled and fell in, directly onto the troopers, taking most of the floor as well.

Flaming debris had set several of the mattresses to smoldering, but Tyler crawled out unharmed. He surveyed his handiwork complacently. Red uniforms poked through the pile of debris, arms and legs thrust stiffly out like pins from a pincushion. From where he stood on the questionable solidity of what remained of the second floor, he could see the greenish-black of reptilian skin through the human flesh.

"What a waste," Ham said, grinning happily. "You would've made nice luggage."

# Chapter 25

Harmony Moore's catering truck bumped along the ancient dirt road so violently that she worried about the kerosene in the stove in the back. She forced herself to slow down, reassuring herself that nothing could have happened to the others in the hour she'd been gone.

She was returning from the new headquarters to pick up another load of supplies—many of the laboratory chemicals and drugs required the refrigeration supplied by the tiny refrigerator in the back of her specially equipped truck. The new hideout was clear across town, an abandoned movie set in a deserted stretch of country.

Quickly Harmy swung the wheel hard right to avoid a particularly vicious rut, then hard left to head straight down the hillside. The path was marked with flattened grass from the traffic today. With relief, she saw Elias, Brad, Donovan, and Caleb sitting on the tailgate of a pickup in the middle of the field. The dark hole of the sewer outlet gaped blackly in the white concrete culvert near them. Harmy shuddered, remembering the nightmare of that hasty scramble through the sewer, clinging to Caleb's hand as he searched out the uncertain footing for them with a steadily weakening flashlight.

When the blast had come, rocking them even underground, the light had dropped from Taylor's hand, and they'd had to grope their way through the darkness. Harmy was pretty sure she'd have nightmares about their escape for some time to come. She didn't like the dark.

As she pulled up, Donovan climbed off the tailgate to meet her. "Everything all right back at the ranch?"

"Father Andrew seemed to be doing the best he could toward getting the place organized. Robin didn't look too good—seemed kind of disoriented. You know how she's been lately."

"Yeah."

Harmy glanced around the area. "What else has to go?"

"Just Willie. He's sitting in the truck. Said the sun was too bright, and he's lost his dark glasses. Mind driving him back to the new HQ?"

"Well . . ." Harmy hesitated. "Would you mind if I didn't drive this time? This is my third trip, and I'm kinda tired."

"Oh, sure—no problem. Elias or Brad won't mind driving the pickup."

"Thanks, Mike."

Several minutes later William sat in the back of Harmy's truck, handcuffed to the stove. When Harmony peeked in at him, he was staring dejectedly off into space. Biting her lip, she hesitated, then went around to the cab of the truck. "Mike? I think I'll ride in back—keep Willie company."

"Sure," he said, starting the truck. "I've got plenty of thinking to keep me occupied."

Quickly Harmy ran around and climbed into the back of the truck. She barely had time to sit down and brace herself, before the truck moved, turning, then growling up the hillside. The jolting was worse in the back.

William was watching her, but when Harmy turned to him, he quickly looked away. She hesitated, then smiled, "Hi, Willie."

He looked back at her, startled, grateful, and wary all at once. "Hello, Harmony. I am glad to see you safely."

"Are you hungry? I have plenty of stuff in here. Vegetables, cheese . . . You can eat cheese, can't you?"

"I am not sure," William said, "but I am not hungry, anyway. Thank you for asking."

"It's the least I could do," she said. "It's too bad they feel they have to handcuff you. It looks so uncomfortable."

"It's not so bad," Willie said. "I understand why they must

do what they do." He hesitated, then gave her a quick, sideways look of embarrassment. "Harmy, why are you being so nice to me?"

"I like you, Willie," she answered softly, looking straight at him. "We're still friends, aren't we?"

"But you saw what I look like!" Shame was evident in every line of him. "You saw . . . my hand. My back." He took a deep breath. "John's face."

"Yeah, I did," Harmy said slowly. "You guys really aren't very handsome—at least to our eyes. But I guess maybe we looked kinda ugly to you at first, didn't we?"

William was visibly taken aback. "Well . . . yes. Of course you people never showed us anything but your true faces." He hesitated. "You are a different sort of person, Harmony. No other human has ever treated me with such . . . uncaringness. Is that the right word?"

She smiled gently. "I don't know. What are you trying to say?"

"That to most people it makes a difference, knowing how I look beneath this covering." He touched his smooth, unlined face. "But to you it does not. You are uncaring of that."

"I think maybe the word you want is 'tolerant,' Willie."

"Tolerant. Thank you."

"Well, to tell you the truth, even before I knew, I wasn't falling in love with you for your looks, Willie." She grinned. "There just aren't that many good people around, that I can stop caring about you because you look different. Life is too short for that."

He looked at her, then very slowly reached over and touched her hand. "Thank you, Harmony. I'll always remember you said that, no matter what happens to me." He smiled timidly. "Even among my own people I am not what you call an ox."

She frowned, puzzled, then burst out laughing. "That's 'fox,' you dope! You've been listening to Robin and Polly, haven't you?"

"I listen, because I like all of you. I want to help."

"I know," she said gently, moving closer to him. She sat braced against him, cushioning the lurching bumps of the truck for both of them.

*   *   *

It took the resistance a full day to unpack and set up their new headquarters in the abandoned movie set. Since many of the buildings were merely facades, they kept the old saloon as a headquarters. Bill Graham, Caleb's friend, found them two old trailers, veterans of many construction jobs. The rebels used one as a lab, and the other to store their munitions. True to his word, Ham Tyler provided them with weapons and ammunition designed to be more effective against the Visitors.

Cal Robinson, Robert Maxwell, and Harmony Moore worked in the laboratory, analyzing samples, running down every biological clue that might lead to a weapon against the Visitors. They were hampered in their efforts by their lack of Visitor guinea pigs—testing substances on William's blood was *not* the same. Certain terrestrial reptiles exhibited some of the same characteristics as the aliens, so the scientists were able to use them in a few experiments. It was slow, discouraging work—especially for Maxwell, who was laboring outside his chosen discipline, striving to pick up the threads in subjects he hadn't studied since getting his Ph.D. eighteen years ago.

The anthropologist also had to fight against letting depression overwhelm him—as it threatened to every time he looked at his daughter. Robin was sinking deeper and deeper into herself. Several weeks after Juliet's capture, the girl attempted suicide, but only succeeded in making shallow, inexperienced cuts across her wrists before Polly, alarmed by her sister's locking the bedroom door, roused their father. After this incident, Robin was never left alone. She made no further attempts, but sat quietly most of the time, staring at nothing. They had to urge her to eat.

The Maxwells weren't the only fighters struggling against a miasma of depression. Most of the time, Mike Donovan was too busy to realize how despondent he was, but when he had a few moments to himself, he spent them wondering why he didn't just take off on his own—nobody could survive under this kind of burden, he thought. Saddened and angered by Kristine Walsh's death, tormented by guilt over Juliet's capture, Mike had to fight his tendency toward action—any action—and play a waiting game. He'd never been a patient man, but during the long days following Julie's capture, he was learning. Hating every inactive moment, but learning.

In Juliet's absence, Donovan had assumed *de facto* leadership of the group, and in doing so, achieved even greater respect for the young woman than he had had before her capture. Julie's brief tirade against the pressures of leadership hadn't even begun to tell the whole story.

It was a full-time job, for instance, just overseeing the acquisition and distribution of supplies—and not just guns and ammunition. People had to eat, bathe, wash clothes—Donovan found himself the target of scathing criticism and scorn a day after the Visitor raid on the sanitation plant, when it was discovered that he'd forgotten to include toilet paper on the shopping list.

Then there were the finances! When Mike unearthed Juliet's records of income and expenditures, he was dismayed by the neat columns of figures, the myriad bankbooks and check-books under carefully established false identities. Running a resistance movement was *expensive*—even though a number of the fighters, Elias for one, channeled all their income into the movement, the underground teetered on the bare edge of solvency. Contributions from people like the Bernsteins helped, but the cash flow was a never-ending drain. Donovan had never liked figures. His nightmares about Sean began to alternate with sweaty, frantic dreams of crouching over the account books, realizing the underground was doomed for lack of money.

But the worst nights of all were when he dreamed of Juliet. They had had no news of her beyond the snippets Maggie Blodgett had garnered from Daniel Bernstein—until the day Donovan took Ham Tyler to meet Martin for their next scheduled encounter.

Tyler picked Donovan up in an L.A.P.D. squad car. He was wearing a police uniform, and as Donovan looked through the window, the older man shoved another at him. "Here, Gooder. This oughtta fit you. Get a move on. We don't want to keep your scaly buddy waiting."

As they turned onto the dirt road leading away from the underground headquarters, Donovan looked down at his disguise. The outfits were a good idea—they would make it a lot easier to get around. "Where'd you get the car and the uniforms?"

"I have my sources, Gooder," Ham said. "Remember, I was in this business when you were still in diapers."

"Really?" Donovan said, with a half-smile. "I had no idea you were so close to retirement. Or is it true that old assassins never die—they just get so hyped on death that they off themselves one day when there's nobody else to wipe out?"

Tyler's hands tightened on the steering wheel. "You shitty little bastard, I oughtta—"

The car swerved, just as Donovan shouted, "*Look!* There's another one!"

Tyler stopped the car and both men got out to stare at the sky. Another huge ship was gliding effortlessly into position over the Mother Ship, even larger than the original. "Where the hell did that one come from?" Tyler muttered.

"Sirius is probably a safe bet," Donovan said. "Christ, the thing covers the whole damn *county*."

"Great. All we need are more of those scaly bastards to fight."

"With *two* of 'em blocking out the sun, there won't be a tree left alive in the whole county." Donovan jerked open the door of the squad vehicle and climbed in. He spent the rest of the drive silently staring at his shoes.

Parking the squad vehicle several blocks away from the rendezvous point, the two men walked, as if on patrol, into the bowels of an underground parking lot. Coming from the sunlit street into the abrupt underground, the world dissolved into pools of gray and black. They stood there blinking, smelling the pungency of gasoline and exhaust fumes. Ham looked skeptically around the echoing concrete darkness. "Okay, Gooder. Where's your gator buddy?"

"He's done more for us than you have, Ham," Donovan scowled, "so watch that kind of talk. He'll be here."

"It's nice that some people in this world are so trusting."

They waited about fifteen minutes before the scuff of a footstep made both men jump. Martin stepped out of the shadows. "Hello, Mike."

"Jeezus! Just like a swamp gator—slides right up on you, no noise at all!" Ham glared at the Visitor.

Donovan gave him an exasperated glance. "Martin, this . . . person . . . has joined us, and is helping us. I don't like him, but I'm willing to trust him, at least during this particular war. I ask that you do the same."

"I trust you, Donovan. That's enough for me."

"Okay, then, meet Ham Tyler. He heads up the U.S. branch of a worldwide resistance network our group is cooperating with. Tyler, this is Martin."

Glancing over at the older man's face, Donovan could plainly see Ham's disgust. Donovan felt a spark of genuine amusement, the first in days. "Any news about Julie?" he asked, sobering.

Martin looked grave. "She hasn't broken yet, but she will. Diana will convert her or kill her. I've never seen her so determined."

Donovan began cursing under his breath, helplessly grinding a fist into his palm. "We've *got* to get her out!"

"Has she talked?" Tyler asked.

"Not that I know of," Martin said. "She has a very strong will, and has shown surprising innovation in getting around Diana's methods."

"If she didn't talk, how did they find the HQ in the sewer plant?" Ham wanted to know.

"Pascal, the counterfeiter. Diana tortured him, and he talked. They had him with them at the raid, and when the explosion went off, they killed him for lack of anyone else."

"Too bad," Mike said. "The guy was a real artist at what he did." He glanced back down at his clenched fist. "Martin, you've got to help us get Julie out."

"She is kept under such tight security that I haven't even been able to speak with her. It's impossible, Mike."

"But if you and the other fifth columnists help—"

"There are too few of us, and too many of them. It's incredibly dangerous for us."

Ham took a quick step forward, balancing on the balls of his feet as he glared at the Visitor. "Hey, scaly, you listen to my friend here, and do what he says. 'Cause if you don't, I'm gonna wrap you up in your human skin and serve you to your buddies up there as an exotic hors d'oeuvre. Get me?"

Martin looked at Tyler for a long moment, then turned a dubious gaze on Donovan. "This man is not like any other human I have met."

Mike rolled his eyes, shrugging. "I know. Fortunately, selective breeding keeps their numbers at a minimum." He turned a long look on the older man. "What I said to you about the others, goes for Martin too. Don't forget it."

Ham nodded, shrugging in turn. "Okay, Okay. Don't be so damn touchy, Gooder." He turned back to Martin. "What's the news on this other ship that's parked over yours?"

"The Supreme Commander Pamela—it's her ship. Diana was talking with her just before I left. That's why I was delayed. She's only been in range of the Earth System for a day, and her first stop was with John, on the New York ship. The Leader wants the schedule speeded up. She brought specially trained engineers and technicians for a new project."

"What kind of special project?"

"I don't know the specifics yet, but she mentioned that if it succeeded, they'll be able to exhaust the fresh water supply of southern California in less than a month."

"Christ on a pony!" Ham said. "Is that possible?"

"I have met the Supreme Commander before. She is not in the habit of making idle promises." Martin sounded grim. "Pamela is famed for her abilities as a skilled tactician and military expert. In her way, she could be even more dangerous than Diana. The two of them hold little affection for each other. Pamela considers Diana corrupt, I believe. She doesn't share Diana's . . . dedication . . . to the more esoteric ways of grasping and holding power. Pamela, for example, favored a straight military takeover, and opposed Diana's conversion and subversion approach."

"A female?" Tyler said skeptically. "As a military leader?"

"Oh, come off it, Ham!" Donovan glared at him, exasperated. "You don't even *know* how much of a jackass you sound like when you make comments like that!"

Martin looked puzzled. "But females hold positions of power in your world, do they not?"

"Probably not as much as they have a right to," Donovan said. "Ham here has problems dealing with people of other races, sexes, colors . . . you name it. Besides . . ." he stopped as though a thought was just beginning to occur to him, "there's no reason that just because the human shape we see is male or female, that the Visitor beneath it has to be the same sex, is there? You guys could make anybody look like anybody, right? Martin, which sex are you?"

"I am male," the Visitor said, smiling. "But you are right, Donovan. Most of us chose to be the same sex outwardly as we are internally, but there were exceptions. Pamela, however," (this was for Ham's benefit) "is female."

"That gives me an idea," Donovan said. "We've talked about trying to assassinate Diana before. Now you say that she doesn't get along with this Pamela. Is there some way we can arrange an assassination attempt so that even if it doesn't work, it will discredit Diana even further with Pamela?"

"I don't know. Pamela did mention that she was disappointed that Diana hadn't managed to wipe out the undergrounds yet. Diana was extremely discomfited."

"That's what we need." Donovan was excited. "But we'll need someone to volunteer for the mission. Someone who can get onto the Mother Ship."

"That would be impossible. Special voice-pattern checks have been instituted. That's part of the problem in getting Juliet free."

"Damn!" Mike said. "I thought that maybe, since you guys are so good with the plastic masks, we could rig somebody up to look like one of Diana's aides, and he could get close to her. Then, if he could kill Diana, good. If not, maybe he could nail Pamela. A breach of security like that would make them lay off Julie until we could mount a rescue mission—using our masks to simulate Visitors who wouldn't be questioned!"

"Whoever we got to go after Diana probably wouldn't make it out of there," Ham said. "Though your idea about the masks is a good one."

Donovan nodded. "It'd be a kamikaze mission, probably," he admitted, "but I'm willing to risk it. Anything is better than sitting down here, trying to add the same column and get the same answer twice."

"But you are needed down here, Mike," Martin said.

"Not as badly as Julie is."

"You are forgetting the voice check," the Visitor officer said. "But I still think the idea has possibilities . . ."

Brian looked up in surprise from the photo Steven had handed him. "But this one is just a young boy. Why do you want him located?"

"A request from higher up," Steven said obliquely. "I'm not at liberty to divulge the source."

"What's his name? If I had his name, I could find him in the computers. Going solely on the basis of visual identification is going to be difficult."

"I don't know," Steven lied, then as Brian looked up at him with undisguised curiosity, his tone became brusque. "I simply want him found. Have your division conduct a thorough search of the ship, and report back to me. One source reported the boy as being on the Los Angeles ship."

Brian nodded slowly. "As you say, sir. You know, you can trust me—I've served you competently for quite a while now. Why do you want *this* boy, out of all the hundreds aboard the Mother Ship?"

Steven smiled. "Let's just say he's a small . . . gift . . . for Diana."

"Yes sir. I'll report as soon as I locate him. Shall I have him revived?"

"Yes, do that." Steven nodded briskly to the younger officer, and walked away, leaving Brian to stare speculatively at the photograph of the boy with the hazel eyes and thick brown hair.


Pounding rock music lapped out from the Bernstein house, savagely tearing the peace of the night. The Bernsteins' neighbors did not complain, however. They knew better.

Daniel Bernstein giggled before sloshing the remains of a bottle of Chivas into his mouth. Maggie Blodgett sat on the floor next to him, also giggling tipsily, but an astute observer, watching her eyes, could have seen that the young woman was sober. Daniel was not an astute observer—in fact, the term "blind" fit him rather well.

"Damn!" He hefted the bottle, peering at its bottom. "Sucker's dead." He looked over at Lynn and Stanley, who sat rigidly on the couch. Lynn worked desultorily at a crewel picture, and Stanley had a book open on his lap. "Hey, Mother! I said this bottle's empty! Didn't you *hear* me?"

Lynn cast a doubtful look at her husband, then quietly went to the liquor cabinet, returning with a fifth of Black Velvet. "I'm afraid this is all we have left, Daniel."

"Shit! We can't drink that piss!" Daniel frowned suspiciously. "Wha' happened to all that Chivas I brought home th'other day?"

"It's gone, Daniel." Stanley spoke for the first time in hours. "You drank it."

The younger Bernstein glared at his father. "Shit, too! I bet *you* drank it—you always want what I get, Pop. Admit it, you envy me. I got everything you never had . . . power, looks, money . . ." He grinned at Maggie. "A pretty woman to do anything that I want."

Stanley's face flushed dark red. Lynn Bernstein hastily opened the bottle of whiskey. "Here, Daniel."

He grinned chivalrously. "Maggie first."

Carefully Maggie poured a small shot into a glass, then handed the bottle to Daniel. "Chicken!" Daniel jeered, raising the bottle to his mouth. He turned back to the young woman after a long swallow. "It's gotta be envy. They envy me, so they treat me like garbage. They *always* treated me like garbage."

Stung, Lynn protested, "That's not *true*, Daniel!"

"Garbage!" Daniel reiterated. "But I'm not garbage anymore! You eat because of me! You have a roof over your heads because of me! You're *alive* because of me!"

Stanley stared at him as though from a long, long distance. "And very tired because of you."

Enraged, Daniel groped for the Visitor sidearm he wore. "You old fart! I'll make you—"

He stopped as Maggie grabbed his face in her hands, turning him to look at her. "*Daniel*," she said pettishly, "why are you screwing around talking to your parents, when you could be talking to *me*?" Digging her fingers into his thick, dark hair, she pulled his face closer, kissing him, her mouth open.

Daniel forgot his anger, leaning into the kiss. Clumsily, his fingers found the buttons of her blouse, then the firm softness of her breasts. She struggled for a moment beneath him, until Daniel realized his gun was digging into her. He pulled it off, along with his uniform. Panting, so excited he could barely contain himself, he dragged at her jeans. It wasn't until he was inside her, thrusting triumphantly, feeling the quiver of satisfaction tell him that despite the liquor, this was gonna be *easy—quick, oh Jesus!*—it wasn't until then that he remembered his parents.

Drunkenly, Daniel turned away from Maggie's mouth,

finding an extra fillip of satisfaction in the idea that they'd have to watch him—but Lynn and Stanley were gone.

Juliet Parrish crouched in the corner of her cell, naked, her hands swollen and covered with blood from places where she'd bitten herself. Pain, she'd found, was the only way to anchor herself to reality in the face of the horrors Diana had managed to call up from her own mind.

She leaned her head against her knees, trying to remember the rest of the lines she'd been reciting. She had always loved poetry, and going over well-loved verses had proved to be a soothing, mindless diversion. She couldn't afford to let herself think too much. That was one of the primary weapons of the interrogator—the subject's own dreadful imaginings of what the next session might hold.

Now, which poem had she been reciting? To her horror, Juliet couldn't remember. The only thing that filled her mind was one verse from a poem—she couldn't remember the title— by Tennyson:

> *"O love, they die in yon rich sky,*
>   *They faint on hill or field or river:*
> *Our echoes roll from soul to soul,*
>   *And grow for ever and for ever.*
> *Blow, bugle, blow, set the wild echoes flying,*
> *And answer, echoes, answer, dying, dying, dying."*

Whimpering, Juliet tried to distract herself with something that didn't hit quite so close to home, but her mind whirled and spun, the words of the verse resounding in her ears—*dying, dying, echoes dying, dying echoes, dying, dying, dying.* She rocked back and forth, tears rolling down her cheeks.

Suddenly the door to the cell opened, and two guards stepped through. Diana stood behind them.

Juliet tried to remain still, but her body and voice betrayed her as she cringed away. "No . . . no, please . . . please, no!"

Grinning, the guards advanced on her. Their hands fastened brutally in her armpits. Julie's legs dragged painfully along the metal grids as they carried her out. "No! No! Not again! I *can't!*"

Diana watched as the small blonde figure stumbled, trying to break away from the guards, then began to struggle. As the guards disappeared around the corner, the screams of protest degenerated into mindless shrieks.

Diana smiled.

# Chapter 26

Brian waited as the laboratory technicians wiped the suspension gel from the face of the boy in the photograph. The child blinked, choked, then began shivering violently. One of the technicians dropped a blanket over him, while the other gave him an injection.

After a few minutes the boy's shudders ceased, and his eyes slowly opened. He coughed, and Brian patted his shoulder. "Are you all right?"

The boy nodded shakily, looking around him at the laboratory. "What's your name?" Brian asked.

The boy's whisper was hoarse and labored. "Sean." He coughed again. "Sean Donovan."

Brian blinked, then a slow grin spread across his face. "Steven, you clever bastard," he whispered to himself. "A gift for Diana, indeed."

Diana watched Juliet Parrish writhe and jerk in the glassy cylindrical conversion chamber. Wires and electrodes monitored and directed the fantasies the technicians were imposing on the human's mind. Juliet's hands were strapped to her sides, so she could no longer bite at them. Diana cast a quick look at the assorted monitors. "Good. Good," she said quietly. "Maybe this time we'll get her. I thought we might the other night, but this time—"

Leaning over, she spoke into a microphone. "Julie? Julie,

listen to me. This is Diana. I want to help you, Julie. Let me help you out of there. Give me your hand, Julie.''

"No . . ." The blonde woman moaned, then jerked, and her legs began to twitch. Her head jerked as though to look back over her shoulder. "No!"

Diana watched the fantasy become more and more real to the human. The technician beside her made a cautioning gesture. "I don't think her heart will take much more."

"Keep going," Diana said inexorably. "Release her arms."

"Julie? Julie, listen. Let me help you. Reach out to me, and I'll get you out of there. You won't have to run away anymore. Reach out to me, Julie!"

"Nnn—" Julie shrieked and twitched. "He's going to get me! Help! Oh, God, please! Help! Diana—Diana! Help!"

"Reach out to me! Give me your hand, Julie!"

Slowly the woman's left hand began to move upward. "Here, Diana! Get me out of here!"

"That's it! We've succeeded in obtaining a right-brain switchover! Get her out of there!"

Hastily two technicians raced over to pull the woman out of the glassy enclosure. "Does this mean she's finished?" the technician next to Diana asked.

"Noooo . . ." the Second-in-Command said consideringly, "but it's a major breakthrough."

The intercom on the wall spoke. "Diana, this is landing bay security. We have a report that Mike Donovan has been captured and is being brought aboard."

"Donovan!" Diana could barely restrain her elation. "Two in one day! Have him brought here immediately!"

"This will be a tremendous help," Diana said to the technician. "In order to instill distrust in her previous companions, I used Donovan as a focal point in the conversion process, making him one of the threatening figures in the pursuit and rape/violence sequences. Observing her reaction to him should prove extremely interesting. It will give me something to gauge her progress by."

Moments later the laboratory door hissed open, and two shock troopers escorted Mike Donovan into the room. "How nice to see you, Mr. Donovan!" Diana said to him, then gestured to her aide.

"How lovely that you could join us for a visit, Mr.

Donovan," Diana said. "Julie will be most happy to see you . . . perhaps."

She beckoned the two shock troopers to bring him closer. Juliet was being assisted out of the conversion chamber by one of the technicians. Diana stepped closer to him, half turning to watch Juliet's face. "Julie," she said, "say hello to—"

Exhibiting an unexpected, violent strength, Donovan abruptly thrust both shock troopers aside, and, equally suddenly, there was a Visitor sidearm in his hand. The pulsing whine of the charge reverberated around the lab. Diana leaped, barely avoiding the shot, bearing Juliet to the floor with her. She heard a thud and saw her aide crumple across the desk, half her torso charred away.

Pandemonium broke loose as the shock troopers both fired at Donovan, who ducked, catching them in a crossfire. One of the technicians grabbed a rifle, loosing a blast at Donovan, who slumped to the floor. The technician lowered the rifle, looking thoroughly shaken, as Diana climbed to her feet.

She walked over to the fallen figure and poked at it with her toe. No response. "He's dead," she said. "Damn."

"Mike?!" For the first time, Juliet showed a reaction. "Mike?" On hands and knees she scuttled toward the limp figure. *"No! Mike! NO!!"*

"Get her out of here," Diana said, annoyed, "and get a team in here to clean up." She watched as the technicians dragged the sobbing woman away from the body, toward the door. "Maybe we're not as far along as I thought," she said, to nobody in particular.

An hour later, as Diana was working in her personal office/lab, the door signal flashed. "Identification?" asked Diana.

"Pamela," said the signal.

Cursing under her breath, Diana opened the door to admit her superior officer. She was barely able to summon a smile to meet the one on Pamela's face. The Supreme Commander bore the outward appearance of a stunningly beautiful thirty-five-year-old woman. "I was just talking to Jake, from Internal Security," Pamela said gently. "I didn't realize we were having problems aboard our vessels."

"Internal security problems?" Diana put down her writing instrument. "I'm not aware of any. I maintain tight discipline and the customary surveillance."

"Oh?" Pamela's perfectly arched eyebrows arched even

higher. "Oh, dear. That *is* too bad. Perhaps we'd better discuss this, Diana . . . dear."

The dark-haired Visitor rose slowly to her feet. "If you're talking about what happened this morning—"

"Jake told me about the assassination attempt."

"Yes, well, I would have disciplined both troopers who proved so negligent, but they were already dead," said Diana in tones of profound regret. "But an assassination attempt by a human resistance fighter hardly represents a problem in internal security."

"I quite agree. However, there's been a new . . . development that must be taken into consideration. I'm concerned in the light of this . . . incident . . . that there may be other attempts. That cannot be countenanced."

"Of course not," Diana said stiffly. "Rest assured that I'm fully in control of this vessel, and perfectly capable of maintaining that control."

"Are you?" Pamela said, a hint of steel underlying the velvet tones of her voice. "I think you'd better come with me, Diana."

"Where?"

"The morgue. I have something to show you that you'll no doubt find very . . . enlightening."

When Diana and Pamela opened the door to the morgue, Steven looked up to greet them, standing beside Martin. A covered form lay between the officers. Pamela spoke. "Martin, I think you'd better show Diana what you discovered earlier."

"Yes, Supreme Commander," Martin said. With a quick, apologetic glance at Diana, he twitched the covering down, revealing Mike Donovan's body. He reached into the corpse's mouth, withdrawing a long, reptilian tongue. "Final identification is pending," he said.

Diana's eyes widened, the hair on the top of her head stirring as her crest, hidden beneath the human scalp and wig, partially elevated. "One of my own people!" Raging, she began to curse fluently, her real tongue flicking as she mouthed the slurring, hissing sibilants of her native language. The skin at the sides of her mouth split and gaped, leaving her jaws unbound, her vestigial fangs snapping wildly. Flying at the body, she raked the face with her nails, exposing the reptilian scales and crest beneath the skin.

A sharp blow from the Supreme Commander on the side of her head made her stagger back, blinking. "Control yourself, Diana!" Pamela said, sharply. "That's an order! Have your face seen to immediately!"

Shaking with fury, her hands partially covering her shredded face, Diana left the room.

Later that day, the four Visitor officers held a staff meeting. Diana's face had been repaired, and icy calm had replaced the white-hot fury of her earlier exhibition.

"The Fifth Column," Steven said matter-of-factly. "I've heard reports on other ships, but this is the first action aboard this one. It's spreading throughout the fleet. Every ship is reporting incidents."

"Not *my* ship," Diana said between her teeth. "I'll have no Fifth Column aboard *my* ship."

Martin spoke up. "If I may, I'd like to suggest that we remove important prisoners to Earth Security Headquarters until we can secure the ship. It would seem safer."

"He's right," Steven said. "As long as this ship is contaminated by the Fifth Column, we're vulnerable. We have Juliet Parrish, one of the most important resistance leaders. We can't afford to lose her."

"I agree." Pamela nodded.

"Yes," Diana agreed. "Implement Martin's suggestion immediately. I want her moved tonight."

"Very well," Steven said, signaling Martin with a look. The two officers made their exit, leaving Diana and Pamela at the conference table.

Pamela scanned a tablet of reports idly. "I'm giving orders to increase security. I'll put it in my report."

"This is my ship." Diana looked up. "I give the orders on my ship."

"Diana." Pamela assumed an air of patience that caused the other Visitor to stiffen in rage. "Your ship is but one in my squadron. You forget my rank."

Diana tapped the table for a moment, then smiled. "I may not have your rank, Pamela, but I *do* have the Leader's special interest. Which, in many cases, is even more desirable than rank."

Pamela put on a gentle, rueful expression. "I shouldn't rely too heavily on your relationship with the Leader, Diana. That road has seen very heavy traffic, you know. As a matter of fact, there were rumors of a new consort under consideration when I left. I hadn't met her, but by all reports, she's lovely. And quite a bit older than you are . . . prime-molted, full-patterned . . ."

"I don't believe you!"

"Diana, sex for favors is as old as ambition, but most people discover eventually that sex is too fragile a foundation to handle the weight of an ambition as . . . extensive as yours. When you were in favor, many people noticed how quickly you became dissatisfied with each achievement."

Diana raised her chin. "I've never seen you lack for ambition, Pamela."

"That's because my ambition has always ranged side by side with my current abilities." She smiled again. "You might take a moment to consider, my dear, that your . . . lover . . . sent you eighty trillion kilometers away from home. Hardly an indication that he couldn't bear not seeing you."

Smiling gently at Diana's discomfiture, Pamela took her leave.

Mike Donovan rapped sharply on the door of one of the rooms in the ancient saloon. "Come in," called Ruby Engels.

Donovan entered to find the elderly woman applying her cleaning-lady makeup. Ham Tyler sat beside her.

"We're ready to move," Donovan said to him. "I handed out the weapons just now. I hope the Teflon-tipped ammo holds out."

"If your people are as good shots as you claim, it'll be plenty," Ham said, watching Ruby as she dabbed a garish spot of rouge on her cheek.

"You don't have to do this, Ruby," Mike said. "You're taking a terrible risk for us, and don't think I don't know it."

Ruby looked at him for a long moment. "If you can get Julie back without me, tell me how, and I'll stay home and knit."

His gaze held hers for many seconds, then his eyes dropped. "Ruby . . ."

"She's a real trouper, Gooder. Something you wouldn't understand at all," Tyler said. "I could'a used this lady in Poland, lemme tell ya. She's pure steel under all that makeup." He fished in a bag under his feet. "Got a couple of presents for

you, Ruby. Here." Carefully he handed her a blackjack, an ice
pick in a leather scabbard, and a walkie-talkie. Drawing out the
icepick, he looked at her, his pale eyes questioning. "You
know where to aim on these gators, babe?"

Ruby nodded. "I think so." She touched her throat, her eye,
and the side of her head, just below the ear.

"Right," said Ham approvingly, "and if they're not wearing
that damn armor, right between the shoulder blades is okay for
a spot in the back."

"Got you," Ruby said.

"Now, on my signal," he tapped the walkie-talkie, "you
pull the plug on the electricity. Nothin' throws a fighting force
into disarray faster than having the lights go out. We'll be
waiting, and we'll move right in when you make your move.
Then you get out quick, understand?"

"Right," Ruby said.

"This entire operation is built around you, babe."

"A star at last!" Ruby grinned. "I didn't have this good a
role when I did the nurse in *Romeo and Juliet*."

Donovan gave her his hand. "Break a leg, Ruby. If this
works, Julie's gonna know what you risked for her sake—
'cause I'm gonna tell her. You've got more guts than any of us,
lady."

"*Shpilkes!*" She shook her finger under his nose in her best
Yiddish-momma manner. "I heard about you, Donovan,
volunteering to get captured just to get a try at Diana. We're all
doing what we have to, that's all."

"Well—" He hesitated, then awkwardly hugged her, careful
not to smudge her makeup. "Be careful, all right?"

"I can take care of myself," Ruby said. "You just tell
everyone in the strike force to pick up their feet."

Visitor Headquarters was lit up like a shopping mall during
the Christmas rush. Ham Tyler squinted through the electric
fence at the distant mansion with the enormous Visitor flag
hanging from a pole in front of it, the landing strip next to it,
and thought of France during the war. Shock troopers in full
armor stood posted on the enormous portico. Several officers
bustled around, obviously hurrying, casting looks now and
then at the great ship overhead.

Ham lowered his binoculars and addressed the others.

"They're expecting that squad ship with those VIP prisoners any second—you can tell from the way they're acting. We're gonna have to shake a leg."

Quietly the strike force gathered its arms, while Tyler eyed the electric fence. He clicked on the walkie-talkie. "Ruby?"

"Here," came the muffled response.

"What about the electricity on the fence?"

"I'm here by the power boxes in the basement. I can turn it off for a minute, but no longer. They've got a monitor in the checkpoint in front of the gate, and if the guard looks that way while the current is off, we're cooked."

"Right." Beckoning to Elias, Tyler handed him a pair of heavy-duty cutters, twin to his own. He thumbed the walkie-talkie. "We're set. Down it."

In desperate haste, the two men clipped a ragged hole in the fence. As soon as the last wire was sheared through, Ham clicked the walkie-talkie. "Power up, Ruby."

Caleb, Elias, Sancho, Brad, Maggie, Donovan, Chris, and the others gathered to hear Tyler's last instructions. "All right. One by one, through the hole, except for you, Gooder. You all set to make the pickup?"

Donovan nodded. "When the lights go down, I ram the gate."

"Right. Get the truck *moving*, 'cause we're not gonna have any extra time." He turned back to the others. "Need I warn you all that if you touch the wire on the way through the hole, you'll look like an overdone french fry?"

There was a combined murmur of assent.

"Good," Tyler continued. "All right, get in there, spread out, and when I fire the first shot, take that as your signal to nail as many lizards as you can until the lights go out. Then grab one of the prisoners and rendezvous on the edge of the landing strip closest to the gate. Any questions?"

There were no questions. Cautiously, the strike force crawled through the fence, scattering into the night. Tyler was the last to go.

A few minutes later, he crouched in the shadows two hundred feet away from the large concrete apron in front of the headquarters. Although a few cars were parked along its fringes, the central portion was bare, a landing strip for Visitor craft.

He scanned the surrounding darkness alertly, but caught no betraying movement. Either Donovan's people were as good as he said they were, or they'd gotten lost in the dark. There was no way to be sure.

Suddenly a shout came from the Visitor guards in front of the headquarters, and the ranks of shock troopers trotted alertly into place. Overhead, a spot of light shone out from the underside of the Mother Ship, then was quickly eclipsed as the comparatively tiny squad vehicle slid out of the landing bay, drifting effortlessly toward the earth.

*Okay, get ready,* Ham thought, taking an experimental sight through the starlight scope on his M-16. A few moments later, the squad vehicle drifted silently to earth, reflecting dimly the wash of lights from the mansion. The hatch came up, and Diana and Steven climbed out, followed by some dazed-looking human prisoners herded along by the shock troopers. Foremost among them was Juliet Parrish. Martin walked beside her. As Tyler watched, the blonde woman stumbled and the Visitor officer moved quickly to catch her arm.

*There's the signal,* Ham thought, taking careful aim. When he squeezed the trigger, Martin went down clutching at his leg, dragging Juliet with him.

A volley of shots rang out. Some Visitor guards began falling, others fired back into the darkness. Ham looked quickly for Diana, but couldn't see her—*damn scaly bitch leads a charmed life*—and continued shooting. When it looked as though the Visitor guards were beginning to regroup, he thumbed the switch on the walkie-talkie.

"Okay, Ruby, kill those lights!"

He heard the explosion from the basement power room faintly, and the lights went out. Tyler heard the crash of the gate as Donovan bashed through it with the big truck, and then he was up, running for the rendezvous point.

Scattered firing pulsed through the night as Ham raced across the landing strip, stopping on his way to catch the arm of a dazed-looking older man. (It was only later, when Tyler really *looked* at the man, that he realized he'd rescued the Mayor of Los Angeles.) Towing his prize stumbling beside him, he legged it toward the truck, identifying its location by sound only—either Donovan didn't want to give the Visitors a visual target, or they'd already shot the headlights out.

Reaching the vehicle, he slung his charge into the back of the truck, seeing Juliet Parrish's blonde head, then tumbled into the cab beside Mike. The air was full of the pulsing of Visitor weapons. Donovan slewed the truck around, gunning it, and took off. Maggie and Elias, still clinging to the side rails, were hastily dragged aboard by their fellow rebels.

Tyler flinched as the flying truck bounced off the gatepost on his side on its way out. "Did we get her?" Donovan yelled over the sound of the engine.

"Smooth as silk, Gooder. Your people did okay."

Glancing over at the newsman, Tyler didn't miss the relief spreading across Donovan's face—even in the greenish dimness of the dash lights, it was palpable. "Don't you think you oughtta turn on the headlights, Gooder?" he asked mildly.

"Oh. Yeah." Hastily Donovan flicked the truck's lights on as the heavy vehicle rumbled along the side road.

Ham grinned. "Since you've gotten hooked up with this bunch, you've really worn a few edges off, haven't you, Donovan?"

"As I live and breathe, the Fixer has turned into a student of human nature. When did you decide to take up psychoanalysis?"

"You oughtta know that any agent who makes it through twenty-five years in this business has to be a pretty observant guy. If you're not observant, especially about people, you're dead."

"I can't figure you, Ham. Sometimes you border on being human—then you come out with some of the most racist, right-wing, bigoted *shit* I've ever heard, and piss me off all over again. What gives?"

"Just natural talent, I guess." Ham heard the tightness in his own voice, and Donovan didn't miss it either.

"What's bugging you?"

"I'm worried about Ruby."

"Why? If things go according to plan, she'll never be connected with the mess. After all, she was assigned to the night shift to clean up the place for the brass—she has every right to be there."

"I know, but I'm still worrying. Everything else went so smooth—not one casualty—that I'm not gonna rest until I know Ruby's all right, too."

"Yeah, I know what you mean."

* * *

Ruby Engels moved cautiously through the dark basement with the aid of the flashlight she'd concealed in her cleaning bucket, along with the plastic explosives and blasting caps. The bucket was empty now. She carried it in her other hand— she couldn't afford to leave any evidence that might point to the identity of the saboteur.

She was almost to the foot of the basement steps when the door swung open with a jerk, and she found herself pinned in the gleam of a powerful hand torch. Daniel Bernstein stood at the top of the stairs. Ruby jumped and screeched, dropping her bucket—and the flashlight. "Mercy, boy, don't scare me like that!"

"What are you doing down here?"

Ruby limped painfully toward the stairs. "I was cleanin' in the main hall when the lights went out. I lost my way, and 'fore I knew what was what, I tripped and fell down these here stairs. Near broke my ankle."

"You're lying," Daniel said, coming down the stairs. "I saw a flashlight beam down here. Where'd you hide it?"

Ruby's armpits were clammy as she forced herself not to glance at the flashlight she'd kicked beneath a storage bin. "I dunno what you're talkin' about, boy. Can you give me a hand t' climb these stairs? It's a mercy I didn't break my leg, an' that's the truth."

"Don't I know you?" The young man shone the blinding beam of the high-power light into her face. "You look familiar."

Ruby cackled with just the right touch of lewd familiarity. "Know me? Honey, I just wish you'd known me thirty years ago. I ain't never seen you before. I'd remember a handsome young buck like you!"

"No." His eyes, in the reflected glare of the flashlight, narrowed. "I *do* know you." He reached out and grabbed her shoulder, shaking her hard. "Who are you?"

As he pulled his hand away, his fingers caught in the frazzled platinum wig Ruby wore, dragging it askew. Daniel reached out and snatched it off her head, baring Ruby's own shock of thick white hair. "I knew it!" he crowed. "Ruby Engels, who lived across the street! The crazy old biddy who ran off and joined the resistance, or so the gossip goes . . ."

Ruby gave up the pretense. "Yes. You know me."

"And you were the one who planted the charge that blew the power boxes, weren't you? When I turn you in, I'm gonna be a hero all over again."

"You'll be a hero, all right, and further disgrace your grandfather's name. Let me go, Daniel. For his sake, if not for your own."

He hesitated, and Ruby thought she saw a shadow of pain flit across his face at the mention of Abraham Bernstein. "No," he said.

"Daniel," she stepped closer to him, keeping her voice soft, coaxing, "I've known you all your life. Remember when you would come over to my house on the days I baked lebkuchen, and you'd watch through the screen door till I took them out of the oven? I used to decorate them like little faces for you, Danny. Little funny faces on the honey cakes?"

His face betrayed a struggle.

"You were a good boy, then, Danny. Could you have changed so much? Betray someone who was your grandfather's friend, who was kind to you? I don't think so."

Slowly she walked past him, her eyes holding his until the last possible moment. Putting her hand on the stair railing, she raised her foot and began to climb. *One step . . . two . . .*

"Stop!" his voice cracked uncertainly, then gained strength and conviction. "Stop! I'm warning you!"

*Three steps . . . Oh, God, let me get away, see my friends again. Let me see the end of this thing—did Julie get away? Four steps . . . five . . . please, God . . . Six steps . . .*

The shot caught her full in the back. Ruby gasped, hearing the pulse of the weapon, and for an endless second couldn't understand why her hand wouldn't hold onto the railing—she was going to fall—

*I'm falling . . .* Livid fire awoke in her back as her body twisted. Then came the terrible slow-motion helplessness of her backstroking plunge off the steps. *No, please, help—*

Ruby crashed onto the cement floor and lay there, stunned, trying to breathe but unable to. The pain was too all-encompassing, too huge. It had swallowed up the world, and now it would swallow her up. It was as simple as that. She could feel it rushing for her, slamming at her with a force so elemental that nothing of what had been Ruby Engels could stand in its way . . .

Reflexively she tried to gasp, but the pain arrived before the air did, snatching her up, taking her down with it, into a darkness where there was no place for anything, not even pain.

By the time Daniel stepped over her to summon his friends, she was dead.

# Chapter 27

Juliet Parrish and Mike Donovan stared up at the gargantuan Mother Ship as it hovered barely a thousand feet above the treetops. Dangling from its belly, like some obscene umbilical cord, was an enormous hose that ran down into a huge pipe. The pipe extended down into the pumping station that stood beside the huge dam.

Donovan made a helpless, wordless gesture with his hands. "Martin wasn't kidding. How can we fight something on this scale?"

"I don't know." Juliet pushed a few wisps of blonde hair out of her eyes. "I just don't know. We can't let the size of the operation hang us up. The bigger they are——"

"Yeah," said Donovan, unconvinced. "How long before they take the reservoir down below replenishable levels?"

"Chris Faber calculated that we have no more than two days to make our move."

"We'd better get rolling, then. We'll need the films of the pumping station to plan our attack." He gave her a quick, concerned glance. "You okay, Doc?"

She gave him a wan smile. "Yeah. Don't I look all right?"

"Sure. You make a perfect Visitor technician."

Slowly the two resistance fighters started toward the pumping station.

It had been ten days since Julie's recapture. During that time Juliet had rested, trying to recoup her exhausted reserves of emotional and physical strength. Her recovery wasn't helped by her profound grief when Lynn and Stanley Bernstein reported that Daniel, in a drunken frenzy, had bragged about killing Ruby Engels. Somehow Ruby's death was a blow that was especially hard to weather—everyone had liked and admired the older woman. Even Robin, who seldom responded to much of anything anymore, had sobbed for days.

Ham Tyler had gone tight-lipped and silent when given the news; it was the most emotion Donovan had ever seen "the Fixer" display. His regret had manifested itself in a driving determination to overthrow the Visitor movement, and, Donovan suspected, a new-found personal vendetta against Daniel Bernstein.

One of the two bright spots in the last week had been Tyler's gift to the group of several small devices that a Japanese network engineer had developed. The small units, when taped to the wearer's chest, duplicated the strange reverberation of Visitor speech in a human voice. The other good news was smuggled out to them from the Mother Ship—Martin was healing speedily from the flesh wound inflicted by Ham during the raid.

When Juliet and Donovan reached the pumping station, they walked completely around it, while Donovan filmed the exterior layout with a tiny video camera, also supplied by Ham. At the entrance, the shock trooper guard scrutinized them suspiciously. "Identification," he said brusquely.

Using their voicebox devices, both gave the ID code the Fifth Column had provided. The guard nodded. "Passes?"

They produced them. The shock trooper scanned them, then jerked his rifle at them. "Okay."

Once inside the station, the two fighters quickly canvassed the interior. They dared not stay too long, however—when they passed one of the technicians for the second time, the Visitor looked up at them curiously. After filming the network of catwalks and walkways strung like fragile spiderwebs from each massive turbine to its neighbor, they hastily made their exit.

Once outside and away from the station, they paused, while Donovan took a quick pan around the hillsides. Juliet frowned as she took in the acres of land surrounding the reservoir and station. "You know, Donovan, we really ought to circle this area and sketch it. It would be a real help if we could find another road to serve as an alternate escape route."

Donovan shrugged. "You're the boss. If you feel up to it, I'm ready."

"I'm fine," Julie said tartly. "Let's go."

They hiked through the area for nearly an hour, and were a little more than halfway around the circle when they came across an old road—hardly more than a bridle path, actually, but it had possibilities. Julie looked up. "Hold on a second, Donovan, while I put this in."

She took out her geologic survey map and busily began sketching a detailed insert showing the old road, using the USGS quad map as a reference. After a minute she realized Donovan was staring at her—or, rather, at her hand. Her left hand. She was drawing with it.

The point of the pencil snapped as it dug into the paper. Juliet stared at her hand for long moments. "Oh, my God, Donovan. Look at me. I'm one of *them*."

He stepped closer to her, his green eyes worried. "No you're not, Doc. You've been fine since you got back—"

"No, I haven't been!" Juliet's words ended in a sob. With a visible effort, she controlled herself. "I've just been hiding it, that's all. This isn't the first time I've caught myself using my left hand, Donovan. That bitch—she's messed up my mind. I might betray us all, and never know it. I should quit before I hurt somebody."

"Bullshit! We need you! The only thing that kept the group together while you were gone was the thought of getting you back!"

"I don't know." She pushed her hair out of her eyes, then determinedly picked up the pencil with her right hand. The point was still broken, however. Quietly, Donovan took out his pocket knife and sharpened it.

After sketching the old road, they decided to continue around the station, then try and locate the outlet for the road using the pickup truck they'd left hidden near the gate.

After a half-hour more walking, they entered a field of mustard grass. It provided a welcome burst of color from the tawny sameness of the turf surrounding the pumping station. They were far enough away that even the throbbing of the giant turbines was gone; there was no sound save the swish of their feet on the grass. Julie walked on a few steps, then, without warning, plopped down. "That's it. Not one more step until I get some rest. Do you have that flask?"

"Yeah." Donovan sank onto the grass beside her, then handed her the water. Julie drank thirstily, then handed the flask back to him.

"I'm out of shape," Juliet said, stretching out. "Those couple of weeks in the Mother Ship wreaked havoc with my muscles. I couldn't climb another slope right now if Diana and the entire fleet hove over the hill."

"I'm beat, too."

"Donovan?"

"What?"

"I wasn't kidding when I said that I'd been feeling . . . funny." She rolled over on her side, propping her head up on her hand, looking at him intently. "It *could* be that I've been converted."

"Wouldn't you know? You don't look converted to me."

She tried to return his grin and failed. "I don't know. My memories of those last couple of sessions aren't too clear."

"What was it like? How does Diana do it?"

Her voice was very low, and just from hearing it, Mike knew that she hadn't spoken of this to anyone else. "They can induce fantasies out of your own mind. They put you into something like hypnosis, using drugs, and I guess they make you talk. I don't remember—but I know that everything I've ever been afraid of—*everything*, no matter how disgusting or private—appeared in those fantasies she sent me."

She rolled onto her back again, looking up at the cloud-strewn blue sky—where the Mother Ship didn't block it out. "I kept being chased into deserted buildings, and men would be hunting for me. I'd try to hide, but they'd find me. They always found me. Sometimes . . ." She swallowed, and Donovan could see the lines of her throat move. "Sometimes I was in a deserted sewer, kind of, and I'd put my hands on the walls to guide me, and the walls would come to life."

Donovan made a small sound, and Julie sat up and looked over at him. "Yeah, it was pretty bad. But no matter how bad I *say* it was, living it was worse . . . if you know what I'm trying to tell you."

"Yeah," he said, pulling up a handful of grass and watching

it drift away in the slight breeze. "Look, Julie, no matter what happened to you up there, you're having doubts. That means you can't have been completely converted."

"Seems to me that being partly converted is like saying a little bit pregnant—you either are, or you aren't."

"They messed with your mind, Julie, that's all. As long as you have no contact with them, they have no control over you."

She was silent for a long time, then gestured toward the reservoir they could no longer see. "The lake is down already—did you notice?"

"Yeah."

"The oceans are next," she said, her tones clear, almost detached—but when Donovan looked at her, he could see tears on her face.

"No," he said, sitting up and putting an arm across her shoulders. "They're not going to get that far."

She swallowed. "Not unless I help them, maybe. And never realize I'm doing it."

"Hey . . . hey, Doc. I'll keep an eye on you, if it'll make you feel any better."

Her eyes were very blue when she looked over at him. "I kinda got the idea you were doing that, anyway."

"You did, huh?" He was very conscious suddenly that the moment had changed—they had crossed some invisible barrier that stands between men and women, an obstacle that is seldom recognized until it is overcome, left behind.

"Yeah," she said. "I did."

"I haven't wanted to . . . well, you know." He cleared his throat, then tried again. "You were so wracked up, and then we found out about Ruby, and—" he hesitated, "I didn't want to push . . . anything, when—" He broke off, staring at her.

She grinned at him. "Y'know, this is the first time I've ever seen you stumble."

"Yeah?"

"Yeah," she said firmly, then, taking his head in her hands, kissed him gently on the mouth.

After a few seconds she drew away, flushed, her eyes dancing. "Nice," she said, a little breathlessly. "You've had some practice, Donovan."

His hands came up to touch her hair, loosen the braid that

held it in back. It spilled down over his fingers as softly as the breeze on the hillside. His voice was husky. "For God's sake, when are you ever gonna call me Mike?"

"I did . . . once," Julie said, touching his cheek with fingers that felt infinitely cool and long.

"When?"

"When you were lying there in front of me, dead, up there on the Mother Ship. If anything snapped me out of the conversion, that was it—thinking *you* were dead." She hesitated, remembering, then said shakily, "I think I really had managed to hide it from myself till then."

"Julie." He kissed her again, harder, feeling her mouth warm and living beneath his, opening like a flower. His arms went out, pulling her against him as his fingers searched for the concealed fastenings of her Visitor uniform . . .

When Juliet woke, she realized she'd been asleep for quite a little while. The position of the sun had changed, and the prickly tightness across her buttocks bespoke sunburn to come. Donovan was still asleep, lying on his back, snoring lightly, his arms still firmly wrapped around her. Juliet grinned, snuggling her head onto his chest. It was so peaceful here, that even if she *had* managed to sunburn her butt—it was worth it.

*A few more minutes,* she thought, feeling a kind of liquid warmth course through her body, as though it were some kind of elixir out of legend. *It's been so damn long since I've felt* alive—*and like a woman.*

Her fingers were splayed against his belly, and for long moments she simply enjoyed the rise and fall of his chest, the taut smoothness of flesh over muscle, the silky tickle of the hairs against her palm. Then, with a sudden indrawn breath, he woke.

Juliet looked up at him. "Hi, Mike," she said with a bright grin. "Long time no see."

"How long have I been asleep?" he mumbled, his arms tightening around her.

"Dunno. Your watch is somewhere behind me. But by the position of the sun, we ought to be getting back."

He peered at the watch. "Jesus," he said. "We've been sacked out here for two and a quarter hours."

Juliet levered herself up on an elbow. "It's a damn good

thing Diana *didn't* come charging up here. It would have been downright embarrassing to be captured in the buff."

He laughed, pulling her down to him, kissing her as though they had all the time in the world. Julie cooperated, her arms tightening around his shoulders as they embraced. But when he rolled her over onto her back, she flinched suddenly.

"What is it?" Mike asked, peering at her anxiously.

"Oh, nothing," she said. "I just wish I'd had the sense to drag one of these damn uniforms across me before I dozed off. I'm sunburned."

He began to chuckle, and she shoved at him. "Go ahead and laugh, Donovan! You darker-skinned types have no idea what it's like to go through life having to worry about sunburn."

"No," he gasped, laughing harder. "I'm full of sympathy, really!"

"What you're full of is—"

He interrupted hastily. "No, honestly! I was just imagining what everyone's going to look like when we come trooping in, hours late, with red noses, and *you* can't sit down. They'll think I'm some kind of animal." He began to snicker again.

"Damn," Juliet said, envisioning it herself. "Especially Father Andrew. Communal living has its drawbacks, doesn't it?"

"You bet," he said. "Do you realize there's not one damn double bed in the whole HQ?"

Juliet thought about it. "We'll work something out."

# Chapter 28

The raid on the pumping station was a flawed success—the resistance fighters were able to blow the installation up, destroying much of the special equipment and killing several of the new technicians Pamela had brought. But they lost Brad in the fighting. The young man fell during the mad scramble to get out before the charges they had set could explode. Sprawled on the catwalk with a badly broken leg, knowing he was unable to climb out, Brad chose to stay behind, guarding the rear, while the others got away. In spite of Brad's protests, Sancho and Maggie would have turned back to get him, but, sharing a long look of final respect with the ex-cop, Ham Tyler ordered them at gunpoint to keep moving.

Wearily, the fighters dragged themselves back together, slogging through each day as though it were something to be fought, like the Visitors. They began to take refuge in silliness—practical jokes were in vogue for a couple of days, then campy movies on the VCR. Donovan and Juliet watched "Attack of the Killer Tomatoes" twice in a row one evening, over a bottle of Liebfraumilch and a joint, careful to keep the grass hidden from Father Andrew and the kids.

Soap operas also tended to gather a following among people who had no regular daytime jobs. Polly Maxwell pounded on the door of Julie's tiny bedroom, now even more crowded due to the mattress from a double bed which had replaced the tiny cot one afternoon. "Mr. Donovan! Mr. Donovan!"

Donovan appeared, bare-chested and bare-footed. "What is it?"

"Come see! On the television!" She dashed off.

"What is it?" Juliet was at her desk, trying to unsnarl the havoc Mike had wreaked on the Bellamy checkbook.

"Dunno. Sounds important."

Dragging on a shirt, he followed Polly down the hall, Juliet behind him. They found most of the group in the common room, avidly watching "The Young and the Restless."

Donovan stood in the doorway. "What's going on?"

"You'll see, Mr. Donovan. They've been showing it every commercial," Josh Brooks looked up at him. "Sit down and wait a minute."

Mike sat on the beat-up armchair, Julie perching beside him. A few minutes later, to a crescendo of organ music, the screen flickered, and Diana's features came into focus. "This is a special bulletin from the Visitors," she said.

The camera drew back as she spoke to reveal the Second-in-Command sitting with a child on her lap. Donovan stiffened. It was Sean. Diana ruffled the boy's hair gently. "We'd like to request the help of all people in the Los Angeles area. This little boy wandered into Visitor Headquarters and is looking for his daddy. If anyone can help us find this boy's father, we'd be most grateful."

The picture faded out, to be replaced a second later by a tiny woman confronting a mammoth toilet bowl. Disgusted, Donovan clicked the set off.

"What are you gonna do, Mr. Donovan?" Josh asked.

"I don't know, Josh," Mike said heavily. His hands were busy, folding and unfolding the battered Dodgers cap he carried like a talisman. "Wait, I guess. Diana'll find a way to let us know what she wants. Probably leak it through the Fifth Column. I'm supposed to talk to Martin tomorrow."

Fran Leonetti looked at him. "What do you think she wants?"

"I don't know. My head on a platter, probably."

Juliet said nothing, but her fingers were gentle as they rubbed the back of his neck.

"What's the story, man?" Elias asked, when Donovan returned from his meeting with Martin the next day.

Seated at the conference table, Donovan didn't look up from the notepad where he was doodling the letter "V" over and over again. "Diana announced it to the entire L.A. ship, knowing, I guess, that it'd get back to us; if I don't notify them that we agree to their terms in the Personal column of the paper by Thursday, Sean dies."

"They wouldn't kill a little kid!" Maggie said, then looked around for support. "Would they?" her voice trailed off.

"Those snakes would do most anything they have to to get what they want," Elias said. "What do they want, Mike?"

"Me. A straight exchange. We name the time and place. They bring Sean, and he goes free. I go with them."

"Shit." Elias' comment seemed to suffice for everyone. The room was quiet once more, for long minutes.

Finally Donovan sat up. "I don't think they'll kill him," he said slowly. "They need my mother as their spokesperson, and, corrupt as Eleanor is, she'd never countenance them killing her only grandchild. She won't let them hurt Sean. I'm not going to do it."

"Mike, no!" Julie grabbed his wrist. "Believe me, I know what it cost you to make that decision, but *no way!*"

"Don't overestimate Eleanor's usefulness to them, Mike," Robert Maxwell said, shaking his head. "Diana wouldn't hesitate to do away with Eleanor Dupres the moment she became a nuisance to her."

"Robert's right," Elias said. "That dragon lady's got a heart as warm as all outer space. She'd off Sean out of sheer spite."

Donovan looked around. "You know what she'll do to me. I'll be in that conversion cell faster than you can say 'evil aliens.' Or in the torture chamber with the blowtorch. Or on the wrong end of a truth serum. *I know too much.* If she makes me talk, I'll destroy everything we've worked for."

He thought for a moment. "There's one way." He grimaced. "God, I wish I hadn't thought of this." He drummed nervously on the table, then faced them all, his eyes level. "I could take poison," he said.

He turned to Juliet. "What could I take just before the exchange, that would let me walk out there under my own steam, but would kill me before they could get anything out of me?"

"An overdose of lots of things would work. Enteric-coated

cyanide would be the best, if we could get it," Juliet said automatically, then shook her head violently. "What am I saying? That's out of the question! No way, Donovan, *no way!*"

"But—"

"I said 'no,' and that's *final*, Mike. There are too many possibilities to resort to something that drastic. You're discounting Martin and the Fifth Column."

"But—"

"Besides, we can make your information obsolete, Donovan," Juliet said. "We'll move HQ again, and you won't know where. We alter the details of our long-range plans. We change the bank accounts, and the codes. We can do it." He gazed at her skeptically. "We *can*," she said. "Don't make this any harder for either of us than it has to be." She made an abrupt little gesture, then straightened. "It's hard enough telling you to turn yourself in, knowing I—we—may never see you again."

"Hey." He took her hand. "Okay, you've made your point. But don't write me off that quick, Julie. I've got the best record of anyone here for getting on and off that Mother Ship. Maybe I can do it again. Maybe Martin can help."

"You hope," Elias said quietly.

"Yeah. I hope."

The exchange was set to take place at night, on a cordoned-off bridge on the L.A. freeway. Ham Tyler and Juliet were the only resistance members openly with Donovan. They'd taken the precaution of stationing Elias and Sancho as hidden sharpshooters. When the lights blinked on the squad vehicle in the agreed-upon signal, Ham flashed the lights on the van he was driving, and turned to Mike. "There they are." He hesitated for an awkward moment, then said, "I'm sorry about this, Donovan. Wish there were something I could do."

"I know." With a wry smile, Mike stuck out his hand. "Take care of things."

When he turned to Juliet, there were no words. He kissed her, then, turning away, began the long walk across the bridge. In the distance, he could see a small figure approaching. Sean.

Donovan quickened his stride, his eyes straining to see his son's face against the glare of the spotlights from the squad vehicle. By the time he could make out the boy's features, he was running. "Sean!"

He grabbed the sturdy young body tightly, picking the boy up.

"Dad—" Sean lifted his face to Donovan's. "Dad, I—"

"Hey . . ." Donovan tousled the thick brown hair, so like his own, his throat so tight that for a moment he couldn't summon words. Then he remembered something, and pulled the battered baseball cap out of his pocket. "Here. I kept it for you."

"Dad—" Sean's eyes were swimming.

"Well, I gotta get moving. You look good, son. Tell Julie I said you need a haircut." He kissed the boy on the cheek, hugged him once more, then set him down, moving on into the glare of the searchlights.

Once aboard the Mother Ship, Donovan was subjected to the most intensive and insensitive body search he'd ever undergone. Diana's technicians made Cambodian prison guards seem like paragons of delicacy and tact. Aching, he was finally allowed to dress, then taken to a cell.

Time ceased to have meaning. Donovan wondered at first why he wasn't tortured immediately, but realized, after several waking and sleeping periods, that Diana had a far greater understanding of human psychology than he'd given her credit for. Leaving him alone in the cell, with the lights burning, without a watch, was a good way to weaken even the strongest will to resist. Without external stimulation, he had too many hours to spend in worrying about what was going to happen to him. Only the increasing roughness on his chin gave him any sense of time passing.

He had fantasies at times that the ship wasn't even orbiting his planet anymore, that he'd been forgotten and was on his way to Sirius, leaving behind a desert, dying Earth. Intellectually he knew he hadn't been locked up for more than a week or two, at most, but at times it was hard to convince himself of that.

Finally, one day he was startled by the sound of his door sliding open. A Visitor entered, carrying a tray of food. Donovan sat on his bunk, eyeing the newcomer suspiciously.

The alien looked at him gravely. "You don't mind the weather in here, do you?"

Surprised, Donovan found the correct response automatically. "Only at night."

"Then you must not be a night owl."

Donovan grinned ecstatically. "Boy, it's nice to have friends! Did the head iguana send you?"

The Visitor nodded at Donovan's code reference to Martin. "Yes. I'm Oliver. But I'm afraid I have bad news for you, Mr. Donovan."

"What do you mean?"

"While you've been locked up here, Diana's been working on a new truth serum that she says is foolproof. She's going to try it on you by tomorrow at the latest."

Donovan swallowed. "Doesn't sound good."

"Yes. And since your other escape, security aboard the Mother Ship has been tripled. It would take nothing short of a full armed assault to get you out this time. I'm sorry, but we can't afford that risk for just one man."

"I understand. I've been there myself."

"We also can't afford to have our people here on the Mother Ship exposed."

"I understand that too."

"Do you? Then you'll understand why I was sent to bring you this."

The Visitor took a small green capsule out of his pocket. "We're not executioners, Mr. Donovan. It's your decision."

Donovan looked at the tiny piece of gelatin-wrapped death for a long, considering moment. *I wanted some warning,* he thought. *Some time to say good-bye to all of it—all of the places, the things, and most of all, the people.* He took a deep breath.

Donovan reached for the capsule. Just as his fingers closed on it, the door slid open again. One of Diana's aides—the one Martin had identified as Jake—stood outside, his gun drawn. Oliver whirled, his elbow accidentally knocking the pill out of Mike's hand, his own hand going to his sidearm. Before he could draw the weapon, Jake fired, and the Fifth Columnist fell.

Donovan threw himself across the room, his eyes fixed on the skittering capsule. He grabbed it, Jake's boot came down on his hand, making Mike's vision blur with pain. The

Visitor stood on his hand, waiting, as Diana entered the cell. "I'm sorry, Mr. Donovan. We can't let you go without a deathbed confession."

Minutes later, Donovan was strapped into a device that bore a disquieting resemblance to a dentist's chair. Diana smiled at him cheerfully as her lab technician prepared an injection. "I suggest you relax, Mr. Donovan. It won't make any difference whether you're tense or not. This shot will make you feel much more cooperative, and we'll have a nice little chat."

The door to the interrogation cell slid aside, and Martin entered. "Here are those reports you wanted—" He broke off, looking at Donovan, his face tight with fear.

"Thank you, Martin. Can you stay for a few minutes to help me? With your knowledge of the Los Angeles area, you can help me pinpoint the geographic locations Mr. Donovan and I are about to discuss." Diana injected Mike's arm.

"Very well, Diana." Martin stood stiffy, watching Donovan. For long minutes, Mike felt nothing—then he began to experience a slight flush of warmth running up into his face, out along his limbs. He felt very relaxed—like someone just awakening from a good night's sleep. Embarrassed, he realized he was getting an erection.

Impersonally, Diana checked his physical reactions, then nodded. "That's fine. How do you feel, Mr. Donovan?"

"Fine," Mike said. What was the point in trying to lie before he had to?

"Good. Now let's talk about the nature of truth. You believe in truth, don't you Mr. Donovan?"

"Depends on whose brand I hear."

She inclined her head graciously. "Clever. But the serum hasn't yet taken full effect. What is your full name?"

"Michael Sean Donovan."

"Such a lovely Irish name. Your mother told me about your father, and how he named you." Diana smiled gently. "And how old are you?"

*Thirty-six . . . thirty-six . . . thirty-six . . .* Mike's mind screamed, and his mouth struggled to form words. "Thir—thirty—sss—sev'n."

Diana cocked her head. "How interesting! A lie! Mr. Donovan, I couldn't have chosen a better subject to give my little concoction what you humans call the acid test. I don't

know which one of you is more stubborn—you, or Juliet
Parrish."

Mention of Juliet strengthened Mike's failing grip on reality.
He had to resist. Had to.

"And what color is your hair, Mr. Donovan?"

"Blue." Donovan said it quickly, without thinking.

"Really?"

"Brown." Mike flinched as he heard the word come
tumbling out.

She smiled, ruffling his hair. "Yes, a lovely shade of brown.
That's much better. Now tell me, Mr. Donovan, about the Fifth
Column. Is there one aboard my ship?"

"Y—yes." Out of the corner of his eye Donovan saw
Martin make a small, convulsive movement.

"I knew that already . . . but there's something I don't
know. Who is their leader, Mr. Donovan?"

Sweat trickled down Mike's face as he struggled to keep his
lips pressed tightly over the name that wanted to burst out in
response to her question. "Nnnnn—"

"Who is the leader of the Fifth Column, Mr. Donovan?"

Donovan gasped for breath, and the name escaped.
"Martin."

Martin's sidearm was already in his hand as Diana, stunned,
swung to look at him. Diana's technican leaped toward the
Fifth Columnist, his gun in his hand, but Martin, ducking
behind the interrogation chair, fired first. The Visitor slumped
to the floor. Martin loosed another shot at Diana as she fled out
the door, then he sprang after her and locked the door panel.

Hastily unstrapping Donovan, who by this time was regarding the world through a rosy drugged haze, Martin dragged
open a nearby ventilation grille, then, lifting the nearly limp
human, hauled him over and stuffed him in. He heard Donovan
swear, then his slurred words. "No, not the damn ventilation
shafts again, Martin . . . I wouldn't be in this whole mess if
it weren't for them . . . wanna go home . . ."

The Visitor dragged the human down the shaft until he
reached one of the larger crawlways and could stand erect. By
this time Mike was giggling. "You're rocked, Donovan,"
Martin said, pulling the human's arm across his shoulders.

Mike stumbled along the metal crawlway with him. "Wha'
you mean, rocked? There's no music in here."

"Stoned," Martin snapped, "I meant stoned. Dammit, Donovan, can't you pick up your feet just a little?"

Donovan peered owlishly at his feet. "But they're so *heavy*."

Martin sighed, and without further argument picked up the human, slinging him across his shoulder in a fireman's carry. He hurried, making the best speed he could toward the lower tunnels. A rasping buzz sounded behind him. Quickly he turned, looking for the source. It came again—still behind him.

Suddenly the truth dawned, and Martin, not knowing whether to laugh or curse, hurried on down the walkway, accompanied by Donovan's peaceful snores.

"*Julie!*" Harmy's cry came from the corridor of the new headquarters. Juliet, who had been in her new laboratory studying the liver biopsy they'd taken from the body of a Visitor killed during a bombing raid, stiffened.

"I'm coming! What is it?"

When she reached the hallway, she saw Robin staring aghast at a green gelatinous-looking fluid puddling around her feet, as Harmony supported the girl. "Her water's broken, Julie! She's in labor!"

Julie reached over to put an arm around Robin's shoulders even as the girl gasped and doubled up in agony. "Find Cal, Robert, and Willie, quick!" Julie ordered. "I'll get her into the small lab with the examination table."

After Julie's initial examination confirmed that Robin was dilated about two centimeters, there was little more to be done except wait. Robert stayed by his daughter's side, coaching her in the Lamaze breathing techniques. Julie lay down for several hours, though she couldn't sleep. She had a hunch it was going to be a long night.

It was. Robin's amniotic fluid had broken just before lunchtime. By midnight, her dilation had not markedly increased and the fetus wasn't dropping. Julie examined her and ordered a half-dose of Demerol, hoping the drug would allow Robin a chance to rest between contractions.

At 4:00 A.M., she did another internal examination, discovering the girl's cervical dilation was still at two centimeters. Robin was exhausted; her eyes purple-shadowed and staring, her forehead beaded with sweat. She kept losing track of her breathing patterns, and was beginning to tense and "go under" with the force of the contractions, instead of panting and staying "on top" of them.

When Juliet's six o'clock examination showed no further progress, she looked up at Cal in anguish. Robin was locked into a private hell of moaning, stabbing pain, and Julie doubted the girl could even hear them, but she motioned him into the other corner of the room just in case. "It's been sixteen hours, Cal, and no significant progress. The fetus isn't dropping—hasn't even budged. I'm afraid we'll have to go for a caesarean."

He nodded. "Yeah. You ever observe one?"

"I scrubbed for one, once. Doctor Bradley even let me do some assisting. If only Fred were here!"

"I'll tell Harmy to prep her, while we scrub."

"Okay."

Thirty minutes later Julie stood beside her patient, her tired eyes intent on Robin's yellowish-orange painted and draped abdomen, the scalpel in hand. "Ready?" she asked Cal and Harmy, who stood by, ready to assist. "Is the incubator ready?"

"Ready, Julie," Harmy said.

Juliet swallowed, reaching forward. At the last second she realized that she was holding the scalpel in her left hand; quickly she switched it to her right. "I'm going to do a bikini cut," she told Cal, as her hand hovered over the girl's freshly-shaved pubic area. "The time I helped Doctor Bradley in the charity ward, that's what he did."

"Sounds good." Cal nodded reassuringly, his own eyes anxious above his mask. Julie's hand pressed the scalpel into the skin lightly, then, as a line of blood welled up, she had to force herself not to jerk back. Biting her lip, she narrowed her world to the six inches of the incision site, and made a quick, firm cut, watching the layers of flesh and muscle draw back. "Sponge, and give me some suction. I have to find the uterine wall."

Yes, there it was. Dipping her left hand into the incision, Julie measured its depth, then she was cutting the uterus, at the bottom of the organ. She could see the problem now. Robin was a bit narrow—not side to side, but front to back. The bulge that must be the infant's head was tilted back. "Here's part of the problem," Julie said. "We've got a posterior presentation."

"No wonder she had all that back labor," Cal said. "Poor kid."

"All right, I've got it open. Here—" Julie reached for the bulge, and suddenly her hands were full of a slithery-red infant, still surrounded by the translucent amniotic sac. Juliet lifted it out. "It's a girl! Suction her mouth!" Harmy did so, and the infant began to squeak, then emitted thin, indignant cries.

"Is she okay?" Robert said, from where he was monitoring his daughter's vital signs.

"Appears to be," Julie said, watching as Harmy carefully wiped the baby's little face and body. Fortunately she was holding the infant over the incubator as she did so, for suddenly the baby opened her perfect little pink mouth, and a long reptilian tongue lashed forth!

Harmy nearly dropped the child, and Willie, who had been standing by, observing quietly, leaped forward to take the baby from her shaking hands. Julie cast a despairing look at Cal, imagining Robin's reaction when she awoke and saw her daughter.

The girl's abdomen heaved beneath Juliet's fingers!

"Wait a minute, we've got something else in here!"

"*Twins?*" Cal leaned forward.

"No wonder there was so much fetal movement." Julie reached deeper, upward, and her fingers encountered another head-bulge. When the figure began to emerge from the uterus, Julie gasped. "Oh, *God! What the hell is it?*"

The creature was small, greenish in color, and clearly of reptilian derivation. Its limbs bore small claws, its head was crested—as Julie's shaking hands tightened on it, it opened two blue-green, very human eyes and stared at her silently.

"Oh, Jesus. I —" Juliet bit her lip, averting her eyes. "*How could this be?*"

Hesitantly, she handed the creature to Willie, who was the only one willing to touch it. Cal stood staring at it, his eyes shocked. "This is *impossible*, Julie!"

"We have a patient, Cal," Julie said, trying to control her nausea. "Robin needs us. We'll talk about this later."

"All right, Julie." He turned back to assist her.

"Sutures ready?"

"Ready. Here."

They continued to work, neither looking toward the two tiny creatures Willie and Harmy cared for. Robert Maxwell stood by his daughter's head, clasping her unconscious hand, silent tears shining on his face in the merciless glare of the overhead lights.

"Mike—another patrol! Get back!"

Donovan made a face as he stepped, not for the first time in the past ten days, into hip-deep black sludge. His feet skidded on the slick metal bottom, and, had it not been for Martin's hasty grab, he'd have gone down. Reaching the other side of the drainage trench, they crawled up onto the narrow service ledge and crouched, hands and faces hidden, as the shock troopers approached. The sludge was an invaluable but nauseating camouflage—in the darkness of the deepest hold on the Mother Ship, the troopers passed them by. They listened to the dying echoes of their footsteps on the deckplates.

Shivering from the wet cold, Donovan followed Martin along the ledge, watching his friend narrowly. Martin didn't shiver—he wasn't built for it—but Donovan had discovered that the prolonged cold made him sluggish and disoriented.

When they reached relative safety beneath the cavernous overhang of a huge pump, both collapsed. Donovan closed his eyes; the momentary energy of fear drained from his body like blood. In another day, two at the most, he wouldn't have the strength to scurry and hide.

"Good thing you heard them, Martin. I was so busy listening for drips of water that I missed 'em completely."

"I didn't hear them, Mike," Martin said. "I sensed the vibration of their feet."

"Well, however you did it, it saved us." Donovan leaned back, listening—then he heard it. "Martin! Water dripping! This way!"

The two crawled among the maze of scummy piping, searching for the elusive sound. When they reached it, Mike gestured Martin to go first. "You deserve first turn for saving us." Donovan didn't watch as Martin lapped at the water dripping from a moisture-laden beam; the sight of Martin's tongue still unnerved him. He heard a quick scuttling of tiny feet, and, knowing what was coming, turned to see Martin lash out with that incredible inhuman swiftness to catch the rat. The creature squeaked and struggled in the Visitor's hold. Donovan looked at it with pity.

Martin smiled sympathetically. "It makes you ill to watch. I will walk away to eat."

"No, don't bother. I owe you more than I ever can repay. If you hadn't given me the contents of those ration packages Lorraine managed to smuggle to you, and lived on what you could scarf up in this dump, I wouldn't be alive. It just takes getting used to."

Out of deference to Donovan's delicate stomach, Martin considerately dispatched the rat before swallowing it. "Our peoples are very similar in some ways," he said, "but very different in others."

"What's your history like? Have you always been scratching to survive, fighting amongst yourselves?"

"No, as a matter of fact, we were much more peaceful in our history than you were, until Our Leader came. Now we have the Fifth Column aboard the ships, and, back home, there is the Alliance."

"The Alliance? What are they, interstellar Marxists, or just your everyday radical movement?"

"They are the ones who opposed the Leader. They are more of a moderate voice, I guess you could say. They were against the plan to take over Earth, for example. They're made up of largely the more . . . intellectual segment of our society. They have good ideas—but they're not big on fighting for them."

"But if you could ally them with the Fifth Column, which has a lot of military experts like yourself, maybe—"

"Maybe." Martin said heavily. "But at the moment, what's the use of thinking about them? They're light-years away, and have no ships, little armament."

"Guess I won't wait for the bugle charge, then." Martin looked at him, obviously not understanding. "They can't help us, then," Mike translated.

"No," Martin agreed.

"But maybe you could help them. If you could take over one of the Mother Ships—"

"That would be a tremendous aid to their efforts against the

Leader—but at the moment there seems little likelihood of that."

"We'll get out of here," Donovan said, trying to believe it himself. "Maybe Lorraine will be able to bring some more food—more weapons—"

"She took an incredible risk the last time. I told her not to do it again."

"She's a gutsy lady."

"Yes."

"All of your people have guts. Did I know the guy who put on my face and tried to kill Diana?"

"Yes. It was Barbara."

"Oh . . ." Donovan felt a quick, intense grief, remembering the way the young Visitor had tried to help him. "I'm sorry."

They were silent for a long time. Donovan felt himself slipping down toward sleep—or something deeper than sleep. He fought it. "How much longer do you think we can hold out down here?"

"I don't know. Without you to keep me awake, share your body heat, I would have slipped off into hibernation days ago. I can probably survive longer than you can, eating the rats escaped from the laboratories, but when you are gone, there will be no one to keep me awake. So I will go too." Martin blinked at him. "Do you mind talking for a while? I must stay awake."

"Me too," Mike said. "What do you want to talk about?"

"I would like to understand you better, you humans. Tell me about yourself. What frightens you . . . and why. What you have learned since this whole thing began."

"I can't remember what it was like before. It seems to have been like this forever," Donovan said. "As to what frightens me—a lot of things, frankly. Some I don't like to admit to." He thought for a moment. "I'm scared to die, yeah. For a long time I was scared of being too close to others. But not so much anymore."

He looked down at his hands, using his thumbnail to scrape some of the filth away, peeling it off in little black strings. "I'm scared of failing," he said. "So much depends on us. I've always had a thing about not failing. Made me kinda reckless, an overachiever. Probably wrecked my marriage, that tendency. I always put it all on Margie, but now when I think about it . . ." he trailed off, scratching thoughtfully at his beard.

He sat for a long moment. "People who hold too much power scare me. Diana scares the living hell out of me. I don't understand people like that."

Martin settled back against the comparatively dry side of the beam. "What else frightens you?"

"Falling. I have dreams about falling from a great height. Looking down from a really high place makes my hands crawl, 'cause I think about falling."

"But you're a pilot. You must've had to parachute at some point in your training."

"Yeah. I jumped twice. I was never thrilled about it, though. It was just something I had to do in order to fly, and I wanted to fly more than anything else in the world. Then one night I was on a photo-recon mission over supply lines leading to Hanoi, piloting a U-2—that Widowmaker was a *bitch* to handle—and I took a burst on my right wing. I ejected about three thousand feet up . . . and my parachute didn't open."

"What? Then how—"

"Oh, my reserve 'chute worked. A bit of a rough landing— but the hike back behind our lines was the real pain. But ever since then, I dream every so often about those first couple of seconds when I was falling, and my first 'chute went bust." He smiled wryly. "I was so scared I damn near wet myself."

They were silent for a few minutes. Donovan noticed Martin's eyes starting to close, and shoved him with his foot. "Your turn. What frightens you?"

"That I may be wrong to be working against my own people—my own leaders."

Donovan looked at him. "Do me a favor. Don't struggle too much with that one until we get out of here, okay?"

Martin smiled.

Donovan hesitated. "You know that I'm really sorry I got you into this mess. If only I'd been able to keep my mouth shut back in that lab . . ."

"It wasn't your fault. It was just a matter of time until somebody discovered me anyway."

Another rat scuttled along one of the overhead pipes. Donovan looked up at it, a struggle going on in his face.

Martin took out his sidearm and offered it to the human. Donovan shrugged, nodded, and shot the creature.

He retrieved the scorched little body distastefully, handing Martin back his pistol. "Well . . . at least it's cooked . . ."

"What's the most unsavory thing you've ever eaten?"

"I don't know. It was better not to identify the stuff they gave us to eat in prison camps." Donovan took out his pocket knife, began skinning the rodent.

After his unsavory meal, Donovan fell asleep. Martin, knowing that he shouldn't sit still, prowled around the hold for several hours, keeping a wary eye out for troopers. He was near one of the hatchways when he saw a small steel box bolted to a beam. Excitedly he opened it, finding two small plastic-wrapped bundles. Then he went back to find Donovan.

Mike awoke to a gently placed foot in his side. "Wake up, Donovan! Look what I've found!"

"Wha—" He rolled over, feeling the remains of the rat move lumpily in his belly.

"Come on." Martin beckoned him to follow. As they walked, he explained, "I've discovered one of the old emergency hatchways. It's our way out!"

"What are you talking about?"

"An obsolete escape system. Abandoned when they built more landing bays and increased the number of squad vehicles. Our ships are assembled in giant grid-networks out in space, but the engineers knew they would be within the bounds of an atmosphere much of the time. So the original engineers designed a system of hatchways, stocking them with emergency slides and parachutes. I've found one of the hatchways, and the 'chutes were still there!"

Donovan followed him, still groggy with sleep and too little food. At last Martin stopped, pointing at a hatchway in the deck. "Help me turn the wheel on top."

The two struggled for minutes, but finally, with a hiss like a pressurized can opening, the wheel moved. They turned it quickly, then levered the hatch up.

Bitter cold fresh air rushed in. Below them were only sky and clouds, and far, far away, like the bottom of a well, the ground. From this distance it looked like a contour map, unreal.

"Here, put this on," Martin said, thrusting his arms through the straps attached to the small plastic square, then drawing a belt out of a slot in the side and clicking it into place across his chest.

"Do you mean," Donovan's voice was very odd, "that we're gonna *jump*?"

"How else?" Martin glanced up. "Fly?"

"But—"

"It goes over your arms like this," Martin said, helping Donovan on with the parachute as one helps a four-year-old with a winter coat. "Now the strap across your chest, like so—"

"I'm dreaming," Donovan said in a tight voice. "I was talking about this before I fell asleep, and I'm dreaming right now. I'm gonna wake up, still sick from that damn rat, and find this is all a dream . . ."

"Don't be an idiot, Mike! This is the only way out! It's a miracle that I even found these 'chutes—they must've been down here for twenty years or so."

"Oh, great. Do they come with a money-back guarantee? There's not even a reserve 'chute with 'em."

"They'll work. They've got to. Come on, Donovan! This is the only way!"

"That's what your buddy Oliver said when he gave me the green capsule. Sure death—"

"It's not. Just close your eyes, Donovan. One step. Snapping the chest buckle activates the unit. The 'chute opens on its own."

"We'll get fouled on the bottom of the ship—"

"No, you'll fall free for the first thousand meters or so."

"Fall free?" Donovan took a quick step backward. "You go first, Martin. I'll follow you."

"All right, Mike. I trust you, my friend." The Visitor walked around the hatch to get a clear shot at the opening. As he passed behind Donovan, his foot lashed out with that blurring alien quickness, catching the human in the seat of his pants, booting him out and down into the free air. Martin heard Mike's yell, composed of equal parts of indignation, rage, and fear, and grinned. "But not too much." Still smiling, he stepped out over nothingness.

# Chapter 29

Diana stalked furiously through the corridors of the Mother Ship. Seeing her aide ahead, she snapped, "I just received your message. Where are they?"

The Captain lowered his voice. "The Deck Five Conference Chamber."

Diana acknowledged the information with a curt nod, then returned to her lab/office. Pressing a button concealed behind one of the drapes in the sleeping area, she watched impatiently as the wall slid aside to present a monitoring system, complete with viewscreen. Activating it, she saw a view of the conference already in progress—the conference she'd only discovered through hearsay.

John, the Supreme Commander, was saying, ". . . know I'm undermanned here. I need to delegate as much authority as I can."

Pamela shook her head reprovingly. "You forget, John, Diana is not a military commander, though I don't doubt she's attempted to assume that role. Her dubious relationship with Our Leader has fired her ambition far beyond her capabilities. When all is said and done, she is only a scientist, after all."

Steven nodded gravely. "And Our Leader himself has warned of the dangers of personal obsessions with power."

"It pains me to say this," Pamela said, "but she is jeopardizing your control of the Fleet, John."

Diana snarled at the screen. "Oh, I'll *bet* it pains you!"

"When you consider the balance sheet," Pamela continued, "her failures outnumber her successes. Look at the hospital fiasco. And then the escape of both Donovan and Parrish. She's frankly becoming a burden we have to clean up after—and I'll bet you're tired of covering up for her mistakes, John."

Reluctantly, John nodded. Diana slammed her hand against the wall.

Pamela's voice was regretful. "Frankly, neither Steven nor I enjoy undermining one of your staff—"

"You love it!" Diana told the Supreme Commander's image, venom flooding her mouth.

"But for the good of the mission, we felt we should discuss it with you," Pamela finished.

"I appreciate your having spoken to me," John said heavily. "I know how distressing it must have been for you and Steven to come forward with this. I'll take the matter under consideration."

Pamela smiled sympathetically. "I'm sure your decision, whatever it is, will be the correct one."

Diana's hand came down on the "off" button with a slam. "You *bitch*!" She spent a few minutes calming herself, then walked to the Deck Five Conference Chamber.

Signaling the door to open, she walked in, smiling. "Ah! John! How nice to see you here! My Captain just notified me that your ship had docked some little while ago."

The three in the room were clearly taken aback. "Greetings, Diana," John said. "We would have notified you of our little conference, but—"

Pamela broke in as John hesitated, "We felt you had enough to deal with. And, since this was a military conference, I'm sure you understand."

Diana smiled, nodding. "Of course. I *am* only a scientist after all." With considerable satisfaction she watched her choice of words spread consternation among them.

"But I wanted to let you three know, as the military commanders of this mission, that I *have* taken it upon myself to make and implement a military decision. One that I think was long overdue."

Pamela's smile became a trifle forced. "Nothing too . . . exotic . . . I hope."

"Exotic to an amateur, perhaps. I should think it would seem inordinately fundamental to a professional." She paused for a beat. "I have planted a spy among the most prevalent and irritating of the resistance groups."

"You *what*?" Steven sat up straighter.

"You've exceeded your authority, Diana!" John said.

"Yes, fortunately," Diana agreed calmly, then turned to Steven. "This should have occurred to you, Steven. *You're* the Military Security Officer."

"You've gone too far, Diana!" Steven retorted.

"Wait a minute." John turned to him. "Why *didn't* you plant a spy, Steven?"

As Steven faltered, Pamela broke in smoothly. "We were going to. A spy working for *us*. Now she's planted one—but who is this spy working for? Diana—or us? We have a chain of command, John, that must be followed."

"Yes," said Steven, with a glare at Diana. "Break that chain, and you have chaos."

"And out of chaos—what?" Pamela leaned back in her chair. "Revolution, perhaps?"

"Now wait just a minute!" Diana flared. "What are you implying?"

"Nothing . . . nothing." Pamela glanced at John, as if to reinforce to the Fleet officer how quickly Diana's temper rose. "What I am *stating*, though, is that, although your idea of a spy may have been a good one, you failed in your responsibility to inform your superior officers of it."

Diana started to speak, then thought better of it and closed her mouth. She was silent, smoldering beneath Pamela's calm scrutiny.

John said nothing.

Juliet Parrish was instructing new recruits in the care of their weapons when Caleb Taylor appeared in the doorway of the room. "Stanley Bernstein is here with a load of groceries," he said, with a hint of a smile.

"So?" Julie asked, puzzled. "Do you need help carrying them in?"

"Yeah, we really do," Caleb said. "He's got some real gourmet items—stuff we haven't seen in a long time."

Juliet shrugged. "Okay."

They found Stanley standing beside a small, hatchback

compact. "Why didn't you bring the station wagon, Stanley?" Juliet asked. "I don't see any bundles—"

"Oh, they're in here, all right." Stanley smiled, opening the hatch. "You like sardines?"

She stared at the two filthy forms huddled in the compact, then whispered, "Mike . . ."

Donovan sat up, grinning. "Hi, Doc," he said. Martin crawled around him, setting his feet on the grass in the backyard as though the feeling of *terra firma*—even if it wasn't his own *firma*—was very welcome.

"Hello, Julie," he said. "We only met for a moment before, and you weren't in the best of condition. I'm Martin."

Tears ran down Julie's cheeks, and Caleb and Stanley looked away, grinning happily. She gulped, wiping impatiently at her face with her sleeve. "Speaking of condition—what the hell happened to you two? I've met bums that looked—and *smelled*—better."

"Long story," Donovan said, climbing out slowly. "Fun and games." Quickly Julie darted to catch his arm, while Caleb assisted Martin. Once standing, Donovan looked around in surprise at the suburban town. "The new HQ? San Pedro?"

"We figured you'd never think of it," Julie explained. "And it's not as if there were anyone left to mind."

"Sean?"

"He's down the street, at school. We set up classes to keep the kids occupied during the day. I'll send someone to get him."

"Wait'll I get cleaned up and eat something," Donovan said, swaying slightly as he took a step. "I don't want to scare him, looking like this."

"Come on, let's get you inside," Julie said, putting an arm around him. "We'll get you clean, then I'll give you a once-over."

"I'll bet," said Caleb, *sotto voce*, but loud enough to carry.

"You have a dirty mind, Caleb," Julie said, grinning. "This man needs *rest*."

"Yeah," said Donovan plaintively, "you have no idea what I suffered to return to you."

Inside the house, the word spread rapidly about Donovan's homecoming, and the four had to push their way through

massed resistance members. Somebody had popped the cork
on a bottle of champagne, and a party was rapidly building.

Leaving Martin to the ministrations of Caleb and Willie,
Julie led the stumbling Donovan into the other bathroom.
"Wait a second," she said. "Don't move." In a moment she
was back with two large plastic bags. "Stand on this one," she
said, "the other is for those disgusting clothes."

Impersonally, she began pulling the filthy rags off, stuffing
them all—even the shoes—into the bag. "You look like you've
been living hip-deep in *garbage*. Donovan!"

"You're half right," he admitted. "Actually, it was garbage
and sewage."

"Yuck. And you're thin!" She stared, dismayed, at the
visible lines of his ribs.

"Yeah." He agreed, looking down at himself. "I look
awful."

In the shower, he revived enough to ask how things had gone
for them during the several weeks of his absence. After Juliet
had given him a quick summary of their military strikes, he
asked about Robin.

"I delivered Robin by caesarean section last week," Julie
said hollowly. "Her water broke, but the labor didn't progress."

The rings on the shower curtain rattled as Donovan turned
off the water and thrust his head out. "The poor kid. Is she
okay?"

Juliet nodded grimly as she handed him a towel. He looked
at her. "Uh, oh. Bad news, huh? *Is* she okay?"

"Physically, yes. She may even be able to have other
children, though she'll always need a C-section. Robin had
twins," She took a deep breath, feeling the memory wash over
her, and told him about the birth. ". . . and since then, the
little girl's molted every few days. She eats like a piranha,
every other day, anything we give her, and then she'll go off to
sleep, and we'll find a shed skin in the crib. She gets bigger
and more mature-looking with every molt. She's taller and
older looking than little Katie now."

He shook his head, water spattering off him. "Poor Robin!
That's *weird*." He toweled his hair. "But you said there were
twins—"

"Yeah." She took a deep breath. "There was something else

in the uterus. It looked very reptilian, but with human-appearing blue-green eyes. It only lived a few hours."

Mike stepped out of the shower, the towel around his waist, and sat down on the hamper facing her. "Julie, how could there be twins like that?"

"I don't know. It goes against every principle of biology I've ever learned. I wonder if even Diana could explain it—frankly, I doubt it. Father Andrew says it's God's way of demonstrating to our two species that all life is one, and that's a better explanation than any Cal and I have been able to come up with."

"The reptilian one died?"

"Yeah. But we saved the body, testing it—don't mention that to Robin, she's close enough to the brink. The day before yesterday, Robert discovered a bacterium in its intestines. Though it's harmless in itself, it excretes a waste product that we think killed the creature. When we tested Elizabeth—that's what Robin named the human-appearing little girl—we found it in her intestinal tract too. But it hasn't harmed her."

Donovan looked at her intently. "But if it killed the other twin, which was more like the Visitors, then maybe—"

Julie nodded. "Yeah. Maybe. We're testing it now on our terrestrial reptiles, to make sure it won't harm them. In a week we'll know whether it might be useful."

"Why do you care whether it hurts—" He broke off. "Sorry. Stupid question. We can't screw up our own ecology worse than it already is just to get the Visitors."

"Well, we cultured the bacterium and exposed the reptiles to it this morning, and so far none seem to be affected. The next step, of course, will be testing it to see if it'll produce the same effect in the Visitors as it did in the dead twin. If it does—" She looked up at Mike, watching the implications sink in.

"If it does, and we can make sure it's harmless to humans, then we've got our weapon! The one we've been searching for all along!"

She nodded, trying to keep her face composed, but she couldn't stop a smile from breaking through. "Maybe."

He stood up, pulling her to her feet. "Hey . . . I just remembered something. I'm not filthy anymore."

Julie put her arms around him and they leaned together in the tiny steamy room. "I'm so glad you're back, Mike. It sounds corny to say it out loud, but every time I wasn't doing something that required my full attention, in the back of my mind I was praying you'd come back safely."

"Maybe that was part of what kept me from giving up that last day. I was so hungry and thirsty I wanted to, but something wouldn't let me." He stroked her hair gently, then kissed her cheek. "I'm getting you all scratched."

"I don't know . . . I kinda like the beard," she said.

He was silent for a long time, holding her, and when he spoke, there was a slight catch in his voice. "I've never been one for organized religion either, but the whole time I was gone something in me was praying I'd see you again."

He hesitated, and his arms tightened around her. "You know, maybe there *will* be a life for all of us after this thing. I never dared think there'd be any end to it, but now maybe there will be a time that I can go back to working at something other than fighting, have some kind of normal existence, with my son—and I'd like to think you'd be part of it, too, Julie."

She laid her head on his chest, not looking at him. "I don't know, Mike. I can't think about that—not until this is over."

Silence above her head, for many heartbeats. Finally Julie looked back up at him. His eyes told her he was trying to understand, but that she'd hurt him. Juliet made a frustrated little motion with her hands against his chest, groping for words. "It's not what you think. You know how I feel—or you should. It's just that having the responsibility for this whole group has left me with nothing that's capable of assuming any responsibility for anything or anyone else—even my own feelings. Am I making sense? Can you understand that?"

He nodded. "Yeah. I think I can. I had nothing permanent to give while I was trying to fill your shoes, and that was just for three weeks. Don't let it bother you. It'll wait. *I'll* wait. It's just that I had a lot of time to think and get things sorted out on that Mother Ship." He shrugged. "I got some priorities straight. You're a big one with me, you and Sean."

He stood up, then glanced over at the doorway. "Guess you'd better dig me up some clothes. And then, I'm gonna scrounge something to eat."

"All right. I'll even cook for you. What would you like?"

"Anything but rats."

She looked at him for a long moment, then gulped. "I have a feeling that remark wasn't nearly as facetious as it sounded."

"You're right."

When they reached the kitchen, they found Ham Tyler waiting for them. He gave Donovan his old, thin-lipped grin. "Talk about bad pennies!"

Mike looked around the room ostentatiously as he sat down. "You got a fly swatter, Julie? Seems I just heard some insect buzzing around."

Tyler snorted. "How'd you get away from the lizards, Gooder? Moralize 'em to death? Can we all go home now?"

Donovan looked at him as though he'd just seen him. "Ham Tyler, as I live and breathe. Hasn't anybody shot you yet?"

Tyler shrugged. "No significant enemy encounters since you left, Gooder."

"I meant somebody here."

Juliet had begun scrambling eggs. "Right back to normal. Don't you two ever get tired of this adolescent macho-put-down stuff?"

Tyler ignored the rhetorical question. "You get him briefed on the current situation, Julie?"

"Yeah." Juliet turned from the stove at the sound of soft, small footsteps. "Oh, hello, Elizabeth."

Donovan stared at the little tow-headed girl who stood in the doorway, unspeaking, clutching a battered old doll. She appeared to be about five years old. "*This* is Robin's daughter?"

"Yes, that's Elizabeth. I told you her growth patterns were . . . unusual." She put a plate of scrambled eggs and toast on the table before Donovan. "Willie says that the Visitor young molt for the first time when they're about six years old, and the change at that time is minimal. He says this kind of growth is unprecedented among their kind also."

Juliet ruffled the little girl's fair hair. "Hi, honey. Want a piece of raisin toast?" She held out a slice to the child, who took it and vanished, munching.

Mike looked up from his eggs with an appreciative grin. "This tastes *wonderful*, Julie. Thanks. Can Elizabeth talk?"

"Nobody's ever heard her say anything. She spends most of her time looking at books. Even technical manuals. She just sits there staring, turning the pages hour after hour. She got hold of one of those spelling toys Polly had, and I caught her one day spelling out the words, perfectly, time after time. But she didn't say a word."

"She must be pretty smart to figure that out by herself."

"Yeah. Harmy and Willie have spent a lot of time with her, and I've helped when I had any to spare. Father Andrew tells her Bible stories, and reads to her. She appears to understand, but she doesn't speak . . . poor little thing. It's hard enough in this world to be a mixture of two *races*—imagine what it would be like to be a mixture of two *species*."

As if hearing his name mentioned, Willie came into the kitchen. "Donovan, I was glad to hear you have retired."

"*Returned*, Willie," Julie corrected, smiling. "It *is* nice to have him back, isn't it?"

"Hi, Willie," Mike said.

"I have finished feeding the animals in the lab, Julie," William said.

"Thank you, Willie."

"Were they all okay?" Ham Tyler asked, glancing over at the Visitor with sharp interest.

"Yes, they were fine," William replied.

Ham gave Juliet a significant glance. "Looks like the stuff has passed the test on our own lizards."

"We'll need at least five days to be sure," she said.

"Then we can *really* see if this stuff is worth anything," Ham said, eyeing Willie speculatively. "I heard you brought another of 'em in with you, Gooder. That was good thinking."

Mike looked at him balefully over the rim of his orange juice. Setting down the glass, he leaned across the table. "No, you don't, Tyler."

"Even *you* wouldn't do *that*!" Julie exclaimed, casting a worried glance at Willie.

Ham grinned wickedly. "What are you all getting so bent out of shape about? Some of my best friends are reptiles!"

# Chapter 30

Ham Tyler stood in the kitchen of the Bernstein house, putting a chicken casserole into the microwave oven. Caleb Taylor stood behind him, at the breakfast bar, twisting a bottle of champagne in an ice bucket. From the dining room they heard Daniel Bernstein's voice. "Hey! Pop! More champagne in here."

Caleb smoothed down his formal butler's tails, with a wry grin at Tyler. "Yassuh, massa. I'se comin'," he mumbled in an undertone, picking up the bottle and carefully drying it on a towel. Flipping the towel over his arm, he went through the swinging door into the dining room.

Daniel, Maggie, Brian, and a short, strawberry-blonde girl Maggie had introduced only as Carol Ann sat at the table with Lynn and Stanley. Places were set with the best formal crystal, china, and silver. A bouquet of tea roses made a splash of color in the center of the damask tablecloth. Daniel turned around as Caleb entered. "Hurry up, Pop! We've got a lot of celebrating to do today!"

"Very good, Mr. Bernstein," Caleb said tonelessly, uncorking the bottle and expertly catching the overflow with the towel. He began to pour.

"Where's the Dom Perignon '79? Daniel protested, eyeing the bottle of Moet & Chandon disdainfully. "We can't drink that swill."

"I am sorry, Mr. Bernstein. There were only two bottles of the Dom Perignon."

"Well . . . okay. Where's the food?" Daniel said.

"It will be ready in a moment, sir."

Stanley leaned forward with his champagne glass raised. "Before we eat, I'd like to propose a toast to our son, Daniel, who has just been named Junior Security Chief for the entire Visitor Fleet. Good work, son. Keep safe, and keep us safe."

Congratulations filled the air as all of them drank Daniel's health. Daniel smiled broadly. "I owe it all to Brian."

"Nonsense, Daniel," Brian said earnestly. "You did it. All I did was supply the opportunity. You're the one who made that spectacular capture of the resistance leader, you're the one who eliminated that saboteur. The credit is yours."

Daniel had tears in his eyes as he patted Brian on the shoulder, then pulled Maggie close to him. "I've got the best friends on the whole damned planet!"

Carol Ann, the freckled little strawberry blonde, smiled vapidly. "Well, I think it's all so *exciting*! Just like having dinner with the FBI or something!"

Daniel rolled his eyes at Maggie. Under his breath, he asked, "For God's sake, where'd you dig her up?"

Maggie shrugged. "I didn't know what type he'd like," she whispered back, "and lots of girls are squeamish about the Visitors."

"The FBI," Brian said thoughtfully. "That was—" he corrected himself hastily, "*is* one of the law-enforcement agencies that help your United States government run the country? The Federal Bureau of Investigation?"

Carol Ann smiled at him. "Is that what it stands for? Hmmm, I didn't know that."

There was a short silence. Finally Maggie said brightly, "Carol Ann is a hairdresser, did you know?"

"Really?" asked Brian. "What does a hairdresser do?"

"Fixes hair," Carol Ann said. "You know, cutting, styling, perms. Stuff like that. You've got pretty hair, Brian." She stood up a ran her fingers through his bronze-colored waves. "Gee, that feels strange. That's not a toupee, is it? Did you get a hair weave, baby?" She peered at the roots of his hair as Brian looked vastly uncomfortable.

"Nope," she said consideringly, sitting down. "Just weird hair."

Brian changed the subject, waving at the kitchen door where Caleb stood, watching them impassively. "These people. These black people. We learned they used to be your slaves, isn't that correct?"

"Yeah." Daniel grinned, deliberately provocative, with a sideways glance at his father, "Y'know, it's too bad we got rid of some of the old ways."

Caleb, who had taken a quick glance into the kitchen, turned back, nodding, in time to catch the remark. Daniel noted his parents' mortification at his comment with satisfaction.

Brian nodded. "It's much simpler to have a class that knows its place is to serve. That leaves the upper class with time to pursue more important matters."

Stanley Bernstein set his champagne glass down, his mouth thinning to a hard line. "We have a word for that kind of thinking in this country."

"Father!" Daniel glared at Stanley. Quickly he beckoned to Caleb. "Hey, Pop, I'm empty over here. Snap it up."

With another glance into the kitchen, the black man moved toward the table.

Brian spoke to Stanley Bernstein. "What is your word for my kind of thinking?"

With a broad grin, Caleb poured the remaining champagne over Brian's head, saying, "It's called racist, Brian." As the Visitor leaped to his feet, Caleb flipped the champagne bottle over and brought it crashing down on the Youth Leader's head. Brian crumpled onto the carpet.

Daniel stood, his hand going to his sidearm, yelling incoherently. Whirling, Carol Ann stabbed his hand with a fork, making him drop the weapon. With a grin, Maggie retrieved the Visitor gun and pointed it at him unwaveringly.

Ham Tyler, Elias, and Juliet Parrish emerged from the kitchen, carrying a large rug. Nursing his bleeding hand against his chest in mute amazement, Daniel looked out the dining room window, seeing that a rug cleaner's van stood across the street. He watched, stunned, as the three resistance fighters began matter-of-factly rolling Brian up in the rug.

Elias grinned up at his father. "Rollin' down to Georgia . . ."

"When we get back to HQ, let's sing him some spirituals. He wanted to know all 'bout slavery, didn't he?"

"You know what they say, Pop. Experience is the best teacher."

Daniel looked pleadingly at Maggie, who blew him a kiss, then raised her weapon in a very businesslike fashion, casually flicking off the safety. "Don't move, Danny honey. Or I'll blow one of your extremities off—and I've got the perfect one in mind."

Seething, but not willing to challenge the hatred in her eyes, Daniel turned to his parents. "Mom? Dad? You're not gonna let this happen in our house, are you?"

His mother stared at him, making no effort to hide her contempt. "So it's 'Mom' and 'Dad' now, is it? No. You're a stranger. A killer stranger who moved into our house, and started off by killing the son we loved. We don't know you."

"I've saved you! Fed you!"

"Disgraced our name," Stanley said inexorably. "Betrayed our faith. Caused your grandfather's death, and cold-bloodedly murdered one of our friends. We have no son."

Stanley put his arm around Lynn's shoulders, and together they walked out the front door. Caleb, Elias, and Juliet finished taping the rug and carried the bundle out through the kitchen. Daniel looked up at Ham Tyler. "Did you hear that? They set me up! My own parents!"

"You deserved to be drowned at birth, you shitty little Judas," Ham said, his eyes like pale blue marbles.

"If you expect me to beg for my life, you're crazy!" Spittle flicked his lips as Daniel laughed hysterically. "I'm *glad* my parents are gone! I've done better on my own than I ever did with everybody on my case all the time. I've done what no other human has managed to accomplish! I'm one of their officers! *They* take orders from *me*! I'm proud of that! Proud!"

"Aw, shut up," Ham said, and flattened him with one blow. Blood trickling from his nose and mouth, Daniel lay sprawled, half under the table. With a flourish, Ham plucked the roses out of their vase, handing them to Maggie. "You done good, lady. You're a winner."

She took the roses, frowning down at Daniel. "I guess we nailed him, Ham—but somehow it's not enough. I want him dead for what he did. To Ruby. To me."

Ham's gray eyebrows went up. "Did I say we were finished with him?"

"What do you mean?"

He grinned at her, then explained, in detail, what he intended. Maggie began to grin too. Walking over to the telephone in the living room, Ham dialed quickly, then spoke to Maggie. "Come on over here. They might recognize my voice. I've called in a lotta bomb threats to 'em."

Maggie took the telephone, listened to the ringing on the other end. A voice said, "Visitor Headquarters."

"I would like to speak to Steven, the Security Officer. Tell him it's a matter of extreme urgency concerning internal Visitor security." She looked up, seeing that Ham was timing the call and would warn her if a trace became likely.

"Yes?" said a male Visitor voice, after a minute. "This is Steven. Who is this?"

"Never mind my name," Maggie said swiftly, "but I'm a human who believes in law and order, and I appreciate the help the Visitors are giving my planet to maintain that law and order. I just saw one of your officers get captured, a Youth Leader named Brian, and I know who set him up. It was Daniel Bernstein. I overheard him say that without Brian around he'd be the eventual head of Visitor Security. He said that to a gray-haired man whose name I don't know, but he called him The Fixer. I hope this will be of help to you."

Maggie hung up, then grinned at Ham, hugging her roses. "Now *that's* more like it."

"You bet, lady."


"How'd it go?" Mike Donovan asked, when Julie stuck her head into the sitting room. Juliet gave him a "V" signal. Donovan left Sean, who had been watching television on the couch beside him, to the perforations of He-Man and Skeletor, and followed the others into the big lab.

Elias and Caleb pulled the tape off the rolled-up rug and, with a dramatic flourish worthy of Cleopatra herself, spilled the now-conscious Brian out onto the floor. Dazed by the sudden brightness, the Visitor officer scrambled up, blinking, and backed into a corner. "What is this place?"

Elias grinned. "As far as you're concerned, this is Harlem, my man."

"Harlem?" Brian obviously missed the reference.

"The end of the line," Caleb explained helpfully, taking off his butler's coat and pulling his white bow tie askew.

Ham Tyler came into the lab, followed by Maggie, who was carrying a bouquet of roses, Donovan noted. Brian looked from one unfriendly face to another, from one drawn weapon to another, visibly daunted by his capture. Robert Maxwell, wearing a white lab coat, walked over to him. "You couldn't have made a better choice, Julie. When do we get to try out the toxin on lover-boy, here?"

Julie pushed back her hair wearily, and her jaw hardened. "Robert, we discussed this. There will be a number of tests performed, but we'll have no unwilling guinea pigs here. Brian will be helpful to us for his security information, and some of his blood and other metabolic responses will be useful in tests. *But that's the extent of it*. Don't forget that."

Maxwell's mouth thinned, but he made no further protest. Juliet gestured the young Visitor into the isolation chamber. Brian scuttled into it as though he was glad to have heavy plexiglass walls between him and the others.

The door to the laboratory opened. Robin, holding Elizabeth (who now appeared to be about nine years old) by the hand, stood in the doorway. Brian called, "Robin!" A microphone hanging from the ceiling of the isolation chamber picked up his words. "Robin, tell them to let me go! Help me, Robin!"

Slowly Robin and her child walked up to the chamber. Robert Maxwell made as if to step out and bar her way, but Donovan held him back. "Let her confront him, Bob. This is the first time she's come out of herself in a long time. Maybe facing him again will help her lay her ghosts." Maxwell looked at the newsman for a long moment, then, nodding, remained where he was.

Brian's voice became lower, more coaxing. "Robin, darling. I'm so glad to see you. Tell these people I mean them no harm. You know that. I love you, Robin!"

She stared at him, as expressionless as the little girl beside her. Brian noticed Elizabeth for the first time. "The child . . . is she your sister, Robin?"

For the first time in weeks, Robin spoke more than a monosyllable. "This is your daughter, Brian. I named her Elizabeth."

The news evidently rocked Brian, but Donovan could see him recovering after a second, see the calculation in his eyes. "I'm glad, Robin. This means we're a family. We can go away together, the three of us."

"Where could we go, Brian?" Robin was *too* calm. Donovan felt his hands begin to sweat. "I don't want to be with your people. I know what they look like, you see. I know what *you* look like. If I'd known that day, I never would have let you touch me, and you know it. You lied to me."

"No, I didn't! I really love you!"

"Bullshit, Brian." Robin's dispassionate demeanor showed a few cracks. "You lied to me about helping me escape, you lied to me with your fake face, and then you wouldn't *stop* when I cried and begged you to! You put a *monster* in me, Brian! Elizabeth had a twin, and it looked like *you*—except it had my mother's eyes! Your people killed my mother! You *killed* her!"

With a sudden, vicious yank, she twisted the outside lock on the isolation chamber and, pulling a vial of reddish powder out from under her baggy sweatshirt, hurled it into the chamber and slammed the door again, relocking it.

Everyone stood stunned, then Maxwell shouted, "It's the toxin! She's got the batch I cultured today!"

"What have you done?" Brian shrieked as he was enveloped by a pale reddish powder that drifted and eddied with his frantic movements. "Help!" He began pounding on the plexiglass. Donovan started forward, but Juliet caught his arm.

"Don't open it, Donovan. It may be harmless, but we can't know for sure. It could be that it won't affect him, but could kill us if you break the seal."

Brian's screams shortened suddenly into choking grunts. He went to his knees, clawing desperately at his throat, gasping. "It's the toxin," Cal Robinson said. "It's entered the breathing passages, and the waste products are clogging the alveoli so they can't take in oxygen. He's suffocating."

As Brian ripped at his face, his human skin shredded and flaked away, revealing his reptilian features. He fell over on his side, still jerking. It was obvious that he was dying.

Ham regarded him with grim satisfaction. "He's a goner," he said, "but he'll twitch for a while yet. Everyone knows a snake doesn't die till the sun goes down."

Robin turned slowly to face the group, her own eyes fever-bright, a hint of a smile on her face. "He's dead," she said. "Now he can't lie to anyone again."

Robert sprang to catch her as she crumpled to the floor. Elizabeth watched dispassionately as Maxwell carried her mother out of the laboratory. Ham watched her go, then turned his hard, cynical gaze on Elizabeth. "Well, she sure blew her chances at child support."

Donovan looked at him, disgusted, then was seized by a sudden, insane urge to laugh. A couple of other members of the resistance poked their heads into the laboratory to see what had happened. Sancho looked speculatively at the red dust, which was now settling to the floor very slowly, falling like red snow on Brian's splayed body. "Hey, maybe I can market this stuff. Put it in fertilizer or something."

"Don't be too anxious, Sancho," Juliet said grimly. "You might end up killing more than you grow. However unpleasant and irrational Robin's actions were tonight—and poor girl, she hasn't been in her right mind for quite awhile—she's solved part of our problem."

"Look, it killed him! What more do you want, Julie?" Elias asked.

"We have to know now if it'll kill us."

"Let's draw straws and find out," Ham said.

Caleb gave him a sarcastic look. "Let's try a popularity contest. I'll hold the door for you, Mr. Tyler."

"Your old man's a barrel of laughs," Ham said to Elias.

"I'll volunteer my mother," Donovan said, only half kidding.

"Why, Gooder, where's all your sweetness and light, those ethics and morals you're always spouting?" Ham cried in mock horror, then, after a beat, he said, "I got a deck of cards in my room. We'll draw for it. Low card wins."

"Now wait a minute!" Donovan said.

"We ain't got a minute," Ham replied. "If we don't get this weapon into production, the damn lizards are going to drain us dry!"

"Well, Tyler, you're gonna have to *take* one minute, while we talk this out. I don't like the way you treat human life. It's all too casual with you. The next step is disregarding human life completely!"

Ham made a disgusted gesture. "I don't believe this guy," he said to the room in general. "We're talking nuts and bolts survival here, and he's talking moral questions. Survival *is* immoral, Gooder! It involves aggression, it involves death, no matter how civilized you get, or how far removed you are from the killing! It's still there, whether you want to admit it or not." He put his hands on his hips, glaring at them. "This is a case of them or us, and I can't think of a clearer cut one in all of history. Survival is the rule—not morals and ethics!"

Donovan shook his head. "That's the difference between you and the rest of us, Tyler. Your argument is just a bunch of gobbledygook that sounds reasonable only because it's so uncomplicated."

"*Julie!*" Caleb shouted.

Donovan turned away from Tyler in time to see Juliet step into the chamber with Brian's body, then use the key to lock the door from the inside.

"*No!*" In one leap Mike was across the room, feeling the plexiglass wall slick against his fingers, staring in at her. "*Julie! Get out! Now!*"

She smiled as he pounded at the door, then deliberately took a deep breath.

"Julie!" Donovan banged frantically at the door, but the lock held. "Open the door!"

"Come on, Julie!" Caleb said, joining Donovan.

"Come on, Caleb. Together!" They prepared to fling themselves at the door of the isolation chamber, but even as they moved, fingers as steely as pistons grabbed their arms.

"No!" said Ham. "Don't bust it in! We're gonna need that isolation chamber!"

Donovan took a wild swing at him, but the motion seemed to return him to his senses, because he dropped his arms and stood, breathing hard, to glare at Ham. "You—" Donovan surged forward, only to be held back by Caleb. "This is your damn fault! If you hadn't been so damn bloodthirsty, she wouldn't have done it!"

"Easy, Donovan. The lady made up her own mind."

Mike subsided, then went back to the door to yank on it again. "Go get the other key. It's in the lab."

"It's too late, Mike. She's been breathin' that stuff for a minute now," Elias said.

"*Get it!*"

As Elias left, Donovan calmed down considerably, seeing Juliet on her feet, showing no signs of discomfort. When Elias came back, Mike grabbed the key from him, but Juliet, grinning wildly, making the "V" sign, unlocked the door herself and stepped out, only to be swept up by Donovan.

"You *idiot!*" he said. "You crazy *nut!*" He hugged her hard.

"We needed an answer. Ham's right. We're running out of time. Besides, I figured it would be more pleasant to die miserably with my lungs choking on bacteria than it would be to listen to you two argue anymore!" She gave Tyler a mock glare past Donovan's shoulder.

"That's the kind of attitude we could use a little more of. Sometimes you gotta take a few risks," Ham said, unrepentant.

Mike pushed her away slightly, scrutinizing her face. "How do you feel?"

"Okay. It has a slight odor, like oregano."

"But not enough to kill you."

She laughed and took his face between her palms, shaking it slightly. "Not if you like Italian cooking, you dope!"

He hugged her again. "You're crazy. I love you."

Ham Tyler made retching noises. Donovan flipped him the finger, then kissed Juliet, long and hard, doing a thorough, slow job of it. "I thought I'd never get to do that again."

She pushed his hair back off his forehead, smiling at him a little shakily. "We may have *lots* of time for that—now."

"All *right!*" Tyler's voice made them step apart. "Back to business! Except for any scientific four-eyed types Julie needs to consult, nobody—and I mean *nobody*—who wasn't in this room is to know what went on. Understand? Elias, you go round up anybody who was in here when scaly croaked, and give 'em the word not to even tell their families. This has gotta be *top* secret."

The door to the lab banged open, and Chris Faber darted in, Robert Maxwell close behind him. "It's the padre!" Faber said. "He's taken the kid and split!"

"*What?*" everyone exclaimed.

"He's right," Maxwell said. "I took Robin back to her room with Elizabeth, and Father Andrew came in. He hadn't heard what had happened tonight, and Robin, when she came back

around, began to cry, telling him she'd committed murder, and
begging him for absolution. She told him she'd killed Brian."

"Did she tell him *how*?" Ham demanded.

"No—no, she was too incoherent to explain. But he did
understand she'd killed the Visitor who was Elizabeth's father.
He told her he'd pray for her, and that God understands that
people are sometimes driven out of their minds by grief, and
that anybody who'd suffered what she's suffered couldn't be
held responsible for their own actions. He told her that Christ
would forgive her. That calmed her down, and I gave her a
sedative and put her into bed. When I came out, Father
Andrew and Elizabeth were gone!"

"I've searched the place, boss," Chris said to Ham. "He's
split, all right. Probably figured Robin might try for the kid
next."

"*Jeezus!!*" Ham slammed one fist into the other. "Well, at
least Father Andrew doesn't know about the toxin, and the kid
doesn't talk—yet."

"All right, gang, start packing," Juliet called. "Donovan,
you help me supervise. Elias, bring up the trucks. I want this
place cleared out in an *hour*. Lock, stock, and barrel,
understand. We've got to move again."


Diana sat in the conference chamber of the Mother Ship,
alone, looking out the observation port at the full moon rising.
From this height it was very large, very clear.

The portal slid open. Jake stood there with two figures, one
large and burly, one small, behind him. "I have some good
news, Diana."

The Second-in-Command straightened. "What is it, Captain?"

"A member of the resistance has turned himself in."

"How extraordinary!" Diana said, her suspicion plain.
"Just like that?"

"He claims to be an emissary of peace. He says he's brought
proof of the ties between our peoples."

"Bring him in, Captain," Diana said. A burly, mustached
man entered, leading a little girl about nine years old by the
hand.

"Be seated, sir." Diana gestured. "Who are you?"

The burly man sat down, and the little girl solemnly climbed into a chair beside him. "I'm Father Andrew Doyle, Diana," he said. "I'm a Roman Catholic priest. This is Elizabeth—the first interplanetary child—interstellar, really."

Diana stared unbelievingly at the little girl, doing some rapid calculations in her head. "Are you trying to tell me *this* is Robin Maxwell's child?"

"Yes."

"But her growth! She can only be a few weeks old!"

"Yes. Is it dangerous, such growth?"

"I'll have to examine her. I suspect the accelerated growth can be slowed to a safer rate. Controlling the secretions of the pituitary gland might be one way."

"Elizabeth here is an extraordinary child, Diana. She doesn't speak, but she's very intelligent—as you'll discover if you test her. She's also a symbol. A symbol of the universal oneness of all God's creations. It's my hope her birth can be the bridge to peace between our two peoples."

"That's every nice, of course," Diana said, watching the priest through slitted eyes, "but I wonder also if you didn't bring her because you were afraid for her. Hmmm?"

He gazed at her for a moment. "It was a factor," he said, "because her mother is only a child herself, and shouldn't be burdened by having to handle something of this magnitude. But it also should be apparent to you that her existence proves that we're all made as part of the same cosmic plan—the same genetic stuff, no matter our outward physical differences."

"Go on," Diana said.

"Well, if you follow this reasoning through to its logical point, then harvesting human beings for food for your people is tantamount to cannibalism. Do you Visitors eat your own kind?"

"No," Diana said, "at least not in several hundred years, we haven't." She leaned forward to study Elizabeth, who stared back at her unblinkingly. "I'm intrigued by your audacity in coming here, Andrew. Courage is a quality I can respect. And your argument, though flawed, is well drawn. I never realized that any of the human religions emphasized clear thinking and logical presentation of conclusions."

Father Andrew smiled. "We Jesuits specialize in that sort of thing. I'd be happy to debate the question with you and clarify my position further."

"And I would like to talk to you again." Diana stood up, speaking now to Jake. "See that Father Andrew is given guest quarters, and is well treated. I must give Elizabeth here an examination." The little girl looked up at Father Andrew as the priest stood up.

"I'll see you later, Elizabeth," he said, putting his hand on her head, almost as though he blessed her. Then he followed Jake out the door.

Diana held out her hand to the little girl. "Come along, Elizabeth." The child hesitated, then slipped her fingers into the Second-in-Command's. Diana looked down at her, ruffling the tow-colored hair for a moment, her eyes speculative. "What am I going to do with you?" she wondered softly, aloud.

Elizabeth looked up at her but did not speak.

# Chapter 31

The next four weeks were hectic. The resistance relocated its headquarters to the Johnson Dairy outside of Los Angeles. The dairy had been closed down due to the water shortage. The owner, Terence Johnson, was understandably opposed to the Visitors for ruining his business—and also because his daughter, a laboratory technician, had "disappeared" during the first major Visitors sweep.

Culturing the toxin in vats of yogurt, the rebels processed and packaged it for shipment around the world. With the international resistance network in full swing, the Los Angeles plant ran twenty-four hours a day, day in, day out. After the first week or two, another plant, located in Switzerland, joined their efforts. Juliet, Robert, and Cal retired into the lab again, this time to work on a vaccine to protect the Fifth Columnists from the deadly red dust.

After a week's work, they came up with a substance that they verified would immunize their Visitor friends against the toxin, but how long its influence would keep them safe, they didn't know. All Fifth Columnists were advised to wear oxygen masks, and to avoid breathing the substance if possible. Lorraine on the Los Angeles ship and Jennifer on the New York ship quietly supervised the distribution and injection of the immunization serum among the Mother Ships. By this time the Fifth Column had spread throughout the Fleet, to an extent that would have horrified John and Pamela if they'd known.

Martin, with his knowledge of Visitor codes and inner workings, proved an invaluable ally. He posed as a mute human, living in the city, monitoring many of the Visitor broadcasts with a receiver he'd put together himself, using communication devices from several stolen squad vehicles.

One day, shortly before distribution of the toxin was slated for completion, Mike Donovan received an urgent message to meet the Visitor in a small Chinese restaurant in the city.

When Donovan entered the restaurant, the small, wizened owner popped up. "Table for one?"

"Wa Chi," Donovan gave the password.

"Of course, sir. This way." Without missing a beat, the man led Mike into the private dining room, bowed once, and left. Martin rose, offering his hand. Donovan shook it firmly and let go, and then, as he sat down, realized suddenly that the coolness of Visitor flesh was something he hadn't noticed in a long time. *Times change*, he thought. *Boy, do they change.*

The Visitor looked oddly unfamiliar, wearing civilian clothes instead of his uniform.

"This is dangerous for both of us," Mike said, keeping his voice low. "Must be important, right?"

"Desperately, Mike. I *had* to see you. The resistance is embarking on something that could be disastrous, if there's the slightest breach in security."

"We know that. If Diana and her cronies get word of this, they'll kick our asses."

"No." Martin shook his head emphatically. "This doesn't concern just the resistance. This concerns the future of your *planet*. Whatever the weapon is that you're working on—"

Donovan's gaze sharpened. "How do you know about that?"

Martin looked down at the battered red tablecloth. "I drove out to the new HQ the other day, and Sancho wouldn't let me through. It wouldn't take an idiot to figure out that the final weapon has been discovered, and that the push is on."

"Okay, yeah. But what's the problem?"

"The Leader is . . . can be . . . less than rational at times. Aboard one Mother Ship in every Fleet, a device was installed that every Supreme Commander or Second-in-Command has been ordered to use if threatened with ultimate defeat or capture. This device links into the gravity drive, turning the vessel into something akin to a thermonuclear device of massive proportions. The equivalent of hundreds of thousands of megatons. Enough to blow a hole in the Earth the size of this *continent. Nothing* would survive if it were triggered."

Donovan stared at him, light-headed with disbelieving horror. "Tell me you're kidding, Martin."

Martin shook his head. "No, I'm not. Your weapon—biological, chemical, whatever it is—had better be capable of *instantaneous* annihilation of all the Visitors aboard that ship, or somebody could trigger that thing. Some do-or-die patriot who is determined to follow the Leader's final order."

Donovan's voice was barely a whisper. "It may be too late, Martin. The weapon is a toxin, and we've already manufactured and parceled it out. The New York group figured out a distribution method that will create a sort of permanent lifecloud, rendering the planet useless for Visitor purposes forever. What can we do? Even if we tell the other groups about the device, one or more of them may choose to act independently, now that they have the means."

"I take it that the toxin is *not* instantaneous?"

"No. Takes about a minute or two to work once it's inhaled. It spreads only as fast as air circulates. They'd have time." He looked up at his friend. "What we were hoping for is that, once the toxin was in the air, your people would realize it was hopeless and split, flushing their contaminated air supply as they did. Less loss of life that way."

"It will probably happen as you hope, except for the ship carrying the device."

"Which ship is that?" Mike asked, somehow knowing the answer even before Martin spoke.

"Diana's. She was one of those who helped pioneer the math to harness the gravity drive to this purpose. And what's worse, aboard her ship are several high-ranking officers who know how to call up that program on the computers, and implement the final code sequence. Diana, Steven, Pamela, and John—if he's not aboard the New York ship—all know about it. Just as I did."

"Okay. I'd better get back, tell the others. Are you still at the same place?"

"No, I've moved again." Quickly Martin scribbled his

address and telephone number—without any name—on a matchbook and gave it to Mike.

Donovan pulled something out of his pocket. "Roll up your sleeve, Martin."

"What for?" the Visitor asked, nevertheless doing as requested.

"Got to immunize you against the V-dust. It won't hurt you, and you'll need it. Here." He took out a hypodermic filled with clear fluid, and injected the substance into his friend's upper arm. "God, you guys have tough skins," he muttered, looking at the slightly bent needle before stowing it out of sight again.

"Thank you, Donovan," Martin said, "you'd better go first."

"All right. Thank *you*, Martin." He looked intently at the Visitor. "Are you sure about this? Could it be that it's just a bluff the Leader conjured up, to keep the troops toeing the line?"

"It is no bluff, Mike. The threat is real." He took a deep breath. "I've seen the results of its use."

Diana watched as Elizabeth sat at the computer terminal in her office/lab, her short fingers dancing over the keys with scarcely a pause. The child never looked up—her attention was entirely for the machine.

"Is that a game she's playing?" Father Andrew asked, watching as the screen in front of the little girl built a fantastic array of colored lines and symbols.

"Sort of," Diana said, watching Elizabeth closely. "It's a programming game we encourage our youngsters to play. But it's very advanced. I've never seen a pre-adolescent even attempt it. And she's *winning*." Her voice held amazement.

"I told you she was smart," Father Andrew said proudly. "Now if she'd only talk."

"Smart?" Diana's laugh held a brittle edge. "The child is what you would call a super-genius. I'm not sure I've even been able to measure her intelligence with any accuracy. It goes off the scale."

The priest watched her closely. "Does that bother you?"

"Her origin bothers me. I'm not sure I did the right thing, experimenting genetically as I did when she was conceived. I've always felt comfortably certain that our species held inherently more intelligence than yours. Now I don't know anymore."

"I see that you've succeeded in slowing her growth."

"Yes, her physical growth. Her mental is something else again. She spends all her time playing with the computer programs I've introduced her to. The other day I saw her playing with one I didn't recognize. She'd written it herself. In our language."

"Speaking of writing, have you looked at that Bible I gave you?"

"Yes, I did. It was very interesting. Strength through love and peace—what an unusual concept! And apparently it worked for your Christ and His disciples."

"Most of the great human religions stress the same ideas, Diana. Inner peace and strength, love for one's fellow man."

"And woman."

"Yes, of course." He gazed off into the air absently. "Can we talk about how to bring peace between our peoples now?"

"And how would you have me do that? Allow you to bring the word of your God to my planet? Persuade the Leader his ambitions are wrong, that he should love his neighbors? Even if they're 8.7 light-years away?"

"I'll volunteer to travel with you, and teach the Word of the Lord to anyone who will listen. If that includes your leader, and God's word makes him decide to put away his plan for destruction, all the better."

"You'd do that?"

"I would."

As Diana hesitated, the signal flashed on her door. "That will be Jake," she said, motioning Father Andrew back out of sight. "Come in, Captain."

"You sent for me, Diana?"

"Yes. I'm worried about a Fifth Column assassination attempt on Father Andrew, the priest. Double his guard."

Jake nodded brusquely, not looking at her. "I will relay your request to Pamela immediately."

Diana sat up straighter, her tones very level. "This is *not* a request, Captain! This is a command from your superior!"

"I'm sorry, Diana. Pamela issued orders this morning that all security or military commands must be cleared through her first. Apparently Our Leader concurred with Pamela and authorized her to implement this regulation."

The Second-in-Command tried to hide her outrage, without much success. "I see. That will be all, Captain."

The portal slid shut behind Jake, and Father Andrew stepped back out into the room, a faint smile on his lips. "I see that more than genetic building material is universal between our peoples. Power struggles plague our planet too."

"You're smiling? It amuses you?"

"The fact that we're not so different does."

She smiled bitterly. "It's ironic that I feel I can trust you as much as I trust any of my own people."

"Perhaps it was meant to be like this."

Diana laughed without amusement. "I'm not a victim of fate, Father. I'm a victim of betrayal. They're all jealous, each and every one of them, and they're bent on my destruction. I've dedicated my mind to the salvation of my planet, my life to this mission, my body and soul to the Leader . . ."

She sank into a chair, her shoulders slumping. "Now he's deserted me too."

"Diana, when I said that perhaps it was meant to be, what I was trying to suggest is that perhaps you've been chosen in some way for a mission of a higher order."

"Your God?"

"Perhaps. Or yours."

Around the conference table at the resistance headquarters, Sancho, Maggie, Caleb, Juliet, Ham, Elias, and Donovan were in the midst of a raging debate. Donovan, who had been appointed the informal presiding official, pounded his hand on the table. "Wait a minute. Wait a minute!" He took a deep breath. "*Shut up!!*"

Reluctant silence descended on the group.

"All right," Donovan said, "we'll go around the table, starting on my right. You first, Ham."

"I'm just sayin', why are we wasting time arguing? We win or we lose. There's no halfway."

Donovan pointed to Juliet, who sat next to Ham. She shook her blonde head. "There *is* a halfway! There's always a way to compromise." She gazed around the table. "If we don't win on V-day, we can still win in the future. Martin is working with the

Fifth Column, and they're steadily undermining the Visitors. Thanks to Elias and others like him around the world, discipline in their ranks is being undercut by drugs and alcohol. We can hold off on using this toxin and still win."

Sancho was obviously bursting to talk. "Go, Sancho," Mike said.

"I'm sorry to disagree with our boss here, but the Fifth Column hasn't helped us to get any of our people back, or even managed to get us many weapons. We're hooked up with them, sure, but the only times we've accomplished anything significant were when we did it ourselves. But I do agree with Julie that we can win without taking this risk. It's just going to take longer."

Ham Tyler broke in. "You listen to slick here, you'd better pack it in, folks. You don't win a war by surrendering before you start!"

"I didn't say to surrender, Tyler!" Sancho flared. "You don't win a war by just screaming 'Victory,' either! And quit calling me 'slick,' or the next raid you may find yourself a casualty of what they call 'friendly fire.'"

"No threats, please," Donovan said, "and the next bozo that talks out of turn has to wash the dishes tonight. Robert."

"We've lost a lot of good people so far," Maxwell said, sorrow shadowing his face. "Ben, though I didn't know him, Ruby, Brad, Chris Faber in that raid last week. Kathleen. If we give up our chance to win, they'll have died for nothing."

"Maggie," Donovan nodded at the slender young woman with the dark-honey hair. "What's your opinion?"

"I don't have one yet. I want to ask a question."

"The most sensible approach I've heard all day," Mike applauded. "Go for it."

"What about this Alliance thing Martin was talking about?"

"I got the impression they were sort of like a League of Nations or UN—long on ideals, but short on clout. Maybe, allied with the Fifth Column, they could get something done, but probably not in time to do us any good."

"Okay," Maggie said. "Next."

"Elias," said Donovan.

"I understand how Robert feels," the young man said, "'cause I'm one of those who lost somebody that meant a lot to me. But it's stupid to risk blowing up the whole world to avenge the deaths of our friends."

"Caleb."

Caleb's deep voice was even deeper than usual. "I'm sick of war, and that's the truth. Sick of it to my bones. But it doesn't make much sense to come this far and throw in the towel before we step in the ring for the championship match."

Elias looked earnestly at his father. "It does when you stand five foot five, step in the ring, and find out the other guy's ten feet tall!"

"And armed with bazookas!" Julie said, leaning forward, her fists clenched.

"I figured that was how *you'd* vote, Doc," Ham said, his voice dripping sarcasm. "Which hand did you use to brush your teeth this morning?"

Donovan slapped the table. "Okay, I warned you. Elias, you wash the dishes," he said inexorably. "Julie, you help him. Ham takes out the garbage—and while you're at it, put yourself in with it, Tyler, 'cause that's where you belong."

A mutter of protest surrounded him. "Okay, now that I've managed to rid myself of my turn at K.P. tonight, I'll open the floor to free discussion. But any more shouting matches, and I'll chuck this whole mess and go play catch with my kid."

Juliet turned to Tyler. "I'd like to enlighten you on your perception of me, Ham. I've never had anything in my mind since the day this group first met that wasn't a full commitment to throwing the Visitors off our planet and pulling in the welcome mat. But we're not talking jungle ambush here; we're talking about the possible annihilation of the *world*. The whole damn *planet*, Tyler, and every life-form on it! You don't have to be *converted* to twig that that's a lousy damn idea!"

Ham glared back at her, not backing down an inch. "Lady, you either kill the predator, or he has you for breakfast . . . and we all know I ain't speakin' metaphorically here."

"You know something?" Donovan said. "We know now what it's like to run the world. Crazy feeling, isn't it? We know what it's like to have the most weighty responsibility a world leader can feel."

He looked at each of them in turn. "There are people in this world—or there were, ten months ago—who would have pushed that button because they didn't give a damn about anything but their little corner of the world, their little grasp at immortality through power. But *we* have that power now. All of us in this room will decide what's gonna happen to the rest of the world. That's a pretty awesome responsibility."

He looked at Ham. "So, how does it feel? *You're Russia now.*" He turned to Elias, "*You're* the United States." He pointed at Juliet. "You're some Middle Eastern religious crazy with the power to destroy the world." He sat back in his chair, his face livened only by his eyes. "How does it feel, gang?"

There was a short silence.

Maggie broke it. "We think we're right, and the others think they're right. *Is* someone nuts enough to obliterate the planet because the world won't bow down to their version of what's right for everyone?"

"Diana's that crazy," Juliet said softly.

"Did she tell you to say that?" Ham asked.

"Shut up, Tyler," said both Julie and Donovan together, then looked at each other.

"You owe me a beer," Donovan said.

"If we're still here, I'll be honored to pay up," Julie said grimly. She thought for a moment. "You know," she continued, "with the Fifth Column gaining recruits every day, just as we are, there's also a chance that the Visitors will evolve into a group that's no longer a threat."

Robert Maxwell shook his head. "That's what Neville Chamberlain said about Hitler. You want to take that chance?"

Silence again. Finally, Donovan stirred. "Okay, everyone has had their say. What do we do now? Call a vote?" He looked at Juliet.

"I guess so," she said. "We're certainly more used to democracy than any other form of government. I'll get some paper and pencils."

"All right," Donovan said when she was back with them. "Write one word on the slip of paper. Write 'yes' if you're *in favor* of carrying our V-day as previously planned; that is, one group releasing the dust while another raids the Mother Ship and attempts to gain control before Diana can push the button. If you've changed your mind about implementing V-day because of that doomsday device aboard the L.A. ship, then write 'no.' Everybody got that?"

Ham Tyler stood up. "I'm not gonna vote on this."

"We all get a vote, Tyler. Even you."

"Nope. Everyone knows what I think. If the group doesn't share my thinking, then I can't change their opinion by sitting here and writing on a ballot. I'm not gonna subject you to a 'better dead than Red' speech, either. But I'd like to remind the group of this: the Visitors came here to this world with the express intent of sucking us dry." He raised a hand to halt any argument. "Okay, I know that most of their people didn't know that we were intelligent life-forms; they were just following orders, and all that other stuff. But the true purpose of their mission still remains—they came to suck us *dry.* And when they're done, they'll throw us over their shoulder like an empty beer can. Not only those of us in this room, but the rest of the world.

"But there won't be a world anymore. Just a squashed beer can. *Now*—at this time and place—we've got a chance against them. We may *never* get another as good, gang. There's also a chance we won't make it, a chance we can't take the Mother Ship in time, before they can trigger that thing. *I think we can.* I've spent over twenty years planning and pulling off this kind of job, and that's my judgment. We're good. All of us. I've never worked with a better team, and I don't say that lightly. Whatever the group decides, I'll stick with you, too, believe me.

"You have to weigh those risks now, the risk of trying to live and risking everything, versus sitting back and taking longer to die. We're not talking deterrence here. We *know* they'll do it. I said there was no halfway in this fight, and there's not. We're dead if we don't win."

They were silent for a long moment, watching each other. Then Maggie looked up at Tyler. "But you think we *can* take the ship in time."

"Yes." Ham turned and walked out, not looking back.

"Anybody have anything else to say?" Donovan asked.

No hands or voices were raised.

"All right. Let's vote."

Juliet shuffled the small scraps of paper together in the privacy of her office, and then counted them once more to make sure. It was definite. By a small margin (*but how could it be otherwise,* she thought bitterly; *we're a small group*), the resistance council had voted for an attack. Julie herself had voted against it. She now had to lead her people in a course of action that made her sweat clammily every time she thought about it.

*Damn, damn, damn,* she thought wearily, feeling a tightness in her throat. *If I'm right and they're wrong . . .*

She leaned her head in her arms. Her own particular demons were haunting her, making it difficult to evaluate the risk correctly. Even as a small child Julie had always been terrified of nuclear war—more so than her friends. For years she'd been physically unable to watch footage of mushroom clouds, knowing that seeing those photographs could make her sick to her stomach.

Many nights she'd awakened, sweating, from dreams where the bombs had fallen and she was always the only one who could keep a cool head, organize everybody, plan the escape routes, nurse the sick and dying. All with her feet encased, in the way of dreams, in invisible lead.

*Is it my old fear,* she wondered now, *making me weak?* She looked down at the hand that was idly toying with ballot scraps. *My left! Damn, damn. Thought I was getting better. Maybe Ham Tyler is right. Maybe it's because I'm converted that I can't . . .*

The door opened behind her and Donovan peered in. "Finished?" He saw her face and began to back out. "I'll come back later."

"No, it's all right. Come on in, Mike."

Eyeing her cautiously, he came into their room and shut the door behind him. "You sure? I understand if you need some space."

Juliet began to laugh, horrified to hear a hysterical edge to it. "Space! Oh, sure! That's what I need, absolutely! Space, and a whole *bunch* of goddamn aliens to play roller-derby with my mind and my life!"

"Hey." He came over to her desk and picked her up bodily, then walked to the mattress on the floor and sat down. He held her tightly, cradling her in his lap, his mouth against her hair. "Hey, I understand. I understand." He held her that way, his hand stroking her back, her hair, for a long time.

Finally he moved, trying to peer at her face. "You crying, Doc?"

"No," she whispered. "It might be better if I could. But this is just too big for tears. I cried for Ben, and I cried for Ruth, and I cried for Ruby and Brad and Chris. I don't have any tears left for this, and I'm afraid the worst sorrow is yet to come."

"If it does, nobody will cry. They won't have time."

"Yeah."

"I take it the vote was in favor of V-day?"

"Yeah." She pushed back and looked at him. "You voted for it, didn't you?"

His green eyes were very level. "Yeah, I did. I think Ham's right. I think we're good enough, lucky enough, to secure the Mother Ship and nail Diana. She's the one we've got to worry about, y'know. Martin says he doubts that either John or Pamela is crazy enough to do it, and Steven is too gutless. I think we can get Diana before she has time, so I voted 'yes.'"

"You going to tell Ham? He'd probably faint if he knew that you'd sided *with* him in something."

He laughed. "I'm sure he would."

Julie looked at him gravely. "I like the way you laugh now. When I first met you, you really didn't laugh, you know. You'd kind of chuckle wryly, just for a second, as though you were afraid to let people see you were amused."

"Oh, I was an emotional *cripple* before you came along, Doc! Ever think of taking up psychiatry instead of bio-med?"

"No, you weren't. You're just trying to make me feel better."

"Do you?"

"Yeah, a little. Enough so I can do what has to be done."

His hand moved to her throat, touching her skin, then traveled down her shoulder. "How much better do you feel?"

She chuckled softly. "You're *insatiable*, Donovan. We're talking about the world maybe blowing up in a couple of days, and all you can think about is making love."

He looked at her, unsmiling. "Can you think of a better way to spend your time, knowing that?"

She kissed him, her hand sliding beneath his shirt, then drew away slightly. "When you put it like that, no, I guess I can't. Besides, we might as well squeeze in a few moments for ourselves now, 'cause once I walk out there and announce the decision to the group, I'll be too busy to sit down anywhere except in the john."

He gave his old wry chuckle. "It would be *terrible* to be annihilated with a full bladder. We must remember to go before we leave." He began undoing the buttons on her blouse, his fingers moving slowly, brushing lightly against her breasts as he did so. Leaning over, he kissed her, his hands still busy, his mouth holding hers with a sensuous, dizzying deliberation.

Julie closed her eyes, feeling her heartbeat quicken. A tiny sound escaped from somewhere in the back of her throat, and he pulled back. She could hear the roughness in his voice as he asked, "You like that?" He touched her again.

"You know I do," she said, kissing him, pulling him down onto the mattress, holding him to her fiercely, trying not to think it might be for the last time.

# Chapter 32

"Hey Sean! Wanna play catch?" Josh Brooks shouted as he came out into the parking lot of the dairy.

Sean Donovan stopped and looked up eagerly. Then the animation went out of his features. "Nah, I guess not," he said.

"Why?" Josh said. "You sick or something? You never want to play like we used to. Are you mad at me?"

Sean hesitated. "Nah. I just don't wanta."

Mike Donovan, who had just stepped out of the office on his way to the processing plant, stopped, listening. "Sounds like a good idea to me, guys. Mind if a dinosaur like me joins in too?"

"Sure, Mr. Donovan! I'll get another glove!" Josh, a wide grin on his freckled features, raced off.

He was back in a minute with a second battered old glove. "Who wants this one?"

Donovan looked over at Sean. "I'll throw to you two first, then you can throw to me."

"All right," Sean said uncertainly, and Josh tossed him the glove. Sean looked at it, then awkwardly pulled it on his right hand. Mike's eyes narrowed. His son had been on the Little League All-Stars team two years running, playing third base.

"Okay, you guys ready?" Mike pitched the ball to Josh, watched the older, less athletic boy make a passable catch. "Good, Josh! You've improved since last summer!"

369

"Thanks, Mr. Donovan!"

"Sean's turn now," Mike said, and lined up an easy one to his son. Sean hesitated, reached for it as though he would catch it with his left hand, then, belatedly, put his glove out. The ball whizzed by, rebounding off the chain-link fence at the back of the parking lot.

"Hey, Sean, what's with you?" Josh was staring at his friend. "That was an easy catch."

"Never mind," Mike said as normally as he could manage, feeling his heart seemingly crawling behind his tonsils. "Even Brooks Robinson had to warm up for a minute. I'll give you a high one. Good practice for pop flys."

Winding up, he loosed the ball so it flew high overhead, forcing Sean to back up rapidly, squinting beneath the brim of his Dodgers cap. After a second's hesitation, the boy's gloved hand went into the air—

And missed the ball by at least a foot. Donovan closed his eyes, anguished, his thoughts tumbling over each other helplessly. *Please, God, let me kill that bitch Diana before I die. Has anyone noticed? If they see, what'll they do? Must get him away, protect him. But the meeting to set V-day is tonight, can't leave . . . What am I going to do? What should I do?*

"Hey, Mr. Donovan . . . you all right?" It was Josh who gazed at him anxiously.

"Uh, yeah." Mike opened his eyes, managed a grin that felt more like a rictus. "Uh, where's Sean?"

"He got real upset when he missed that ball, and ran away. I think he might have been crying. What's wrong with him, Mr. Donovan?"

Mike shook himself mentally. "Oh, nothing, Josh. He told me earlier his history essay for school was giving him a hard time. He probably went to study."

"Sure," said Josh, his brown eyes troubled. "That must be it."

"Of course it is," Donovan said heartily. "Anyone can have a bad day."

Diana looked up when the portal signal flashed. "Enter," she said. When the burly man stepped through the door, she smiled coldly. "Ah, Father Andrew. Thank you for coming. I wanted to tell you I have finished reading your Bible."

"And?"

"I've found it very intriguing. I even found myself experiencing an emotional response during certain of its lovely poetic passages."

"That's wonderful! I'm so glad to hear that."

"I've also been considering what might happen if your Earth religions of love and peace—which you humans seem to have such difficulty adhering to—were to be introduced on my planet. If such teachings could affect and sway me, what might result if my less—what's an appropriate idiom—my less . . . hard-boiled . . . kinspeople were to be exposed to them?"

Father Andrew smiled warmly. "It might change the course of history for your planet and all its people."

"Yes. It might. You've impressed me very much, Father Andrew, both you and your God. There is something very attractive about your words. They fall with great impact on the ears of those who are . . . troubled."

"I'm only the mouthpiece, Diana. I try to hear what the Lord wants me to say, and relay it."

"You're too humble. Our discussions over the last few days have been extremely enlightening for me. I've found new strength of purpose because of them. I must thank you for that."

Father Andrew's mouth stretched into a broad grin. "I must admit, this praise is unexpected, coming from someone who is so self-assured."

"Self-assured? Several days ago, I would never have thought of myself as anything else. But you've helped to show me that I do have vulnerabilities. I never allowed myself to express or feel these things before. Indeed, I never even knew they existed."

With considered deliberation, she drew her sidearm and shot the priest point-blank in the chest. As Diana watched him sink to the floor, his eyes wide with shocked betrayal, she finished: "And I won't allow them to exist any longer."

Tossing the Bible down beside the body of the priest, she charred it into slag. Father Andrew, moments from death, looked at her in mute shock. "Vulnerabilities, my dear priest, are exploitable weaknesses. My strength has always lain in being able to do what must be done, without worrying about the consequences to myself or others."

She leaned over to key the intercom. "Jake?"

"Yes, Diana."

"Send a clean-up squad to my quarters immediately."

"Yes, Diana."

A small noise from the other room made her turn. Elizabeth was framed in the doorway, her eyes huge.

The resistance council sat around the table, while Ham Tyler stood before them, writing on a battered old blackboard. Chalk dust made a white haze in the morning light filtering from behind the venetian blinds. "So while the L.A. group is busy at Edwards, the D.C. group will be busy at Andrews, the Portsmouth group will be taking Pease, the Saint Louis folks will be raising hell at Scott. And so forth. Coordinating our efforts like this will leave the Visitors so stunned that it'll take them a few hours to get a unified course of action, and by that time the toxin will be in the air, and it'll be too late."

"Now, has everyone got that straight?" he asked. "The plan, the time, the date? We can't have any screwups, folks."

Everyone indicated that they understood. "Good," Tyler said. "Best of luck to us all. Keep your heads down."

When the group didn't move, he said, "That's all. Reveille at three-thirty A.M. Don't eat too much."

The group broke up, people milling around, talking in smaller groups.

Caleb Taylor looked up as his son came through the door carrying a stack of Visitor uniforms. "Seven, Pop!"

The older man grimaced. "You were supposed to get *ten*. And you're late. You missed the special briefing Ham Tyler called. Where've you been—toking up?"

"No," said Elias, his face hardening into the old "jive" impassivity. "No, Pop. I thought I'd do it right, and shoot up this time." Dropping the uniforms on the table, he marched out, his back stiff.

His father made a wordless noise of disgust.

"Come on, Caleb," Juliet said, putting a hand on the older

man's arm. "Elias is only dealing to the Visitors. He's not doing drugs anymore, and he wouldn't sell them unless it was necessary for our cause. He's changed, Caleb! Can't you see that?"

Caleb refused to look at her. "He's nothin' but a lousy pusher."

Julie's mouth dropped open in sheer indignation. Grabbing Caleb's arm, she hauled him around to face her, her anger making up for her size. "You listen to me, Caleb Taylor! Elias is one of the best we have! I won't have you put him off his stride just hours before this raid—*I won't have it, do you hear me?* Dammit, Caleb, what's he got to *do* to make you care about him? Die, like Ben?"

Taylor stared at her, shocked, angry, defensive. Then, as Julie held his gaze unwaveringly, his face sagged. "Is that what I've been doing? Punishing Elias because he's alive, and Ben is dead?"

"Something like that," Julie said softly. "I know you didn't mean it. I think you'd better make your peace before the raid. You don't want something like that on your conscience if—" She took a deep breath, looking down, then raised her eyes to his again. "If something happens on V-day, God forbid."

Caleb nodded. "Thanks, Julie," he whispered after a second, then walked out of the room after Elias.

Donovan had already left the conference room, looking for Sean, his strides coming quickly, his eyes anxious. He finally found the boy in the room next to the conference room, a history book propped open in front of him.

Mike stood in the doorway. "Sean?"

His son sat up with a startled jerk, his eyes wide. "Oh, hi Dad. What is it?"

"I want you to come with me, son. We're going for a ride."

An expression Donovan couldn't read flickered across Sean's features. "Where, Dad?"

"To see your grandma."

He took Harmy's truck after taking the precaution of putting on a white catering uniform and dark glasses, with a white cap to pull down over his eyes. Donovan tried to make conversation as he drove, but Sean replied mostly in monosyllables, until his father gave up.

Two blocks from Eleanor's house, Donovan pulled over to the curb. "Okay if I ask you to walk from here, Sean? It's not safe for me to go any closer." He tugged on the boy's beat-up old Dodgers cap.

"Sure, Dad." The boy hesitated for a second. "How come you're sending me away, Dad?"

"I can't tell you that, son. It's a secret. But it's only for a little while, so you'll be protected, no matter what. Tell your grandmother I said to keep you safe. I know she will."

"Okay, Dad." Sean's eyes held a shadowed appeal as he looked up at his father.

"I love you, son, remember that." Donovan leaned over to hug the boy tightly, kissing his cheek. "Be good for your grandma."

"Okay. Bye, Dad."

Robert Maxwell knocked on the door of his daughter's room. "Binna? It's Daddy. I need to talk to you."

After a minute or two he heard a laconic, "All right. Come in."

He walked into the room, his pupils dilating in the near-darkness. With a muttered curse, he walked over to the blinds and twitched them up. Sunlight flooded the room, showing clearly Robin's lank hair and purple-shadowed eyes. She rolled on her side to avoid the brightness, then lay still again.

Maxwell walked around to sit down on the bed beside her. "Robin, you've got to snap out of this. V-day is only hours away, and you've got to pull yourself together and be prepared to look after the kids. None of us can be spared."

She didn't answer, and there was something fetal about the way she lay curled on the bed. Her father reached out to shake her shoulder. "You look terrible. Your hair's dirty. When was the last time you showered? Or ate a decent meal instead of picking at your food? Or went for a walk with your sisters? You're all the mother they have now. They *need* you. Are you going to let them down? What would your mother say if she could see you?"

Her voice was muffled. "Leave me alone."

"Dammit, I *can't*. I need you too badly, Robin. I know you've been through a lot, but so have I! So have all of us. Are you just going to let the rest of your life slip through your fingers because you're too *cowardly* to pick up the pieces?"

He felt her jerk convulsively, then she lay still again. "Don't try and shut me out, Robin. It's time to grow up, whether you want to or not. You were the firstborn, and we spoiled you. Frankly, in many ways Polly is a nicer child, because we learned a few lessons with you and didn't make the same mistakes."

He took a deep breath. "But soon she'll be thirteen. Do you want her to suffer problems because she's growing up lonely, without her mother, with a sister who doesn't care about anyone but herself?"

"I've been doing my chores."

"Bullshit. You've been dragging through each day like some kind of zombie, never smiling, never speaking. It depresses people to look at you!"

He heard a muffled sob, but went on relentlessly. "And your schoolwork. Before, you wouldn't study because all you cared about was yakking on the phone with your girlfriends and chasing boys. Now you won't study because life has treated you rotten. What excuse are you going to use in ten years? Or twenty? Unless you try and make up for lost time, you're going to have a life that's so empty you'll try suicide again. You want that?"

She was crying harder now. "I've left you alone as long as I can, Robin. But you have to pull yourself together now. I mean *today*."

"I'm not Mother! I can't be that strong!"

"And I'm not a fighter, or at least I wasn't when this all started. Now I can put an M-16 together in the dark, and nail my target at three hundred yards. I can rig plastic explosives and throw a grenade. I *learned*, Robin, because I wanted to live. And you're going to have to learn to want that too."

He reached over and stroked her hair. "I've said some very honest things today, Binna. Things I could only say to an adult. I think you're strong enough to make it, to take control again. We need you so badly, honey."

For long moments he thought perhaps he'd gone too far—or that she had gone so deep he couldn't reach her. But then she moved closer to him. "I'm sorry, Dad. I've let you down."

He reached to gather her up, hold her close. "No you haven't, sweetheart. Nobody can blame you for being so down. It's just that it's time to wake up and smell the coffee."

"I'll try, Daddy."

"I know you will, Binna."

Maxwell stood up, then heard her voice behind him. "Dad? That responsibility you were talking about extends to my own child, too, as well as Polly and Katie. Doesn't it?"

"Robin, we may never see Elizabeth again."

"I know. But if she's returned to us, you won't try and stop me from seeing her, will you?"

Maxwell took a long breath, then laughed bitterly. "Heal thyself, Doctor Maxwell," he mumbled. Choosing his words very carefully, he said, "Robin, I can't deny that I have a lot of bitter feelings toward the Visitors. But Elizabeth is my granddaughter." He shook his head. "All I can tell you is that of course I wouldn't attempt to stop you from seeing her. I can't promise that I'll open our home to her, either. You can't quell months of anger and bitterness just with good intentions. But I'll try and remember that she's just a child, and not responsible. I'll try my best to accept her."

He turned and looked at his daughter. Her face was more alive than it had been in months. "We'll both try, Dad. Maybe I can't really be her mother, 'cause Willie says they don't raise their children like we do. They grow up too fast. But if she comes back, I can try to understand and help her. I can try to be her friend."

"It's some kind of germ. I don't know what kind," Sean said around a mouthful of peanut-butter cookie.

"What are they planning to do with this germ, darling?" Eleanor asked.

"They're going to use a bunch of jets to spray it in the sky."

Steven leaned forward. "Where are they going to get all these jets?"

"From Edwards Air Force Base. They're going to steal them."

"A common thief. What won't Michael *do* to disgrace us further?" Eleanor asked of the air.

Sean's small face darkened. "Don't talk about Daddy that

way, Grandma. I love my Daddy. It's just that he's mixed up. Diana said he's sick inside, and that she could make him better if I helped her. She showed me pictures of him in my head, and in some of them he was sick, and then she showed me how she would make him well."

Steven glared at the older woman. "Don't antagonize him, Eleanor," he whispered. "Conversion can be a chancy thing, especially when you're trying to combat emotional ties this strong." He addressed Sean again, who was wiping a milk moustache off his upper lip. "This is very helpful, Sean. Do you know how many jets they're planning to steal?"

"A lot, I think. They've got friends in other cities. They're going to attack them all at the same time."

"When do they plan to do all this, honey?" Eleanor asked.

"Can I have a piece of cake?"

Steven and Eleanor, who had been leaning close, were taken aback. "It's not polite to change the subject, dear," Eleanor chided.

"But I'm still hungry. It's been *two hours* since lunch!"

"Of *course* you can have a piece of cake, darling. Grandma will cut it for you just as soon as you answer my question."

"The raid's going to be tomorrow, at dawn. I'd like chocolate, please."

"Are you *sure*, Sean?" Steven asked.

"I'm positive. They all had a big meeting and I sat in the next room and listened to them. I could hear fine."

"Well, you were a good boy." Hurriedly Eleanor cut the cake and sent Sean off to eat it on the deck.

Steven looked at Eleanor, a speculative smile playing on his lips. "This information will be invaluable. Now my only problem is whom I should inform first—Diana, or Pamela?"

Eleanor gave him an understanding smile. "Well, which one will do you the most good if you gain her gratitude?"

"That's what I'm trying to decide."

She gave him a coy look. "You won't forget your old friends when you're a Supreme Commander, will you, Steven?"

His gaze was speculative. "Not the ones who control their ambition." He touched the copy of Machiavelli's *The Prince* that lay on the counter with a bookmark in it. "A book on how to prosper by political intrigue, isn't it, Eleanor?"

"Well, yes, but that doesn't mean—"

"It had better not. I had to dispense with the Bernstein boy, you know. He became a security risk. An *ambitious* security risk."

Eleanor's hazel eyes held a growing unease. "What did you do to him?"

Steven smiled. "I assure you, dear lady, you'd rather not know."

Diana stood outside the conference room and keyed the door. "Pamela? This is Diana. I'd like to speak to you."

"I'm very busy right now, Diana. Can't it wait?"

"I'm afraid not. It's about the rebel raids planned for tomorrow morning."

The portal opened, and Diana entered, the full skirt of her red lounging robe swishing against the doorframe. Pamela was seated at the table while her aide stood by the observation portal, looking out at the waning moon.

"How did you find out about the raids, Diana? That is classified information."

Diana inclined her head haughtily. "I'm entitled to know about the raids, Pamela. *I* provided the source from which you gained that piece of intelligence."

Pamela's face was a cold, impassive mask. "You are entitled to information that pertains to our scientific mission—nothing more."

"I walked by the landing deck on my way here. There are no troop carriers or fighters being readied. Is it possible you're not taking the boy's report seriously?"

"It's not standard practice to base troop movements on the tattlings of human children."

"I converted him myself. His information is reliable."

"I've told you before that I don't trust your conversion process. However, I will have someone look into it, if that will ease your mind."

"When? The raids are due to begin in about eight hours."

Pamela gave her aide a sidelong glance, and a mock-tolerant smile crossed her perfect features. "You scientific types are so easily ruffled."

Diana smiled back at her sweetly. "And you military types are so easily predictable. I, on the other hand, am not."

Pulling a gun from the folds of her gown, she shot the startled Pamela in the shoulder, then, whirling, fired the weapon at the aide before he could ready his sidearm. He fell to the deck, mortally wounded. Diana walked around the table to regard Pamela, who was trying to crawl to the gun her aide had dropped.

"You rely on cunning, Pamela. Intrigue. Trying to turn people against each other. I prefer the more direct approach myself. Don't worry, Commander. I'll do my scientific best to command your fleet. First I'll save it from the rebel raid tomorrow morning, thus earning the Leader's undying gratitude and approval. Then I'll eliminate the only remaining opposition to his plan, all in a few hours' time." She smiled charmingly. "Good-bye, Pamela. Consider this early retirement."

She raised the gun, aiming carefully, and depressed the firing button.

"Nice party, Juliet," Robert Maxwell said, watching the resistance members serving themselves in the cafeteria of the dairy. They were laughing and talking, though the tension in the room was palpable. "The glass of beer apiece was a real bonus. None of us expected it."

Julie laughed. "I figured it was better to hold the festivities here, rather than have folks sneaking out on what might be their last night to sample a few last-minute . . . delicacies. And the beer may help everyone get a few hours sleep, at least."

"When's curfew?"

"It's almost ten. I'll have to make an announcement in a couple of minutes." She looked across the room to the table where Robin, Polly, Josh, and Katie sat with Harmy. "Robin looks so *different* tonight. She's such a pretty girl. Did you say something to her to get her out of the funk?"

"Yes, I talked to her today. I guess she listened."

"Good. Tomorrow we'll really need her."

Donovan joined them, balancing a plate of fried chicken

and coleslaw, with his allotted beer teetering precariously on the side.

"If you drop that, you don't get another," Julie warned severely.

Donovan cast a quick glance at Robert. The latter was watching Elias set up a record player and speakers. Donovan leaned over to whisper, "I compromise my honor and sleep with the boss, and I don't even get the privilege of an extra *beer*? What good are you, Doc?"

She gave him a wide, knowing grin, not answering.

"Attention, everybody," Elias called, waving for emphasis. "I'd like to say a few words."

The babble of conversation decreased not a whit. After a second, Caleb Taylor jumped up on the tiny raised speaker's platform beside his son. "Hey, you turkeys! *My son* wants to speak with you, and the least you can do is listen up!"

Caleb's rafter-trembling tones got the desired quiet.

Elias gave his father a warm smile and a nod. "Thanks, Pop." He turned back to the group. "Julie is gonna tell you all to toddle off to bed in a couple minutes, but before she does, I'd like to say a few words and play you a song, symbolizing how I feel.

"We owe a lot to one special lady tonight," he continued, and everyone glanced quickly over at Julie, smiling. "If it weren't for this lady, none of us would be here. She brought us together, and it was because of her that we've been welded into a fighting force that tomorrow is gonna finish this thing we've started, so we can *go home*."

Everyone clapped and cheered, their eyes on Julie, who smiled back at them graciously. "And so, my friends, my brothers and sisters, tonight I would like to dedicate my favorite song from my favorite artist to—Diana!"

A mutter of surprise raced around the room, then Elias, with great solemnity, dropped the arm of the phonograph onto the record. After a second, everyone began to laugh, realizing they'd been royally had. It was Michael Jackson's "Beat It."

The laughter swelled and grew, dispelling the last of the tension. Donovan leaned over to whisper in Julie's ear, "You knew about this, didn't you?"

"Yeah," she said. "I came up with the idea to make everyone think it was *me*."

The laughter rolled on, competing with the throbbing beat of the music, filling the night.

# Chapter 33

Diana sat in solitary mastery over her Mother Ship's military communications and control center, listening to the report from the force she'd dispatched to Edwards Air Force Base. "The troops are in place, Diana. The fighters are about to take off to maintain holding positions out of visual range."

"Then you're completely prepared for them, Commander?"

"Completely."

"No sign of them yet?"

"No, but it's still nearly an hour before full dawn. They probably overslept."

Both Visitors laughed. "Very well, Commander. Stay in contact. Mother Ship out."

"Acknowledged. Out."

The portal to the room slid open, and the Supreme Commander, John, strode in, scowling. The silver-haired Visitor leader wasted no words. "Why the hell is Pamela deploying so many troops Earthside? Our defense forces aboard the Mother Ships are understrength!"

"Pamela's dead," Diana said, looking at him levelly. "She was careless enough to select a Fifth Columnist as one of her personal guards. *I* am in charge now."

Obviously shocked, John displayed a moment of skepticism when he heard her explanation, but dismissed the issue of Pamela's death in favor of the more pressing matter. "How *dare* you deploy troops planetside without my authority?"

"Pamela had begun the preparations to eliminate the resistance before she was killed." She looked at John blandly. "I'm simply carrying out her orders. The waiting is almost over. The rebels are in the process of mounting a nationwide—possibly worldwide—series of raids on air force bases. We have an opportunity to wipe out the entire network in one blow."

John frowned. "That's ridiculous. What could they hope to accomplish by raiding air force bases? Their jets are useless against our fighters."

"Their plan is to use the jets to disperse a toxic bacterial weapon."

"I thought you had inoculated us against all Earthly bacteria and viruses."

Diana shrugged. "They apparently think they've developed a new one."

"Is that possible?" John was plainly disconcerted.

"Of course it's possible." Seeing his face, she continued, "Don't worry. We're going to insure that that toxin never enters the atmosphere." Standing up, she relinquished the Commander's seat, waving John toward it gracefully. "Now that you're here, John . . ."

Inclining his head, John sat down, studying the troop deployment shown on the strategy board before him. "You've amassed quite an army."

"Pamela wanted this victory to be absolutely decisive."

"That shouldn't be hard," he said, favoring her with an approving smile.

"And if by some wild chance we should fail . . ." Diana opened the center of the board with a key.

A shiny metallic box with a lock on either side rose out of the board. A red light blinked in its center, and a small computer keyboard and terminal were placed beneath it.

"Do you have your key, John?"

The Supreme Commander nodded. "Right here. But isn't this a little . . . premature?"

She gave him a surprised look. "Our orders are clear on the subject. During any major military engagement, we must be prepared to take the ultimate reprisal."

"But . . . the device will destroy this vessel. And us with it."

"I can program the timing of the final destruction sequence to remain open, leaving us the option to set the number of times the counter cycles down. That way we can plan plenty of time to escape to one of the other ships. If anything happens to us, and we don't implement that option, it will default to its originally programmed time to detonation."

"All right then. Is it armed?"

"It's armed."

John began checking troop status. Diana stood behind him, fingering her own key, watching the strategy board.

Martin sat at the controls of a squad ship, wearing a Visitor uniform. The landing bay of the Mother Ship loomed ahead as a voice came over the communications channel. "Squad ship triple-ought twenty-eight, establish voice check."

William, seated beside him, leaned forward. "This is squad ship triple-ought twenty-eight requesting permission to land and download."

Behind Willie, Juliet, Donovan, Sancho, Harmy, Maggie, Caleb, and Elias, all dressed in Visitor uniforms, stood crowded into the squad ship's corridor, listening tensely.

The bored voice of the controller came again. "You're not on the download schedule, triple-ought twenty-eight. Hold your approach to minimum speed while I check this out."

Donovan made a throat-cutting gesture, receiving an elbow in the side and a glare from Julie. She winced, rubbing her elbow, which had struck something hard concealed by the breast flap of Donovan's uniform. "What've you got in there?"

Donovan pulled out the hand-held video camera. "I stuck this in at the last minute. Figured I'd try for some footage." He stowed the small camera in his pack.

"Okay, triple-ought twenty-eight." The controller was back. "I'm clearing you to land. I can't find your bill of lading, but that's nothing new. The computer's been up and down all week."

The huge bay doors opened before them. "They're just about empty," Donovan said, peering out at the viewscreen.

Julie chuckled. "The Air Force bases all over the U.S. must look like the L.A. freeway during rush hour by now."

Donovan's expression mingled pain with bitter amusement. "Sean did a good job."

"You did a better one," Julie said, mirroring his feelings. "It's not easy to lie to your son."

"We should all get Oscars for that performance, especially Ham Tyler. I sat there and hated every moment of it."

"At least it worked. He picked it up and passed it on. We made his conversion work *for* us. Remember, he's not a traitor, Mike. He's not a spy. He's just a little kid who didn't have the ability to fight back against Diana."

"I wonder if he'll ever get back to normal?"

"If we're successful, and the Visitors leave, I should think so. He may require some therapy to work out his own feelings when he realizes what was done to him."

The squad ship set down with a gentle hiss of braking jets.

Each resistance fighter carried a pack with an aerosol supply of the toxin in it. Sancho was equipped with a portable blower he wore on his back like a backpack, covered with the same material as the Visitor uniforms, to minimize its visibility. All were equipped with the voice-changers.

When they stepped cautiously out of the vehicle, Juliet directed Harmy to set up her "infirmary" in the only other squad vehicle, which was located in the southern end of the landing bay. This larger shuttle was designated the "escape shuttle" for the Fifth Columnists. The fighters had come with extra gas masks and a supply of the vaccine, so they could immunize any Fifth Columnists who had not yet been protected. Security aboard the L.A. ship had been extremely tight. Lorraine had reported that she hadn't been able to contact several of her people.

Juliet, Donovan, and Sancho left, to rendezvous with Lorraine on their way to Master Control. Caleb and Elias remained in the loading bay, to distribute the toxin through the air system, while Maggie, Willie, and Martin stood guard.

As Caleb and Elias worked to open one of the nearby ventilation shafts and begin blowing the dust into the Mother Ship's air system, two guards wandered into the northern end of the landing bay, glancing at them curiously.

"They probably think we're just conducting normal downloading procedures," Martin said, nudging Willie, "but we can't let them get too close. Distract them!"

William walked casually toward the patrollers. "Hi! I've just come off-shift from Richland," he said, "and I haven't heard anything since last night. What's happened since Diana received that message from John?''

"What message?'' asked the foremost guard, intrigued.

"Someone told me she'd received a message from John saying that the Leader had announced that he's chosen an Official Consort, and you can *imagine* Diana's reaction!'' He kept strolling toward the entrance, keeping the guards' backs to the ventilation shaft.

"Space, I can imagine, all right! What did she do?''

"Well, *first* she told John he could insert his announcement in his . . .'' Still talking, Willie led the guards out of sight.

Martin looked at Elias and Caleb. "How much longer do you need?''

"Just a minute or two, then we can turn it on and the pump will keep blowing automatically, as long as the supply of dust in our cargo hold holds up.''

"*Hurry.*''

Donovan, Julie, and Sancho walked cautiously down the dim catwalk, peering anxiously ahead. A hiss from the shadows made them all jump. It was Lorraine. She led them quickly down the corridor, checking her chronometer. "A group that hasn't yet been immunized is taking this route to the escape shuttle,'' she said quietly. "They should be along any second.''

A minute later they rounded a corner and came face to face with a group of Visitors. The three humans froze, until Lorraine stepped forward. "Scott! You must hurry! Martin is waiting at the escape shuttle!''

"Pull up your sleeves, quickly!'' said Julie, stepping forward with an air-inject gun. Quickly, she inoculated each of the Fifth Columnists.

Lorraine fidgeted as Julie worked. "You must hurry. Diana is a poor loser. She'll blow your planet right out of this solar system if she perceives defeat.''

"I know,'' Donovan said grimly.

"I don't know if you really do,'' she said. "You don't understand her the way one of her own can. I sneaked a look at the monitor showing the military center before I came down here. She and John are sitting there, listening to the reports

from the ground troops and growing more and more concerned. *She's armed the device*. It only needs the insertion of
two keys, hers and John's, plus a final coded sequence to begin
the countdown."

"Martin told us this would be the way she'd play it. We
voted on it, and we voted to take the chance."

"It's an insane plan. You're risking your world. I'd have
voted against it."

"Your argument's a little late," he said wryly. "We're
committed, and the only thing we can do is see this through.
How do we reach Master Control from here?"

"I'll show you. You'll never find it otherwise."

They continued on into the dimness of the monster ship.

Ham Tyler stood in an open field, beneath a rosy-flushed
dawn sky. He checked his watch, then gave the signal. "Okay,
it's six A.M.! Let 'em go!"

At his signal, hundreds of hot-air balloons, varying in size,
color, and decoration, began rising into the air. One or two
balloons were clear, and in their depths swirled a reddish cloud
of dust. Ham watched his own balloon, purchased specially for
this occasion, go up. It was a huge black one, and on it was
painted a blood-red "V."

He thought of the signal that would be going out all over the
world, and of balloons rising over Cairo and London, Paris,
Moscow, Sydney, Hong Kong, and New York. All the major
cities of the world, and many of the smaller ones, with
balloons rising on the air currents, their internal pressure
carefully calculated so they'd explode within the specified
portion of the atmosphere.

Some of the dust would drift back to earth, mingle
harmlessly with the dirt and the water. The rest would become
an organic, self-perpetuating adjunct to the atmosphere,
making the planet forever unusable to the aliens.

Ham watched the balloons drift and skitter upward, smiling.

Sean Donovan awoke suddenly when a hand grasped his
shoulder. He rolled over, frightened, and relaxed when he saw
it was Arthur Dupres. "Grampa Arthur? What's going on?"

"Quiet." The big balding man put his finger to his lips.

"There's a wonderful sight outside. I'm going to drive you up to the cabin in the mountains, and we'll see it together." He motioned Sean to get dressed.

"What is it?" asked the boy.

"Balloons, son. Thousands of 'em. All floating upward. It's beautiful."

"But why?"

"I'm not sure, but I think it's Earth's way of telling the Visitors good-bye. Hurry, Sean."

"Is Grandma coming?"

Arthur hesitated. "No, I don't think so, Sean. You know she doesn't like to get up early."

"So it'll be just you and me?" Sean had always liked his stepgrandfather Grandpa Donovan had died before he'd been born. Going to the mountains with Grampa Arthur would be fun. But Sean frowned as he thought of something. "Grampa Arthur? My Dad's coming back for me. I've got to wait here."

"We'll be back tomorrow. I'll let him know you're with me."

"Okay," Sean said happily.

Dressed, they padded silently along the corridors of the big house, then down the stairs and out to the car. As Arthur started the engine, he looked back at the house, and there was something so sad in his face that Sean suddenly wanted to cry. "Grampa Arthur? Do you miss Grandma already?"

His stepgrandfather glanced at him, then put the car in gear. "Yes," he said, "I miss your grandma very much. I've missed her for a long time now."

The car headed down the street. Sean watched the sky, then shouted, "Grampa! I see the balloons! Aren't they beautiful?"

"They sure are, Sean," Arthur agreed. "I think they're the most beautiful sight I've ever seen."

Martin and William herded the Fifth Columnists aboard the escape shuttle, while Harmy nervously kept lookout. "Hurry up!" Martin urged them. "You've got to get out of here as quickly as possible! Diana's bound to pick up on the dust in the ventilator system soon!" A hose connected the cargo hold to the shaft.

As if his words had been a signal, an alarm began to chime,

while a voice announced, "Defense alert for hostile humans. Defense alert. All personnel report to—" The voice continued, giving battle station locations.

William looked up at him. "I wonder if Donovan and Juliet made it?"

"You won't know till later," Martin said. "You, Maggie, Harmy, Elias, and Caleb have to go with Scott and the others. Drop the humans off near HQ before you head back to another ship." He looked up at the sound of Maggie's whistle, to see a squad of shock troopers trot into the northwest end of the docking bay, their guns ready.

At the same moment, Harmy, who was watching the south entrance, shouted, "Look *out*!"

The warning resounded through the cavernous docking bay, intercut by the pulse of weapons. Elias and Caleb ripped loose the hose from the shaft, spraying the toxin directly at the north-end troopers. Some fell, but others, unaffected, continued to fire. A blast resounded from the weapon in the tail section of the escape shuttle. Looking up as he scuttled for cover, Willie saw Scott firing at the troops near the southern entrance.

A row of stored chemical canisters went up with a whoosh, and suddenly a fire was raging in the southern portion of the landing bay. Willie heard Martin, dimly, above the mayhem: "We've got to get out of here! Come on, Willie!"

William waved at the northernmost troopers. "Why are they still alive?"

"Those helmets are equipped with gas masks, if they were smart enough to use them in time. They've got about five minutes' worth of air. Get to the shuttle!"

Willie nodded and, gathering himself, rushed for the entrance to the escape shuttle, trying to spot Harmony in the chaos. He heard her scream, "Willie!"

He checked, trying to locate her, then suddenly she was in front of him, between him and the pulse of a rifle. She fell forward with an agonized scream, and only William's alien speed kept him from tripping over her. Quickly he grabbed her arms, dragging her behind the shelter of some loading equipment. Dimly, he saw Maggie race and dodge to cover, firing as she went, and saw the trooper who had shot Harmy fall.

Willie pulled her head into his lap, trying to find a pulse in her throat. "Harmony?"

Her eyes were open, but she didn't seem conscious. William found her pulse finally. It was very fast, and weakening steadily. "Harmony?" William said again. She'd been shot in the back, but he hated to pick her up to examine the wound. He didn't want to see it. It was obvious, even to his limited experience with human physiology, that she was dying. Her breath came in more and more painful gasps.

He bent over her, numb with grief and shock, wishing his people had the surcease of tears. Humans cried when they felt grief, and it seemed to help. He could do nothing but touch her fading pulse and wish it had been him. It would have been so much easier that way.

"Harmony?" he called again, without much hope, and this time she heard him. She blinked, and the blue eyes that had been so fixed in pain focused on him.

"Willie?" Her voice was so faint the sounds of battle drowned it out, but he knew she'd spoken his name.

"Harmony." He held her against him, feeling her bones suddenly sharp and brittle beneath her skin. Her skin that was real, not a covering. Her fragile, broken skin, covering a fragile, broken body.

"Willie . . ." She made an effort, and her words reached him. "You've got to go. It's not safe."

"Please, Harmony." He didn't know what he was begging her for. Not to die? That was ridiculous, but perhaps to wait for a second. He said it again. "Please, Harmony . . ." Then the words were there, the words he could probably never have voiced, if it hadn't been for this sudden knowledge that there was no more time in which to speak them. "I love you, Harmony."

She made the faintest nod. "I know. Go, Willie."

"No, I won't leave you." He held her tightly, as though he could contain the life in her body with his arms. "I will stay with you forever."

Her mouth curved upward infinitesimally, the fading shadow of a smile. "Forever, Willie."

He crouched over her in the flaming landing bay, holding her, waiting. When the shock troopers had been beaten back, and the escape shuttle was ready to close its hatches, Martin found him there.

Martin dropped to his knees beside them, putting a finger on Harmy's throat. "She's dead, Willie."

"I know." William stared dully at nothing.

"You have to get out. I'll help you carry her."

William didn't answer.

"Come on, Willie. She'd want you to get away."

"I know," William said. Harmony *would* want him to get away, go back with his people. He thought about what would happen when they returned to their planet. Martin had spoken of contacting the Alliance, using captured Mother Ships to help defeat the Leader and bring peace. He looked down at her face again. Peace. Harmony had believed in it. She would want that.

"I'm ready," he said, climbing to his feet. "I can carry her myself."

Diana's mouth was an ugly gash as she leaned forward to speak with the ground forces. "Commander, I want you to return immediately with as many troops as you can muster within three minutes."

"We're on our way."

She turned to John. "Whatever they're trying to pull, they don't stand a chance."

John nodded, then stiffened, his fingers dancing over the strategy board. "What's this? Airborne images, thousands of them!"

"Fighters? Jets?"

"No, they're much too small, most of them. They're climbing, but straight up, as though they're lighter than air."

Diana switched on the viewscreen, and they saw them. "Balloons?" she said incredulously. "Is this some kind of joke?"

"They aren't attached to anything."

"No. Why would they release thousands of balloons and just let them . . . rise? Into the atmosphere?" She froze, staring horrified at the colorful display as a possible explanation occurred to her.

"They don't actually think these balloons are going to divert us from the raid on the air force bases, do they?" John was puzzled.

Diana whirled on him savagely. "Don't you understand yet? The air force bases were just a diversion. They're not going to use jets to disperse their toxin; it's in the balloons!"

"How primitive. Even millions of balloons could hardly deliver enough toxin to do us much harm."

"You—" She threw up her hands. "Don't you *see*? All they need to do is release a comparatively small amount into the atmosphere at the proper altitude for the bacteria to survive, and it will *reproduce*. The damned stuff will multiply, contaminating the water, becoming part of the living organisms—the whole food chain! Very quickly, everything on Earth is going to be poisonous to us!"

"But perhaps we can collect them before they burst—"

"If they're smart enough to figure this out, they're smart enough to have filled them with enough pressure to get them as high as they want them, then they'll burst. They're much cleverer than I ever gave them credit for."

"A fatal miscalculation . . . for all of us."

"We're safe in here," she said.

"So far," he reminded her grimly. "But frankly, I don't much relish the idea of spending my life locked up here with you."

"Be quiet," Diana said absently. She turned back to study the colorful wind-riding flotilla, her mind racing as she tried to come up with a solution. "Damn them!"

Steven looked out the third-floor window at the troops scattered over the lawn of the Visitor Headquarters, sprawled where they had died. The resistance forces advanced steadily. "What am I going to do?" he asked Eleanor frantically.

"I don't know," she said, clutching his desk as if it would anchor her to the earth, keep her from flying up off the chair in sheer panic. "That red dust they exploded in those bombs—I suppose it would kill you too?"

"It killed them," Steven said. "It would be nice to imagine that I'm immune, but also rather silly."

"Don't be sarcastic! I don't know what to do! I came here

for protection from the mob that was surrounding my home. I barely made it here!"

"You've got to help me," he said, looking out at the approaching fighters. A man with steel-gray hair was in the lead, another, younger man with dark brown hair beside him. "Tell them I surrender. Tell them I ask for mercy!"

"All right," Eleanor said, joining him at the window. "That's Robert Maxwell. He's my neighbor—he won't let anything happen to me. Go into the other room. We don't want them to think you're using me for a hostage or a trap."

"Very well," Steven said, crossing the room toward his secretary's office.

Eleanor waited until he had closed the door, then opened the window all the way, leaning out so they could see her. "Don't shoot! I'm Eleanor Dupres, Michael Donovan's mother! I'm one of you! The leader of this headquarters is here, and I'm being held prisoner by him. Help me!"

As they looked up at her, hesitating, Steven's voice came from behind her. "You double-crossing *bitch*! Did you think I'm so stupid I wouldn't listen?" His gun pulsed.

The fatal shot thrust Eleanor through the window, her body toppling the three stories to the concrete drive below.


"Master Control is just ahead," Lorraine said, then tensed. "There's someone coming up behind us. Fast."

Donovan, Julie, and Sancho turned and drew a bead on the corridor. "I don't hear anything," Julie said, peering anxiously into the dimness.

"Neither did she," Mike said. "They can sense the vibrations of movement."

A figure darted in view, moving with the blurring quickness of a Visitor. "Don't shoot!" It was Martin.

"Did the escape shuttle get away?" Julie asked.

"Yes," said Martin. "But Harmy didn't make it."

"Oh, no," she whispered.

"Martin, do you have your access card?" Lorraine asked.

"Here," he replied, walking to a portal ahead, inserting the bit of plastic. After a moment he looked up. "Diana must've jammed the opening mechanism!"

Donovan aimed his weapon. "We'll have to blast it, then.

Somebody keep watch. We don't want to tangle with any more shock troopers.''

Diana activated the monitor screens that filled the room. Visitors lay sprawled everywhere in the corridors of the Mother Ship, and a flashing readout of the air circulation systems verified that the toxin was continuing to spread death aboard. The monitor of their L.A. Headquarters showed the body of Steven slumped in the hall, where he'd been caught as he'd attempted to escape. From the way he was lying, it was impossible to tell what had killed him. The resistance fighters were having a party on the lawn, toasting each other with the contents of several kegs of beer. The Visitor flag was down.

The international monitors revealed similar scenes of human victory and alien death. Diana's jaw hardened. ''Silly children. They celebrate nothing but the death of their world.''

She turned to regard John. ''Your key?''

''The Fleet is beginning to leave orbit. We'll have to hurry,'' he said, tongue darting in his nervousness.

''Oh, we'll get away,'' she said, ''but first I'll scatter this planet to the solar winds.''

''Why?'' John stared at her. ''We've lost, Diana. They've defeated us. Our ground troops aren't going to make it back. It's *over*. Don't you understand? Or can't your vanity handle that?''

There was a tiny sound from the emergency hatchway on the other side of the control room. The small hatch opened on a ladder that led down to a shuttle that could be launched from Master Control, designed to be the final escape for those manning the communications and military center. Diana strode over to the hatch and opened it, her weapon ready in her hand.

Elizabeth stared up at her expressionlessly from the deck below. She was sitting on the floor, hugging her knees. Diana motioned her to climb the ladder.

''Who is that?'' John asked as the child emerged. ''A human?''

''Not exactly. We'll take her with us when we go, I think. Her mind has too much potential to be lost to our people. She's Robin Maxwell's daughter, by Brian.''

John looked skeptically at the child. ''Whose side is she on?''

"Ours, of course," Diana snapped. "Hurry, John. Your key."

The sound of laser pistols came from the main portal. "They're breaking through," John said. "We must hurry and get aboard the escape vessel!"

"Your key, John!"

He stared at her. "No. I'll not be part of this. It's obscene, destroying a world just to salve your ego."

The muzzle of her sidearm centered on his face. "Think again, John."

Reluctantly, he handed her his key. Moving with quick precision, she inserted both keys. The countdown began.

John looked at the second-in-command disgustedly. "Pamela said you were ambitious, Diana, but she underestimated you. There's a level of ambition that transcends rationality. You killed Pamela, didn't you? You're insane!"

"Shut up," Diana said, and shot him.

"We're almost through!" Sancho shouted, as the lock of the portal began to glow cherry-red. From inside they heard the pulse of a Visitor weapon.

Even as he spoke, a discordant whine echoed through the dead corridors. Martin held his ears. "It's the device! She's activated it!"

"We're through! Watch it!"

The door sprang outward. At the same moment a laser blast seared toward them. Donovan flung himself down, rolling, firing as he went. Diana went down.

They threw themselves into the Master Control center. Elizabeth stood backed against a wall, while Diana and John lay sprawled next to each other.

"Can you stop this thing?" Donovan asked Martin as he looked at the metallic box with its pulsing red eye.

"No," Martin said. "It's programmed to a specific countdown. The standard default is three minutes to detonation."

"It took us damn near thirty seconds to get in here!" Julie cried, feeling her lifelong nightmare threatening to overwhelm her. She wanted to throw down her weapon and run shrieking down the corridor. She was shaking so violently she nearly dropped her gun.

"All I can do is try and pilot us out of the orbit," Martin

said, working desperately at the controls. "Then, at least it will only be the six of us who die. But I don't think there's enough time."

While Julie, Donovan, and Sancho stood guard at the door, the two Visitors worked feverishly. The Mother Ship seemed to shudder, then the vibrations of its engines increased. It strained upward. The blue of the sky began to darken to indigo.

"Julie," said Diana softly.

Juliet turned, wondering if she were hearing things, and walked over to the fallen Second-in-Command. She gazed at Diana's face, that face so much a part of her subconscious horrors of the past months.

"Julie, I can help you . . . Let me help you." The words were nothing but a drifting breath from the shattered creature lying sprawled on the deck. Only Juliet heard them. "Who is the one who hurt you, Julie? You must kill him . . ."

Juliet turned uncertainly to look at Donovan's back. Her left hand trembled, inching toward the gun in her right. "Kill him, Julie . . . kill him . . . kill him . . ."

Then, somehow, the gun was in Julie's left hand as she aimed at Mike's back. The muzzle wavered in her hand, as her finger groped for the firing stud. "Kill him . . ."

"NO!!" Juliet flung the weapon out the door and, turning, dragged Diana up. With a savage hatred like nothing she'd ever felt, she shoved the wounded officer through the open hatchway in back of her, feeling her fall, then hearing a thud.

"What happened?" Donovan and Sancho turned to face Juliet, staring at her uncomprehendingly.

"We've got less than a minute, by my watch," Martin said from the pilot's seat, ignoring the humans. "We're not going to make it, I can't get the altitude."

With an abrupt, darting swiftness Elizabeth stood before the console, her eyes intent on the keyboard. She punched in a command, her fingers flying with single-minded swiftness. A glowing sequence of Visitor code came up on the monitor.

"What's she doing?" Donovan asked.

"She called up the main destruct-sequence program. She can't hurt anything," Lorraine said wearily. "What difference does it make?"

Elizabeth's eyes scanned swiftly, her hands moving again,

entering a command. Then she turned to smile up at Julie and Donovan, slipping her hand into Juliet's. Kneeling, Julie hugged her. "Poor little thing. She doesn't understand."

Donovan put his arm around Juliet as they watched the seconds tick by on the chronometer of Martin's pilot's console. The droning whine of the alarm continued inexorably. Julie looked up at Donovan, her eyes welling up. "For what it's worth in the last twenty seconds of our lives, I love you."

"It's worth a lot. I love you too."

"Eight," said Martin, staring at his watch. "Seven . . . six . . . five . . . good-bye, everyone. It's been fun . . . three . . . two . . . one . . . Here we go . . ."

Juliet held her breath, waiting for the wash of nova-energy to obliterate her body.

After a long, long moment, she let her breath out. Drew another deep breath. *So Martin timed it wrong by a couple of seconds—here we go . . .*

She was forced to breathe again, feeling dizzy. The alarm continued to sound. "God!" Julie threw up her hands. "I can't stand this! Get it *over* with!"

"This is crazy," Martin said. "It should've detonated ninety seconds ago."

They all looked at each other, wondering if they'd gone mad.

"If this is heaven," Sancho said, "I think I want to try the other place."

"What's going on?" Donovan demanded, then, as a thought hit him, looked at the little girl standing pressed against his side. "It has to be Elizabeth. *What did she do?*"

Martin was already at the doomsday console, his eyes scanning the program still glowing on the screen. "It's been a long time since I messed with these things. Lorraine, can you tell what's going on here?"

The Visitor female moved to the console with the flashing red button, eyeing the Visitor characters intently. She began reading the program, mumbling to herself. "Here's the default . . . three minutes, that's right . . . but—"

She looked up at them. "She did it! Diana left a timing option in the program, I suppose so she could get away. Elizabeth reprogrammed it to feed back into itself. It'll cycle infinitely."

Julie had taken an introductory programming class as an undergraduate. "An infinite loop?" she asked cautiously.

"That's it," said Lorraine. "We can dismantle the device at our leisure." Bending over, she hugged the child. "*Thank you*, Elizabeth."

"You're welcome," Elizabeth replied, staring at her solemnly.

"You mean we're gonna live?" asked Donovan, dumbfounded.

"For a while, anyway," Julie deadpanned. "Maybe another fifty or sixty years."

Donovan stared at her, then grinned. "Hey . . . *hey*! This is wonderful!" He sat down on the floor suddenly, as though his legs would no longer hold him. "I don't know whether to laugh or cry."

"I have a feeling I'll do both, maybe at the same time, as soon as I stop shaking." Julie said, slumping down beside him, pulling Elizabeth into her lap.

They all sat there for several minutes, grinning at each other, light-headed from relief.

Finally Martin stirred. "Maybe I'd better check our heading. We must be past your moon, and still picking up speed. We don't want to pay a visit to your Sun or something."

He busied himself at the controls for a moment, then the viewscreen came alive before them. "Take a look, Donovan. This is the highest you've ever flown."

"Yeah," Mike breathed. "This is something for the records. Wonder if I'll make the papers—the papers! Oh, damn!"

"What is it?" Julie asked.

"Here's my camera. I forgot about it. All this wonderful dramatic footage, and I missed it all."

"We *were* rather busy," Juliet said. "It's probably going to take some getting used to, to go back to *recording* the news."

"As opposed to making it? I'll be only too happy to trade in my grenades and laser pistol for something more peaceful. Maybe I'll do weddings. Speaking of which, will you marry me, Julie?"

She frowned. "Oh dear. That's so . . . permanent. Our generation gap is showing."

"Come on, make an honest man out of me. Please."

"I'll think about it. Maybe we should live together for a while first."

"I'll give you a pre-nuptial agreement . . . anything you want. We can go to Mars for a honeymoon."

"You're babbling, Donovan."

"Damn straight."

"That's funny," Martin said. "The escape shuttle was just launched out of the Master Control deck."

"How do you get to it?"

"Through there." He pointed to the hatchway with the descending ladder. Juliet crawled over to look down it. Diana's body was no longer sprawled where she'd pushed it.

"Diana?" Mike guessed.

"Maybe," she said. "But she was badly wounded."

"The escape shuttle doesn't have the range to get back to Earth from here," Martin said. "And if she goes back, she's doomed anyway."

"You're right." Mike looked up at his friend. "Julie and I have decided on our plans. What are *you* going to do now, Martin?"

"First I'm going to disconnect the destruction device and shut off that alarm. Then—" He thought for a moment, looking at Lorraine. "We'll go home. We've got a lot to do there." He stood up, saluting them all, and went out into the corridor.

Lorraine watched him go, then nodded somber agreement. "What about Elizabeth? We could take her with us . . . but a planet at war is not the place for a child."

"Earth probably isn't the most peaceful place in the galaxy," Mike said, "but at least ours is no longer a global conflict. Until tomorrow, maybe."

"She can come with us," Julie said. "Perhaps now we can actually fulfill that bargain John offered us—" She looked at the Supreme Commander's body. "But for real, this time. We have things you need, you have things we need. Maybe we can trade. Elizabeth might turn out to be the bridge Father Andrew thought she was." She looked pensive. "I wonder if he's still alive?"

Elizabeth shook her head and whispered, "Diana killed him."

* * *

Several hours later, Martin reappeared. The alarm had stopped about an hour before. "Everything fixed?" Donovan asked.

"Yes," the Visitor Officer said, nodding, then resumed his seat at the pilot's console. "The device is dismantled. We can go home now."

"Good," Julie said, checking her watch. "How long will it take?"

"Not long. About an hour."

They sat on the floor, staring at the viewscreen as Martin skillfully reversed the mammoth ship. They could see the Earth now. Donovan watched the small bluish crescent that was his world grow steadily, seeing and appreciating its loveliness as never before.

*Too bad Tony couldn't see this*, he thought. The memory of his friend sparked another in his mind. "When we get back," he said, "you'll have to layover for a day or two, Martin. We're gonna be so busy, Julie, it'll make V-day seem like a Sunday picnic. It's a good thing we can rest for a few minutes now."

"Why do they have to stay?" Julie asked.

"The people in the hold. We have to revive them. Martin, unless the authorities disagree, I guess you folks can keep the water. As a gesture of good will."

"Thank you, Mike," Martin said. "Frankly, I can't think of a feasible method for returning it."

"Neither can I."

"How awful!" Julie exclaimed, sitting up straight. "I forgot all about those poor people. That's terrible! How could I?"

"As you said yourself, you were kind of busy." Mike smiled at her, then sobered. "What's terrible," Mike said, "is that the other Mother Ships won't return their shipments."

"Perhaps, if we win," Martin said, "we can bring them back."

"Yeah, maybe someday," Julie agreed, trying not to sound ungrateful. It wasn't Martin's fault. But thoughts of the others reminded her that no joy is completely unsullied, no victory is won without many individual deaths and defeats. She sighed, looking up at Donovan. "You're right," she said. "Tomorrow we're going to be *very* busy."

"Responsibility," he said, with his old wry grin. "If you prove that you're someone who can handle it, they're not going to let go of you. But look on the bright side, Doc. There's gonna *be* a tomorrow. There almost wasn't."

They sat side by side, watching the Earth grow in the viewscreens, resting while they could.

**COMING IN SEPTEMBER!**

The alien forces hold all of Earth in an iron grip of
repression and terror.

But as long as one human soul struggles to resist,
hope remains alive.

The resistance grows as the saga continues in . . .

**V**

**EAST COAST CRISIS**
by A. C. Crispin and Howard Weinstein

*WATCH FOR IT!*

**FROM PINNACLE BOOKS**